THE WRONG HOLIDATE

CATE ASHTON

All rights reserved. No part of this publication may be reproduced, distributed, or transmitted in any form or by any means, including photocopying, recording, or other electronic or mechanical methods, without the prior written permission of the author, except in the case of brief quotations embodied in articles or reviews.

The Wrong Holidate

Copyright © 2024 by Cate Ashton

Edited by: Abigail Owen | Authors on a Dime

Proofreading by: Tracie Owens

Cover Design and Illustration: Mitxeran

This is a work of fiction, created without the use of AI (artificial intelligence) technology. Names, characters, places, and incidents either are the product of the author's imagination or are used fictitiously. Any resemblance to persons, living or dead, business establishments, events, or locales is entirely coincidental.

Any use of this publication to "train" generative AI technology to generate text is expressly prohibited.

Print ISBN: 979-8-9884194-1-9

❀ Created with Vellum

"I'm not great at the advice. Can I interest you in a sarcastic comment?"
Chandler Bing

"There's nothing better than a world where everybody's just trying to make each other laugh."
Matthew Perry

Thanks for making our world brighter, Matthew.
Rest in Peace.

New Year's Eve

LAINEY

No, not tonight.

I swipe my mom's call away. It's after 10 p.m. on New Year's Eve, and I refuse to have her hijack my night. I told her going on a blind date was a bad idea.

My phone lights up with another call.

"I told you I wasn't going to bail you out, even if it was horrible," I say to my ringing phone and swipe the call away again, feeling only a smidge of guilt. While it's nice she's walking away from bad dates instead of making relationships out of them, I've already helped her out of three dates over the last two months. Not tonight of all nights, when I have my own date and staying on it is literally part of my job.

Dating for work might be unconventional, but it's part of a new series called Holidating in the City for the online magazine *What's Good, ATX*. I'll be visiting different places around the city and meeting new people. Plus, it's a guaranteed job for a whole year. Surely with all this variety, I'll stick it out that long. I really do think I finally picked the right job.

As long as my mom doesn't ruin it.

Right on cue, my phone buzzes with a text message this time.

I refuse to look at it. I'm not dealing with her terrible taste in men and broken red flag radar. Instead, I glance around the swanky hotel ballroom, looking for my holidate, David, who went to get us drinks forever ago. *What's Good* is hosting a party downtown and partnered with several local distilleries and restaurants, which I've already featured in videos and pictures so I can enjoy the rest of the night focusing on David.

David's my neighbor so, technically, he's not a blind date. We've flirted whenever we see each other but have only exchanged small talk. When I learned he didn't have plans for New Year's, I knew he'd be my perfect holidate. He checks all the right boxes—good job, gorgeous, funny, and smart. And I have every intention of kissing the hell out of him at midnight.

My phone buzzes again.

That is, if my cockblocking mother would leave me alone. What the hell could be so important? Shit. My stomach suddenly twists with worry. What if something is really wrong? I sigh. And look.

MOM

Answer my call!

My date is having a heart attack. I'm at the hospital. I need you!!!

Fuck. My. Life.

I drop my hand with the phone in it and quickly look for David. I finally spot him at the bar, chatting with Mona, one of my coworkers I haven't really gotten to know yet. She's laughing at something he said and puts her hand on his arm, letting it slowly drag down toward his wrist.

Oh. Hell. No.

My phone rings again. I reluctantly turn away from David and Mona and take the call, making my way to the patio so I can hear.

"I'm here," I answer, burrowing into a spot against the wall that gets me out of the cold air.

"Lainey," my mom sobs. "Oh my God, it's horrible. I'm so afraid he's going to die."

"You're already at hospital, right?"

"Yes."

"Okay, just be there for him. That's all you can do. Does he have family?"

"A son. He's a widower, and his son is all he has. His son works at a bar in South Austin, and Mike doesn't think he has his phone on him. It could be hours, and he really needs his son here. Lainey, you have to help."

Oh, no.

"Mom, what can I do? I don't know who this guy is. There has to be someone else you can call."

"There's no one," she says so theatrically that I pull the phone away from my ear and look at it. My mom can be dramatic, but this is a bit much. I press the phone back to my ear to hear her say, "I know the bar. You need to go and find him."

"Are you serious? Mom, I told you already. I'm on a date. For *work*. This is my first assignment for my brand-new job. I can't just leave. Call Harper."

"Why would I call your sister when I can call you? You're already out."

I roll my eyes. Because, of course, I'm available over my married with a kid sister—who I know for sure is staying at home tonight.

"What if he dies, Lainey?" This wail's even more drawn out than the last one. "If it was me, wouldn't you want someone to find you?"

I sigh. Great...lay on the guilt.

"Mom..." It's on the tip of my tongue to complain, but what good would it do? I'm still going to help. Because she's right, I'd want someone to find me if the roles were reversed. Plus, my mom is usually not this over the top, so she must truly be worried.

"Fine. Text me the bar and what hospital you're at, and I'll do my best."

"Oh, baby, thank you so much. His name is Ben."

"Do you have access to your date's phone? Can you send me Ben's number? I can keep trying it."

"Alright, I'll do that. Bye, honey. Love you." She suddenly sounds way less dramatic.

"Love you, too."

I end the call and sigh again, defeated, before heading back into the party to find David. Thankfully, he's not at the bar with Mona. I glance around and find him doing the same with two champagne flutes in his hands. I wave to catch his attention and make my way to him.

"There you are," he says, and his face falls as my expression registers. "What's wrong?"

"My mom's date had a heart attack."

"Oh my God, that's awful. Did he die?"

"No, but she needs me to help locate his son. I'm really sorry, but I have to take off for a while."

His brows bunch in confusion. "Are you serious?"

"I really wish I wasn't." I take the champagne flute from him and down half in one gulp. "She's afraid he's not going to make it, and he really wants his son there."

My phone buzzes, and I glance at all the information my mom sent me. Wonderful. The bar is a good fifteen to twenty minutes from here, and the hospital is way north, more than half an hour from the bar. Why isn't this guy's phone in his pocket?

"I have to go south to this bar."

"Ah man, that sucks." He gives me this pitying smile that immediately rankles. Shouldn't he be offering to come with me?

"Um, so you want to stay? I hate to leave you here not knowing anyone—"

"No, it's fine. I'm having a good time with everyone," he says and glances back to the bar where he was earlier—with Mona. Then his gaze comes back to mine, and I see realization register. "Oh, you want me to come with you?"

Is that an offer or a question?

"No, no. It's fine. It's New Year's. You should stay. I have just under two hours before midnight. I'll try to make it back."

He immediately looks relieved that he doesn't have to leave, though he tries to mask it with faux concern. "If you're sure."

I resist the urge to kick his shins. Jeez, I really can pick them. I suppose I'll give him points for pretending. Then he surprises me by closing in and pressing his hand on my lower back. "Hurry back. I'd really like to spend midnight with you." He brushes his lips across my cheek, and even though he just waved a big red flag, my body lights up. See, this is what happens when you've been celibate for far too long. You go colorblind. Because I'm seriously considering downgrading his red flag to yellow for a little midnight action.

I kiss his cheek and promise to get back as soon as possible. Getting a rideshare on New Year's Eve is costing me a fortune. My mom is so paying me back. No, this Ben guy is paying me back. This is all his fault as far as I'm concerned.

It doesn't take as long as I thought to get from downtown to the bar—probably because everyone's already at their parties having fun. On the way, I text Ben a few times, but he never answers. When I arrive at Red Poppy, it hits me why I've heard of this place. It used to be a dive bar called Red's Place but has been recently revamped into a swanky bar with speakeasy vibes. It's actually on my list of places to check out for work. They kept the original sign that says *Red* with its old-school look and block lettering and *Poppy* in cursive, giving the moniker a more modern and feminine look. Through the windows, I can see it's packed, which probably isn't going to make my task easy. I ask the driver to wait and thankfully he agrees.

Inside, pushing myself up to the bar is a nightmare, and I get a lot of evil looks along the way. There are two men behind the bar, but they're on the far end so I approach the woman bartender that's closer.

I lean in over the bar as she's busy making a drink. "Hey, I need to talk to Ben."

She barks out a laugh, lifts two bottles of booze, and starts pouring them into a glass. "You and every other woman in here."

Oh-kay.

"Look, it's important—"

"Lady, I don't have time for this. Ben's at the end of the bar. If you want to talk to him, go over there." She turns away to deliver her drink and doesn't come back.

Great. I head back into the crowd and force my way to the other side. There are two guys, but one's clearly the barback, so I focus on the other guy making drinks. And, *Holy Sexiest Man Alive*, he's gorgeous. Bright blue eyes, deep brown hair, and facial hair that looks more like he didn't bother to shave for a week instead of being intentional. He's wearing a black button-down with red suspenders, though his are off his shoulders and hanging at his sides. The look is ridiculously sexy on him. The shirt is straining against his biceps as he shakes a shaker. Damn, who knew that would be so sexy? If this man takes after his dad, then I absolutely see why my mom was interested.

The thought of his father springs me back into action. I wedge my way to the front of the bar as several people start cussing at me. "Hey! Ben!"

He glances my way and quickly notices all the angry people

around me. "Sweetheart, you need to wait your turn," he says as he pours the martini he made.

"I don't want a drink."

His jaw ticks as if he's annoyed, but then he looks at me, and his expression is pure sex. He raises the hem of his shirt, showing off his flexed abs. "That's all you get tonight. You can leave your number on a napkin." He winks and nods toward a stack of red napkins with a pen sitting on top.

Um, what just happened?

"Now, please move so all these people you cut in front of can get their drinks." He turns to the computer to input the order he just delivered, acting like he didn't flash his abs out of nowhere.

"Hey, asshole. Your dad's having a heart attack and is in the hospital."

Ben freezes, and his gaze snaps to mine, his face paling. Okay, maybe that wasn't the best way to tell him.

"What?" He comes back to the bar and leans closer to me. "Are you serious?"

It's on the tip of my tongue to say *as a heart attack*, but I'm not that tactless. "I'm your dad's date's daughter. My mom called and they couldn't get a hold of you. He's in the ER now."

Ben runs his hand through his hair as his eyes turn glassy. He looks around frantically, seeming not to know what to do. Finally, he rushes to a spot in the back of the bar and pulls out a phone. He quickly looks over it, then rushes over to the woman bartender and starts talking to her. Her gaze flicks to me, and her shoulders slump. She nods and gives him a hug.

He comes back to me. "Meet me out front." His expression leaves no room for argument.

I fight through the crowd and go to my Uber to tell him I'll be another minute.

"Which hospital?" Ben asks as he joins me outside. "Do you know if he's okay?"

I check my phone and there's nothing new from my mom, but I see an unread text from David. "North Austin Hospital. No update, but I'll text my mom that you're on your way."

"Is this your ride?"

"Yeah."

"Okay, let's go." He opens the backseat door and gestures for me to get in.

"Whoa, I'm going back to my party and date. I found you. My job is done. Don't you have a car?"

He looks at me like I'm crazy. "I let the DJ block me in. Are you actually going to delay me even more while my dad might be dying?"

Jeez, I'm really being a bitch.

"No, of course not. You can have the ride. I'll order another."

His brows bunch. "You're not coming?"

"No, why would I?"

"To deal with your mom."

I want to tell him to just send her home, but considering how hysterical she was on the phone, she might be a bit much for this guy to deal with while worrying about his dad.

I slump as the realization I won't be making it back to the party weighs down on me. "I suppose you're right."

I slip into the backseat, and Ben joins me, giving directions to the driver. I text my mom to tell her we're on our way then read David's text. It's a group picture with his message saying they're all missing me. Mona is cozied up next to him and he has his arm around her waist.

Seriously. Fuck my life.

I text him back to have fun and that I probably won't make it back with a bunch of crying emojis.

"Which one is your date?" I glance up to see Ben looking at my phone. I raise my brows in question, and he shrugs. "Distract me. Please."

The pain etched on his face makes my heart twist. This man is seriously worried about his dad, and all I can think of is my ruined New Year's Eve. What is wrong with me? I blow the picture up and point out David. Ben winces.

"What?"

"Sorry to tell you, but he'll be banging the girl in the red dress tonight."

"Well, if someone had kept their phone on them, he would have been banging the girl in the black dress." I gesture to myself.

"No, he wouldn't have." His voice is very matter-of-fact.

"What? Why would you say that?"

He rolls his head to look at me. "Because if he was really into you, he'd be with you now." He points at my phone. "And he would have said *he* missed you instead of the whole group. *And* he wouldn't have his arm around another woman. My guess is he'd already zeroed in on Miss Red Dress before you left."

He looks at me expectantly, but I stay silent, which is enough to tell him he's right. He picked up on the red flags I went color-blind for because I was horny for a midnight kiss. My red flag radar is as busted as my mom's.

"Let me guess. This was more of a group hang than an actual date?"

"No, I asked him out. He didn't know any of those people before tonight. It's kind of a work thing."

His eyes narrow as he seems to process this information. "The party is work-related, or you date for work?"

I sigh. "Both, kind of. Those are my coworkers. I work for *What's Good, ATX,* and my assignment is to go on dates featuring Austin businesses and sights for each holiday. David's my neighbor, so I thought he would be a good first holidate."

He studies my face as he contemplates this. "So, are you

upset you're missing time with your date or because you're bailing on your job?"

I hesitate a second too long, and he raises his brows at me.

"Did you see him? Do you really think I don't want this date to end with a kiss? Or more?"

He chuckles and shakes his head. "It was never going to work out like you wanted."

His laugh takes away the pain in his eyes, which I love, and distracts me enough that it takes a moment for his words to register. "What do you mean?"

"You would have gotten a decent kiss at midnight to see if he was horny enough to take the risk of sleeping with you but would have decided it's not worth it."

A choked sound comes from my throat as I stare at him.

He shrugs. "You don't shit where you eat, and this guy doesn't want a one-night stand to turn into a stage-five clinger with the chick next door."

My jaw drops. He grins, takes his thumb and rubs it along his bottom lip. Déjà vu washes over me. I've seen him do that before, but it was way more sexual. Suddenly, it clicks, and it all makes sense—the flash of abs, the napkins with the pen, and why Red Poppy was on my radar. He's social media famous because of videos where he makes cocktails in a sexually sugges-tive way. They're total thirst traps.

A sly smile pulls across my face. "You're the Bare-chested Bartender."

He winces and glances away.

"Oh my God," I snigger. "That's why you raised your shirt at me, which was really weird, by the way. How many numbers do you have behind the bar?"

He looks back at me, now sporting a cocky expression. "That stack was twice as high at the beginning of the night."

I roll my eyes as my fuckboy radar goes off. "That's gross."

"By the second hour we were open, I lost count of how many times I was asked to lose my shirt. The ab peek was a quick way to give the women, and some men, what they wanted. They freely gave over their numbers. And in a few days, they'll be added to the Red Poppy's newsletter."

I bark out a laugh. Not that I believe for one second he doesn't take advantage of having all those numbers. "Probably not the response they're expecting. As icky as those videos are, they're marketing gold."

"Icky?"

Okay, his videos are hot. I might have watched them on replay a few times, but I'm not about to admit it. "You slapped a watermelon like it had been a bad fruit, then went all *Watermelon Sugar* on a wedge."

Amusement dances in his eyes before his gaze roams down to where the hem of my dress hits my thighs. "Like that one, huh?"

As if he was talking directly to my pussy, it answers in a rush of tingles. Damn, he's making me want a different kind of midnight kiss.

I squirm in my seat, and his gaze jumps back to mine. I swear he's promising to give me that kiss with those gorgeous eyes. It's tempting, but he's the kind of guy who keeps his red flags hidden behind his charm, and you don't see them until it's too late. The kind of guy I learned the hard way to stay far away from.

"My point is you should do more of them."

It takes him a minute to remember what we're talking about. His mouth tightens briefly and he shrugs.

I hum at that. "By the way, I definitely wouldn't be more than a stage-two clinger, tops. Totally worth the risk."

An amused smile lifts his lips just before my phone buzzes. I look down and see my mom responded.

MOM

> He's calmer knowing Ben is on his way

I show my screen to Ben. He stares and stares as if he can't comprehend what he's reading then suddenly his face cracks with emotion. He folds over, cradling his head in his hands, as he takes in deep shuddering breaths. This has to be horrible for him, and I've been terribly selfish. I put my hand on his back and rub up and down his spine, then give the spot between his shoulder blades a deeper massage. His body immediately relaxes, and after several minutes, he leans back. I go to put my hand in my lap, but he surprises me by taking it and lacing it with his.

"What's your name?" he asks. "Sorry, I've forgotten what your text said."

"Lainey."

"Thank you, Lainey, for coming to get me. Sorry it ruined your night."

There's something about the warmth of his hand in mine that soothes me, and I accept the fact I'll ring in the new year in a hospital. I relax fully into the seat and settle into our mutual comfort.

"It's okay. What's another New Year's gone wrong? I guess it got you out of working and fighting off all the ladies."

"Except I hate leaving my employees in a bind."

I jerk to face him. "Wait. Red Poppy is yours?"

"Yeah."

I stare at him, and I can feel my jaw falling again. This guy owns Red Poppy? But he's so young. "How old are you?"

His mouth twists in amusement. "Twenty-five."

"We're the same age. And you own a bar? Are you a young billionaire or something?"

He laughs. "I wish. No, my Uncle Red used to own the bar.

Well, technically, he still does. I've bought into it as much as I can afford for now, and I run it exclusively. Uncle Red retired and offered the bar to me instead of selling it outright."

"So, you're responsible for the re-brand. He didn't care?"

"No, he knew things were changing, and it wasn't going survive much longer as it was."

He's right, especially in that area, which is quickly becoming a trendy spot for a younger crowd than what Red's Place was probably drawing in. "I like the new name. Any reason you picked it?"

"Poppy was my mom's name. Redford was her maiden name, which is where my uncle got his nickname, he's actually Gary."

My heart melts as I remember my mom mentioning her date was a widower.

"She passed five years ago on December twenty-first after a two-year battle with breast cancer." He swallows hard. "I don't think I can handle losing another parent in December."

I squeeze his hand. "You won't." I have no right to say it, as we have no idea how bad things really are, but I need to reassure him somehow.

"Thanks."

We fall silent and he leans his head back against the seat, closing his eyes. His thumb gently rubs my hand. It should be weird since I've known this guy for less than thirty minutes, but it's actually nice. Plus, I like that I can give him comfort. So, I stay silent and let him hold my hand.

As the car pulls up to the emergency entrance, Ben lets go of my hand and scoots closer to the door. I text my mom that we're here. Inside, I hang back as Ben talks to the nurses. A woman who looks like she's trying not to laugh eventually leads us back to a curtained area and leaves us there. Ben pulls open the curtain, and we both stop and stare at our parents making out.

Not just that. Ben's dad's hand is groping my mom's boob, and there's a clear tent in the blanket.

Ben looks at me, his eyes wide with an ashen tint to his skin.

"I think he's okay," I whisper.

My words break our parents apart.

"You're here!" my mom says with a nervous giggle as she fumbles with her shirt.

"Ben!" His dad says as he sits up, thankfully making his boner less noticeable. He immediately tears up and reaches toward him.

"Hey, Dad." Ben walks over, takes his hand, and leans down, giving him a half-hug. "Um, you seem to be okay."

"Right as rain," he says with a wide grin. This does not look like a man who was supposed to be knocking on death's door an hour ago. Did they give him some sort of pain medicine or something? "Hey, do you have any food on you? I really could go for a hot dog. No, nachos!"

"Yes, we definitely need nachos. And maybe a burrito," My mom proceeds to try to roll her r's as she says burrito over and over. She and Ben's dad suddenly burst into laughter.

What the—

"Oh my God, are you high?" I ask, my question like a pin drop.

They stop laughing and stare at us with big, guilty eyes before bursting into laughter again. I throw my arms up in exasperation. I can't fucking believe this. I left my job and date to run all over Austin—all because my mom got high with her date. At least this explains my mom's odd behavior on the phone.

"Dad? What the hell? Lainey said you were having a heart attack."

After his dad gets his laughter under control he says, "Turns out I was having a bad reaction to a gummy."

Ben blinks at his dad.

"Two gummies, actually."

"You had *two*?" Ben's eyes practically bug out of the sockets.

"I didn't know they took a while to kick in. Or that half of one was plenty."

Ben covers his face with his hands and mutters a curse.

"I started having chest pains and seeing things. It was actually really horrible. I thought I was dying. We didn't know if maybe the gummy had something else in it. So, we rushed here."

"Are you fucking kidding me?" It takes a couple of seconds to realize I actually blurted that out loud. Everyone turns their gazes toward me. I look at my mom. "You didn't think to tell me you were high on the phone?"

"Lainey," she scolds in that warning voice that tells me I'm being rude. "It felt very serious in the moment. The doctor said we did the right thing by coming in. These kind of bad reactions can be dangerous. But now we're so relieved, we're a little delirious."

"You're not delirious, you're still high. And horny, apparently, since you decided to grope each other in the hospital room."

"Lainey." My mom's cheeks turn apple red.

I look at Ben's dad and he has a matching blush. "I really am glad you're okay, but if you don't mind, I'm going to try to salvage my New Year's."

He nods sheepishly, and I turn to leave the room. I can't believe pot gummies ruined my night—and I wasn't even high. Now I have no midnight content for my New Year's Eve post, which hopefully doesn't get me fired. To add insult to injury, my mom has gotten more action than I have in more months than I care to count—in a freaking hospital room.

Fuck. My. Life.

I exit through the sliding doors of the emergency room and pull out my phone to order a ride. Maybe I can get back to my party and kiss David. Or get there in time to see David kiss Mona.

The rideshare app doesn't show any rides nearby. I order one, but I have no idea when someone will accept. I look at the time and realize there's no use in hoping, it's almost midnight. Not even the rideshare drivers want to spend the new year driving a sad stranger around.

I use my phone camera to snap a picture of the emergency room sign, which I guess I'll use for my post. Then I go to the bench in a darkened corner and plop down.

"Hey."

I look up to find Ben standing in front of me, his hands stuffed into his pockets. We stare at each other for ten seconds before he bursts into laughter.

"Oh no. Not you, too. This isn't funny!"

"It's fucking hilarious, and you know it."

I sigh and sag further into the bench with a grumble. "Maybe."

He gives me a look that makes me laugh. He joins me on the bench, and we let the laughter take us. When I finally stop, I say, "It would be funnier if it hadn't been such a shit year."

No relationship that got past date three. Four jobs I hated. And this overwhelming feeling that I'm never going to get it right. Never going to be happy.

"Starting this year alone in a hospital parking lot doesn't feel too promising for the next 365 days."

Ben doesn't say anything but pulls his phone out of his pocket and starts swiping. A moment later, I hear a countdown starting over the phone. One minute to midnight.

He puts the phone down between us, stands, and holds out his hand. "You're not alone." I look at him but don't move. "Dance with me."

"Here?"

"Come on, Lainey. Would you rather bring in the new year sulking on that bench or dancing with a handsome stranger?"

I raise my brows. "Someone thinks highly of himself."

"I know you've drooled over my thirst trap videos."

"Charming shirtless bartenders aren't my thing."

"Liar," he says with a seductive smile. This guy is everything I avoid, but it seems resisting him is beyond my willpower tonight.

I take his hand, and he immediately pulls me into him, wrapping his arm around my waist. We sway together as our gazes stay locked on each other. He really is handsome. Ridiculously so.

"Your date is an idiot. That girl in the red dress has nothing on you, Lainey."

My heart lurches at his compliment. It's not that I don't think I'm attractive, but Mona is gorgeous. Like red carpet kind of beautiful. "Do I need to show you the picture again?"

"Nope." His hand shifts on my back, pulling me tighter against him. His face is so close I feel the fan of his breath on my skin. His eyes roam my face, and with every sweep of his gaze, my body gets hotter and hotter. "I know what I saw and stand by what I said."

I swallow the sudden emotion in my throat. I want him to kiss me more than I want to breathe. Not because it's New Year's, but because he's made me feel more with those sweet words than my last orgasm.

Vaguely, I hear the countdown. Three...two...one.

Blaring applause and a chorus of Happy New Year's come over the speaker as *Auld Lang Syne* starts to play.

"Happy New Year, Ben."

I hate that this moment is almost over, and I'll have to step away from the solidness of his body.

"Happy New Year, Lainey."

He stops dancing and leans in. Anticipation tightens my belly. He lingers a breath away from my lips, as if asking permission. In answer, I run my hand up his neck and sink my fingers into his hair, adding just enough pressure to encourage him to close the distance between us.

And he does.

Fireworks explode. In the air. Inside my body. His lips move over mine in a soft caress—sipping, tasting. It's a slow, tender torture and maybe the most seductive kiss I've ever experienced. He presses his hand into the small of my back, pulling me fully against him.

He doesn't hold back anymore.

His kiss is no longer sweet, it's ruthless. And it doesn't take long before it's out of control. We're grasping at each other, seeking more. Suddenly, he picks me up and moves us around until he's sitting on the bench, and I'm straddling his lap. I hear the slit in my dress tear.

I grind against him, and we both groan.

"Fuck, Lainey. You feel so damn good." He trails kisses along my jaw, down my neck. His hand cups my breast, sending a shock of heat all through me.

"God, yes. Don't stop."

"Never." He takes my mouth again, and I grind on him like a sex-starved woman.

A loud ping jerks us apart. It takes me a few seconds to realize it's the rideshare app on my phone.

I check the screen. "My ride will be here in twenty minutes."

And our heated moment bursts. I stare at him as this awkwardness settles over us. I'm suddenly very aware I'm straddling him on a bench in a hospital parking lot. We untangle ourselves from each other and stand, straightening our clothes. What is wrong with me? I just dry-humped my mom's date's son mere minutes after she was being groped by his dad. My mom has always been a fuckboy magnet, and considering tonight's circumstances, Ben's dad is probably no different. Is this situation like father like son or like mother like daughter?

What I do know is I have no desire to get wrapped up in any of it. I take a big step away from him and wrap my arms around my suddenly cold yet still aching body. "So, I'm glad your dad is okay."

I swear a look of disappointment comes over his face before he clears his throat. "Thanks. Me, too. I guess I should go back in and see about getting him home."

"Oh, shit. I guess I should see about my stoned mother."

He cracks a grin. "Probably."

We both turn toward the sliding doors, but before I can take a step, Ben grabs my wrist and pulls me back into his arms. He kisses me again—quick but potent.

"Thanks for the fireworks, Lainey."

New Year's Day

BEN

Okay, admit it, if my dad hadn't had a "heart attack," your NYE post would have been way more boring. Our parents getting high and my dad's boner are comedy gold.

LAINEY

I hope he doesn't get upset about it because my mom is not happy with me. She thinks if he finds out about my article, he'll cancel their next date.

BEN

Too late. I already showed him. He laughed his ass off.

LAINEY

Whew! I'll tell my mom. Or not...maybe I'll let her sweat it out.

BEN

You're evil. I like it.

I am disappointed in the ending. You could have mentioned you had the best kiss of your life at midnight. I mean, my dad's boner gets a mention, but nothing about me?? I'm hurt, Lainey. Hurt!

LAINEY

Will you please stop mentioning your dad's boner? I literally cringed writing about it and am trying really hard to erase it from my brain.

BEN

Same, Lainey. Same.

So, what is the date plan for NYD?

LAINEY

No date. Going to my sister's for dinner. I'm grabbing some cabbage and black-eyed peas from Betty's Table so that's my Austin plug for today.

BEN

Lame.

LAINEY

Well, if a certain someone had kept their phone on them, I'd probably be cuddling up on the couch having takeout with my new fuck buddy, completely satisfied.

BEN

Or doing the walk of shame out of his apartment, unsatisfied.

LAINEY

Doubtful. What amazing thing are you doing today?

BEN

Hanging with my dad. Bar's closed so everyone could have a break.

LAINEY

How's your dad today?

btw, it's really nice to give your employees a day off. I bet they were slammed after you left.

BEN

Embarrassed. But laughing through it. And thx, I really owe them after last night.

LAINEY

I gotta run. Nice meeting you, Ben. Tell your dad to stay away from pot gummies.

BEN

Ha, for sure! I enjoyed meeting you, too. Thanks for the kiss and mini dry-hump.

LAINEY

Omg! You're the worst.

BEN

Maybe. But you like it.

Two hours later...

LAINEY

I can't believe I'm admitting this, but...you were right. Just saw Miss Red Dress do the walk of shame out of David's apartment.

BEN

It's a gift, what can I say?

LAINEY

You know, you could be a little sympathetic about my date going home with someone else.

BEN

Why? He wasn't the guy you were thinking
about when you went to bed.

LAINEY

Wow. You really do think an awful lot of yourself.

BEN

Am I wrong?

...

BEN

Look, I know a good kiss. And that was a really,
really, good kiss. I would have risked you being
a stage-five clinger. No question.

LAINEY

I can't tell if that's really sweet or really weird.

BEN

If you had been my date, I wouldn't have left
your side.

Groundhog Day

BEN

So, what date option did you choose for today?

LAINEY

Are you reading my posts?

BEN

Of course. I'm all locked into this assignment of yours.

LAINEY

You and everyone else. It's gotten way more attention than I expected. Not sure if I like that or not.

And we're watching Groundhog Day.

BEN

Are you doing the quote-along theater showing?

LAINEY

No, he wanted to stay home, so we're renting it.

BEN

Abort mission!! Do NOT go on this date!

LAINEY

What? Why not?

BEN

He only wants to have sex with you. Or kill you.

LAINEY

I highly doubt he's going to kill me.

And maybe I'm okay with sex.

BEN

Your option was to watch the movie at the Alamo Drafthouse for the quote-along. How is this an "Austin date" if you're at home?

LAINEY

It's called takeout. Like I did for NYD.

BEN

I'm telling you, this guy is using this opportunity to get some ass then never talk to you again. He's not interested in another date.

LAINEY

Hmm, how are you so certain? Sound familiar?

BEN

Look, all guys look for the easiest route to pussy.

LAINEY

You're a pig.

BEN

This guy is beyond lazy. The whole town was just stuck at home with the snowpocalypse that blew through. He should be ready to go out and have fun. If he can't be bothered, do you really think the sex will be good? Don't go to his house!

LAINEY

Fine. I'll think about it.

. . .

THREE HOURS LATER...

LAINEY

Ugh. You were right. Again.

BEN

What happened?

LAINEY

Said I needed to go to Alamo for work. He canceled.

BEN

Told ya. Lazy.

He probably would have made you be on top to do all the work and wouldn't even have made you come.

LAINEY

Ha! That's highly likely. And I really hate telling the guy to do his job.

BEN

Oh really? Do tell.

LAINEY

Sex is supposed to be fun for both people. If he finishes first, then it's my turn. This isn't a one-way street.

BEN

Man, I like you. More women need to be open about their pleasure.

LAINEY

Having a hard time with ladies, Ben?

BEN

Trust me, that's never been a problem. The woman comes first. And hopefully, second and third, too. I never leave a woman unsatisfied.

But not all women come the same way, so if a woman tells me what works for her, it'll make it even better. Just saying, I like your style.

LAINEY

Thanks. I like yours, too.

BEN

Maybe we should "style" together.

LAINEY

I'm not sleeping with you, Ben.

BEN

No, not sleep. Let's fuck.

LAINEY

Omg, you're still the worst!

BEN

Yeah, yeah. But you're curious.

LAINEY

Our parents are dating.

BEN

So? A little curiosity isn't a bad thing.

LAINEY

You're clearly forgetting what it did to the cat.

Besides, I already told you…charming shirtless bartenders aren't my thing.

BEN

Whatever you need to tell yourself.

So, what are you going to do for your date? Need someone to go to the quote-along with you?

LAINEY

No, it's sold out. I never had tickets. Just wanted to see what he would do.

BEN

Smart.

LAINEY

Since that damn groundhog saw his shadow, I'm going to bundle under some blankets and watch Groundhog Day by myself. Canceled dates happen.

BEN

I could come and watch it with you.

LAINEY

Sorry, someone already warned me about guys like you.

BEN

I think we established that the sex would be good. Great. Phenomenal. Mind-blowing.

LAINEY

Bye, Ben

BEN

Happy Groundhog Day, Lainey

Valentine's Day

BEN

THE DARK BAR TOP IS NOW GLEAMING AS MUCH AS THIRTY-YEAR-old wood could gleam. I might have fancied up Red's Place to make Red Poppy, but the original bar top is one thing I didn't touch. Not only is it too beautiful to destroy, it has too much history. The scrapes and scores marring it are part of this place. One carving, in particular, is the reason I could never part with it. I take my rag to the end of the bar and wipe over the deep mark where it says *Poppy's spot.*

Uncle Red said he'd been furious when he caught his sister carving up his brand-new bar top before Red's Place even opened. But when he saw what she wrote, he couldn't be mad at her.

When I told her I wanted to open a bar, she promised she would be my first customer. And she was. She always supported me, so if she wanted her own spot, then I'd let her have it. I still wish she'd let me make her a sign instead of tearing up that pretty cherry finish.

After she died, Uncle Red said he'd never been so happy she left her mark. No one has sat in that spot since. I moved the garnish tray in front of it, and the barstool has a permanent ribbon over the seat that says *Reserved.*

I toss the rag into a bin and look out over the room, letting the silence settle around me. In a few hours, it will be filled to the brim for Valentine's Day. We aimed our marketing toward singles and came up with a wristband system that acts like an icebreaker for those looking to meet someone. The idea has gotten a lot of social media attention, so I know we'll be slammed. And after New Year's, I made sure we'll have all hands on deck tonight.

At the thought of that eventful evening, a smile forms as my mind instantly brings up the image of Lainey Langford. The moment she pushed herself to the bar, she'd grabbed my attention, even if I expected another pushy drunk woman. I suppose you'd call her hair dirty blonde, but all I could think was how it reminded me of the shades of autumn—an earthy brown covered in golden leaves. Those honeyed highlights brought out the tints of the amber in her rich brown eyes. And don't even get me started on how she looked in that black dress. Yeah, the red dress woman had model looks, but she didn't hold a candle to Lainey. The plunging neckline had me constantly wondering how that slinky fabric was staying in place—and how I wished I was the person taking it off her.

I pull out my phone and check her post, seeing what dates she suggested for tonight. Of course, she mentioned dinner with lots of restaurant options, ranging from upscale to hole-in-the-walls. She also suggested other options like a chocolate-making class, wine tasting, and a sunset dinner cruise on Lady Bird Lake.

I don't celebrate Valentine's Day. My parents never did. Mom always said they didn't need a day designated to make them celebrate their love, so I never gave much thought to the holiday past forced participation in elementary school.

However, I'd be willing to do every cliché in the book if it meant spending time with Lainey.

I open my texting app and bring up her contact, smiling as I read through our Groundhog Day texts. There's something between us. Fuck...that kiss. I recall it with complete clarity. Sweet. Spicy. Sexy. Intoxicating.

The fact that she demands pleasure from her partner? *Damn*, I love that about her. When you can get in sync like that with a lover, it's the best fucking kind.

And I really, really want to have that kind of sex with Lainey.

I don't understand why she's keeping me at arm's length with all the chemistry between us. I'm not used to women turning me down. Not sure if it has to do with the fact she has to date for her job or because our parents are still dating—and I don't see that stopping any time soon.

My dad called me today to help him plan a "traditional" Valentine's date, so I made reservations at a swanky restaurant and ordered red roses to be delivered to Kathleen's house this morning. He asked me to pick out a good red wine and come by the house to see if it looked romantic enough. The idea I'm helping my dad get laid makes me a little queasy, but the man has smiled more in the last month than he has in five years, and I'm doing my best to be supportive. But that doesn't mean I'm going to stop talking to Lainey, so I type out my message.

ME

Don't keep me in suspense about tonight's date. What's the plan?

I press send, and the back door opens, the voices of some of my employees filtering in. Janice emerges from the back hallway first. Jan has her thick, dark hair piled on top of her head, with her trademark cat-eye makeup and red lipstick on. She's wearing a vintage rock band t-shirt and jeans, which she'll change out of and into the Red Poppy uniform of a black button-down with red suspenders.

"Hey, sweetie," she says as she takes in the room. "Looks like you already did our job."

I shrug. "Don't worry, there's plenty more to be done. I couldn't take all the fun."

She joins me behind the bar and gives me a tight hug. I've known Jan since she started working for Uncle Red ten years ago. Being twelve years older than me, she's always been like a big sister. "Gonna be a good night. Don't worry."

I nod and squeeze her back. I can't seem to quell my nerves before opening on big nights like this. Hell, I still can't quite believe this is all mine. That I created something people show up for, let alone like and enjoy. I haven't even been out of college a year—even if I am older than most college graduates.

"The Valentinis are going to be a huge smash. We'll have to keep an eye on how they're hitting." Jan has always been supportive of the changes I've made and has been a crucial part of making Red Poppy what it is. "We might have to enforce a two or three drink limit. It packs quite a punch."

Creating signature cocktails is one of my favorite parts of my job. Twists on martinis are my specialty, which is why Red Poppy is mostly a martini bar. They really draw people in— especially when I make them shirtless. I've reluctantly done two videos since New Year's after Lainey mentioned I should do more. The Valentini one added interest to our mingle night and blew up my DM's. All the attention is definitely a stroke to my ego, but it's a bit much. The image is a little too close to my college days and not exactly how I wanted to portray myself as a business owner.

Nora, Tyler, and Bonnie mill around the room, heading over when I motion them for our staff meeting. I go over everything we need to take care of before we open the doors in just over an hour. The DJ I hired should be arriving any minute. Thankfully, the weather's mild enough for me to put him on the outdoor patio. As we wrap up the meeting, my phone buzzes in my pocket, and I pull it out to see Lainey replied. A little thrill zips through me as I excuse myself to my office.

LAINEY

Are you going to bug me every holiday?

ME

Obviously.

LAINEY

Maybe someone needs to get a social life.

ME

Don't worry, my social life is just fine.

Okay, that might be an exaggeration. My focus has been all Red Poppy since I graduated college last May. For the first time in a long time, I'm content. I'm a pro at pretending. It started when my mother got sick right after high school, and I pretended college was too hard so I could drop out to be with her. I pretended to be cheerful and positive when I was fucking scared shitless. When the cancer took her two years later, the last person I wanted to be was grieving Ben. Motherless Ben. So, I went back to college at twenty and became Frat Bro Ben. And I rode that cliché for four years. Some thought I was a god. Others thought I was a douchebag. Almost everyone thought I was a good time—which is exactly what I wanted.

ME

Stop avoiding the question.

LAINEY

If I tell you, I'd be spoiling it for you

ME

I love spoilers!

LAINEY

Fine. I let my date pick. Dinner, then cocktails, and listening to live music.

ME

Solid choice, but I wouldn't have picked that.

LAINEY

What would you have done?

ME

Dinner at home in sexy lingerie, of course.

LAINEY

Yeah, that option was for committed couples, not blind dates. This is a fine first date for Valentine's.

ME

I suppose. Tell me about the guy.

LAINEY

Software engineer, avid rower, likes to read.

ME

Hmm, nerdy but athletic. Another solid choice. You'll have a decent date but won't want a second.

LAINEY

You don't have to poo-poo on all my dates.

Yeah, I do.

ME

Don't you want to know why?

Dots float across my screen. Stop. Start again.

LAINEY

Fine. Why?

ME

He'll be too boring.

LAINEY

He sounds pretty well-rounded. We've had some good text conversations so far.

ME

Not as good as ours. Trust me, this guy isn't as interesting as his profile.

LAINEY

I knew I shouldn't have asked.

ME

Fine. Sorry. I hope your date goes well.

No, I don't. I hope it's an epic fail. Preferably one that sends her in tears to my bar looking for a shoulder.

ME

When is your reservation?

LAINEY

5 p.m.

I roll my eyes. Is this guy sixty? Who goes to dinner that early for a date?

LAINEY

I can practically feel you biting your tongue. It was the only time slot left. It is Valentine's Day, you know.

ME

I wasn't biting my tongue. But you have a point. I'll retract my eye roll.

LAINEY

What are you doing tonight? Working or got a hot date?

BEN

Working. All the singles love to drink on Valentine's Day. Though first I have to stop by my dad's to drop off wine and make sure everything is romantic enough. Pretty sure I'm helping him get laid tonight.

LAINEY:

gif of woman shaking her head with her eyes closed and hands over ears singing lalalala

Stop!! I'm still traumatized from NYE.

ME

I was going to bring a nice Cab. Maybe I should bring over something really wretched. Like sweet raspberry wine.

LAINEY

My mom loves raspberries.

ME

Well, damn.

LAINEY

I still can't believe she's letting him call her Kathy. Thought she hated that nickname. Though she did say he was the only person that could. You might as well bring the good stuff. It's Valentine's, after all. I have to finish getting ready. My date will be here soon. Happy V-Day, Ben.

Disappointment fills me that we're done. I text her back to have a good night, but I don't really mean it. The thought of her liking this guy enough to kiss and take home makes me want to do something stupid like stalk and sabotage their date.

I get distracted with the bar until my dad texts about the wine. I need to get over there before the night gets going. I imagine we'll be open for a couple of hours before things really start picking up. With traffic, it takes me almost forty-five minutes to get to my dad's house. I let myself in and immediately notice almost every available surface is covered with candles. Instead of romantic vibes, it looks like the power went out. Where did he even get all of them? Only a few are lit. Did my dad realize he went too far and stopped? I have a feeling when they're all lit, it'll be a bright, roaring inferno instead of a golden glow.

I find an empty spot on the kitchen counter and set the wine down.

"Hey, Dad," I call, but no one answers.

Music or maybe television noise comes down the hallway from his bedroom. I head that way, and the door's ajar, so I push it open.

"Hey—"

The sounds register a second before my eyes comprehend what I'm seeing. And what I'm seeing is Kathleen riding my dad like he's a bucking bronco.

"Oh, shit!"

They both stop and stare at me just before Kathleen lets out a scream. I stumble back, trying to get the hell out of the room. I spin and smack my head right on the edge of the door.

"Ow, fuck!" I grab my forehead and immediately feel liquid.

"Are you okay?" Kathleen yells.

"Fine. Fine. I'm going to, um, go." I wave a hand behind me blindly. "Uh, carry on."

I race down the hallway, almost tripping over a box of candles. My head's already throbbing and blood's dripping into my eye. I stop long enough to grab the bottle of wine. At this point, I need it more than they do. I get in my car and immediately flip down my visor. A huge gash gushes blood at the top of my forehead.

My stomach rolls. I look like something out of a horror movie. I grab some napkins out of my console and wipe my hands, snatch my phone to take a selfie, then press my makeshift bandage on the wound. Using my free hand, I text Lainey.

ME

We have another holiday medical emergency on our hands.

It doesn't take her long to respond back.

LAINEY

Please tell me you're kidding. Are our parents high again?

ME

Nope.

selfie pic

LAINEY

OMG, what happened?

ME

I was running for my life after seeing your mom ride my dad.

LAINEY

WHAT?

ME

Yep. You saw my dad's boner, and now I've seen your mom's boobies.

LAINEY

gif of woman covering her head in embarrassment

ME

Mostly side boob...thank God.

LAINEY

gif of Jim Carrey gagging

ME

I'm pretty traumatized. I think I need stitches.
Probably shouldn't drive.

LAINEY

Are you trying to hijack another holiday
from me?

ME

Technically, my dad hijacked your last one.

LAINEY

I'm in the middle of my date, Ben. Again.

ME

And I'm your excuse to get out of it.

LAINEY

What makes you think I want to get out of it?

ME

You're texting me in the middle of it.

LAINEY

You caught me on a bathroom break. I wouldn't
text at the table. That's rude.

ME

Lainey, come on. Admit it. It's not going well.

LAINEY

Ugh. Will you stop being right! Do you know
how annoying it is?

ME

It's a gift.

He ordered oysters after I said I didn't like them and wasn't interested in sharing. Proceeded to pressure me to eat them. He only reads non-fiction. Has talked about a true crime book almost the whole time, and I'm pretty sure he sympathizes with the murderer. Trying to decide if my job is worth being the victim of a copycat killer.

I laugh then wince at the spike of pain shooting through my head. I make the mistake of lifting the napkin only for more blood to ooze out. A gag works its way up my throat. I reapply the napkin. Hell, I definitely need stitches. A cold sweat breaks out on my forehead.

Well, I'm your perfect out. I'm not kidding about the stitches. Did I tell you I hate needles? And blood. I'm really queasy.

Where are you?

My dad's driveway.

Send me the address.

I do and she sends me back a text saying she'll be here in twenty minutes.

Be prepared to hand over that good Cabernet you were talking about. And chocolate. This Valentine's will not die in vain.

Deal

I text Jan to let her know what's going on, then lean back in the seat and close my eyes. My head hurts like hell, but I get to see Lainey, and that makes the thought of getting stitches worth it.

"OH MY GOD, are you about to faint?"

Fighting off mortification and the black hole threatening to swallow me isn't easy.

"No," I reply weakly. It doesn't even sound convincing to me.

Lainey shakes her head, but she takes my hand in hers. "Look at me."

I turn my head toward her.

"Don't move," the doctor orders.

"Right." I catch the sight of the needle in his hand, and my stomach lurches.

"Close your eyes," Lainey says gently. "It's better if you don't watch."

I do as she says and concentrate on her hand in mine. How her thumb is making sweet circles in my palm.

"That feels good." I slightly move my hand in hers.

"Hmm." Her hand shifts and she opens my palm and draws on it with her fingertip. It tickles a little but mostly feels really sensual. The pattern changes to something more deliberate, and I realize she's making letters. I concentrate on each one: M-O-M-B-O-O-B

A laugh bursts from me and the doctor sighs in frustration. "Unless you want a scar down the middle of your forehead, you have to be still."

"Sorry." I open my eyes long enough to glare at Lainey, who's biting back her own smile. She mouths sorry before I close my eyes again.

"You'll look like a sexy Frankenstein after all this," Lainey says.

"You think I'm sexy, Lainey?"

"Look, you can't talk," Dr. Elliott snaps. "You're moving your forehead when you talk."

He'll probably give me a scar for being so annoying.

Lainey traces on my palm again. T-R-O-U-B-L-E

I manage to grab her hand and concentrate on making letters without looking or scrunching my forehead. A-L-W-A-Y-S

Then, I go for it.

I point to her, back to myself, and scribble B-E-S-T-K-I-S-S on her palm.

She makes this contented hum I take as agreement and write M-O-R-E.

"Trouble." She laughs softly.

I open my eyes and glance at her without moving my head. I see the interest in her expression.

Her hand folds around mine again. "Almost done."

I close my eyes and focus on the gentleness of her hand as the doctor finishes up. He gives directions on how to take care of the stitches and when to follow up to get them removed. He's clearly aggravated with us and exits the room as soon as possible. When we're alone, Lainey and I look at each other and burst into laughter.

"He hates me."

"Oh, yeah. You're the worst patient ever."

"I wouldn't have been if you hadn't spelled out mom boob."

She giggles. "I mean, I'm completely repulsed by the thought of my mom screwing your dad, but it's seriously funny."

"I have two words for you: Dad. Boner."

Her smile falls. "So not cool."

A nurse comes in. "Okay, Mr. Kelley, here are your discharge papers. You're free to go."

I take them and glance at Lainey, who's looking at me with a furrow in her brow. "What?"

"Nothing." She shakes her head and looks away. As we walk back to her car, an unsettled feeling stirs in my stomach. Her walk is agitated. Her expression's contemplative but her skin seems pale.

"Something's wrong," I say once we get inside the car. "What happened?"

She looks at me. Her expression is blank, but purposely so. "Nothing. Just thinking. What's your address so I can put it into my phone?"

She's lying, but I decide not to push. "Take me to Red Poppy."

Emotion floods her face like I've lost my mind. "The doctor said to take it easy for the rest of the night and watch for signs of a concussion. He didn't say go to work at a busy bar on Valentine's Day."

"I need to check in on them. I brought in extra help, but we have a Valentine's special going on. It's going to be busy. You can stay and make sure I don't pass out. Drinks on me."

"You want me to play nurse while sipping on cocktails? Sounds like a brilliant idea." Her voice is dripping in sarcasm.

"Let me see how things are going. I promise not to push it, okay? And you can sit and watch all the singles hit on each other."

She hums. "That does sound fun. What about me, though? I'm single."

I don't like the idea of watching her get hit on in front of me, but what am I supposed to do? "You can pick your poppy, Lainey. What you want is up to you."

"What do you mean *pick my poppy*?"

"You'll see."

Our conversation seems to have distracted her from whatever was bothering her. When we arrive, I have her park in my spot in the back. Since we're not going through the front, I steer her to my office where the extra bracelets are kept. The elastic bands are different colors and have a poppy design on them. I grab a handful and show her the one I hope she chooses first. "Lavender means taken or not interested. Red means interested in women. Blue means interested in men. If you're interested in a combination, take all colors that apply." I wiggle the bands at her. "Pick your poppy, Lainey."

She looks at me. "So, everyone here picks a band, and that makes it open season to hit on someone?"

"Pretty much."

"What about the orange ones?" She points to the ones left on my desk.

I grin at her. "We were going to do a Down to Fuck band but thought it might lead to trouble once people were deep into their drinks. In the end, it didn't seem too romantic."

She laughs. "I have to admit seeing this orange band in action would have been really fun."

"Alright, so which will it be?

Her gaze touches them all, and my stomach is in knots.

Pick lavender, pick lavender, pick lavender.

Her fingers graze the blue one and my stomach sinks. Then she snatches up a lavender one. My gaze jumps to hers.

She shrugs. "I've already had one date tonight. I'd much rather watch this experiment than participate."

I do my best to appear cool and collected, but I can feel the wide-ass grin on my face as I place the lavender band on her wrist. "Here you go. Not that this is going to stop men from hitting on you."

"Why would you say that?"

"I have eyes and see the way you're wearing that dress."

A blush seeps into her cheeks. She's wearing a red sweater dress. Nothing about the dress itself is sexy. It's all in the way it fits her, hugging her curves in all the right places. Her above-the-knee boots make me want to see her wearing nothing *but* them.

"Thanks. I don't think other men will agree. From the look my date gave me, I guess this dress wasn't revealing enough. I have every faith in your pale purple band."

"Further proof your date was a tool. I bet you get hit on within an hour."

Her brows raise. "A bet?"

"Yeah. I'll do a Bare-chested Bartender post if I lose. You can pick the humiliating sexual thing I do."

"And if you win?"

"You owe me a favor."

Her eyes narrow. "What kind of favor?"

"Whatever I need."

She tilts her head. "I would be an idiot to take that bet."

"No, it makes you adventurous. You know you want to. I can see it in your eyes."

She smirks. "Fine. You have one hour."

"Then let's get you a drink."

We enter the bar, and it's packed. The room's already decorated in red, gold, and black, but we added a bunch of hearts and extra red lights and rearranged the furniture so there's plenty of standing room. People seem to be mixing and mingling more than usual, which means the music plan with the DJ is working like we hoped. The bar area is jammed with one empty barstool at the end. I need her close by so I can watch as I win my bet, so I go to the barstool at the end and rip the ribbon off. "Sit here."

When I round the bar, my staff's staring at me like they've

seen a ghost. Yeah, my scalp and forehead don't look the best with the stitches, but it's not *that* gnarly.

"It's not as bad as it looks," I say, but that doesn't seem to jar them out of their stupor. I look at Jan, whose gaze bounces to Lainey and back to my hands. Oh shit. I'm holding the *Reserved* ribbon. I let Lainey sit in Poppy's spot. Fuck. I didn't even think twice about it. Lainey's expression is rife with confusion.

"Should I move?" she asks.

I swallow. It's not obvious why the chair is reserved unless you notice my mom's carving, which is too hard to see in the dim light. When I don't answer right away, she starts to slip off the stool.

"No!" She stills at my outburst. "You're good. Please sit."

She nods slowly and scoots back on the seat, her gaze darting between me and my staff. I turn, and they're still looking at me with shocked expressions. "Those drinks are about to be watered down. Let's get back to work."

My order seems to snap them out of their trance, and they jump back into action. I pull out a martini glass, add ice water to chill it, and grab a shaker to make Lainey's cocktail, not wanting to think about the significance of what I just did. I cut my gaze to her, but her focus is glued on my hands, her eyes sparking with interest. I shake the drink. Her gaze moves over my arms, and she bites that damn bottom lip. I'm no stranger to women watching me as I mix drinks, but I've never enjoyed it more than having Lainey watching me.

I dump the ice water and pour the drink. "Your Valentini, ma'am," I say, unable to contain my smile as I hand her the glass.

"Mmm, clever." She takes a sip, and her eyes light up. "This is really good. What's in this?"

"Strawberry basil vodka, pomegranate juice, blackberry liqueur."

She gives a moan of satisfaction as she takes another sip, and all I want to do is jump over this bar and kiss her until she moans for *me*. Instead, I turn to Jan and get a quick update on how things are going. It's mostly smooth sailing so far, but the bar is drowning, so I start taking care of Bonnie's patio orders. Lainey and I keep stealing glances at each other and pretending we're not.

It doesn't take long before women start lining up in front of me. For every drink I hand over, I get a phone number on a napkin. Any time I try to glance at Lainey, she's looking elsewhere, her demeanor stiff. Is she jealous? Mad?

I gesture toward Jan, and we switch places. Ten minutes in, we switch again. This usually breaks up the attention. Not only has it done that, but a man has closed in on Lainey. He eyes her band, but it's not going to deter him. I glance at the time. Oh yeah, I'm about to win our bet just under the wire.

Seeing her glass empty, I start making her another drink, but address the man, "What can I get you?"

"I'll take a Red Bull and vodka and a Valentini for the lady." He nods toward Lainey. She blinks and looks between him and me, and I know her annoyance is more because she knows I won. I ignore his order for now and pour the Valentini I'd already mixed into a glass and set it in front of her. "Too late."

"Let me get that for you," he tells Lainey.

She holds up her wrist to show him her poppy. "Thanks, but I'm good."

"From what I can tell, you're here alone. What's the harm in a drink and some conversation?"

I knew this guy would push it.

I grab a band from the bowl behind the bar, then set his drink in front of him. "The lady is taken."

I lift my wrist with a lavender band on it. The man looks between us with an annoyed sneer before he pushes away from the bar.

"*Now* you put a band on?" She shakes her head. "I guess it makes sense. You already have the numbers of half the women here."

"Jealous?"

"No."

I actually believe her. No, there's something more to her agitation. I almost wonder if she's about to bolt on me.

And I can't let that happen.

"Good. Because all you need to worry about is the fact that I won our bet."

"Yeah, yeah," she says, then takes a sip of her drink. "The bet should have been how many numbers you'd get in the first hour. Or how many times you'd call a woman sweetheart or beauty. I can't believe no one gets bothered by that."

Her voice is tight and annoyed. Okay, yeah, she's really pissed. Doesn't she realize this is just a game? Flirting is practically a job description of a bartender. I lean in close. "Because I know which ones like it, even want it."

Her mouth tightens, telling me she doesn't like my answer.

"I had a line of women waiting specifically for me. Why would I disappoint them? Give them a smile, pay them a compliment, and they walk away feeling good. What's wrong with that?"

"You're playing with their emotions. Giving them hope when there is none."

These women aren't looking at me with hearts in their eyes. They're looking for a good time. A bragging right. I traded Frat Bro Ben for Bare-chested Bartender Ben. "Trust me, they've forgotten about me as soon as another man talks to them. I'm just the shiny object behind the bar." There's a bite to my voice that surprises me. Or rather, I'm surprised I let it out.

She blinks at me, her brows furrowing as her mouth parts, but I'm called away before she can respond.

After another hour, the constant noise and music has my head pounding. I take a credit card from someone and turn to run it through. I squeeze my eyes shut and let my head hang for a minute. When the transaction processes, I turn around to see Lainey behind the bar.

"What are you doing?"

"Give him back his card. You're done. I already cleared it with your other bartenders."

I blink at her but return the card and let Lainey take my hand.

"Wait." I turn back and grab the reserved ribbon and give it to Jan. She immediately nods in understanding.

Lainey leads me to my office and immediately goes to the small sofa along the wall and sits. "Come on, put your head in my lap."

I grin. "Really?"

She rolls her eyes. "Get your mind out of the gutter. I'm going to give you a head massage."

Now the head that's throbbing is below my belt. "Sorry, Lainey, that did nothing to get my mind out of the gutter."

"Seriously?"

I shrug. "I'm a guy."

I do my best to fold myself on a couch that's much shorter than me and rest my head on Lainey's lap. Her fingers gently tease through my hair, and I immediately moan. I don't even understand how something can feel so erotic and comforting at the same time.

"Does your cut hurt?"

"My whole forehead is throbbing."

She moves her fingers through my hair, careful of my injury, then gently massages my temples. I close my eyes and get lost in the sensations. My body relaxes, and soon I feel myself being pulled under.

No idea how long it is before I open my eyes and blink a few times. I look up to see Lainey still holding me, one hand on my chest while the other is typing on her phone. She glances down, a gentle smile on her lips. "Hey. Feel better?"

"How long was I out?"

"About an hour."

"Wow, I'm sorry." I slowly rise so I'm sitting next to her.

"It's okay." She goes back to her phone, her brows bunching in concentration. "Just finishing notes for my post."

I wait, loving how adorable she looks as she focuses. A few minutes later, she sets down her phone. "I hope you don't mind if I use the pic of you getting stitches. I think if I tell my boss I had another failed date, I could be out of a job. And I can't lose another job in less than two months."

I raise my brows and wince at the sharp twinge of pain. "Another?"

Her mouth flattens. "They never seem to work out. Either it's not what I expected or what they promised. Or I hate it. Or I screw something up. I can't seem to hold on to a job for very long. But this one is guaranteed for a year, as long as I stop fucking up these holidates."

It doesn't escape me that this was probably a big admission for her. No one likes to talk about their failures. While I love our flirty banter, I love that she allowed me to see this vulnerable side of her, too. The urge to lean over and press a soft kiss to her lips is overwhelming.

Fuck, this woman has me all tied up. When have I ever cared about a woman being vulnerable with me?

"You can use me anytime for your holidates."

She shoots me an amused grin. "Thanks." Her gaze shifts to my wound. "How's your head?"

She raises her arms to stretch and my gaze zeroes in on her chest. The memory of her breast in my hand has my palm itching to feel its full softness again. Except this time, I want to bare it and sink my teeth into her hard nipple.

My cock jerks, and I look away. Fuck. "Just sore, no headache. Thanks for taking care of me, Nurse Lainey."

She laughs. "It would be nice to have a holiday that's not hijacked by a trip to the hospital."

"To be fair, stitches were not in my plans."

"What about your plans? Do you spend every Valentine's Day working?"

"I usually worked here when my uncle ran it. This is Red Poppy's first Valentine's, but I don't usually make holiday plans."

She tilts her head. "Why not?"

"Usually never dating anyone."

She stiffens, and that same uneasy feeling returns from earlier in the hospital parking lot and after I won our bet. She clears her throat, "You went to Central Texas University, right?"

"Yeah."

"I heard of a Ben Kelley at CTU when I was there. My junior and senior years."

My stomach clenches. Fuck. While I was busy being Frat Bro Ben, I didn't really think how his reputation might follow me. Now, I'll probably never see Lainey naked. "Um, that was probably me."

"I heard you had sex with four girls in one night."

I wince. Damn, my reputation is shit.

Her mouth drops. "Wow, it's true."

"*Technically*, it was three. And it was more in a twelve-hour period."

She narrows her gaze. "*Technically* three? Yeah, that's not suspicious at all." She shakes her head. "So, what did you do? Jump from woman to woman with a water break in between?"

I want to laugh, but she seems really pissed. I can't tell if she's judging me or what.

"Are you slut shaming me, Lainey?" I ask it with a bit of a laugh, but it kind of stings. After her talk about being open about your pleasure with your partner, it doesn't seem like her to judge.

Her expression softens, and her cheeks redden. She looks down at her lap. "No. At least, I don't mean to. I'm all for a healthy sex life. It's just...I'm thinking of those women and how they probably felt. I know how I'd feel if I was only a fucktoy." I flinch at that, and she shrugs. "I shouldn't jump to conclusions. That's not fair. Sorry about that."

I let out a long sigh. She's not exactly wrong. On one hand, I'd felt like a sex god at the accomplishment. But I also felt like shit because everything blew up, and those girls were hurt. But I hate that she thinks I'd treat them as fucktoys. At least, that's not how I looked at it at all.

"They weren't fucktoys, Lainey. Yeah, I've had a lot of casual sex, but I've never thought of any woman that callously."

She glances at me, her brown eyes searching my face. Eventually, she nods.

I slump back into the couch. "It was the night the Toros played the Tigers, and we had an all-day tailgate at the frat house. This girl and I had been flirting hard, and eventually, we moved things to a room. Afterward, she had to leave with her friends. Then I went to the game and ended up standing next to these two girls. They said if we won, they'd have a threesome with me. If you remember, we won by a field goal." I shrug. "When a guy is offered a threesome, he doesn't turn it down."

I pause and wish I could decipher her expression. She seems a bit amused, but not fully. "Why do I have a feeling that's not the end of the story?"

"Yeah...so we went back to the house. We immediately hit my room and afterward they passed out in my bed. I went back to the party and ran into the first girl and ended the night with her."

I take a breath. This is when my stomach usually churns with shame. "The next morning wasn't great. The two girls saw me come out of a room with the other. So yeah, they were embarrassed and pissed. Hell, I was embarrassed, but I put my charm on and tried to smooth things over before the whole frat got wind of it. Even though I wore a condom, we agreed to all get tested and report back. In the end, it wasn't the best feeling."

"So, technically three because it was twice with the same girl." She lets out a soft laugh, but it's not a true amusement.

"Yeah, but I didn't correct anyone when they said four."

"Why not?"

"Look, I'm not going to lie and say that night isn't up there in the top five of my amazing sexual moments, but the morning after felt so cringe. I honestly try not to think about it. But Frat Bro Ben was going to milk it for all its worth. He had a reputation to uphold."

"Frat Bro Ben?"

I give her a crooked smile. "That's me."

Her expression turns contemplative. It feels like she's cutting straight through the bullshit and seeing me. Just Ben. Not that I really know who Just Ben is anymore.

I wonder if I'd met her in college if it would have been the same. Would she have seen through the façade? Would I have dropped Frat Bro Ben for a chance to be with her? The clench of my stomach tells me no. I would have let Frat Bro Ben reign. I wasn't ready for her.

But I am now.

"It's who I needed to be at the time," I confess.

She continues to watch me and after a moment, her body relaxes, and I realize how tense she's been this whole time. I still don't understand why. It doesn't feel like jealousy. Is she freaked out by my body count? Or did someone hurt her?

"So, Frat Bro Ben never had a Valentine's date. What about Ben Kelley?"

I want to press her on why this bothers her so much, but I'm actually thankful for the subject change. I'm so tired of Frat Bro Ben. I'm not that guy anymore.

"I never grew up celebrating it. My mom said every day she and my dad didn't kill each other was celebration enough. She had a sarcastic sense of humor. They were completely in love until the day she died, so it made sense to me. However, I could get behind the sexy lingerie striptease."

Her brows pop up. "Sexy lingerie striptease?"

"I thought sexy lingerie was a Valentine's must for women." As her expression grows more skeptical—and amused—I raise my hand. "Stop. Don't say a word. If that's not a thing, it just proves this holiday is stupid."

She laughs, and it's a real laugh—and fucking music to my ears. "And the striptease? Is that also a must?"

"If not a must, then a big fucking bonus." I give her a completely put-out look. "Well, it's settled. There's no reason to celebrate this day. It's officially ruined for me."

She's pressing her lips together in an attempt not to laugh, but her brown eyes are practically dancing. She's cute as hell. She releases her lips, and my gaze dips to them. Her lipstick has worn off and her mouth's a sexy shade of faded pink that I desperately want to taste again. I want to kiss her until that pretty pout's swollen and wet. Until she's begging for more.

Her lips suddenly part, and her breath hitches. My gaze jumps to her eyes and her dilated pupils. As the air cracks and sizzles between us, I know what I want for winning tonight's bet.

"Lainey, I believe you owe me a favor."

Her throat works through a swallow. "What do you want?"

Everything.

That thought should scare the shit out of me. Instead, what's coursing inside me is that same feeling you have right as the roller coaster crests the first incline. I'm more excited than afraid —and ready for the ride of my life.

"I want you to give me my first Valentine's present."

Her breathing increases, and I can practically see her mind working ninety miles an hour on what she wants to do. If she says no, I won't push it. But I seriously fucking hope she doesn't.

She stands directly in front of me, her decision apparently made. She bends forward and takes hold of the hem of her dress.

I sit up, my heart slamming against my chest. "Really?"

"You deserve at least one Valentine's Day, um, tradition." She slowly pulls up her dress. "You can't laugh. Getting this dress off isn't going to be sexy, and I've never done this before."

Holy fuck. "Laughing's the last thing on my mind right now."

No, my body is at full attention. She hasn't even shown me anything, and my cock's already straining against my zipper.

She smirks and pulls the dress over her head, letting it fall at her side. Damn, she's gorgeous. She's wearing a black half-sheer bra and matching panties that don't leave much to the imagination. I soak her in—her dark nipples erect and straining against the translucent material, the hint of her pussy appears mostly bare, but there's a strategically placed piece of lace concealing the part I really want to see.

"Turn around." I don't even recognize my voice.

She hesitates. "Okay, listen, I don't have one of those perky round asses. Flat bottoms run in my family."

"Lainey, turn around."

She casts me a doubtful look but does as I demand. The back of her panties is all lace cut in a boy-short style. No, her ass isn't overly rounded, but I don't give a fuck. Her ass looks fantastic in those panties.

She looks over her shoulder. "Well?"

"Do I look disappointed?" I hold her gaze as she takes me in. I lean back and reveal the obvious bulge in my pants. Her throat moves through another swallow. "Lainey, you're fucking gorgeous. Never doubt that."

A softness fills her deep brown eyes at my compliment before she faces me again. She takes a step, then lowers herself down onto my lap, straddling me. I ball my hands into fists. I want to touch her so badly, but don't know if I should.

"I think this might be more of a lap dance than a striptease," she says as she lowers all the way down.

"You don't hear me complaining." My voice comes out rough.

Her lips quirk up as she moves her hips against mine. "Is this what you want?" Her voice is smoky and sexy as fuck.

I groan. "God, yes."

She grinds down on me and, fuck...I've never had a lap dance feel this good. "I want to touch you."

She takes my hands and places them on her hips. I grip her tightly and pull her down hard on my cock. She shudders, and I guide her hips up and down, loving how I can feel how hot and wet she is even through my jeans. She moans and starts moving on her own, taking her pleasure. If we keep going like this, I'm going to come in my pants.

The sudden ringing of my phone stops us. We stare at each other, breathing heavily, indecision hanging in the air. Do I answer or ignore it? Finally, I pull it out of my pocket, fully intending to turn it off, but it's my dad calling.

"You should answer it." She nods at the screen. At my hesitation, she says with a mischievous smile, "Maybe it's a heart attack for real this time. He has been active tonight."

I scowl at her and swipe to answer, even though it's the last fucking thing I want to do. "Hey, Dad."

"Are you okay?" Panic is evident in his voice.

"Yeah, I'm fine."

He emits a harsh sigh. "Oh, good. There's a trail of blood all through the house and a bloody handprint on the front door. Kathy and I just saw it."

I don't even want to think about how long my dad has stayed in his bedroom with Kathleen. So much for the dinner reservations I made. "Yeah, I was a bit in a hurry to get out of there."

My dad clears his throat nervously. "Yeah, um, sorry about that. Are you sure you're alright? It's a lot of blood."

"The cut was deep. I had to get stitches."

"Damn it, did you drive yourself to the hospital?"

"No." Thanks, Dad. I'm a little smarter than that. "I called Lainey, and she helped me out."

Lainey's eyes go big, clearly surprised I mention we're together.

"Lainey? Kathy's daughter?"

"Yeah."

He relays the news to Kathleen, and I hear her whisper, "*Why?* How does he have her number?"

"From New Year's," I answer, wanting to regain control of this conversation and return to enjoying my prize. "Thought I'd share my awkward parent moment with her, and she graciously offered to take me to the ER."

Kathleen continues her not-too-subtle whispering. "Are they still together? I thought Lainey had a date."

My dad repeats the question as if I can't hear. Unfortunately, Lainey doesn't miss her mother's words either. She jumps off me, grabs her dress, and pulls it over her body.

Shit. No, no, no.

"She, uh, went home after the hospital. Look, Dad, I'm at the bar, and we're slammed. I'll talk to you later." I hang up before he can respond. "Lainey—"

"Can you get a ride home?"

"Yes, but I'd rather you take me home."

She cocks a hip, and I feel the best thing that's happened to me in a long time slip away. "Our parents are dating."

"So?"

"So, I'm not going to mess that up. That," she points to the couch, "was your Valentine's Day gift."

I want to argue *that* was inevitable. There's a pull between us, and the fact our parents are dating isn't going to stop it. I can tell there's no use arguing tonight though, so I nod. "Thanks for the best Valentine's Day present I ever got."

She cocks her head at me. "It's the only one you've gotten."

"I stand by what I said."

National Drink Wine Day - February 18th

LAINEY

"IT'S NATIONAL DRINK WINE DAY!"

My sister stands on the other side of my front door with a bottle in her hand. Harper never comes by without a text and usually three days' notice.

My stomach clenches. Is something wrong? Shit, my apartment is a wreck. "What are you doing here?"

Her smile deflates, and the arm with the wine drops. "Did you hear what I just said? It's National Drink Wine Day. It's a holiday, and I'm your holidate."

My mind immediately jumps to Ben and what I did on my last holidate. A flash of heat with a dash of mortification ripples through me. I've been doing my best to forget the fact I gave him a lap dance in my underwear—in his office with a bar full of people mere feet away.

"Lainey? Seriously. Are you going to turn me away while I have a top-notch Pinot in my hand?"

I shake my head. "Sorry, come in. No, you've just surprised me. But it's a good surprise."

I haven't seen her since New Year's Day so it really is nice to see her.

We hug as she comes into my apartment. "Well, I saw what day it was on social media, and I thought it would be a good excuse to come over. Plus, I need a break from Cassie. She's been extra-extra this week."

"I don't believe that. My niece is perfect."

"That's because you don't live with her. You should have seen her on Valentine's Day. She threw a fit through dinner then refused to go to bed until after eleven. By the time we were done with her, Chandler and I couldn't be bothered to talk to each other, much less anything else."

Harper stops as she fully steps into my living room and takes in the laundry, dirty and clean, strewn around the room. My kitchen isn't any better with a sink stacked full of dishes.

"Jeez, Lainey. How can you live like this?"

This is why I need notice before Harper visits. She already lectures me enough every time I change jobs. I don't need to give her any more ammo.

"If you're going to criticize my apartment, you can take your precious Pinot and leave. You didn't exactly give me notice to tidy up."

"Fine. Sorry. But while I open the wine, can you at least move any dirty laundry away from the couch?"

I roll my eyes but scoop up all the clothes and toss them in my room. I'll probably have to wash them all over again since I now have no idea what's clean and what's dirty. Thankfully, Harper says nothing about how I "cleaned up." She settles on the couch, hands me a glass, and we clink them together.

"Happy National Drink Wine Day."

"I can't believe this is a holiday, though you won't hear me complaining," I say as I bring the glass to my lips.

"Me either."

It's hard to believe Harper came over simply because she wanted some sister time. It's not that we're not close. She's only three years older than me, but she spent a lot of time taking care of me growing up when our mom was either at work or caught up in some guy. Or getting over a guy.

Harper hasn't let go of that caretaker role—hence the lectures. However, she did have her reverse harem phase in college—something she pretends doesn't exist or that I don't know about. Her sister/mom mode is firmly back in place and has only intensified since becoming a mom.

"So, what really brings you here?"

Harper's overcome with a hurt expression, but I'm not buying it. I raise my eyebrows at her, and she drops the pretense. "Okay, I might have a couple of ulterior motives, but that doesn't mean I didn't want to see you or spend time with you."

While her visit might not be completely altruistic, I know she's being truthful. Since having Cassie, her life has become a different kind of busy. Honestly, I don't think she takes enough time for herself. If she needs a reason to come see me without having mom guilt, I'm good with that.

"I believe you. Now hit me with these ulterior motives."

"Well, would you mind babysitting Cassie one day so Chandler and I can have a date night? We're at our wits' end after this week."

"Of course. You know I'll watch her anytime."

Harper sags in relief, and her eyes go glassy. Shit, it must be bad if she's on the verge of falling apart. My sister prides herself on keeping it together. I take her hand in mine and give it a squeeze.

"Thanks." She blinks a few times, erasing the evidence of tears.

"And the second?"

"I want to talk about Mom and Mike."

My stomach hitches, and this irrational thought that she's caught me being naughty with Ben comes over me. Then I remember she doesn't know anything. As far as she knows, I haven't talked to him beyond New Year's Eve. I did confess to my best friend, Josie, that we kissed at midnight, but that's all I've even told her.

"Lainey, this guy sounds legit." Her voice is full of excitement and wonder, and I totally get it. Could Mom have finally met a decent guy? "She told me he had his house decked out in candles and sent her two dozen roses for Valentine's Day. Two dozen! You know how expensive that is?"

"Yeah, and you know what she did? Jumped his bones."

Harper's face scrunches in horror. "Oh, I didn't need to know that. How do you even know that?"

"Because Ben walked in on them."

"His son? How do you know?"

"Because he told me. He split his forehead open trying to escape. I ended up taking him to the ER to get stitches."

"Okay, wait. How are you talking to his son?"

"He has my number from New Year's Eve. Thought it would be funny to share his humiliating encounter." It's not a lie. It might omit several key details about our relationship, but they're not really needed to tell the story.

Harper takes a sip of her wine. "Of course, Mom would jump straight into bed with him. She can never take it slow. Mom says he hasn't really dated since his wife died." She looks at me, her expression now more concerned. "You probably know more about him if you spent time with his son. Think he'll run soon?"

"I don't know. We haven't talked about him much. I know he and his wife didn't celebrate Valentine's Day, thought it was an unnecessary holiday. But he asked Ben for advice on how to give Mom a good Valentine's date, so the fact that he went through the effort seems promising. I think he's a good guy."

"What about Ben? He a good guy?"

"Yeah."

Her brows bunch. "Why did you say it like that? Like *yeah, but…*"

But he's another frat bro asshole.

Except he's not an asshole. The whole label doesn't sit well. Which is incredibly naïve of me, especially after he was recognized in my Valentine's post. There were several suggestive comments from women who seemed intimately familiar with him. I even got a few DMs warning me away from him.

"In college, he was a well-known player. I even heard of him."

Harper slumps into the couch. "Great. Another fuckboy. Well, let's hope his dad doesn't take a page from his book."

"I don't think he is, Harp. Seriously, I have the same good feeling you do. But I guess it's hard to get excited about it."

She sighs. "I know. Some of them have really fooled us." She winces as she says it and glances at me. After all the assholes that came around our mom, you'd think I'd possess a special radar for them, but nope. I met a charming frat boy and fell in love. And was blissfully unaware I was an experiment in *how many virgins can I fool at the same time*. So, yeah, I have experience being a fucktoy.

Finding out Ben is the infamous Ben Kelley hit a little too close to home. I wanted to throw up when the nurse said his last name. Then watching him flirt with girl after girl at the bar didn't help. But hearing his story…it didn't sound like what happened with me and Isaac. I really shouldn't judge him for having a robust sex life like most college students.

"Well, I was looking forward to meeting Ben too, but not so much now," Harper says.

"No, you should meet him. He doesn't come off as a tool. He's actually funny and easy to talk to and—" I stop when Harper straightens and stares me dead in the eye. "What?"

"You cannot get involved with Mom's boyfriend's son."

"I'm not. I just said he was nice."

"No, you got this dreamy look on your face and started singing his praises."

"No, I'm only saying he might not be the douchebag player like the DW's. Or Isaac."

DW is short for dick wad, which is what we'd started calling Mom's boyfriends.

"But he's still a player."

I shrug. The way he so easily flirted and accepted numbers still rankles. I also wonder if it's all a show. If he even likes it.

I'm just the shiny object behind the bar.

It's who I needed to be at the time.

But I barely know him so it's hard to trust if he's being real.

"Lainey, you can't pull your little stunts like in high school and fuck this up for Mom."

A small sliver of shame fills me. I'm not exactly proud of the few times I purposely sabotaged my mom's relationships. Harper had gone to college, and I found myself all alone while my mom continued to constantly date. I finally got fed up. I erased texts so she'd think she'd been ghosted. I deleted her dating apps. Acted like a brat if I met them. There was one guy she was really falling for, but I overheard him answer his phone calling someone baby. I sent him a nasty text from her phone then blocked him. One night while she was crying over that DW, I confessed and told her I was sick of her ignoring me for a bunch of assholes. Everything changed after that night. She stopped dating and didn't start again until I was in college. It was the first time in all my childhood that my mom was fully present, so even if it wasn't right, I don't regret it.

"Are you kidding me, Harp? This isn't remotely the same."

Harper folds her arms. "Maybe not exactly. But what happens if this guy pisses you off? Breaks your heart? You can't go all revenge crazy again and break up Mom and Mike."

Whoa. Seriously?

"Are you really comparing the actions of a desperate fifteen-year-old to this situation?"

"It's just..." Harper stops, looking contemplative before sighing. "Mom is happy, Lain. Really happy. And yeah, she wasn't perfect when we were growing up, but she deserves *this* chance at love. You can't take it away from her."

That seems a little dramatic. And why does it feel like she's holding back something? I don't think that's what she was originally going to say. But she has a point. I do want to see Mom fall in love with a good guy and have the happiness she's always wanted. Getting involved with Ben any more than I already have would make things messy.

I have no business wondering if he's reformed fuckboy or not. My heart has been eviscerated once, and I have no desire for it to happen again.

So, I respond with the truth. "The last thing I want to do is fuck this up for Mom. Don't worry about Ben. Promise."

President's Day

You seriously made me spit coffee all over my
phone.

BEN

It's clever, right?

LAINEY

No one's going to order that.

BEN

You'd be surprised what people order. Folks
love themed drinks. Especially naughty ones.

I can do some sort of bourbon martini.

LAINEY

An Old Fashioned! Now that's funny.

BEN

It is?

LAINEY

Because presidents are old-fashioned. Get it?

BEN

If you have to explain the joke, it's not funny.

LAINEY

Whatever.

BEN

I'll come up with something. Check IG later.

LAINEY

Speaking of your IG...I saw you advertising for
Mardi Gras. A Jazz Night sounds awesome.
And a hurricane in martini form? Yes, please! I
was thinking of putting Red Poppy as a date
option for today's post for tomorrow. Are you
good with that?

BEN

Yeah, I'm not going to pass up free advertising.

What is your date for tomorrow anyway?

LAINEY

Not sure. We partnered with this new dating app so I have to pick my date from that. I've narrowed it down to two guys.

BEN

Need help?

LAINEY

I can pick out my own date.

BEN

You do remember your last one, right?

LAINEY

Oh, I came up with some screener questions based off that date.

BEN

Ha! Good idea. You're not planning on wearing sexy lingerie again, are you?

LAINEY

And if I am?

BEN

I think that's more of a 50th-date thing.

LAINEY

Me wearing lingerie on a 1st date worked out for you, didn't it?

BEN

Absolutely! And you can wear it for me any time!

LAINEY

Goodbye, Ben.

BEN

Happy President's Day, Lainey.

LAINEY

The Smoky Martini seems like a nice presidential choice. But why do I feel like the cigar in the pic has a dual meaning??

BEN

What? It's a smoky martini, so a smoking cigar fits. It has nothing whatsoever to do with a certain president's scandal.

LAINEY

Sure...

Well played, sir.

BEN

gif of a man tipping his hat

Mardi Gras

LAINEY

As our Uber pulls up in front of the Red Poppy, my stomach knots. I never should have added it as one of my date options. Because, of course, my date picked it. Now, it's like returning to the scene of the crime.

What happened in Ben's office on Valentine's Day has lived rent-free in my head for the past two weeks. I still don't know what possessed me to take his bet, knowing the direction it would go. He's Ben-freaking-Kelley, after all.

Yet, despite all the reasons I shouldn't have, I wanted to be the person to give Ben Kelley his first, and possibly only, Valentine's gift.

I wanted to be special to him.

And here I go again, romanticizing the fuckboy. What I need is to forget Ben and focus on my date, Duncan.

Duncan helps me out of the car with a kind smile. He's good-looking, tall with shaggy dark blond hair and an honest charm that instantly puts you at ease. He's got a great job at a marketing firm and has had some fantastic ideas on what we can do for my post. He's also been genuinely interested in what I have to say and is turning out to be my most invested and attentive holidate by far.

He's the total package. I should be experiencing some serious butterflies right now, but...nothing. Zilch. Nada.

"I'm excited to try this place. I've heard great things," he says.

"I've only been here once," And gave the owner a lap dance, "but the drinks were amazing. I'm excited about the jazz band."

"Yeah, I've seen the videos of the Bare-chested Bartender. Those reels crack me up. Gotta appreciate good marketing."

I glance at him, and he seems truly excited. This man really loves his job. Honestly, if he wants to take the reins of this date, I'm happy to let him. This job hasn't exactly gone in the creative direction I thought it would, and the dating part has been a flop—except for Ben.

Nope. Not thinking about him.

The bouncer at the door offers us disposable masquerade masks to wear. Duncan immediately puts his on, and I follow his lead. We enter the dim room, and my gaze immediately cuts to the bar area.

There he is.

The charming bartender who makes the dormant butterflies in my stomach take flight.

Fuck.

As if he feels my gaze, Ben looks in my direction and a category-five hurricane might as well have blown through me. The corner of his mouth lifts as he takes in my purple and gold sparkly dress. Duncan's hand lands on the small of my back and guides me further into the room. The small smile on Ben's face fades as his gaze slides from where Duncan touches me. As if a switch flipped, his focus snaps back to the woman at the bar, effectively dismissing us both. He flashes her a megawatt smile before leaning over and letting her put a string of beads over his neck. While she has him in her clutches, she stuffs a rolled-up napkin into his shirt pocket. And he winks at her. Ugh, I'm surprised he didn't flash his abs.

"Let's find a table." I need to be as far away from the not-yet-bare-chested bartender as possible.

Duncan frowns. "We can sit later. Let's go to the bar. I want to see this guy in action."

Wonderful.

We make our way through the crowd and finally get a spot in front of Ben—after wading through a plethora of women. His gaze meets mine again, and those damn butterflies strike up their own Mardi Gras party.

"Lainey." My name is like warm honey off his lips, and I find myself squeezing my thighs together.

"I'm wearing a mask. You're not supposed to recognize me."

Ben leans over the bar, his gaze intense. "I'll always recognize you."

Heat fills my cheeks as his seductive voice moves over me. He winks, and I hate how potent it is, especially when he gives it so freely. He turns his attention to Duncan. "Hey man, welcome to Red Poppy. What can I get you?"

Duncan glances between us before asking me, "What would you like?"

"Hurrican-tini," Ben answers. I narrow my gaze at him. "You said you wanted to try it. Am I wrong?"

"You two know each other?" Duncan's tone cautious.

"Sorry, yeah. Duncan, this is Ben Kelley. His dad is dating my mom."

"Oh wow, that's cool. It's nice to meet you, Ben. I really like Red Poppy's online presence. It's genius." Duncan holds out his hand for Ben to shake, which he does.

"Nice to meet you too, man. Not sure about genius, but thanks. Want to try the Hurrican-tini, too, or something else? My treat for you and my future step-sis." Ben shoots me a cocky grin, and it takes all my willpower not to flip him off.

"I'll take one as well." Duncan looks at me. "It'll make a good picture."

I nod, agreeing. Yes, this is all about the Mardi Gras date. Focus on Duncan, not the man behind the bar. "The band sounds great. We should dance."

"Absolutely." His gaze dips down my body as his arm comes around to my waist. He pulls me into him a little more and leans until his mouth is next to my ear. "You look gorgeous. That dress is hot on you."

I should be melting at the sexy compliment. Instead, I'm trying not to visibly squirm and wishing I'd heard those words in Ben's voice.

Duncan straightens and hits me with the full force of his charming smile. I really need to give the guy a chance so I force myself to relax in his embrace and say, "Thank you."

"Here are your drinks."

Ben's voice jerks us apart. I glance at him, and his expression is thunderous. A surge of desire suddenly pulses through me. Ugh. There is seriously something wrong with me that Ben's angry gaze turns me on more than Duncan's sweet smile.

Thankfully, my holidate doesn't seem to notice Ben's annoyance and asks him to take a picture of us. Ben agrees but is clearly not happy about it. Duncan pulls me close, and we hold up our glasses, posing for the camera. Ben returns Duncan's phone and I pull mine out to take a video of the bar and the music playing then grab a shot of us cheers-ing with our martini glasses. I finally take a sip of the drink and, *damn*, it packs a punch. It's also probably one of the best drinks I've ever had.

I look over to Ben, who is still in front of us making another drink. "This is amazing."

He smiles then. "Thanks, step-sis."

Oh, no, you don't...

I lean forward. "Stop with that crap."

"That's how you introduced me."

"Not exactly."

A hand lands on my hip. "Lainey, you ready to dance?"

I give Ben one last glare, and turn to Duncan. "Yes, ready."

We head toward the band and enjoy our drinks while we listen. Very deliberately, I keep my back to the bar. We take off our masks and talk a little, but most of our discussion focuses on what we should do to document our date next. We decide to wait for an upbeat song before we dance, and when the band finally starts to play one, I down the rest of my drink before we hit the floor. Duncan pulls me into him. Taking out his phone, he shifts it to selfie mode and videos us dancing and laughing. Duncan might just be worth a second date—if he'd focus more on me than posting to social media. It hasn't even been two full months, and the constant obsession with being online all the damn time is already overwhelming.

Soon, I have a pleasant buzz going. Duncan has gotten more interesting and my glances toward the bar have gotten further apart. Watching Ben flash his abs for beads is churning up feelings I haven't experienced since Isaac, and I don't like it. I'm shocked he's not slumping over from the thick stack of necklaces around his neck. The jazz band ends their set, and a Zydeco band sets up. When they start, I'm ready to cut loose. But as soon as we're on the dance floor, Duncan has his phone out again, taking more videos and pictures.

Annoyance fills me. I'm so over his damn camera.

After a couple of songs, I yell over the music, "I need a break."

Of course, Duncan beelines it toward Ben. He orders us more hurrican-tinis, and as Ben goes to make them, Duncan leans into me.

"We should kiss."

My stomach drops. I lean back slightly trying to hide how badly I want to scramble away. "What?"

"For your post. A kiss picture would be great. It would also be an awesome plug for the dating app."

He's right. I'd actually already thought of it, except I don't want to kiss Duncan, even if it's only part of the job. He already has his phone camera ready and pulls me closer with that sparkling smile on his lips again.

Fly, butterflies. Damn it, fly!

But they don't.

I want to tell him to stop, but the word lodges in my throat, battling with what I know would be a good job move. He leans in and I press my hand to his chest, trying to figure out if I push away or not. But I don't get a chance. Sprinkles of water hit us both in the face and we jolt apart.

I look over to find Ben holding the soda gun in his hand. "Shit, sorry!" he says, looking appropriately surprised. "Got away from me there."

Yeah. Right.

He replaces the gun in its holder and sets fresh martinis on the bar in front of us. "On the house. Really sorry about that."

I glare at him then look at Duncan, who is wiping his face with a napkin. He got a lot wetter than me.

"It's okay, man," Duncan says, but I'm pretty sure he's annoyed.

His eyes meet mine, but before he can suggest the picture again, I pick up my drink and take a healthy sip. A drink this strong really shouldn't taste like candy. Ben gives me a growly look.

"Hey, Ben. A call for you." The female bartender who blew me off on New Year's Eve shouts at him.

Ben doesn't tear his gaze from mine. "I'll take it in my office."

I refuse to watch him walk away. Instead, I polish off my martini. I glance at Duncan and he's eyeing my empty glass with concern. Before he can propose the kiss photo idea again, I make a break for the bathroom, telling him I'm going to clean up.

Except once I'm in the hall toward the restrooms, I stop in front of Ben's office door. Not about to question what in the world I'm doing, I try the handle. It opens, so I push my way in, closing the door quickly behind me.

He's sitting at his desk, leaning back casually in his chair watching me with a smirk on his lips that is far sexier than it should be. All the beads are discarded except for a couple of strands—and he's not on the phone. No, he looks like he was expecting me.

"Back hurting from the weight of all those beads? Or just getting ready for the next round of ab flashing for your adoring fans?"

"It's Mardi Gras, Lainey. Can't expect me to be a saint on a night all about sin." His smirk grows into a knowing smile as he leans forward. "How's the date going?"

Of course, he'd be all laissez-faire about his actions. "I can't believe you sprayed water on us. What the hell, Ben?"

He stands and stalks toward me, his cocky expression now something much darker. I step back until I'm suddenly against the door, and he's left only inches of space between us. "You didn't want to kiss him, but for some stupid reason, you were going to let him."

Anger mixed with a spark of desire flares in his eyes. The fucking butterflies take over my body, fleeing my stomach and flying north into my chest. I bite back a scream of frustration— at him and my reaction.

"You don't know that. Duncan is nice, smart, and good-look- ing. He's actually been interested in this date, which is more than I can say for any of my past holidates. Why wouldn't I want to kiss him? He's a fucking catch!"

Ben puts his hand on the door behind me and leans in, so close his breath heats my cheek. "Want to know what I think?" His voice is low and gravelly, and the butterflies go berserk. "I think you're trying to convince yourself that you like him, but you really don't. I think you haven't stopped thinking about what happened the last time you were in this office. You haven't been able to stop from glancing at me every time his head is turned. In fact, I think this whole evening, you've thought of nothing but...*me*."

You arrogant...

"How would you know unless you're watching me," I fire back. "Though not sure how you could have with all the numbers being tossed at you." I pluck the napkin from earlier still in his pocket.

He takes the napkin, balls it in his hand before tossing it over his shoulder. He inches closer, his gaze intense. "Maybe I haven't been able to stop thinking about what happened in this office either. Maybe I really don't like that you brought a date to *my fucking bar*."

He's so close the tips of my breasts now brush his chest. I can't breathe properly. And I'm pretty sure the butterflies are all dead because now all I feel is the roaring inferno he's created inside me.

"If you liked him so much, you'd be out there with him getting that kiss you don't want instead of sneaking in here with me."

I go to disagree, but my gaze falls to his lips and whatever false denial I could have come up with, disappears.

His mouth flattens in annoyance and he steps away from me. "That's it. We're establishing a safe word."

I blink out of my mental haze. "A safe word?"

Our eyes meet, and he may as well have me pinned in place.

"You tell me no when you mean yes. You tell him yes when you mean no. I don't want any fucking confusion between us. We need a safe word."

"Ben—"

"Acnestis."

I pause, trying to figure out what he said. "*Ack* what?"

"*Ak-nees-tis,*" he says slowly. "It's that part of your back that you can't reach to scratch." He reaches around and presses his hand into the spot between my shoulder blades. "Your acnestis."

"Why that word?" And why does his hand there have every part of me focused solely on him?

"It's a word you'll never accidentally use. If you say that word, it's because you really mean it. Now, repeat it back to me."

The authority in his tone sends a flood of desire right to my pussy.

"Acnestis."

"Good girl."

Oh fuck. Now my panties are soaked. He just unlocked a kink I didn't realize I had.

"That's your safe word. Use it only if you want to stop anything between us. Okay?"

"Okay," I repeat, breathless.

He takes a few slow steps, his gaze never leaving mine, until his hard body's brushing my soft breasts again. "Now *I'm* going to give you the kiss you really want."

He leans until his nose brushes mine, his mouth a hesitating breath from mine. The safe word hangs between us—unsaid. Then his mouth takes mine in a kiss that immediately claims. It's rough. Messy. Almost painful.

And I fucking love it.

I wrap my arms around his neck, pressing my body fully into his. His hands roam down my body until he reaches my thigh, pulling my leg to his waist, but my dress restricts the movement. He growls, rips his mouth from mine, and yanks my dress until it's pooling around my waist. His gaze captures mine, daring me to stop this. I hold his stare.

And say nothing.

A knowing, arrogant smile pulls his mouth before he kisses me again, this time with even more ferocity than before. He brings my leg up and pushes his hips into mine. I arch into him, shamelessly rubbing myself over the hard cock straining against his fly.

"Fuck, Lainey." He thrusts against me.

We continue like that for I don't know how long. Kissing and thrusting against each other frantically. I'm so wet I'm probably making a mess on his pants. I swear it won't be long before he makes me come like this. His hand slides between us, and his fingers brush my soaked panties. I shudder, crying out. He breaks our kiss and looks at me—another chance to say the safe word.

Another chance I don't take.

He groans as he presses his fingers harder against me before moving my panties aside and slipping his fingers over my bare skin.

"Ben..."

"Fuck, you're so wet. You want to come, Lainey?" His touch is soft, barely there. A tease. A promise.

"Yes...*please.*"

"You want *me* to make you come. Only me." His fingers brush my clit, and my hips jerk, begging for more.

"Yes," I sob.

"Say it." He strokes me again, giving me only a taste of pleasure. "Be a good girl and tell me. I'll make you come so hard you'll fucking see stars."

"You. Only you."

A low, primal moan comes out of him as he thrusts his fingers inside me, fucking me with long strokes before pulling out and rubbing my clit with the perfect amount of pressure that pushes me over the edge. I come hard and fast, screaming so loud I'm sure anyone on the other side of the door heard me.

"Your cum feels so fucking sweet. I can't wait to taste it."

I groan at his words as I ride his fingers, wave after wave of pleasure continuing to crash over me. I grip his shoulders so I don't melt onto the floor in a puddle of bliss. He presses his forehead to mine, our labored breaths mixing. Our gazes meet and all I can think is...finally. This moment was inevitable the second his hand slid over mine in the car on New Year's Eve.

Holding my gaze, he takes his fingers out of me, brings them to his mouth and sucks off my cum. "So. Fucking. Sweet."

A broken moan escapes me. I want to sink to my knees, take him in my mouth, and suck until I get a full taste of him. But before I can move, a loud beep sounds, and a voice erupts from the phone speaker. "Ben, we need you back out here."

He mutters a curse and slowly untangles himself from me. I tug at my clothes while we hold each other's stare. Those butterflies are back, their wings flapping heavy with realization.

I just let a man who wasn't my date give me an orgasm.

He must see the panic in my expression because he sighs and turns away from me. "I've got a private bathroom." He goes to a door on the opposite wall that I assumed was a closet before. Rushing water sounds, and he steps back into the room, tossing a spent paper towel in the trash can beside his desk. "Feel free to use it before you leave. And if you could press the lock, I'd appreciate it."

I nod. This has to be the weirdest post-orgasm conversation I've ever had. And I really hate it.

He gives me a quick nod back and goes to leave. But before he passes me, he stops, and our gazes meet again. His expression is somber, yet a spark flares in his blue eyes. "Don't kiss him. Not tonight. Not after that." His voice is steel, and he doesn't wait for me to answer—because he knows I'll obey.

It takes a few moments before I can move. I use his bathroom to clean up and try to get myself back under control. Though that's a battle I won't win. Holy hell. I have to go back out there and face my date with my body still tingling from Ben's touch.

Wow, I never thought I'd be a fuckgirl.

Once I gather enough courage, I reenter the bar area and scan the room for Duncan. I wouldn't be surprised if he left me. I was gone much longer than any normal bathroom break. I finally find him near the front window, leaning in close and talking to a woman, his hand on her hip. Normally, I'd be pissed he's chatting up another girl on our date, but considering what I just did, he has every right. My stomach churns with guilt as I approach him.

"Hey," I say once I'm beside him.

He stops talking to the woman and gives me a quick scan. His eyes flick behind me toward the bar. He returns his gaze back to me, and a resigned smile graces his lips, which is a lot nicer than I deserve. He should be pissed. "You're back."

"Yeah, sorry about that."

He nods, not looking too put out. "Lainey, this is Rachel."

I smile at her. "Hey, it's nice to meet you. Can I borrow Duncan for a few minutes?"

Rachel looks between us, seeming unsure of our relationship. "Yeah, sure."

I nod toward the corner, but when I move, I sway a bit on my feet. Duncan grabs my elbow to steady me. "You okay?"

"Yeah, I think that last Hurrican-tini is hitting me."

He lifts his highball glass with an amber liquor in it. "My drinks are on the house for the rest of the night."

"Oh really? I guess it was worth it to get a little sprayed, huh?"

"I don't think that's the reason. But I'll take the guilt drinks."

My face flames. Thank goodness it's dark in here. "Look, I'm really sorry. I've never acted like this on a date. I promise there's nothing between me and Ben."

Duncan tilts his head and raises his brows at me.

I am such a terrible liar.

"Okay, there's something. But we've never acted on it." Until tonight. Lie, lie, lie. "I shouldn't have brought you here."

Truth.

"Lainey, it's fine. I was the one who wanted to come here. You suggested other places. As soon as I saw you two together at the bar, I picked up on the vibes. Look, I don't think it's a secret I went on this date because I wanted to be part of your post."

I smile at him. "I got that. I really was looking forward to getting to know you, though."

He nods. "Me too. I mean, I wasn't going to rule out the possibility of sex."

I laugh and sway a bit again but balance myself before Duncan can.

He glances at Rachel. "I know we should probably finish the date for the post, but..."

"No, no. You should totally go back and talk to her. You deserve a good night."

"Thanks. Look, if you mention that we didn't work on the post—"

"No one needs to know how the date ended. Don't worry, I'll make sure everyone knows you're a good guy."

"Thanks, Lainey." He leans and gives my cheek a kiss. "Happy Mardi Gras."

He goes back to Rachel, who looks relieved that we're clearly not a couple. I should go home, but instead, I turn back to the bar. Surprisingly, there's an open seat in front of the female bartender. I don't try to get her attention for a drink. I don't need to lose my inhibitions anymore tonight. I have enough repercussions to deal with tomorrow. Instead, I people watch. The place is rocking, and it looks amazing. Ben replaced the usual red accent lighting with purple and gold, giving the place a real Mardi Gras feel, not to mention some appropriate decorations spread throughout the bar. And this band is electric. I take out my phone and get some video. Hopefully, my post will get Red Poppy some good exposure.

I turn back to the bar and a Hurrican-tini is set in front of me. I look up at the female bartender. "I didn't order this."

"I know. But since you let go of Prince Charming over there, I thought you deserved one. Now, if you decided to keep the date to make my boy jealous, your ass would have been kicked to the curb. I'm Jan, by the way."

"Lainey," I say. "And thanks." I lift my glass in cheers, knowing this isn't a good idea, but too dazed to turn it away.

I sip the martini slowly, not that it makes the effects of the alcohol take hold any less. The whole place has a certain softness to it now, but the music is louder and feels like it's closing in. I should go home. I glance at the front door, and it hits me that I didn't lock Ben's office. Fuck. I make my way unsteadily back. Sure enough, the door opens. I go in, shut it, and press the lock. I blink a few times. What was I going to do next? If the room would stop spinning, maybe I could figure it out. Or maybe I should sit on the couch. Just for a few seconds.

Ash Wednesday

BEN

I LOST TRACK OF LAINEY. LAST TIME I SAW HER, SHE WAS SITTING on the other side of the bar talking to Jan. Then she was gone, and no one knew where she went. Duncan left with another woman. Gotta give the guy credit for not seeming too upset that his date disappeared with another man. Jan said Lainey had started to sway in her seat, so I pray she got a ride home. I've sent her texts, but it doesn't look like she's seen them.

I give the bar one last wipe-down. We had a hell of a night, but now it's three-thirty in the morning and exhaustion is setting in. I let Jan and the rest of my crew go ten minutes ago. I toss the rag in a bin and pull out my keys to unlock my office. As soon as I step in, I stop. Lainey is curled up on the couch, sound asleep. Well, passed out might be a better description. But she's here.

Instead of going home, she came here.

This woman. She's driving me the best kind of crazy. What we did earlier was hot as fuck, but it's not nearly enough. No, it only made me want more of her, which is why the look of panic that came over her face after she came on my fingers disappointed the hell out of me. How can she deny this thing between us when it's this explosive?

Fuck, I can't let my thoughts turn that over anymore. I'm too tired. I set my keys on my desk and flip off the overhead lights, leaving my desk lamp on, and cross over to the couch. I get rid of the remaining beads around my neck, belt, suspenders, and untuck my shirt before gently easing her head up and sit down, letting her head rest on my lap like she did for me on Valentine's Day. She doesn't even stir. I lean back, close my eyes, and let my exhaustion take me.

"Ben?"

The voice pulls me from sleep, and I open my eyes to find a very tousled-looking Lainey blinking at me. "Morning," I say, my voice thick with sleep, though I have no idea what time it is.

"How did I end up here?"

"Not sure. I came in here after we closed, and you were asleep."

She blinks a few times and presses her hands to her temples. "I think I came back because I forgot to lock your office."

"Then Goldilocks found the just right place to go to sleep?"

She snorts a laugh. "I guess. Those martinis hit me like a hurricane."

"Yeah, I had to cut some people off. Your date left with another woman. What did you tell him?"

She winces. "Nothing really. He pretty much guessed. I can't believe I..."

"What? Came like a fucking rockstar on my fingers?" I grin at her, and her blush deepens.

"More like let someone other than my date..."

"Make you come?"

She gives me a frustrated look.

"Regret it?"

Surprisingly, she keeps eye contact with me. I was sure she would try to escape the question.

"I didn't say the safe word," she says quietly.

"That means you wanted it in the moment, not that you don't regret it now."

She sighs. "It shouldn't have happened. Our parents are dating, and unless your dad has a side he hasn't shown yet, Mom is finally dating a decent guy. She'd probably marry him tomorrow if he asked."

I roll my eyes. "That's a bit much for two months of dating."

She shrugs. "My mom has never dated a decent guy. My sister's dad stayed the longest. He waited until she was born before he moved on. My dad took off two hours after she showed him the positive pregnancy test. There was Vince, the firefighter, who ended up being married. Jason, the schoolteacher, who was also banging the principal at his school. And countless other guys who loved and left her, always staying just long enough to give her hope." She pauses and sighs. "Ben, she deserves a good, honest love. If there's a chance to be happily married, I promise she'll take it. And I don't blame her."

Shit. That's a lot to process, but what really sticks out to me is what Lainey said about her father. "You don't know your dad?"

"I know his name. Never met him. Never tried."

"Damn, Lainey. I'm so sorry."

She shrugs again. "It's easy not to give a damn about someone when they never gave one about you."

Tough sentiment and I'm sure she means it, but I imagine they're covering a lifetime of hurt.

"Lainey, my dad isn't like those guys your mom dated. My parents were together for over twenty years. They were dedicated to each other. But this is the first time he's dated since her death. I don't think he'll treat your mom poorly, but it's hard to say if he'll ever be ready to be married again."

She snorts a laugh. "It would be my mom's luck that the first decent guy she dates is just dipping his toe in the dating pool after thirty years. Still, Mike's good for her. And I can't mess it up by having a one-night stand with his son."

"One-night stand? What makes you think it'll only be one time?"

She blinks at me. "Because..." her words trail off.

"What?"

"Look, no offense, but...I don't go out with guys like you."

"Like me?"

"Players." She gestures to the mound of beads on my desk.

Hurt pierces my chest. "I had a Mardi Gras theme night. What did you expect to happen?" I don't get why she thinks me getting beads makes me a player. Then it hits me. "Do you think I'm being Frat Bro Ben with you?"

She doesn't need to confirm it. I can see it on her face. This is why she was so upset about my college reputation on Valentine's Day. She's seen her mom get screwed over by guys like Frat Bro Ben...or whatever she thinks I was like. I didn't cheat or trick women.

My heart plummets and I feel a little sick to my stomach. I was hoping she'd be the one person who saw past Frat Bro Ben, but I'm starting to wonder if I'll ever escape him.

But I have to try.

"Lainey, you're the only woman I've touched since I graduated college."

She looks at me doubtfully. "How is that possible with all the women who give you their number?"

"Because I don't call them."

"Why not?"

"Because Frat Bro Ben's lifestyle got old. I was twenty-four when I graduated, kind of time to stop fucking around. He served his purpose."

"And what was his purpose?"

I sigh. "To get me through my grief. Or rather, to help me ignore it."

A thick silence fills the room.

"Ben." Her expression softens, and she intertwines her hand with mine.

I don't talk about how hard my mom's death was on me. No one who knew me in college realized Frat Bro Ben was a mask. What I didn't get was how hard it would be to shed it once you're used to wearing it. How exposed it makes you feel. How you don't recognize yourself anymore. How you don't even know who you are.

"Want to talk about it?" she asks.

A jumble of nerves fills me. I never talk about the time during my mom's illness. I never wanted anyone to see past the mask. But when I look at Lainey...I want to give her all my secrets. I want her to see all of me.

I clear my throat and hope I can actually get the words out. "She was diagnosed the summer after I graduated from high school. I was going to be an architect major, not because I knew a whole lot about it, but thought it sounded fun. I was dating this girl, Emily, and she was also going to CTU, so I was looking forward to not sneaking around with her anymore. But..."

Emotion clogs my throat and I have to clear it again. "My mom's diagnosis fucked with my head, and I didn't want any of that anymore. I dropped out after two weeks. Emily eventually dumped me since I wasn't exactly a lot of fun to be around. I got odd jobs, but mostly worked here and spent time with my mom. We were starting to feel positive, and then..."

My sinuses burn at the sudden rush of tears, but I force them back. Her grip on my hand tightens even as she uses her thumb to gently stroke my skin in comfort. "We found out the cancer had spread, and just before Christmas, she passed away. I don't remember much about the months after that, but one day, Uncle Red said if I went back to college and got a business degree, he'd turn over the bar to me. So, I did. But I refused to be the dorm's resident sad sack, so I became Frat Bro Ben."

We sit in silence for a while as she continues to give me comforting touches. I think she knows I need a moment to collect myself.

"Then, as a graduation present, Uncle Red turned over the bar to me. I wasn't expecting it so soon, but I'd already told him my vision, and he thought it was time. So, I immediately threw myself into making Red Poppy."

"A reformed fuckboy?"

Achieving that title wasn't ever a goal of mine, but I wasn't interested in love. I didn't want to feel that much, especially for another person. Frat Boy Ben's lifestyle was exactly what I needed. What my parents had was the end game, and since meeting Lainey, I've remembered it was a goal I once wanted—and maybe it could be a possibility for us.

But if I tell her all that, she'll bolt out of this office faster than the Roadrunner. So, instead, I say, "Do you go out with *reformed* fuckboys?"

Silence fills the room as she looks down, her gaze on our interlocked hands. "We can't date, Ben." Her voice is soft, yet there's a finality to it that makes my stomach turn.

"Lainey, we're adults. It doesn't matter that our parents are dating."

Her gaze darts to my desk before she eases her hand out of mine. "Yes, it does. It's what really matters. They're mending their broken hearts together. They deserve this piece of happiness."

"And we don't? Last night was good. Every time we're together, it's good. More than good."

"That's lust."

"So? You never said you regretted it. I think you're not answering because you don't want to admit that *this* can be more than lust."

"It was a mis—"

"Stop." I jump up, my body and voice tight with tension. We can call what we did last night a lot of things, but that was no fucking error in judgment. I pace away, turn back and hold her gaze. "It wasn't a mistake."

Her mouth flattens. "It won't work."

"Why not?"

"Because it *never* works!" Her shouted words vibrate through the room, the anguish in them lingering in the air.

She stands and attempts to leave, but I step in front of her. I can't let her go like this. Her gaze snaps to mine. "Acnestis."

The word hits me like a gut punch. I wasn't expecting that. And as much as I hate that she said it, it's probably best she did. I can't keep pressing her. Not after everything she just told me. So, I nod to let her know that I accept her request to stop.

But that doesn't mean I'm giving up.

I don't just want her. I want to be with her. I want to see if these feelings are as right as they feel.

"Lainey," I say when her hand grips the doorknob. "There is a time for everything and a season for every activity under the heavens."

Her brows furrow in confusion.

"It's a Bible verse. There's more to it, but that's what I remember. Happy Ash Wednesday."

St. Patrick's Day

LAINEY

Happy St. Patrick's Day!!!

BEN

Whoa, this is a surprise. Happy St. Patrick's
Day!

LAINEY

Why is this a surprise?

BEN

Because you never initiate the holiday text.

LAINEY

Oh, I like to initiate. *smirking emoji*

BEN

Lainey, are you drunk?

LAINEY

Maayybeeeee

BEN

Well, at least you're celebrating the holiday
properly. We've been slammed at the bar all
day. Are you on the Irish pub crawl?

LAINEY

Did that already with Ryan.

BEN

Who's Ryan?

LAINEY

pic of a half-drunk margarita in front of basket of chips and salsa

Margarita specials all night!!

BEN

Whoa, wait. You're at a Mexican restaurant? It's St. Patrick's Day, not Cinco de Mayo! You're supposed to be drinking Irish beer or whiskey.

LAINEY

Polka music and skunky beer are not my thing.

BEN

YOU'RE DOING IT ALL WRONG!!

LAINEY

Ugh, don't be a Ryan. Margaritas are green! Joey says it totally counts!!

BEN

Who the hell is Joey?

LAINEY

idk

BEN

You're not making any sense. Who is Ryan?

LAINEY

Holidate.

BEN

And Joey? You're out with two guys?

LAINEY

I ditched Ryan hours ago. Way too serious about a pub crawl.

BEN

You still haven't said who Joey is.

LAINEY

Autocorrect, lol!!!

BEN

gif of man rubbing his face in frustration

I think it might be time to stop drinking.

TEN MINUTES LATER...

BEN

Where did you go? Are you okay?

LAINEY

Not really.

BEN

What's going on?

Seriously, Lainey! Where are you?

LAINEY

Mexican restaurant

BEN

That's specific. There are at least 20 Mexican restaurants just on the street I'm on.

LAINEY

Which one?

BEN

omfg! Where's your date? What's going on?

LAINEY

Next to me. Got kicked out. You spill one drink...

BEN

Jesus. Where are you? I'll pick you up.

LAINEY

No, I'm on a holidate.

BEN

And you're texting me.

LAINEY

Okay, I'll stop.

BEN

Lainey!! Fuck. Please be careful. Don't drive.

An hour later...

LAINEY

I'm not driving.

BEN

I've been going crazy. Where are you?

LAINEY

On way home. Driver just dropped off Josie.

BEN

Josie?

LAINEY

pic of Lainey and a dark-haired woman with margaritas in their hands

Meet my holidate and bff. Josie not Joey.

BEN

I'm thinking the spelling mistake was more user error than autocorrect

You okay? I don't like that you're drunk and alone with a stranger.

LAINEY

Feeling better. Got water while we waited for a ride.

BEN

Good.

LAINEY

Why don't you meet me at my place?

BEN

That's not a good idea.

LAINEY

idk, I think it'll be good. Really really good. *winky face emoji*

BEN

You're drunk. I'm not taking advantage of you.

LAINEY

It's not taking advantage if I invite you. I don't want a gentleman right now. I don't want gentle at all. I want rough and hard.

BEN

Fuck, Lainey...you're killing me.

LAINEY

Come over.

BEN

The first time I fuck you, you're going to be stone-cold sober.

LAINEY

That was hot. That doesn't solve the problem that I'm horny now though. One little fuck...come on...

BEN

Little? That's not how you convince a man to get naked with you.

LAINEY

Then come over and show me I'm wrong.
Sending you a pin of my address.

BEN

Tell you what, if you feel the same way when
you wake up in the morning, text me and I'll be
at your place before your phone goes dark.

LAINEY

Tomorrow is not a holiday. Don't we only do
holidays?

BEN

It's National Awkward Moments Day. Just
looked it up.

LAINEY

Sounds like the perfect day to have sex. *rolling
eyes emoji*

BEN

It's also National Sloppy Joe Day. I can bring
lunch.

LAINEY

Omg, you're not making it any better!

BEN

Sloppy Joes can be sexy

LAINEY

No, they can't! What is wrong with you?

BEN

It's also National Biodiesel Day

LAINEY

wth?

BEN

There's more...

Wait, I got it! National Corn Dog Day. Corn Dogs are definitely sexy. They have wieners. *winky face emoji* *eggplant emoji*

LAINEY

Omg. Carnival food is NOT sexy! And why is one day getting so much attention? That's too many holidays for one day. This conversation has definitely sobered me up. Just come over.

BEN

Text me tomorrow.

LAINEY

Ben!!

BEN

Goodnight, Lainey.

National Supreme Sacrifice Day, National Corn Dog Day, National Sloppy Joe Day, National Lacy Oatmeal Cookie Day, National Awkward Moments Day - March 18th

LAINEY

I KNOW I'M NOT THE ONLY PERSON WHO'S PRAYED TO THE porcelain god after St. Patrick's Day, but I don't think many barfed up copious amounts of tequila and an enchilada plate. I should vow not to drink margaritas or eat Mexican food again, but let's be honest, that'll never happen. Though I might take a break until Cinco de Mayo.

I groan as I reach for the glass of water on my nightstand that I was thankfully smart enough to put there. I have zero plans to leave my bed today. I can post about my date from here and I'll consider my workday done. I'll just have to figure out a way to make my disastrous holidate sound good.

Ryan was one of the many guys who had emailed *What's Good, ATX* interested in being one of my holidates. He was perfect on paper, but who knew he'd take St. Patrick's Day so seriously? He had a schedule of when we would hit up each pub, and God forbid we deviate. He was more than happy to end our date after I suggested we ditch the pubs and get Mexican food. Thankfully, my BFF, Josie, is always on board for margaritas and Mexican food, so I roped her in as my second holidate.

Hopefully, I have enough pics of the pub crawl with Ryan for my post because the drunken photos of me and Josie downing margaritas will *not* be included.

God, what a mess we were. I'm pretty sure I spilled my drink into a basket of chips. Then—

I gasp as I jack-knife in bed.

My head immediately reacts to the quick movement with a sharp stab of pain, and I press my hand to my temple as if it'll help. Even through the throbbing, I remember snippets of the end of the night. Us getting kicked out of the restaurant. Me texting Ben.

Oh God. Why do I have a bad feeling about my texts?

My stomach rolls and I pause, wondering if I'll need to sprint back to the bathroom.

I sit here and breathe, eyes closed, waiting for the wave of nausea to pass. Once I know my stomach isn't going to revolt, I reach for my phone and scroll through our messages, and my stomach is back to sloshing around as my chest tightens. Oh, my God. I don't think I can be more humiliated. Seriously, what is wrong with me? I can't tell him I don't want to date him then beg him to fuck me.

I am the worst sort of wishy-washy that I can't stand.

When did I become that person? Maybe when the margaritas had me confessing to Josie that Ben and I exchanged flirty texts, and let her convince me a booty call text was a good idea.

I can't even work up the courage to text him and thank him for being the voice of reason last night. I toss my phone away and burrow back under my covers.

No idea how long it is before I hear a ring through a fog and blink open my eyes, disoriented for a few seconds before I realize I fell back asleep. I glance at the clock beside my bed and see it's now early afternoon. Shit, I've been asleep for hours and still haven't posted about my date. I grab my phone and see a few texts from my boss. Just great.

I text her back, letting her know it'll be posted within the hour. I don't even know how I'm going to pull that off, but I will. I throw the covers off and get out of bed. My stomach seems to have settled, but my head still feels fuzzy. I pull on pajama bottoms and make my way to the kitchen. A little toast, coffee, and ibuprofen will get me through my post.

As I pass my front door, I remember the ring. It was my doorbell. I open it to see a box on my welcome mat. It's not properly addressed but has a card taped to the top that says, *Don't worry, it's not a bomb - Ben*

I snort a laugh, pick up the box, and take it to the kitchen. I open it up to find another card that reads:

Happy:

National Supreme Sacrifice Day

National Corn Dog Day

National Sloppy Joe Day

National Lacy Oatmeal Cookie Day

National Awkward Moments Day

Oh my gosh, he didn't. I glance inside and see a can of Sloppy Joe mix and a package of buns, a container of lacy oatmeal cookies, a box of frozen corn dogs, a bottle of ibuprofen, and Gatorade.

I open the card and read his note.

Lainey,

I doubt you'll be interested in <u>Sloppy Joe's</u> today, but a <u>corn dog</u> would be a nice greasy hangover lunch. It's the sexiest carnival food around! And if you aren't going to eat those <u>lacy oatmeal cookies,</u> then I request you return to sender. Can't let those babies not be celebrated on their big day.

The ibuprofen and Gatorade don't have a special day (at least not today), but I thought it might help with the hangover you're probably experiencing.

Last night it was <u>supremely</u> hard to not accept your invitation *and you might be suffering an <u>awkward moment</u> this morning after remembering our text exchange, but please don't give it another thought. Drunk texting happens to the best of us. Plus, I definitely experienced an <u>awkward moment</u> this morning while I stared at my phone anxiously hoping for your text to come through.*

I'm <u>sacrificing</u> my pride to give you this package, hoping it'll convince you to text me (not the point of the holiday, but I thought you'd appreciate some humor).

It's not too late to save me from this one. Just saying.

Happy March 18th!

Ben

P.S. It's also Goddess of Fertility Day. So, if you decide to text me that invitation to come over, I'm properly prepared with the special weapon to fight off the Goddess' gift.

I laugh out loud at that last line, and my head reminds me loud sounds are a no-no. I can't believe he did this for me. He's made it impossible for me to ignore him. I go get my phone and text him.

ME

You're kinda funny, you know that? Kinda sweet, too.

BEN

I really want to take those compliments to heart, but I have a feeling that "funny and sweet" is not going to get me an invitation to come over to be rough and hard.

Even as embarrassment washes over me at the reminder of my text, intense tingles fire up between my legs. I don't know how my hungover body can even contemplate getting turned on. But Ben never seems to fail to push those buttons.

ME

> Thank you for being a gentleman last night.

BEN

> You're welcome. And today, I can be as ungentlemanly as you want.

The problem is, I really, *really* want to invite him over. Not only do I want him, but I just plain like him. As humiliating as it is that I begged him to fuck me, I still had a stupid smile on my face reading our text exchange.

I shift back and forth on my feet, staring at my phone for the longest time. I think about the way he smiled at all the women giving him beads on Mardi Gras. Then about everything he confessed about his mom and being Frat Bro Ben. I really don't think he gets how potent his charm is. And while I feel he was genuine on Ash Wednesday, it's still hard to believe his flirting is all for show. Too many men have fooled me before.

Fuck you very much, Isaac and DWs.

The thing is, even if I decide to ignore my issues with fuck-boys, what really matters right now is my mom. I can't intervene on her chance at happiness. Not again.

I have my holidates and a perfectly good vibrator that can take care of my tingling parts. So, I avoid his offer.

ME

> Tequila is the worst!

BEN

> Drink that Gatorade. And next year, stick to Irish beer and fish and chips.

April Fool's Day

BEN

LAINEY

I'm at the hospital. Our parents have struck
again.

I BITE BACK A SMILE. I HAD A FEELING I WOULD HEAR FROM HER
today. Very curious where she's going with this.

ME

What??

LAINEY

They're stuck. Together.

ME

What does that mean?

LAINEY

Um, it seems your dad has a piercing.

I bark out a laugh. At least she's inventive.

ME

No, he doesn't.

LAINEY

It's not somewhere you'd see. And it's new. He and my mom have been...experimenting. *shudders*

ME

You're funny.

LAINEY

I'm not joking! I wish I was. You think I like the picture of our parents stuck together by their hoo-hahs in my mind?

ME

Lainey, it's April Fool's Day. I'm not falling for it. You can stop now.

LAINEY

I'm serious!!

ME

No, you're not. My dad is the last person in the world to get a piercing. Especially through his dick.

The next text that comes through is a picture of a nurse with a mask on holding up an admissions chart with my dad and Kathleen's names on it. Impressive.

ME

Wow, you've really taken this far.

LAINEY

The only other proof I can get is going into the room and taking a picture of them in a very compromising position. I don't think they'll appreciate that. And trust me, that's the last thing I want to see. Besides, the doctor is in there now. I'll update you in a bit.

I shake my head. I dip out of our text exchange and text my dad. I'm going to catch her in her lie.

ME

Okay, sure.

LAINEY

I'm serious!!

ME

I texted my dad.

LAINEY

Have you heard back?

I don't answer since I haven't. Not that he's the most timely when it comes to responding to texts.

LAINEY

You can call him. I'll wait for you to tell me he didn't answer.

ME

Fine, I'll call. But I still don't believe you.

I call my dad, and it eventually rolls into voicemail. In all the times I've called my dad, he hasn't answered maybe three times. Doubt creeps in, but I refuse to entertain it. It's April fucking Fool's Day. I'm not going to fall for it.

LAINEY

I'm calling you. The doctor just came out.

A moment later, my phone rings with a video call and when I answer, I see her in what looks like a hospital hallway. She immediately says, "Hey, here's the doctor."

The screen shifts, and I'm eyeing what looks like a real doctor, scrubs and all. "Hello, Ben, I'm Dr. Wheeler. Your parents are in a lot of pain, so I think it's best if we put them under to separate them. It's a delicate situation, and any movement or, um, stimulation could make things worse."

I'm silent for a beat. There's no way this is real. Yet, my heart-beat has picked up, and worry has set in.

"Are you serious?" I demand. "This isn't a joke?"

"I'm sorry, it's not. I understand it's not the best day for a situation like this." He gives me a sympathetic smile. "It's actually more common than you'd think. It's a complicated surgery with their positions, but they should be able to go home this afternoon, depending on how they respond to the anesthesia. And, of course, I'll have to assess any damage first."

"Damage?"

"There could be some extensive tearing for both patients."

I wince and resist the urge to cover my own dick in protection.

"Of course, they should abstain for—"

"Um, yeah, I think you can leave the aftercare instructions to them."

"Right. Of course. I need to prep now. The sooner we take care of this, the better. I'll talk with y'all post-op." He gives me a nod, and then I see him squeeze Lainey's shoulder. There's no doubt she's in a hospital.

Jesus. I look around my office for my keys. If my dad's having surgery, even if it's the most ridiculous surgery I've ever heard of, I need to be there.

Lainey comes back on screen. "Believe me now?"

"I can't believe I'm saying this, but yeah. What hospital are you at?"

"Gotcha Memorial."

I pause. "What?"

"Happy April Fool's Day, Ben!" Several people's laughter rings through the line before she ends the call. I drop my head, kinda hating myself for falling for it when I knew it was a prank.

ME

I fucking knew it!

LAINEY

And I still got you.

victory dance gif

ME

Who the hell was that guy?

LAINEY

Dr. Wheeler. I guess I never told you that my friend Josie is a nurse. Once I told them the plan, they were all in. Your dad was a good sport, too. I asked him to ignore your calls and texts.

ME

You're diabolical.

LAINEY

I had to be. I knew you'd expect it.

ME

I'm going to get you back.

LAINEY

Give it your best shot!

I smile. She might have won this round, but the game's not over.

LAINEY

Why are there trombone players at my desk playing Pharrell's Happy?

ME

Happy Trombone Players Day!

LAINEY

There's no way you pulled this off in a couple of hours.

ME

I've had this planned for two weeks. Had to get your office's permission and everything.

I knew you wouldn't fall for an April Fool's joke, so I went for another "holiday."

LAINEY

The whole office is staring and videoing me. I can't believe you did this.

ME

hahaha, I know. Your boss just sent me a video. Man, it's so fucking awesome.

LAINEY

It's really fucking loud!

ME

Enjoy the next hour of some fine trombone music. They're paid to follow you wherever you go.

Oh, and your boss assured me you can't leave the office early. Go ahead ask her.

Send me a selfie with the players.

LAINEY

pic of a middle finger with trombone players in background

Easter

LAINEY

I'M GOING TO HELL.

I'm pretty sure getting turned on during Easter service is way up there on the sin scale. No amount of prayers is going to save me. Not with Ben pressed against me in the overcrowded pew.

I knew Mike was joining us for church and at my sister's house afterward for lunch, but I wasn't expecting Ben. My brain and body have been going haywire from the moment I saw him. Now with every brush of his body against mine, my panties are getting wetter. My nipples are already so hard they actually hurt.

I glance over, and Ben meets my gaze. His pupils have taken over those gorgeous blue irises, and his breathing is way too erratic for just sitting in church. His hot gaze dips to my breasts, and a tiny groan escapes him before he faces forward again, his hands balling into fists. The fact he's fighting to keep in control only makes me hotter—*wetter*. I cross my legs to give my pussy some relief.

"Jesus." He picks up a hymnal and places it on his lap.

Oh, we are so going to hell.

Somehow, we get through the rest of the service without bursting into flames. As soon as we stand, Ben jumps into the aisle and says he'll meet us outside. Thankfully, the next hour is busy with getting back to Harper's and helping set out food. When I stop, I catch him flirting with Mrs. Abbott, Harper's sweet elderly neighbor, from across the living room. And she's eating up every bit of it. I can't help but smile. This is probably the happiest I've ever seen Mrs. Abbott. His charm is so effortless, making her feel young and carefree. It's hard not to admire that part of him right now.

She laughs at something he says then gives him a playful pat on the arm before walking away with flushed cheeks. His smile lingers—until our gazes collide. It's suddenly as if we're back in that pew, our bodies pressed against each other. Everything stills. Heats. And I'm imagining straddling him and begging him to make me see heaven.

Jesus. Why can't I seem to remember he's all sorts of wrong for me? One text, one look, and I lose all reason.

"Why is Ben eye fucking you from across the room?"

I startle and look to Harper. "What? No, he isn't."

My sister raises one perfect eyebrow. I've always envied her ability to do the evil one eyebrow raise while also glad I couldn't do it since it's so very Harper. "Yes, he was. And you were taking every bit of it, too."

My face feels like it's on fire which is probably a big red sign telling Harper I'm lying, but I roll my eyes and head toward the kitchen. "You're ridiculous."

Unfortunately, I don't escape her that easily, as she follows right on my heels. "It was like a porn scene out there. It's *Easter*, Lainey."

"Oh my God, Harp, you're being a little dramatic." I stuff a deviled egg in my mouth and look around for something to distract me from this conversation.

Harper's gaze narrows as she cocks her hip against the counter. She hates it when I call her dramatic, and I can tell she's doing her best to not let it get to her. "Look, I get it. He's hot. Really hot. Which you totally forgot to mention, by the way. But you can't go there." She glances back into the living room. "I've never seen a guy like this with Mom. She's so happy." Her voice is almost dreamy.

I follow her stare where Mom and Mike are standing, his arm around her waist as he watches her tell a story with the most adoring expression on his face. No man has ever looked at her that way.

Harper's right. Not that I didn't already know that. Still...it makes me want to throw something—preferably at her.

Harper looks back at me. "Seriously, don't fuck this up for her."

"Jeez, thanks." I pop another egg in my mouth before I decide to smoosh it all over her silk blouse.

"You know what I mean."

I swallow and face Harper, now pissed. "No, I don't, actually. What do you mean? Go ahead, spell it out."

"For one, you said he was a fuckboy. Do you really want to get involved with another guy like that?"

"Harp—"

She holds out her hand. "Yeah, yeah, he's a nice guy, but you thought Isaac was nice too. Come on, you don't exactly have a great track record when it comes to guys. Your relationships tend to pan out as well as your jobs. He's Mike's son, Lainey, you need to stay the hell away before this blows up in your face. You can't fuck this up for Mom. Again."

Her words spear me right in the chest. I don't even know where to start with her tirade. She's acting like I purposely set out to sabotage my dates. And Mom's. I don't get why she keeps reminding me about something I did when I was sixteen. Like I've repeated that behavior over and over. It was a four-month period in my life, and she benefited from my intervention just as much as I did.

"What the hell, Harp? I thought it was Easter not *Throw Lainey's Mistakes in her Face Day*?" I hate that my voice shakes with hurt instead of the anger I really want to throw at her. "You really need to stop bringing up what I did in high school like I'm some villain trying to make Mom's life miserable. I was a fucking kid needing my mom to step up as a parent."

A tense silence fills the room as Harper stares at me open-mouthed. Suddenly, tears flood her eyes before she covers her face with her hands and slumps over. "Oh my God, I'm so sorry," she says in a muffled voice. She takes a few broken breaths before dropping her hands, tears slipping down her cheeks. "That was really horrible of me."

"Yeah, it was." I wrap my arms around my middle, my own tears threatening.

She comes over and pulls me into a tight hug. I don't move, still feeling to raw to hug her back. "I don't know what came over me. I guess...she's been doing so well, and I don't want to see her revert back to her old self if things go south. I can't handle it again, Lainey."

My anger immediately dissolves, and I relax in her arms and hug her back. I don't tell her it's okay, because it's not. But I get it. Our mom has handled relationships so much better since her dating break, but no one has caught her attention like this. If it doesn't work out, the fallout could be momentous.

"Maybe it's *Harper's Childhood Trauma Day*," I say to lighten the mood.

She barks out a laugh and pulls back to meet my gaze. "You might be right." She wipes away her tears and shakes her head at herself. "Man, what a mess. Forgive me?"

"Always. Keep it up though, and I'm enrolling you in drama school."

Her body relaxes in relief. "Deal." She takes my hands in hers. "I'm just so hopeful about this one. And I haven't felt that way in a long time. I know you feel it too, Lain."

"I do."

Which is why I need to double-down on my resolve to stop this thing between me and Ben.

Putting our fight behind us, we move on to hiding Easter eggs. Harper's Easter party is not a simple family affair. She pretty much invites her whole neighborhood and to call it hectic is a massive understatement. Kids dressed in pastels run amok, high on sugar, squealing at an octave that usually has my ears ringing for forty-eight hours. As torturous as it is, there's nothing more entertaining than seeing dozens of sweet-looking cherubs go full-out Hunger Games for some candy-filled plastic eggs. And while Harper might drive me crazy, I love her and the amazing niece she's given me. The few hours of chaos are totally worth it.

The tricky part will be avoiding Ben for the rest of the afternoon.

Once the eggs are hidden in my sister's giant backyard, all the adults gather as the children line up, armed with their gingham-lined baskets. Their expressions grow more and more fierce as they scan the lawn before them, plotting their route.

A whistle is blown, and they're off.

"Holy sh..."

I glance over my shoulder to see Ben standing behind me, his expression horror-stricken at the scene before him. So much for avoiding him. I dart a glance at Harper and see she's preoccupied with the hunt.

Suddenly, he winces, so I turn back to see what I missed.

"Your niece just took out a boy twice her size. Like literally body-checked him."

I look around until I locate Cassie and the carnage she left behind her as she picks up a blue Easter egg. "That's my girl."

Ben chuckles. His chest brushes against my shoulder, and it takes all my willpower not to lean back into him.

"Man, this is brutal," he says. "Cassie scares me a little bit now."

I laugh. "She is Harper's child. You've met my sister. She's super scary."

I feel his laughter more than hear it. "She is, but I like her. Chandler, too. Actually, your whole family is really great, Lainey."

The genuine tenderness in his voice melts my heart. I have a lot of love for my brother-in-law. He doesn't let Harper get too lost in her own head, he's her rock. He's so good for her that I can't even be annoyed that she found her perfect match so easily while Mom and I have struggled. Mike and Ben fit right in, too, like they should be family. I look over my shoulder at him again. "Thanks."

Our gazes lock, and suddenly, our sentimental moment turns scorching, and all I want to do is everything I just resolved myself not to. Lean into him. Wrap my arms around him. Kiss him. Climb him. Sink down on his—

I jerk my gaze away. Fuck! I need to get a grip.

His chest presses in on me as he leans closer, his head bending down toward my ear. "Never in my life did I think I'd have to fight so many boners on Easter Sunday."

I choke back a laugh. "Yeah, well, keep fighting," I whisper back. "And stop eye-fucking me from across the room. Harper noticed."

He inches even closer, his mouth brushing the lobe of my ear. I feel his fingers brush the back of my thigh. "I'd rather be fucking you."

My whole body flushes as the image of him ripping my dress

and burying his cock inside me flashes in my mind. It's so vivid and tempting I have to suppress a moan. "Stop it!"

He laughs and drops his hand, the deep rumble of his voice against my body way more erotic than it should be. Thankfully, the hunt takes over our attention and gives us time to cool down. After the eggs are found, lunch is served then the kids settle (mostly) in the living room with a movie as the parents lounge outside with wine. I head into the kitchen to start cleaning up, letting Harper enjoy this moment with her friends. As I enter, I get yanked into the laundry room. Before I can process what's happened, Ben has me pressed up against the dryer.

"What the hell are you doing?" I whisper-hiss.

"Getting you alone. Your family is impossible to escape. Your sister talks *a lot*." He brushes his mouth at my temple as he boxes me in.

"Because she's probably trying to prevent you from hiding away in the laundry room with me. She's banking on you being my future stepbrother."

"Lainey, it's only been four months."

"I know, but she might not be wrong. Our parents are silly over each other, so we really shouldn't be in here together."

"Hmmm...probably not."

Yet, he doesn't move away. No, he leans closer.

I shake my head. "Does anyone ever tell you no?"

His blue eyes roam my face, lingering on my mouth. "Not often."

One of his hands wraps around to my back, slowly moving up until it finds that unreachable spot between my shoulder blades. He adds pressure and holds my gaze, "You know how to tell me no."

Yes, I do. And yet, I stay silent.

His hand slips from my back and makes its way to the hem

of my dress. "This has been killing me all day. Do you even realize how sexy you look?"

"It's an Easter dress. It's not supposed to be sexy."

His gaze soaks up my body. "It fits you like a fucking dream. You have no idea the fantasies that have been playing over and over in my mind. Are you wearing panties?" His fingers trace where my inner thighs and dress meet.

"Ben, you don't go commando on Easter. I wore this to *church* this morning."

"I'm well aware. Every time you crossed and uncrossed your legs, I broke into a sweat." He nuzzles his nose over my cheek, letting his lips brush my ear. "I needed to be alone with you. I want to touch you." His fingers keep brushing my thighs causing little fires to ignite all through my body. I feel my panties grow wet. Again. "Fuck, I can smell you. So damn sweet...let me touch you, Lainey."

I grip the edge of the dryer to stop myself from jerking my hips toward him in invitation. "Ben, you can't finger me on Easter."

"I can make you feel alive. Isn't that what Easter is all about? Being alive."

"I think that's playing fast and loose with the translation."

He chuckles. "I'm pretty sure there are lots of loose translations out there. What's one more?"

I can't help but laugh and wrap my arms around his neck. I press my forehead to his. "You're something else, you know that?"

"Yeah, but that's why you like me."

Suddenly the air around us seems to still—thicken. There's simply this pull toward him. I'm caught. Mesmerized. And powerless to fight against it.

"I do like you."

The admission feels...good.

I don't know how it happens, but we're kissing. It isn't hurried but soft and achingly gentle. It feels like a promise. It feels powerful—like it could break my heart.

I need to pull away. Stop this before it becomes a wrong we can't right. Instead, I dig my fingers into his hair, and our kiss goes from tame to feverish. We're pulling at each other as if we're trying to crawl inside one another. I grab his shirt and pull it up so I can splay my hands over his flat stomach. He lifts me onto the dryer, my dress bunches at my waist as I wrap my legs around him. He presses his cock against me, and I moan, shamelessly rubbing myself against him. Fuck, he feels so good. So wonderfully hard and thick. I want him like I've never wanted anyone in my life. God, I want him inside me.

He rips his mouth from mine and looks at me with a dazed heat. I don't know if I said that out loud or if he's thinking the same thing. His expression morphs into, *do we dare?*

The silence between us is deafening until voices come into the kitchen. We both freeze. I jump off the dryer, and we frantically straighten our clothes.

"Think we should take two bottles back out? There's still so many people." The voice is my mother's.

"I think we should take three," Mike says.

My mom laughs and there's some clinking sounds then my mom squeals and laughs. "What are you doing?"

"Dancing with you."

"There's no music."

"We make our own music. And maybe I just want an excuse to touch you."

I lock eyes with Ben. I really hope our parents aren't planning to jump into the laundry room for a quickie like their children. We edge closer to the door and squint to see between the slats. Our parents are slow dancing, then Mike twirls her and pulls her back in.

"Today has been a great day," Mom says. "I'm so glad you're here."

Mike stops their dancing. "I love you."

My hands fly to my mouth to stop my gasp. Ben looks equally shocked before his expression morphs into one of concern.

"What?" my mom says a little breathlessly.

"I love you. Today has been such a perfect day. Your daughters and granddaughter are amazing, and our families get along so well. It feels like coming home, Kathy."

I squint to see my mom still standing in his arms, a shocked expression on her face and maybe some tears in her eyes.

"It's okay if you're not ready to say it back. I just want to be with you. You're the first thing I think about in the morning and the last thing before I go to bed. And I—"

"Let's live together." My mom's sudden outburst has Ben and me jerking in surprise. We look at each other, and I mouth *what* at him as he shakes his head in disbelief.

"Really?" Mike says.

My mom nods. "You're the first and last thoughts of my day, too. I love you, Mike. So much."

They kiss and I turn away quickly. Ben does, too. I can't believe this. They're moving in together? After four months?

"Okay, okay, we have to stop," Mom says breathlessly.

"No, we don't. There's a laundry room."

My eyes round in horror. So do Ben's. We look around for I don't know what...a place to hide? There is none because it's a freaking laundry room!

"You're terrible. How about we deliver this wine then I say I'm tired and we can get out of here?"

"That's definitely a better plan."

Ben and I both release a heavy breath. I hear more kissing sounds before they leave. Once they're gone, we're silent for several moments. Ben looks shell-shocked, and I can't tell if he's upset his dad moving in with my mom or not.

Ben finally meets my gaze. "He's happy. Really happy."

I nod.

He runs a hand over his face. "It's been a really long time since I've seen him like this. Since before my mom got sick."

I reach out and touch his arm. "Are you okay with it?"

He releases another deep breath. "I think so. I'd almost forgotten him this way." He gives me a small smile. "How are you feeling about your mom shacking up with my dad?"

"It's a bit of a surprise. My mom used to fall fast, but never lived with anyone. Well, there was one guy who stayed with us a couple of weeks, but turned out he just needed a place to crash until he convinced his ex to take him back."

"Lainey, I can tell you with a hundred percent certainty that my dad didn't say those words lightly. If he moves in with your mom, he's serious about her."

I nod. Mike is different. This really is our mom's chance at happily ever after.

Ben sighs heavily. "Okay, I get what you've been saying." He looks at me, his expression somber. "Maybe what almost happened in here isn't a good idea. I don't want to mess anything up for my dad."

This is exactly what I've wanted. For us to be on the same page. So, why does hearing him agree feel like I'm drowning with no hope of reaching the surface?

Maybe it hurts because it's right.

I let myself get caught up in him two hours after resolving to stay away from him. I can't keep making these bad and selfish decisions, or I'm going to wreck my family.

"I don't want to mess things up for my mom either," I finally say, and our gazes meet. The heaviness between us is so thick it's almost suffocating.

Damn. How can being right feel so wrong?

No. This is right. It has to be. Because this is the one thing I can't be wrong about.

He blows out a breath. "Well, it's a good thing we didn't christen your sister's dryer."

I bark out a laugh. "Yeah, pretty sure that's not the kind of christening you should do on Easter."

"I don't know. I imagine this room would have heard plenty of, *Oh God!, Oh God yes!*"

We stare at each other for a second before we start laughing. When we finally get ourselves under control, we smile, a soft sadness filling the air. It feels natural when we move into each other and hug. I burrow my face into his chest and inhale his scent as if it'll somehow stay with me when he steps away.

"Friends?" he asks.

I nod against his chest. "Friends." I ignore the pinch of pain in my heart and step out of his arms. "It's time to wash the dishes. Want to dry?"

"I think I can handle that."

Cinco de Mayo

BEN

I TOLD LAINEY I WANTED TO BE FRIENDS, AND HERE I AM, THE VERY next holiday, on a date with her. Actually, it's a double date with her sister and brother-in-law, and *technically* it's a holidate. But, still. Probably not the direction I should be going if I want to think of her as a friend and not the woman I want to fuck so badly I can't see straight. Of course, she looks gorgeous tonight. She's wearing a low-cut bright red blouse with loose ruffles along the neckline that draw the eye to her amazing tits and a pair of skintight jeans hugging her curves perfectly. With her lips glossed to match her blouse, I can't keep thinking how I want my cock covered in that exact color.

Damn, I really need to get my lust-addled brain under control.

"Here you go," the waitress says as she sets down our second round of margaritas. "Anything else I can do for y'all?"

"Oh, we need a photo before we drink. We forgot before," Lainey says. "Would you mind taking one?"

"Of course," she says, but her smile is strained. The place is packed so this is probably the last thing she wants to stop and do.

Chandler and I stand behind Harper and Lainey with our glasses up for the picture. Once that it's taken, I take the phone and glance at her nametag. "Thanks, Jill. You're taking such good care of us. It's too bad you can't sit and enjoy one with us."

Her body immediately relaxes, and her smile turns genuine. "Aww, thanks. Don't I wish. But a Mexican Martini is waiting for me as soon as we close."

"They're amazing here. I've tried to replicate it, but it's never as good. You must have some secret ingredient."

Her eyes light up before she leans in. "The secret is our specialty olive brine."

"Oh man, who do I have to charm to get that info?"

"Just me." Her grin turns mischievous as she closes the distance between us and whispers a couple of ingredients into my ear then presses a finger to her lips.

I zip my lips with my fingers and pretend to toss the key away, causing her to laugh. "Can I get you anything else?"

"How about an order of nachos?" I ask the table as I sit back down. They're all staring at me with slightly stunned expressions. Finally, Chandler agrees.

"Thanks, Jill." I give her a big smile and she pats my shoulder before walking off.

"Wow, I totally see the player in you now. I think we'll get stellar service for the rest of the night," Harper says with a laugh.

My brows furrow and I glance at Lainey. She's taking a drink from her margarita and looking away. What did she tell her sister?

"I wasn't being a player. I was being nice."

Lainey snorts. "You were flirting. Trust me, you're going to have another number to add to your pile by the end of the night."

"Flirting isn't the same as being a player."

"I didn't mean anything by that," Harper says quickly. "Just hadn't seen your charm in action yet,"

I'm still looking at Lainey and she holds my gaze for a charged moment before saying, "You're right."

Except I don't believe her.

Am I taking my flirting too far? I thought I was just easing Jill's stress. Thankfully, the subject moves on, but a twisting feeling stays in my stomach for a little longer.

"Okay, seriously, Lainey. What happened with the hot hockey player?"

Harper has tried a couple of times to get Lainey to talk about her Kentucky Derby holidate yesterday, but Lainey has deflected. He was supposed to be her date today, too, but for whatever reason, that didn't happen—not that I'm not sad about it. The guy was good-looking and on the local NHL affiliate hockey team. The comments on her post had all been about how good they looked together.

Lainey lets out a frustrated laugh. "Oh my God, Harper." She tosses a tortilla chip at her. "Why are you obsessing over this?"

"Because you're being weird. Was there an awkward morning after today?"

My stomach lurches and my gaze jerks to Lainey. Did she sleep with him? She's rolling her eyes at Harper. "I didn't sleep with him. It was a first date."

Harper gives her a look. "Pretty sure that hasn't stopped you before. Something must have happened for you to call us as your emergency holidate."

Lainey sighs. "He was fine. He just wasn't second-date worthy."

Harper tosses her hands up in a give-up gesture. "None of them are."

Lainey takes a sip of her margarita.

"What happened to that guy we met last year? He was nice. What was his name? Tim?"

Chandler laughs. "Come on, Harper, you can't be serious. That guy was about as exciting as watching paint dry."

"He was nice!" Harper insists.

"They had nothing in common. I'm honestly surprised the guy lasted as long as he did."

Lainey waves her hands at the couple. "Um, you know I'm sitting right here?"

"Sorry, Lain," Chandler says. "But all the guys I've met have been totally wrong for you."

Lainey's mouth flattens as she leans back in her seats and folds her arms across her middle.

"Come on, spill the tea about the hockey guy. You guys looked great together, and he seems so genuine. Did you see all the charity work he does? The videos of him teaching kids to play hockey...so hot. And there are lots of Big Dick Energy thirst trap videos out there with him." Harper wiggles her brows.

Lainey barks out a laugh. "Harp, it sounds like you want to go out with the guy."

Harper waves her comment away. "I already have my BDE man."

"Harp!" This is from Chandler.

"TMI," Lainey says at the same time.

I can't help but laugh. This conversation has taken quite a turn.

"Come on, how was this guy so bad? Because I'm not buying it."

I want to come to her defense since she clearly doesn't want to talk about it, but I'm also curious.

Lainey and Harper engage in some sort of glare-off before Lainey finally relents. "Maybe what you see on social media isn't necessarily what you get."

The sisters seem to have a silent conversation that appeases Harper's curiosity.

"Oh." She sighs. "Don't you hate it when they have the wrong kind of big dick energy?"

This makes us all laugh and successfully diverts the conversation away from Lainey's love life. After our second round of drinks, Lainey and Harper are having a blast together. The restaurant has a band on the patio, and the girls eventually leave us to join the people who have started dancing.

Watching them, they definitely seem related though they have some stark differences in their looks. Lainey's skin has a natural sun-kissed tone to it with deep brown eyes, while Harper's skin is pale, like Kathleen's, and has light hazel eyes. Their hair color is probably similar, but Harper's is dyed a cool blonde while Lainey's is all warm autumn colors. Guessing their dads look quite different from each other, or possibly different races.

"I love it when Harper enjoys a few drinks," Chandler says, smiling as he watches his wife let loose on the dance floor. "She doesn't let herself stop since we've had Cassie. She needs these moments in her life, and it's good to see them have fun together."

"What's their deal? They seem to have a bit of a contentious relationship."

"Harper has always been protective over Lainey. Sometimes it's hard for her to remember Lainey's an adult now and can take care of herself."

They've stopped dancing and have interlocked arms to take sips from their margarita glasses much like a groom and bride would do. Once they're successful, they start laughing and dancing again.

"Look, I know your dad is dating Kathleen, and I love her, I do," Chandler says, "but she wasn't exactly always there for the girls."

"What do you mean?"

"She was a single mom, so she worked a lot, but whenever she started dating someone, she'd let them consume her. At least, that's how Harper described it."

"Yeah, Lainey makes it sound like she had some really bad luck with guys."

Chandler snorts. "That's an understatement. I think Kathleen is so eager to be loved that it seems to attract the kind of guy who takes advantage and when the girls were younger, she allowed it. The girls had to rely on each other a lot and pick up the pieces when she got dumped."

And now their mom's in another relationship that's going ninety miles an hour. My dad invited me over the week after Easter to tell me he'd fallen in love with Kathleen and asked permission to move in with her as if he was a teenager. He acknowledged it was fast, which is why he and Kathleen agreed they'd look at it as a trial instead of making a permanent move. So, my dad's keeping the house and only moving the bare minimum for now.

At least they're thinking it through. Which sounds like it's more than Kathleen usually does.

"This thing with your dad could be the real deal, though," Chandler says. "Kathleen took a dating break when Lainey was in high school and started seeing a therapist. I think it's helped her navigate dating better, but things still haven't ever worked out for her."

I rub a hand up my face. "All this has been a bit surprising. After my mom died, my dad said he would never love again. And now...sometimes I wonder, can it be real if it's happening this fast?" However, my feelings for Lainey seem to grow with every text we exchange. "But if he says he loves her, he means it. He would never abuse those words."

Chandler nods. "I think the girls know that too. I've never seen Harper this excited for her mom."

It seems like he wants to say more but stops himself. "What are you not saying?"

A hesitant smile forms on his lips. "Harper worries about you and Lainey being together—"

"Lainey and I aren't together."

Chandler gives me a deadpan look.

"We're not. We're friends." I deliver the line with surprising ease considering how much I want to choke on that f-word.

"Bro, you should see the way you look at her. If you're just friends, you definitely don't want to be."

I sigh and take a drink of my beer. "Nothing's happened between us."

Another doubtful look from Chandler.

"Okay, nothing *much*. We mutually decided to only be friends. We realize how important our parents' relationship is and don't want to mess it up."

Chandler doesn't say anything for a while.

"For what it's worth, you two have a good vibe going. Better than any other joker she's dated."

My heart stutters.

"But the girls don't trust guys easily—not after what they saw their mom go through. It took a lot to earn Harper's trust. And Lainey went through a bad breakup in college, so that didn't help. You'll need to be patient with her."

Because it never works.

Her words from Ash Wednesday, right before she used our safe word, come back to me. I understand them so much more now. Some asshole broke her heart, and whether it was bad luck, poor taste, or judgment, she's seen her mom get screwed over again and again. And here I am, telling her I want her then flirting with the waitress.

I glance at her on the dance floor. Her skin is shiny with sweat, and her hair is frizzing out of control, yet she's never looked so beautiful. Fuck. I've got it bad for her. How am I supposed to be just friends with her? I want to say fuck it and take Chandler's advice. But what if she's right and it doesn't work out? It's not like I know a lot about being in a relationship either.

My dad had been a shell of the man he used to be until he started dating Kathleen. I don't want to be the cause of him reverting back to that.

The band transitions into a slower song, and Harper runs back, grabbing Chandler and dragging him to the dance floor. Lainey laughs at them before she turns back to look at me, still smiling. I should let her sit while we awkwardly watch Harper and Chandler dance, but I don't. No, I stand and take her hand, not even giving her the option of saying no, and lead her to the dance floor.

The music still has enough liveliness to it that I can twirl her around without pulling her too close. I dip her, making her laugh, so I dip her again. When I pull her back up, we're both grinning like loons. The music slows. Our smiles dampen, but her eyes still shine as she looks at me. Unable not to, I pull her closer and wrap my arms around her waist. Her hands rests on my biceps, and we're moving together like we're at a middle school dance.

"Why aren't you here with the hockey player? What really happened?" I murmur.

Her mouth flattens, and I get a sickening feeling in my stomach. It takes everything I have to keep dancing, to not draw attention. "Lainey, did he hurt you? Touch you?"

Her eyes dart away, and my fingers dig into her waist as fury fills me. "I'll fucking ki—"

"No," she says quickly. "He got a little handsy as the date

went on but didn't cross a line. He wanted me to have a three-some with him and one of his teammates."

Forget not drawing attention, I stop dancing. "For real?"

"They like to share. It was a very enlightening conversation." She glances away and shrugs.

"But you didn't do it." I really fucking hope she didn't, considering she said she didn't sleep with him.

"No." Her deep brown eyes meet mine. "I don't want to be shared like I'm a dessert they can't finish."

No. She deserves to be owned. To be treasured.

I let my hand wander up her back until I find that special spot between her shoulder blades. I press my fingers into her and her breath turns shallow as she melts into the touch.

I let my fingers tell her what I can't say. What I just told myself not to feel.

I'll be patient.

You're mine.

Mother's Day

LAINEY

9:27 A.M.

ME

Here I am, pumping myself up to handle lunch with my mom and Harper's crew, then I think of you. I imagine this day must be hard for you and I wanted to say, I'm thinking of you and hope today is full of all the good memories you cherish. If you want to talk, I'm here.

BEN

Thanks. It'll be fine. My dad and I spend the day together. Enjoy your time with your mom.

ME

Thanks.

7:37 p.m.

BEN

Today's been shit. Will you come over?

ME

Send me your address.

WHEN BEN OPENS THE DOOR, the first thing I notice is how tired he looks, as if he hasn't slept in days. His hair is spiking in all directions, his eyes are dull and sunken in looking, and there's this agitated tension radiating from him. But when he sees me, his body seems to instantly relax. A sad smile forms on his lips.

"Thanks for coming." He steps aside for me to come in.

"Of course." I enter, and he closes the door behind me.

We just stand there, an awkward silence between us.

He rubs the back of his neck. "I feel a little silly for asking you to come over. You know what, it's fine. I'm fine. You—"

I rush to him and wrap my arms around his waist and pull him into a tight hug. "I'm not going anywhere."

"Lainey, seriously, it's fine. I was—"

"Ben." He looks down at me, his chest moving up and down in heavy breaths. "We're friends. You had a bad day. I'm here. For you."

After a moment of standing stock-still, he collapses into me. He wraps his arms around me and pulls me until I'm crushed against him. He buries his face into my neck and releases a shaky sigh. I pull him closer and let him take all the comfort he needs.

"I'm sorry," he mutters against my shoulder.

"There's nothing to be sorry for."

I slide my hand up his back and gently rub the spot between his shoulder blades—our spot. He sighs and relaxes into me even more. We stay like that for a long time, and when he pulls back, he swipes at his shiny eyes, avoiding my gaze. "I'll, um, be right back. Make yourself at home. There's wine in the kitchen."

He disappears down a hallway. I go into his kitchen and search around until I've found wine glasses and pour each of us one. Heading into his living room, I note how nice his apartment is. It's a newer complex, so his kitchen has a marble-looking counter with modern cabinets. His couch is contemporary but looks comfortable with a simple coffee table and stylish lamps sitting atop the two end tables. He has a narrow table under his giant television that's mounted on the wall with pictures of his family and a few people I don't recognize.

For a guy who was considered Frat Bro Ben a year ago, his place is anything but frat-ish. It's an adult's apartment.

I bend to look at a picture of him and his mom. She's beautiful, and Ben favors her a lot, especially her bright blue eyes. Those pictures are the most decorative items in the place, other than two large canvas photographs behind his couch. One is of the Red's Place sign, and the other is the sign as Red Poppy.

Ben emerges from the hallway. There's still some sadness lingering around his eyes, but mostly, the pain has disappeared. He sits on the sofa next to me, a sheepish expression on his face as I hand him a glass of wine. "I have to say, for all the reasons I've invited a woman over for, crying on her shoulder's definitely a first."

"I'm truly honored." I keep my tone light, hoping to inject some humor into the situation.

He looks at me, his gaze roaming over my face, settling on my lips before moving back up to my eyes. "You should be."

I swallow and look away, unable to handle the fierceness in his voice. I take a sip of my wine. "So, um, I'm sorry today was tough."

"I didn't think it would hit me so hard. The past Mother's Days were difficult, but I got through them. When she was sick, we got used to focusing on the good days, so that's what we always did even after she died. This year was different. It's the fifth Mother's Day since she's been gone, and something about it being a milestone year made it seem so much more significant. Then...and I really don't mean any disrespect to your mom or anything, but...he's moved on. And..." Emotion clogs Ben's throat. "And even though I'm happy for him, it also made me really fucking sad. It means she's really gone. And how stupid is that? She's been gone for five years."

He stops, his jaw clenching as he works through his emotions. I weave my fingers through his, squeezing his hand. "It's not stupid, Ben."

"He was different this year, too. And it really fucking pissed me off. I'm sorry to say, it made me resent your mom a little. And I don't. Not really. I don't know. It's just been a hard day."

I don't know how to respond. I understand what he's going through to an extent. Father's Day isn't easy for me. Harper's dad eventually stepped up and wanted to be part of her life. He didn't live nearby, and the times she left to spend time with him when we were younger, I always resented her a little bit. But I've never experienced the same immense sense of loss like Ben. His world has suddenly shifted with my mom entering the picture and that must be hard.

"Tell me about your day," he says.

"Do you really want to know?"

"Yeah, distract me."

I sigh. "We met at the restaurant and there was an hour wait even with our reservation. Cassie was not having it. Lots of squealing and breakdowns. Harper got her panties in a twist when I took the last glass of mimosa from the carafe. When Mom went to the restroom, she asked me in dramatic fashion if I planned to share or drink it all. It's not my fault I drink faster than her. I ordered another carafe and didn't drink a drop, but she was still all twitchy. Then Mom showed me a picture of her new yoga instructor and suggested I take him on one of my holidates."

"A Memorial Day yoga date?"

I pause, then huff a laugh. "You know, that might work. Because guess what his name is?"

"What?"

"Eagle."

Amusement lights up his bright eyes. "Eagle? Is that a name?"

"Apparently."

He starts laughing in earnest now. "Oh, my God. Dating a guy named Eagle on Memorial Day is so fucking perfect. Actually, the Fourth of July might be better."

I'm laughing, too, and give him a shoulder bump at the suggestion. "Lord, can you imagine? But wait, it gets better." I grab my phone and swipe to the picture my mom sent, showing him Eagle with his shaved head. "He's literally a *bald* Eagle!"

Ben nearly falls off the couch he's laughing so hard. Good tears are running down his cheeks. "Damn, Lainey, that's got to be one of the best stories I've ever heard."

"This is my life. Being set up by my mom with a bald Eagle."

He starts laughing all over again. When he finally gets himself under control, he slouches into me. "Ah man, thanks, I needed that."

As I watch him sip his wine, his face is now relaxed and happy. I kinda love my mom for trying to set me up. Ben looks at me, and a small smile forms on his lips. There's nothing particularly amazing about it, but my heart starts beating faster and little flutters take flight in my stomach. How does he do this to me with just one look?

"What did you do today with your dad? Or what do you normally do?" I ask, needing to stop this moment between us before it ignites.

He stiffens. Damn, maybe I shouldn't have brought it up. Then he slowly relaxes, and a tiny, wistful smile forms. "When my mom was alive, all she wanted to do for Mother's Day was take a hike, watch her favorite movie and have Chinese take-out for dinner. So, that's what we'd do. Dad and I continued the tradition after she died."

"What's her favorite movie?"

"*Singin' in the Rain*. Sometimes she'd pick a different musical. Musicals were her favorite. Not so much for me and Dad, so it was the one day of the year she got us to watch one with her."

"And y'all did it today?"

"Sorta...it wasn't the same. For one, the house is different now that he's moved in with your mom. You can tell it's not lived in anymore. While my mom would pick different musicals, we've always watched *Singin' in the Rain* since she died. Today, he said that Kathleen recommended *Hamilton*."

I suppress a groan. I'm sure my mom was only trying to be helpful, but she really shouldn't have gone there.

"And he wanted to do lunch instead of dinner, probably so he could go back to your mom's early."

Oh God. My heart clenches, and I want to wrap him in my arms all over again.

"The restaurant was always the same. My mom loved the soup dumplings from this place not too far from our house. My dad ordered and when it arrived today, it was from a different restaurant, another recommendation from your mom."

No wonder he was such a mess today. I don't blame him for resenting my mom.

"I'm sorry, Ben. That's a lot of change for one day."

His shoulders slump. "I shouldn't make such a big deal. Things are supposed to change."

"No, don't discount your feelings. Your dad's already in a new relationship, and to mix up the rest is a lot." My mom should really mind her own business. And his dad should have damn well known better. Love can make people so oblivious. How many times did my mom pick the DW of the month over me and Harper?

Ben squeezes my hand. "Thanks for understanding."

"Of course. Now, what's the restaurant your mother loved?"

"Snow Pea."

"Okay, order for us, and we'll watch *Singin' in the Rain*."

"You don't have to do that, Lainey."

"I know. I want to. I've never seen it." He looks at me like he doesn't believe me. "I'm serious. I've seen the clip where he dances in the rain, but that's it. I like musicals, so let's watch it."

He stares at me, his expression fierce. I can't tell if he's trying not to let emotions overcome him again or if...his gaze dips to my lips, and I think I have my answer. This is a kissing moment. But if we kiss, it'll be so much more than a kiss. The emotion's too high. Things will escalate, and I don't think either one of us will have the willpower to stop it.

Suddenly, he looks away, takes a harsh breath, then looks back at me, his expression relaxed. "Okay, let's do it. Thanks."

An hour later, I can't stop smiling. Donald O'Conner might be my new favorite actor. He sings. He dances. He's hilarious. Oh, and he flips. The scene where he flips off the walls just ended, and it was brilliant. Suddenly, the film pauses, and I look over to Ben and he's smiling at me.

"What?"

"You should have seen your face during that scene. Like a kid on Christmas morning."

I laugh. "It was so awesome. I mean, he's so good!"

"I know. That was my mom's favorite scene too."

"Really?

"Yeah, that and Good Morning."

"Good morning?"

"It's another song. You'll see."

He restarts the movie and we continue watching. I totally agree with his mom, the Good Morning song is adorable. When it's over, I turn to him on the couch and tackle him in a bear hug. "Thank you!"

"Whoa, for what?"

"For sharing this with me." I pull back to look at him. "For sharing your mother with me."

His eyes turn shiny. "Fuck, Lainey, you're going to make me cry again."

"You can if you want."

His throat works around a swallow. "I'd rather do this." He gently takes my face in his hands and kisses me. It's soft and chaste. It's a friendly kiss. Except it's not. Because a friendly kiss shouldn't cause my heart to beat so fast.

The kiss is over as quickly as it began, and he looks as regretful at stopping as I feel. I can't shake this longing, this pain. Not kissing him feels wrong, as if I'm robbing my body of something vital—depriving my very soul. "Thanks for making today a good day."

"You made my day better, too."

The problem is, he makes all my days good. And as I look at him, I wonder if he's thinking the same thing. Because even as the air charges between us, there's a sense of melancholy to it. A question of why are we fighting this?

Before we can contemplate the answer, he pulls me into him and we snuggle into the couch. If we can't see the questions in our eyes, we don't have to answer them. So, I take his comfort and cuddle into him further. "Tell me about Poppy."

He doesn't say anything for a few moments, then releases a soft, slow breath. "Her favorite colors were red and gold. I think she favored red because poppies are red. She liked to play cards and was super competitive. Her favorite music was from the '60's and '80's. She loved to make meals out of appetizers."

I listen to him go on about her, and I wish I'd gotten the chance to meet her. She doesn't sound like my mother at all, but

I think they would have been friends. I close my eyes and enjoy the feel of his body against mine and the smooth sound of his deep voice.

"Lainey?"

I blink. "What?"

"You fell asleep."

Crap, I'm practically in his lap. I push myself to sitting. "I'm sorry."

"It's fine. I drifted off a bit myself." He stretches his arms up and rubs his sleepy eyes.

I pick up my phone from the coffee table and see it's 1:00 a.m. "I should go," I say as I stand slowly, then can't make myself move. It feels like I'm standing in quicksand. Finally, I take a step, but his voice immediately stops me.

"Stay."

My heart seizes and I look at him. "What?"

His eyes look as heavy as mine feel. "I don't want you to go home this late being so tired."

Oh. Disappointment settles heavily in my belly.

"I'll be okay. It's a short drive."

He takes a step closer. His expression is resolute, yet his eyes implore. "Okay, how about I want you to stay? Just tonight. To sleep."

All the heaviness that came over me disappears and the need that won't lessen seems to build between us again. This time it's not sexual, at least not fully. It's vulnerable. Comforting. More...

I should say no. I know I should say no.

I don't. "Okay."

His eyes widen in surprise a bit before he looks away. A beat later, he stands, takes my hand, and leads me to his bedroom. We get in bed fully clothed, and he wraps an arm around my waist, pulling me into him, but not so close that we're completely touching. I stiffen at first then slowly relax into the bed, into him. I've never really snuggled with any of my past boyfriends or hookups. I'm not a super touchy-feely girl, but this feels good. Really good. He finds my hand and interlocks his fingers with mine, I close my eyes and let his warmth lull me to sleep.

World Whisky Day, National Eli Day - May 20th

BEN

"Fuck, man, I still can't get over this place. I can barely tell it used to be Red's, and the pics don't do it justice." Eli, my oldest friend, meets my gaze from across the bar. "So proud of you, man."

"Thanks. That means a lot."

"I wish I could have been here for the grand opening."

Eli has been working in Seattle for the last year.

"I'm just glad you're back. I missed your ugly mug," I say.

He laughs. "I guess now that we're living in the same city again, I'll have to compete with your pretty boy blue eyes." He raises his highball glass. "I welcome the challenge. To finally being back in Austin."

I nod and cheers. Red Poppy doesn't open for another three hours, but I wanted Eli to see the bar before it got busy. Plus, I won't have time to catch up once it opens. He got into town at the perfect time. Turns out it's National Eli Day and World Whisky Day, which is Eli's preferred liquor, so I thought it was the perfect day to get together.

Since I started paying attention to the odd national holidays in case there's an opportunity to talk to Lainey, I've learned there's a shit ton of national drink days. I don't keep up with them all, but every once in a while, I'm inspired to feature a drink to draw in crowds. Today I've made a Whiskey Smash as a special.

"Damn, this is good," Eli says after he takes a sip. It's a high compliment since Eli is more of a whisky neat guy. "I could get in trouble drinking these."

"Which is why I made you get a ride here."

"Cheers to that." He raises his glass again before he takes another sip.

My phone buzzes on the bar and my stupid heart picks up at the sight of Lainey's name. I haven't seen her since she slipped out of my bed in the early morning after Mother's Day. I let her think I was still asleep since I was too tempted to pull her back into bed and do all the things I'd dreamt of doing to her.

LAINEY

Are you at Red Poppy?

ME

Yeah

LAINEY

Be there in 10. Fix me that whisky drink you put on IG. Make it a double.

ME

It's already a double.

LAINEY

Quadruple, then.

I LAUGH AT THAT. There's no way I'm fixing her a four-shot drink.

ME

Wow. Bad day?

LAINEY

You have no idea.

ME

SYS

"What's so funny?" Eli asks.

"My friend is having a bad day and asked me to make her a quadruple shot drink." It really pains me to call Lainey a friend. Even as it feels right, it also feels really fucking wrong.

"Whoa. Well, that one drink would do the trick. She'll be passed out before four."

It must be a really bad day if she's leaving work this early.

"So, who is this *she* friend? Anyone I know?" A curious gleam lights up his eyes. Eli is who gave me the nickname, Frat Bro Ben, recognizing it as a mask for my grief. Other than the occasional tease, he accepted it. He enjoyed the benefits of the female attention I attracted whenever he visited. He went to college in Colorado, so we didn't see each other often.

"No, it's Lainey. I met her on New Year's Eve. Our parents are dating."

His mouth drops open as he leans back on the barstool. "Whoa, wait. Mike's dating?"

"More than that. He's shacked up with her."

Eli's eyes bug out. We've been friends since elementary school and practically lived at each other's houses as teenagers, so he's almost as close to my dad as I am. "No. Way."

"Oh, it gets better."

I go on and tell him about how Lainey and I met and the situations we've caught our parents in. I don't tell him how close Lainey and I have really become or the fact that I know what it feels like to make her come. Or how I'm afraid that if I'm not careful, I'll probably fall in love with her. I already feel like I've got one foot over the ledge after Mother's Day. The way she understood and listened...it was exactly what I needed. I don't think I'll be able to spend Mother's Day without thinking of her.

It's been almost ten minutes, so I start making her drink. I've told her anytime she wants to come by that she can park in the back and use the code I gave her to get in. A minute later, the back door squeaks open.

She emerges from the hall, and the moment Eli sees her, he sucks in a breath. He looks at me and mouths, *whoa*, with an interested gleam in his eyes. My stomach twists. Fuck. I didn't think about Eli finding her attractive. I mean, of course, he would, but I didn't think about him hitting on her.

And he definitely will.

Lainey beelines straight to the bar and the drink I've set down. She settles on the stool next to Eli, takes the glass, and starts drinking—no, she starts gulping.

"Whoa, whoa." I gently take the glass out of her hand. "You don't chug this like a beer, Lainey. Do you want to kill yourself?"

"Not really," she mutters. "But a two-week coma should do the trick."

Eli chuckles, and she looks at him, seemingly noticing him for the first time. I can see the appreciation in her gaze. Eli is a good-looking guy, and I've seen firsthand how easy it is for him to hook up. My stomach twists again.

"Your future stepsister is awesome," Eli says.

Lainey looks at me with narrowed eyes. "Is that who you told him I was?"

"Definitely not." I fire a hard glare at Eli. "I told him our parents were dating. This is Eli Burke, my oldest friend. He's been living in Seattle for the past year and just returned to Austin."

She reaches out her hand. "Lainey Langford, nice to meet you. So, are you here for good?"

"For good. Unless work ships me off again."

Eli works for a major hotel chain and was in Seattle to oversee the opening of a new hotel and conference center.

"So, what's been so horrible about today?" I ask her, wanting to get her attention away from him.

She groans and takes a drink from her glass, this time a proper sip. "It's the holidate posts."

"Holidate?" Eli asks, and I explain Lainey's assignment to him.

She drops her head to the bar with a heavy sigh. "They told me that not only do I have to find a real date for Memorial Day, but I also have to plan a whole weekend full of activities. Which means I have to spend a whole weekend with some stranger."

"Hey," I lift my arms, presenting myself. "I can be your date again."

"*Real* date. My boss wants someone new. Even though you're the most popular post so far. You got more comments than the hockey player."

I can't help but smile. I did notice her Cinco de Mayo post got more attention than the Kentucky Derby, and everyone was shipping us together, noticing we've been in more than one post together. I also saw some comments from past hook-ups. Some were kind about my, um, skills, and some were not. Despite those cringe comments, the exposure has been positive. Red Poppy's socials have even gotten more hits since then.

"I can't use Josie again either or anyone in my family," she continues. "The posts when I have a true holidate are too popular. Now I have to find someone in the many emails of guys vying for a holidate or use that dating app again."

"I'll be your date," Eli pipes in.

Lainey jerks her gaze to his while my heart slams into my chest. The word "no" is at the tip of my tongue.

"Really?" she says, like he's just thrown her a life preserver.

"Hell, yeah. A weekend full of fun with a beautiful woman. Sounds perfect."

Fuck. Me.

Lainey looks at me hesitantly, then back to him. "I don't know. You're still a stranger." Her voice is now a bit wary.

"Technically, but I have a reference." Eli points at me. "Ask him anything about me. We've known each other since we were nine."

Lainey looks at me. "Well? Any skeletons in the closet I should know about?"

Damn it. Even if I dig up the dirtiest thing I have on him, it's on par with something Frat Bro Ben did. No, Eli is a good guy. I would easily recommend him to any of my friends.

Just not Lainey.

No choice, asshole.

"Unless he's gathered some fresh ones while away, not really. He likes to drink but doesn't get drunk often. Though don't let him drink tequila, he gets super stubborn. Not into drugs that I'm aware of." I look at him and Eli shakes his head. "Was a bit of a ladies man in college, but he's never cheated on any of his girlfriends. His biggest fault is he prefers hot tea over coffee."

Lainey looks at him. "Eww. That might be a deal breaker."

Eli laughs. "I might not drink it, but I know how to make it." He gives her a confident and charming grin. I've seen that look. Bare minimum, that look gains him a phone number, but more times than I care to remember, it leads to the bedroom.

"Well, I suppose that's something."

I start making another drink to distract me from noticing the spark in Lainey's eyes. Why did I have to make it so fucking easy for her to fall completely in love with him?

She bites her lip as if contemplating, then takes a sip of her drink. My eyes meet hers, and there's something in her gaze that makes me think she wants me to give her a reason to say no. Or is that what I want to see? Because the thought of her and my best friend hooking up is like a knife to the gut.

"Why don't I take you out to dinner tonight?" Eli says, breaking into our moment. "We can get to know each other, then you can decide if you want to spend the weekend with me."

She looks at me, seemingly conflicted. "I haven't even eaten lunch yet."

I pour her Whiskey Smash into a glass, but since she hasn't finished her last one, I take a sip and set it between us.

"We can order some food, and y'all can get to know each other here," I offer with a smile.

Eli glances at me, not appreciating my suggestion, but when Lainey agrees, he goes along with it. I order a pizza and suffer through watching Eli flirt with her.

"Oh, and get this," Lainey says. "They want me to go camping to promote a local outfitting company. *Camping.* I've never been camping in my life, and they want me to go with someone I've just met? Like that's safe!"

"I'm an Eagle Scout," Eli says with a shit-eating grin.

"No fucking way!" Lainey says on a laugh.

Shit, she's warming up to him.

Eli's hand slides over hers on the bar, and it takes all my willpower not to slap it away. "Lainey, pretty sure this date is destiny."

She grins. "I think you might be right."

I throw back another gulp of her whiskey smash.

Eli goes on about where they could go camping, and the more he talks, the more Lainey looks unsure. "Wait, you want to sleep in a tent for three days?"

"Yeah, that's camping," he says in a *duh* kind of way.

I swear she looks paler.

"Depending on where we camp, we could go tubing down the Guadalupe or Comal, and we can..."

As Eli goes on, Lainey looks more overwhelmed and panicked. Her gaze finds mine, and I can't take it anymore.

"Let's do a group thing. I'll join you," I blurt.

Eli raises his head from where he'd started looking up things and narrows his gaze at me.

"And bring Josie. Or anyone else," I continue so he doesn't think I'm trying to sabotage his date. I'm not really trying to, but I refuse to let Lainey get roped into a weekend she's not completely comfortable with.

"You know, that's not a bad idea," she says, her expression relieved.

"I thought it was supposed to be a real date," Eli says.

"We'll focus the pictures solely on us for the post. It'll be good to have others around to help document the date." She scoots off her stool. "I'm going to run to the restroom, and I'll text Josie."

As soon as she's out of earshot, Eli pins me with a look. "What the hell? Why do you keep cockblocking my date?"

"I'm not."

"You totally are!"

I glance away and take a calming breath before I face him again. "Look, you were going a little fast and furious. Spending the weekend with a guy she doesn't know while camping in the middle of nowhere for *days* isn't exactly something a woman is comfortable with. Her holidates haven't exactly gone well."

That seems to deflate him some. "It's not the middle of nowhere, but I guess I did get a little ahead of myself. It's been a while since I've gotten laid."

I ball my hands to stop myself from grabbing him and telling him he better not fucking touch her. "Look, don't push Lainey."

"I don't push women, Ben." He looks at me like I've lost my mind. Maybe I have. "But if you think I'm going to give up the idea that Lainey will end my dry spell, you're sorely mistaken." I slam my teeth together to stop myself from completely losing it on my best friend. Thankfully, Lainey comes back before I do something stupid.

As she approaches the bar, she pauses by the reserved bar stool. "You know, I meant to ask you, why is this always reserved?"

My heart seizes. Shit.

"That's Poppy's Spot," Eli says. He might not have been here since I reopened as Red Poppy, but he knows about my mom's carving and the significance behind it. "You can see where she carved her name in the bar top."

Lainey's gaze bounces from him to me before she inspects the bar and finds my mom's script. She gently runs her finger over it. "No one sits here."

It's a statement, but when her gaze rises and meets mine, I can see the question in them.

"No. Never."

Except not never. Only her.

Her mouth parts in surprise even though her expression softens. My heart is beating so fucking fast. I feel raw and exposed, as if I've just revealed my deepest darkest secret. I watch her throat in a swallow before she dips her gaze back to the carving. She gives it one last touch.

"That's beautiful, Ben." She keeps her gaze down, and I can't help but think it's because if she looks at me, it'll reveal too much. Hell, I've probably revealed too much in mine.

I glance at Eli and he's looking at me with a sympathetic expression. At least, he thinks this tense and somber moment is due to thinking of my mother. I'm internally grateful for him for easing the pensiveness surrounding us when he raises his glass and says, "To Poppy."

Lainey returns to her seat and raises her glass. Since I don't have my own drink, I grab a bottle of tequila and pour a shot. "To Poppy."

My gaze catches Lainey's as we take our drinks. It's weighty. Significant.

"So, did you get a hold of your friend?" Eli asks.

Lainey blinks. "Oh, yeah. Josie's in."

"Is she single?" Eli asks.

"Yes."

"Awesome!" He looks back at me. "Now it's a double date."

Lainey and I lock gazes as we both respond with a hollow sounding, "Great."

Memorial Day Weekend - Saturday

BEN

"WHOA. *THAT'S* HER FRIEND?" ELI SAYS AS WE PULL UP TO LAINEY'S apartment.

I peel my gaze away from Lainey and her gorgeous legs on display in a pair of cutoff jean shorts and look at the woman standing next to her. She's already familiar to me since I saw her in the picture Lainey sent me on St. Patrick's Day. She's attractive —dark hair, seafoam green eyes, and a nice curvy body. It's too bad I feel zero attraction to her. But if Eli does...

"Yeah, that's Josie. I haven't officially met her yet."

"Nice. Looks like you're in good hands."

Well, damn. Eli thinks I'm interested in this double date, but I'm mostly focusing on keeping my cool while Eli hits on Lainey all weekend. We park and get out of Eli's SUV. Lainey introduces Josie, and I do the same for Eli.

"So, you're the famous Eagle Scout?" Josie asks Eli.

Lainey and I look at each other at the mention of Eagle. Last I heard, Kathleen was still keen on Lainey meeting her yoga instructor, and Lainey was doing her best to ignore her.

Eli smiles charmingly as he glances between the women. "I'm famous?"

"I was told you could do all the camping things. Have to admit, it's one of the main reasons I agreed to go. Nature and I have a love-hate relationship."

"Don't worry, I know my way around a campsite." He winks at her.

Josie laughs. "Oh my God, did you just wink? Man, this is going to be fun."

Eli looks a little taken aback by that before he shifts his focus to Lainey. He gives her a kiss on the cheek. "Hey, gorgeous."

Lainey blushes. "Hey." She glances at me and quickly averts her gaze. "So, ready to get this show on the road?" She gestures to the stuff waiting to get loaded.

While Eli brought his own tent, Lainey's company provided one too, which is still in the box. Lainey and Josie provided most of the food and drinks, so there are two giant coolers. Lainey only has one backpack that's stuffed to the gills, but Josie has three bags at her feet. Eli picks one up, his expression slightly annoyed. "You know it's a camping trip. You don't need a wardrobe change each day."

Josie gives him a sassy look. "One of them is a first aid bag. I don't leave home without it."

"I've got a first-aid kit. We don't need two."

"It's going. You can leave yours if you want."

"Yours is twice the size as mine. We're already low on space." Eli's frustration is clear.

Josie puts her hands on her hips. "Look, Scout, this bag is going. I'll keep it in my lap the whole time if it bothers you that much. I'm a nurse, and this bag covers almost any emergency situation. There's no way I'm going camping without it."

Eli puts his hands up in surrender. "Fine."

He turns toward the back of the car and looks at me, then rolls his eyes. So much for hoping Josie would woo his interest away from Lainey. Once we're packed, Eli opens the passenger door for Lainey, so I get relegated to the backseat with Josie. We have a campsite off the Guadalupe River with close access to the river, so we have over an hour's drive ahead of us. She gives me a sympathetic look. Does she know how "close" Lainey and I have gotten these past months? Something tells me she isn't completely in the dark.

Another laugh comes from the front seat thirty minutes later. That's the tenth time he's made her laugh—not that I'm counting. I tear my gaze away from the video Josie was showing me to see Lainey lean closer to Eli and give his arm a playful push. And that's the sixth time they've touched. I can't wait to get out of this fucking car.

When we get to our campsite, we unload, and the girls assign us to tent pitching. Eli gets his tent up with relative ease, but struggles with the bigger, newer one Lainey brought.

He presses his fingers to his forehead and mutters a curse as he stares at the instructions.

"What's the problem, Scout? I didn't think it would be so hard for you to pitch a tent," Josie tosses to Eli as she lounges in a camp chair with a beer in her hand.

He glares at her. "I can pitch a tent just fine."

Josie smirks and lets her gaze fall to his crotch. "Sure you can."

I'm pretty sure if Eli could shoot lasers from his eyes, he'd eviscerate Josie. He turns back to the pile of poles and the groundsheet, wincing and pressing his hand to his forehead again.

I go to the drink cooler and pull a couple beers from it and hand one over to Eli. "How about a beer break?"

Eli's mouth flattens as he tosses the instructions on the ground. "Why not? Already have a headache. It can't get any worse," he says, as he takes the beer.

"You sure? I can grab a water instead. I bet Josie has some great headache medicine in her first aid pack."

Eli glares at me and I cover up my laugh by taking a sip of beer.

"A tent this fucking fancy shouldn't be this hard to put together. Isn't it for bougie campers who don't know shit about camping?"

"I don't know, man. You're the professional."

Eli actually laughs at that. We finish our beers and tackle the tent again. Eli hands me the instructions this time, saying his headache is making it hard for him to focus. This does the trick, and we have the tent up within fifteen minutes. Eli falls into a camp chair like he's just run a marathon.

"Tent pitching really took it out of you, huh, Scout?"

Eyes closed, Eli's only response is to raise his middle finger in Josie's direction.

"Now that we're settled, do we want to tackle a hike? The trailhead down that way is supposed to have a great view of the river. It's only one and half miles," Lainey suggests.

"I suppose I can handle that," Josie says.

"That's one-way. Three miles total."

Josie scrunches up her nose. "Um, no thanks. I'd rather put my swimsuit on and lounge in the water with a bevi."

I look at Eli, who still has eyes closed. "Eli?"

He blinks an eye open. "Yeah, sure."

He sits up and goes to stand then winces and sits back down. Josie sits up and looks at him with concern. "Hey, not trying to bust your balls or anything, but I don't think a hike is a good idea right now. Professional opinion."

Surprisingly, he doesn't argue. He looks at Lainey apologetically. "Let me take some meds and hydrate so I can enjoy this evening. Just gotta get rid of this headache."

Lainey nods. "I think that's a good idea. I'm sorry you're not feeling well." She glances at me. "Do you want to hike or hang here?"

Like I'm going to pass up a chance to spend alone time with her. "I'd like to hike, if you're up for it."

Her smile is brilliant as she nods. We grab daypacks and water, then head off toward the trailhead.

"You think Eli is okay?" she asks, as we hit the trail.

"Must be a hell of a headache, because it's not like Eli to miss out on a hike. Hopefully, he'll be back to normal when we get back."

Okay, maybe there's a part of me that hopes he doesn't recover too quickly. It's not the best look on me, but I'm really enjoying having Lainey all to myself for the next couple of hours.

"So, um, you and Josie seemed to be getting along in the car."

I glance at her. "No more than you and Eli."

The way Lainey's mouth tightens tells me that wasn't the answer she was looking for. Yeah, Josie seems great, and we were having fun in the car, but there's zero spark between us.

"She's nice," I concede.

"That's it?"

"What do you want me to say?"

"I don't know."

"What about you and Eli?"

"What about us?"

"You seem to be getting along. Flirting."

She stops walking and puts her hands on hips. "Are you kidding me? You're accusing me of flirting when you and Josie had your heads pressed together the whole ride."

"We were laughing at videos. You were the one that was all up in Eli's business while he was driving."

"I was not, but we're supposed to be on a date. What do you want me to do? *Not* talk to him?"

"I don't know, Lainey. You're the one who started this whole conversation."

Her mouth opens as if to argue then she snaps it shut. A frustrated look comes over her face right before she starts walking again. After a few steps though she stops and looks at me. "He's nice."

I can't stop my grin, and her eyes narrow at me, but there's no real malice behind the look. Actually, her own grin forms before she starts walking again. "Come on, we have a lot of ground to cover.

Despite the rocky trail, the hike is fairly easy. Lainey and I talk about superficial stuff, avoiding anything related to our complicated friendship. After an hour, we get to the overlook.

"Oh my God, it's gorgeous," Lainey says, but I can't tear my gaze off her to see what is making her so happy. The only gorgeous thing I see is her. The way the deep orange and purples in the late afternoon sky kiss her face and how it makes a wistful smile on her lips even more magical. The way it gives vibrance to her brown eyes.

I get my phone and take a picture of her. She looks at me, and I don't know what she sees in my expression, but hers shifts, and awareness sparks between us. All I want to do is reach out, pull her into my arms, and kiss her until we're both breathless. My ultimate fantasy would be to strip her bare and grind her up and down my cock until she comes so hard the whole park hears it.

Her breath hitches, and I wonder if I said that out loud or if my thoughts are that transparent. I clear my throat and show her my phone screen. "This will be perfect for your post."

She smiles at the photo with a flush on her cheeks. "It's actually not bad. Thanks," she says and looks at me. "Now, you need to look at the view."

"I was."

The flush in her cheeks deepens as she smiles shyly. Then, she takes my face in her hands and turns it toward the river. The view is well worth the hike, but I'd still rather look at Lainey. We find a place to sit and rest and enjoy the benefits of our work. She takes several pictures before scooting closer and puts her phone in selfie mode.

"I thought you could only post pictures of your real date."

She shrugs. "This is for us."

I try not to smile at that.

We take a picture of ourselves. Then we move so the view is behind us and take a few more pics. I can't help it, but in the last one I press a kiss to her temple. She doesn't say anything, but when she scrolls through the photos, I notice she lingers on that one longer than the others.

"Send those to me please."

She nods and seems to be purposely not looking at me. After a bit more of a break, we hike back to the campsite. We find Josie lounging in the water on top of an inner tube with a drink in her hand.

"Where's Eli?"

She glances toward his tent. "He laid down. Think Scout will feel like making us dinner? I'm more of a take-out burger girl than making my own, so I'm banking on his expertise."

Man, Eli is going to seriously regret telling people he was an Eagle Scout before this weekend is over.

"I can grill the burgers," I offer.

"Woo-hoo!"

Lainey shakes her head. "Josie, you might want to consider learning some new skill sets. You're a nurse, you know eating out all the time isn't good for you."

"Hey, I can cook. When I want to."

Lainey crosses her arms. "I've had your spaghetti, and it leaves much to be desired."

"Um, it's a jar of sauce and pasta. How am I messing that up?"

I laugh. "If you don't know what's wrong with that sentence, then that's where your cooking skills falter."

"Seriously," Lainey agrees. "You could add some ground beef or Italian sausage. Or throw in some pre-cooked meatballs, at the very least."

Josie waves off Lainey's suggestion and takes a sip of her drink. I dip my head into our tent and see Eli waking up. "Hey man, how are you feeling?"

"Headache's not gone, but better. I still have no desire to sit in the light right now." He lowers his voice. "Don't tell Josie, but her meds are better than mine."

I chuckle at that. "Just chill. I'll get the burgers going. Sun should be tolerable in about an hour."

"Thanks, man. Oh, and please don't let Josie cook. Her cooking skills sound like a nightmare."

"No kidding."

An hour later, I have the burgers finished, and Eli joins us around the campfire. He looks a little pale but says he's feeling better, though he barely eats.

"Let's play Truth or Dare," Josie suggests after we finish our meal.

We all groan.

"Oh, come on. It'll be a fun way to get to know each other. Oh, wait. Let's do Never Have I Ever instead."

"Fine. I don't have it in me to try a dare," Eli says.

Josie claps and passes out fresh beers. "Okay, I'll start. Never have I ever been an Eagle Scout."

Eli glares at her as he takes a sip of his beer. "Never have I ever been a nurse," he returns.

"Mine was funnier." Josie drinks then says, "Never have I ever drunk texted someone begging them to fuck me."

Lainey glares at her. As she starts to drink, her gaze darts to mine, then away. Eli drinks, too, with a raise of his shoulders.

"Never have I ever been a frat bro," Eli says, forcing me to drink.

"Never have I ever gone skydiving," I toss out randomly to get us out of these personal strikes. Only Josie drinks.

"Never have I ever had sex this year," she says and takes a drink, her eyes taking on a mischievous gleam. Eli drinks, too.

I glance at Lainey. She doesn't drink, which means she hasn't been with anyone since I met her. And what happened between us on Mardi Gras *technically* wasn't sex.

Eli looks at me curiously while Josie looks at Lainey. "You haven't had an orgasm in six months?" she asks her.

Lainey lifts her brows. "That's a completely different question."

"I mean by someone other than yourself."

"Again, completely different question."

"Never have I ever had someone give me an orgasm in the last six months," Josie counters, then drinks.

Lainey sighs before she takes a drink, purposely not meeting my eyes. Josie looks at me, noticing I don't drink this time either. "Aren't you some legendary CTU fuckboy?"

Eli snorts a laugh. "Maybe I should have nicknamed you Fuckboy Ben instead of Frat Bro Ben."

I give him a look that makes him grimace a silent apology before turning back to Josie. "Legendary?"

"Not anymore, it seems," Eli says. "It's hard to believe you haven't seen any action all year. How the hell did you go from sixty to zero?"

"I hit the brakes."

Eli narrows his gaze at me. "You haven't had any sex. At all?"

"What's your definition of sex?"

"Cock inside pussy."

Josie snorts a laugh, but looks at me expectantly, clearly

interested in the answer.

I sigh. "No, I haven't."

Eli leans forward. "No BJ or handy?"

I shake my head.

"But you've given someone an orgasm," Josie says confidently.

"When did the game change to twenty questions?" I ask, but Eli and Josie continue to stare at me, waiting. I look at Lainey and finally take a drink.

"I knew you hadn't been a complete monk." Eli slouches back into his chair.

I can't help but notice Josie is looking between me and Lainey, who is suddenly engrossed with her beer can.

"I have one," I say to take the heat off myself. "Never have I ever had Mexican food on St. Patrick's Day."

Josie and Lainey groan but drink.

"What?" Eli says. "That's sacrilege."

"Don't worry. I prayed a lot that night in repentance." Lainey shudders. "It's a good thing my love for Mexican food is strong."

"Oh, I have another," Josie says. "Never have I ever been an Eagle Scout and forgot how to pitch a tent."

Eli groans and tosses his beer down. "I'm going to bed."

"Come on," she calls after him. "Don't be a sorry sport."

Eli flips her off and disappears toward the set of bathrooms.

Lainey looks at her friend. "You're evil."

"I know, but that was too easy." She glances between us. "So...Lainey has received an orgasm, and Ben has given one. That's really interesting."

Neither of us says a word.

"I wonder if it happened on the same day. Now that would be a real coincidence."

Lainey and I look at each other, and both take sips of our beers. Josie busts out laughing as she stands up. "Yeah, that's what I thought. I'll grab the s'mores stuff."

LAINEY

I NEVER THOUGHT I'D BE SO THANKFUL FOR AN AIR MATTRESS, BUT that thing saved my life last night. There was no way I would have gotten any sleep in just a sleeping bag on the hard ground. I barely slept as it was. Crickets, noises from other campsites, and my stomach rolling from the beer/s'more combination made for a not-so-great night. Plus, I've had to pee for hours but didn't want to trek to the bathroom in the dark. I don't think camping is for me. If it wasn't for the smell of coffee coming through the tent, I'd pack it up right now.

I get out to see Ben pouring some into a thermos from a French Press.

He glances up. "Hey, there's not much, but it'll do the trick. Hopefully."

"You're a godsend." I rush over as he hands me the thermos. I prefer it with some cream, but I'm not going to turn this away.

"No promises on how good it is."

I take a sip and moan. "It's coffee. It's wonderful."

He takes his own sip then winces. "A tad strong, I hope Josie doesn't want any, because I'm not making more."

"We'll just get rid of the evidence."

"I heard that," Josie's voice comes from the tent. A minute later, she emerges and sits next to me, taking my thermos. "We'll share."

We take in the scenery. It really is beautiful. The river is running and fairly clear. It's almost as if time has pressed the pause button, it's so quiet and peaceful. Okay, at this moment, I get why people enjoy camping.

"It's so nice right now, I think I'll actually go hiking today," Josie says.

I glance at the guys' tent. "Eli's still sleeping?"

"Yeah. He was kind of restless last night," Ben says.

"Maybe I should check on him," Josie says.

"I don't know. He was finally sleeping good when I got up."

His headache must have been a killer, because I have a feeling this is not Eli's normal M-O.

Josie eyes Eli's tent. "Okay, I'll let him sleep and check after we get back."

We eat a quick breakfast of protein bars, take restroom breaks, and get changed for hiking. Surprisingly, Josie doesn't complain on the hike even though the trail is rocky and has a steady incline. Once we get to the view, we take pictures and lounge around for a few minutes.

Thankfully, Josie didn't press me anymore about my relationship with Ben last night. I've told her enough that she knows we've kissed and that he's the reason my date didn't work out on Mardi Gras, but I didn't tell her how far things went. She also knows me well enough that this attraction, or whatever it is, isn't gone—despite my declarations that we're just friends.

We get back to the campsite and Eli is lounging in a camp chair with a bottle of water in his hand. He's in his swim trunks, and while I could tell Eli was a fit guy, I wasn't expecting the impressive chest and defined abs. Or the script tattoo on his ribs that I can't quite make out what it says.

"Hey," I say. "How's your head?"

He gives me a small smile. "Not as bad as yesterday, but still lingering. I took some meds, so hopefully, it'll go away soon." He reaches out and takes my hand, and his is clammy. "Hey, I'm sorry I've been so lame so far. This isn't exactly how I wanted this weekend to go."

"It's okay. Glad you're feeling better."

Josie comes by and looks him over. "Do you get migraines often?"

He waves off her concern. "I'm fine. I can handle hanging in the water today." He gives me a weak smile. "I really want to spend time with you."

I smile at him, but my stomach clenches. I don't get it. The man is seriously hot, plus nice and funny. Even his grumpy side is kind of adorable. The thought of spending time with him shouldn't make me uneasy.

I don't even know why I question myself. The obvious answer is standing on the other side of the fire pit.

"Yes, let's have a fun day," I say and squeeze Eli's hand.

We eat lunch, then all get ready to swim, and when I get back to the campsite, the guys are standing next to each other as Ben shows Eli something on his phone. The sight of Ben in his swim trunks shouldn't send my body in a full-out tizzy, but it does. I've seen his chest before in his Bare-chested Bartender posts, but there's something about seeing it in person that's much more potent. Especially since now, I can see that sexy little V muscle at the band of his low-riding trunks. I ball my hands so I don't walk up to him and yank that string and fall to my knees.

As if sensing me, he glances up. His body freezes as he takes me in in my swimsuit. Josie's is skimpier and revealing with lots of cutouts. I'm wearing a more standard bikini, but I will admit my halter top makes my boobs look fantastic—which is exactly where Ben's hot gaze is.

Ben suddenly turns and walks away, and I swear I hear him mutter *fuck me.*

I shouldn't get a little thrill from that, but it makes me ridiculously happy. We all make our way to the water. At first, it's a little chilly, but it quickly feels amazing since the sun is already blazing. We've attached our tubes to a nearby tree branch with some rope so we stay together and don't float away.

"How are y'all not cold?" Eli asks, visibly shaking. "The water is *freezing.*"

We've been in the water for at least half an hour now, and the temp is perfect. "It feels great," I say. Ben and Josie agree.

"So....f-f-f-freaking....cold." His teeth are chattering now.

Josie is next to Eli, so she leans over and presses her hand to his forehead, then gives a small gasp. "Oh my God, Eli. You're burning up."

"No way. I'm freezing."

"Fuck! Get out of the water now." She immediately jumps out of her inner tube and starts helping him up. When Eli's knees buckle, Ben kicks into gear and helps support him back to the campsite. I make sure our inner tubes are secure and follow them.

"Get a blanket or towel and get him dried off. I'm going to grab my med bag." Josie rushes to our tent.

Ben helps dry him off and wraps a blanket around him. Josie returns and pulls out a thermometer. "Open up."

Eli doesn't argue. A few minutes later, it beeps, and Josie inhales sharply. "It's a hundred and four. Eli, how long have you felt this bad? I thought you were having a migraine."

"Me, too."

"What are your other symptoms?"

"I'm a little achy. Head fucking hurts. Tired. Cold."

Josie shakes her head in disbelief. "You might have the flu or pneumonia. I'm taking you to the hospital."

"What? No. I probably just need to go home and rest."

"No. You need to see someone first. I saw an urgent care on our way in, we can stop there."

He groans. "It's Memorial Day weekend. Not flu season."

She rolls her eyes. "Germs don't have a season."

"I'll take him," Ben offers.

Josie looks at him as if he's said the most idiotic thing in the world. "I think it would be best if the nurse takes him."

"We'll all go. I can pack up real quick," I say.

"I'm taking him now. You need this for work, so y'all stay and enjoy. I'll call you when I know more and let you know when I can get back with the car."

Ben glances at me right as the realization hits. We're going to be alone. Possibly all night. With no way to leave.

Oh, shit.

It doesn't help that before Josie slips into the driver's seat, she gives me a knowing smirk. If I didn't know better, I'd think she planned Eli getting sick. We stand there and watch the dust kick up as they leave before we turn to each other. An awkward but electric silence hovers between us.

"What now?" he asks.

Suggesting we disappear into a tent and fuck our brains out is probably not what I should do with someone who's supposed to be just a friend.

"Jesus, Lainey."

I jerk my gaze to him, realizing I was looking at my tent, with my thoughts probably playing out on my face.

He's looking at me intensely. Almost painfully. "I don't think you were having friendly thoughts."

Busted.

"Um, how about we tube the river? There's an entrance point down the road, and the park has a shuttle at the exit point that will bring us back. It's supposed to be a three-hour ride."

"Perfect," he says a little too quickly. "Let's do it."

We jump into action to get everything ready so we're away from the campsite as quickly as possible. Tubing turns out to be exactly what we needed. It wastes the afternoon and we have just enough drinks to loosen us up and make friends along the way. When we get back to the campsite, we make sandwiches for dinner and devour what's left of the chips. Then we take our camp chairs to the river, staying as far away from the tents as possible.

A text pops up on my phone from Josie. She had texted earlier saying Eli had the flu. "Josie again," I tell Ben. "She's back home with Eli, and he's resting. She'll pick us up in the morning."

We pretty much figured that would happen, but now that we know for sure, the sexual tension we've been ignoring all day comes roaring back. It's dark enough I can't see his face fully, but I feel his gaze on me.

Unsure how to handle it, I look up at the sky. The sheer amount of visible stars is impressive compared to being in the city. "It's beautiful, isn't it?"

"Yes," he says, and there's something about the way he says it that makes me wonder if he's still looking at me. But I don't dare move to find out.

"I wish I could take a picture and it would show the true beauty of what we're seeing, but I know it'll just look black."

"It's awesome. I haven't seen this many stars in a long time."

I take out my phone anyway and mess with a bunch of the camera settings, but none of the pictures truly show what I'm looking at. "Oh well," I say, giving up. "Would have been good for my post."

"What are you going to do now that Eli is gone?"

I shrug. "Roll with it, I guess. It's not like every other holidate hasn't been a disaster."

"Have they?"

I know he's looking at me now—what he's asking. And the truth is, no. Every time I ended up with Ben...those have been my favorite days of the year. But I can't confess that. Not when our parents are living together, and we've decided to be friends.

"Think we'll see a shooting star?" I say, changing the subject.

The silence between us feels heavy, and I wonder if he's disappointed I didn't answer his question, or if he understands why I didn't.

"What would you wish for?"

I glance over at him and he's now looking back at the sky. "I can't tell you. It wouldn't come true."

He looks at me. "And all your secret birthday candle wishes have come true?"

"Maybe."

He shakes his head at me. "Come on, Lainey. It's a game. What would you wish for?"

You.

In this moment, that's my answer—the one thing I can't let myself fully admit and won't now. So, I think of the next thing that frustrates me the most, that I struggle with the most: "I wish I could trust myself."

"What are you talking about?"

"I can't seem to get anything right. I changed my major three times and still don't know what I want to do. This will be the longest job I've had since graduating if I can see it through the year-long contract, which I already want to tear up. Every time a new opportunity comes up, I think this will be the one, and then it falls flat."

I'm always wrong about men too.

But I don't say that out loud.

"What if I keep making wrong decision after wrong decision? It's like I'm constantly going up on a down escalator. It's exhausting."

"Lainey...you know you're not alone in that feeling, right? Everyone questions themselves."

I suppose. It's still isolating. Frustrating.

"You're only twenty-five. I think you need to give yourself a break. Lots of people our age are still figuring it out and making mistakes. And those who seem like they have it all together are probably just pretending."

"Twenty-six."

He leans forward in his seat, spearing me with an agitated look. "When did you have a birthday?"

"March first." I want to say it was before we got close, but he'd already given me an orgasm at that point.

He practically growls. "Why the hell didn't you tell me?"

"Because I don't announce my birthday to people. When's yours? Were you going to tell me?"

His mouth tightens as if he sees my point but doesn't want to agree. "June ninth. I expect a birthday text, at the very least," he says with a teasing smile.

"Noted."

He leans back into his seat. After a few moments, he says with a soft voice, "I get your frustration, but...I don't think you realize how fucking amazing it is that you don't stay in a job you hate. That you don't yield to the pressure to stay in a life you don't want. Do you know how many people stay in shitty jobs because they're afraid to leave? Or in a bad relationship? I think as long as you can support yourself, go ahead and keep searching for what makes you happy. Embrace your tenacious-ness, Lainey." He holds my gaze then. "Because it's not a fault. It's admirable."

My throat constricts and tears burn my eyes. That might

have been the nicest thing someone has ever said to me. God, I want to launch myself at him. Soak up all his faith in me.

"What would you wish for?" I ask instead.

His gaze holds mine, his answer intensifying with every passing second. I blow out a breath and glance away. My body is practically vibrating with need.

I hear Ben shift back into this seat, and after a moment, he says, "I want to be a real businessman, not just eye candy."

"What are you talking about? You *are* a real businessman."

"Not the way I want to be."

"Explain, please, because the bar is amazing."

"I'm the pretty face who brings in the customers. The hot bartender who rakes in the tips. When I started Red Poppy, I never thought I'd be making viral thirst trap videos. I thought I'd be a respected bar owner, not social media porn. I don't want to have to take my shirt off to make it successful. I want more. Maybe invest in another bar or a restaurant one day. Start a local chain. Ten years down the road, I don't want to be a bartender who's still flashing my abs."

"Oh my God, Ben, what you've done with Red Poppy in less than a year is remarkable. You can't attribute all that to those videos. That might lure some people in, but that's not why they stay or come back. That's all because you've created an atmosphere that's both comfortable and exciting."

He shrugs. "It doesn't feel like that some days." He studies his water bottle with a frown. "I don't think I'll ever outrun Frat Bro Ben."

I have to admit that's one of my fears, too. I got even more comments and DMs from women about him on my Cinco de Mayo post, and they're not exactly kind about his college days. But this man before me—he's so much more than a pretty face. More than a party boy.

What would it have been like if I'd met him in college?

Would I have fallen for his charm? Been another forgotten one-night stand? Or would I have been the one who made him want to drop his fuckboy ways? I actually snort at that fantasy.

"What?" he asks.

"I was wondering what it would have been like if we'd met in college."

I probably shouldn't have voiced that. Could be asking for trouble.

His head dips and he twists the cap to his water bottle, as if he's giving it considerable thought. But he doesn't say anything, which is probably for the best. Because the real answer is another frat boy would have broken my heart.

"It would have been explosive."

His sudden, rough words have me jerking my gaze to his. That earlier intensity is back, and it's impossible to ignore the heat between us.

"Whatever it would've been..." he says. "It would have been explosive."

I swallow, feeling his answer all through my body. It's not specific, but I feel the truth in it. He's right. I wouldn't have been some random girl to him, even if it had been only one night. No, our acquaintance would have become a core memory. Just like we can't seem to escape the explosiveness between us now.

There's a crunch of plastic as he crushes his water bottle in his hand, then stands. "Guess we should head to bed."

"Yeah, I'm tired."

I'm not, but we need to get away from this conversation. We both go to the bathroom, but I stay there long enough that Ben's already in his tent when I get back to the campsite. I slip into mine and it takes a bit to get comfortable. Every little rustle and sound have me staring at the tent flap to see if someone's trying to get in. I toss and turn, finally flipping on my back and willing myself to go to sleep. That's when I feel it. A distinct tickle of something moving up my leg.

I scream, jerking my leg, then scramble toward the door, trying to work the zipper as fast as I can. I can hear Ben calling my name, but I'm still squealing. Finally, I burst through, immediately falling into Ben's arms.

"What happened? Are you okay?"

"There's something in there. It was...it was crawling up my leg. It..."

"Okay, okay. I'll take a look."

He goes to his tent and comes back with his phone flashlight on. He pulls back the flap and moves the light around, heads inside and looks under the covers and mattress. After a few minutes, he says, "It's a spider."

"Nope," I say taking several steps back. The only worse thing he could have said was snake.

He comes out and goes to our supplies and grabs some paper towels then returns to my tent. When he comes back out something is clearly in the paper towel, I back up another ten steps. He goes to the edge of the campsite and tosses the paper towel, retreating himself. I see him shudder before he looks at me. "I fucking hate spiders."

"Well, you put on a good show." I put a hand over my heart. "My hero."

"Yeah, well, I can't have you sleeping with those eight-legged fuckers."

"Oh, I'm not going back in there. What if there's another one?"

The side of his mouth quirks up. "Is this your way of trying to sleep with me, Lainey?"

"I'm not trying. I *am* sleeping with you."

His smile is full out now.

"Sleep," I say pointedly.

His expression deflates a bit. "Is this a friends let friends sleep in their tents kind of thing?"

"Absolutely. Especially when spiders are involved."

He laughs softly then gestures with his arm, "After you."

I slip into his tent and immediately stop when I don't see an air mattress. "Wait. Where's your air mattress?"

"Don't have one. We have these padded pallets."

I whirl around. "That's it?"

"The air mattress is in your tent. You're welcome to go back."

I shudder. "No way." I turn back to the pallets. "Which one is yours?" Ben points to the one to my right so I sit down on it.

"Whoa, what are you doing?"

"I'm not sleeping on Eli's germy blankets."

"I'm not either."

"Then it looks like we're sleeping together."

His eyebrows pop up as an interested gleam lights up his blue eyes. "Oh, yeah?"

"Sleep. Friends."

"Sleep friends, huh? I did enjoy the last time we were sleep friends. Are you going to sneak out of my pallet in the morning again?"

"I didn't sneak."

I totally did.

"I watched you. You tiptoed out of my room like you were doing the walk of shame. Meanwhile, the most shameful thing that happened was the fact that we *didn't* get naked."

I raise my brows, ignoring him. "Are you coming down here or are you going to take your chance with the flu germs or the spiders?"

He smiles as he bends to his knees. "Oh, I'd much rather be sleep friends with you than germs or spiders."

"I'm flattered," I say with a laugh.

"If you want to be more than sleep friends, just say the word."

I swat his chest. "Behave, or I'll smother you with Eli's blanket."

He laughs and we try to get settled and find a comfortable position that works for both of us. The good news is his pallet is more padded than I expected and large enough to hold both of us. The bad news is it's still not an air mattress. Or a real mattress. We shift around until we finally end up on our sides with him spooning me, much like Mother's Day. That night it had been comforting. Tonight, it feels as if I'm surrounded by electricity. Every inch of his skin touching mine is sending fiery signals all through my body. My nipples are hard and tight. My pussy is throbbing and practically begging to be touched. The need to wiggle my ass into him is hard to resist.

I will myself to be utterly still. I'm not even breathing, which makes it easier to hear Ben's harsh breaths. His hand flexes where it rests near my stomach as if he's trying hard not to touch me. His forehead presses into the back of my head, and all I want to do is expose my neck so he'll press those talented lips to my skin. I want him to kiss and suck until he's marked me as his. The thought only makes the throbbing between my legs more insistent. And before I can stop myself, I press my ass into him and his cock, hot and hard, presses right back. Ben hisses and buries his face into my neck, but he still doesn't kiss me.

We stay like that, pressed tightly against one another, for I don't know how long. I want to cry I want him so badly. I want him to ignore all my protestations and just take me. Take the decision out of my hands. I want him to fulfill this ache that I know only he can. But he won't. This isn't like the times before when he's waiting for me to say the safe word to stop things before they start.

No, this is five months of built-up sexual tension coming to a head.

Suddenly, Ben rolls away, taking his arm around my waist

with him until we're not touching anymore. I squeeze my eyes shut against the pain of the loss. And yes, it feels painful. All the electric feelings that were coursing through me seem to be reaching for him. Begging for him. Begging me.

I turn to face him. He's on his back, one hand over his chest and the other behind his head. His eyes are closed, but he looks far from peaceful.

"Ben?" I ask in a small voice.

It takes him a beat to answer, but finally, he opens his eyes and looks at me. "Yes?"

"Can we not be friends for just a minute?"

He immediately turns back over, pulling me to him. "Abso-fucking-lutely."

His lips crash over mine. The kiss is instantly frantic and fiery. He shifts, rolling on top of me, and I spread my legs, and his thick cock presses into me. I arch into him more, moving my hips against him. He groans, trailing kisses down my throat.

"Maybe another minute," I gasp, as I give him more access to my neck. I don't care if this is wrong. If I'm wrong. I'm running on pure need.

He moans his agreement. "Five more minutes," he says as he nips and sucks along my neck, exactly like I wanted him to. I'm on fucking fire. Every ounce of my body needs more. Nothing less than everything will do.

I reach down between us and grasp his cock through his pajama pants. "I want this. Now."

"Fuck, Lainey."

"Hurry. We only have five minutes."

Suddenly, he's shoving down his pants, and I'm pushing down my sleep shorts and panties. I spread my legs, and he settles between them again, his cock pressing into me just enough to feel how wet I am.

"My God. Lainey..." His head falls so our foreheads are pressed together. "I have to stop. I don't have—"

"Don't stop. I'm safe. IUD. As long—" He thrusts inside me, and we both cry out.

Finally.

Finally.

I knew it would feel good, but I've never loved the feel of a cock inside me more than having Ben's thick one filling me.

He fucks me fast and hard, grinding on me in that perfect spot that has my orgasm building higher and higher. I move my hips with him, grip his ass in my hands, demanding more. "Yes, God, don't stop. I'm going to come. Please...don't fucking stop."

"Never," he growls. "Come, Lainey. Come all around my cock. Let me feel you."

And I explode.

It has to be the most intense orgasm I've ever had. It's so overpowering I can only scream out and let it consume me. Ben doesn't stop fucking me. He slams into me over and over, groaning into my neck. "Your pussy is the best fucking thing I've ever felt. So fucking good."

His cock suddenly feels like steel inside me and I clench around him. "Lainey..." He shudders and moans as he finds his release, fucking me with long, hard strokes until he collapses on top of me.

After about ten seconds of only our labored breaths filling the air, applause suddenly breaks out, as well as some cheering and crude jeering that has both stiffening. Oh, no. Oh, shit. Our words might have been hushed, but our other sounds were definitely not. I can't believe the whole campsite just heard us have sex.

Ben is still on top of me. Inside me. He maneuvers so he's resting on his elbows and not crushing me. Our gazes meet in the dim darkness a second before we both start laughing.

"Shit, you can't laugh while I'm still inside you. Fuck, that hurts so good," he says as he rolls off me and onto his back. "I can't believe the whole park heard me come faster than a speeding bullet."

"I think we still have time left in our five minutes."

"I *know* we do."

We both softly laugh as we continue to lay there in our post-sex bliss. Ben props up onto his elbow. "I've never not used a condom, just so you know."

"Me either."

I've never been so far gone with a guy that I wanted to forgo a condom, but I wanted him too much. I liked that there were no barriers between us. And I don't even want to think about the significance of that thought.

He smiles and leans in, placing a soft kiss on my lips before he takes off his shirt. He reaches between us and gently cleans me, then himself, before tossing the shirt away. I pull my underwear back on, and he puts on his pants before he pulls me to him and spoons me like earlier.

"I'm sorry, but I'm going to fall asleep as fast as I came."

I laugh softly, feeling sated and sleepy. "Me, too."

After another couple of moments, he says, "Lainey..." His voice is already thick with sleep. "I really liked not being friends with you."

My throat tightens and tears suddenly threaten. I close my eyes and burrow closer to him, taking his arm so it tightens against me.

Me too.

Memorial Day

BEN

WHEN I OPEN MY EYES, A LOT OF THINGS HIT ME AT ONCE.

The fact that I'm in a tent and my back is stiff from sleeping on maybe five inches of cushion. That the muted light filtering through tells me it's morning, but late enough that it's already warm and humid. And I'm hot. But most of it has to do with the fact I have a sleeping Lainey plastered to my body. The same Lainey I had sex with last night.

Lainey and I had sex.

Even repeating it to myself, it doesn't seem real. There's a part of me that doesn't understand how it happened. One minute we were kissing, and the next thing I know, my cock is buried inside her. It happened so fast, it's almost like it didn't happen.

Except it absolutely did.

And it was fucking fantastic.

I don't remember ever experiencing such a raging need like that before. We were so in sync for our first time together and both so crazed for each other...I've definitely never had that kind of connection with another woman. And all I know right now is I want to do it again. And again.

But when Lainey opens her eyes, will she feel the same?

I want to believe she'll wake up and have the same goofy smile I'm wearing and be ready for a repeat. But my practical side tells me she's going to freak out and run. So, until she opens those pretty brown eyes, I'm going to soak up every second of bliss in this moment.

I bring my hand up and gently brush a lock of hair away from her face then my fingers trace down her arm before letting it rest back around her waist. Her eyes flutter open. I watch as her mind catches up to her surroundings. Her gaze shoots up to mine, and her eyes are wide, not with panic, but with startling realization of what happened between us. Then the barest of smiles lift her lips as her cheeks flush. My heart soars and my dick hardens.

"Morning." My voice is rough and deep in the quiet around us.

"Morning," she returns shyly.

Not wanting things to start off awkward between us, I decide to address the elephant in the tent. "So...we did a thing last night."

To my delight, Lainey bursts into laughter. "Um, yeah. But does it really count when it happened so fast?"

Considering she came faster than me, I'm not taking it as an insult to my manhood. Fast and furious was exactly what we needed. "When it feels that good, trust me, it counts. And it seemed to entertain the masses."

The red in her cheeks deepens even more just before she covers her face with her hands. "Oh my God. I forgot about that."

"We could always give it another try this morning," I suggest. "Take our time. See if slow garners as much praise as fast."

I see the interest in her eyes, but I also see the doubt. Last night could be labeled impulsive, but if we do it again today then we're deliberately entering a relationship—what kind, I don't know—but definitely a relationship. And that's something she doesn't want.

Suddenly, there's a loud clearing of a throat outside the tent. We both freeze.

"Hate to interrupt, but I don't really want to sit out here and listen to you two, um, *wake up*."

It's Josie. I bite my lip to stop from laughing, but Lainey looks panicked. She pushes away from me and sits up.

"We're up."

"Hmmm-mmm, bet you are," comes Josie's reply.

"Oh my God, Jo, we just shared a tent. There was a fucking spider in mine," Lainey says as she raises the covers and looks down. Her underwear is on, but her pajama shorts are wrapped around her leg. Unfortunately, her top is on since we didn't even get that far in undressing. And it's a fucking shame I didn't get a chance to put my mouth on her tits. She pulls up her shorts, crawls away from me, and unzips the door. Josie's standing there with an amused and knowing look on her face.

"Sure, you did."

Lainey scrambles out, and I hear her softly hiss, "Nothing happened."

Like hell, it didn't. I knew she'd panic, so I'm really trying not to read too much into it. But her denial leaves a burning sensation in my chest.

"Lain, no one looks this sated and rested after sleeping in a tent. Besides, your neighbors already ratted you out." Josie nods her head to the campsite next to us. Lainey looks over and her cheeks go dark red as she gives an awkward wave.

I can't help it, I start laughing. Lainey looks back at me with a hard glare.

"I brought coffee. Think of it as a sorry for interrupting." Josie holds up a drink tray.

Lainey takes one. "You didn't interrupt anything."

Josie looks at me questioningly as I step out of the tent, pulling a clean t-shirt over my head. "Not yet, at least," I say and take the other coffee. I'm greeted by some applause from our neighbors. I give them a sweeping bow which earns me more laughter and cheers. When I turn back to Lainey, she's glaring at me again.

"Seriously?" Lainey says with a narrowed gaze.

"Gotta have some fun with it." I close the distance and dip my head closer to her ear. "You know you had fun, so maybe you can stop fucking denying it before I prove it to you again." I lean in enough to meet her gaze and sink my hand into her hair, curling it at the nape of her neck. "I'm happy to give all these people a real show instead of just the audio version."

Her pupils blow. Hell. She's tempting me to actually make good on my threat.

"Damn. Too bad I missed it," Josie says.

I smile and give Lainey a quick kiss, then step away before I bend her over the picnic table. "How's Eli?"

"The meds have helped. His fever broke, and he got a good six hours of sleep."

"You stayed with him?" Lainey asks.

"Yeah."

Lainey's brows shoot up in surprise, and I feel the same way. I mean, I understand that as a nurse, Josie would feel some sort of responsibility for him, but I didn't think she'd spend the night —especially since she didn't seem to like him.

Josie throws up her arms. "What? It's no big deal. I mean, someone needed to make sure he was okay through the night."

"Thanks, Josie," I say. "That was really awesome of you."

She waves off my apology. "Since Scout's not here to flex his skills, let's get decamped."

We don't argue and get to work. It takes us about forty-five minutes to pack everything up. Since Josie returned in Eli's car, she hands over the keys to me and climbs in the backseat. Lainey seems hesitant at first but gets in the passenger seat and immediately starts scrolling through her phone.

"Has your dad mentioned that he and Mom are having people over for Memorial Day?" she asks me.

"Yeah, but I said no to the invite since I thought we'd still be here."

"My mom and sister have both texted this morning and asked if I changed my mind."

I glance over at her. "Want to head over there?"

"Yeah, probably should. But I want a shower first."

I nod. "Same. We'll need to do a car shuffle, too."

Lainey looks back at Josie. "Want to come?"

"Thanks, but I'll check on Eli, then head home to catch up on sleep."

A few hours later, after car swaps, drop-offs, and showering, I arrive at Kathleen's.

I pause outside.

Is this going to be weird? I haven't visited Dad at Kathleen's. To see him living amongst another woman's things. His house, the one I grew up in, hasn't changed much since my mom passed.

"Sack up, Ben," I mutter to myself and open the front door.

Lainey's already here.

I really wish she would have let me pick her up, but I have a feeling she's trying to make sure we aren't alone together. I give Dad a hug, and he leads me into the kitchen, where everyone is gathered. Harper and Chandler are here, along with several people I don't know. My gaze immediately seeks Lainey. I find her across the room talking to an older lady with flaming red hair. Her gaze flits to mine and holds. That awareness we can't seem to escape sparks between us, and a faint blush seeps into her cheeks before she looks back at the woman talking to her.

All of a sudden, a hand grips my elbow and I'm being pulled out of the kitchen by Chandler. "What the hell, man?"

Once we're in the living room and away from people, he hands me a beer. "I thought Harper was being dramatic about the eye-fucking between you two. I'm going to have to take that sangria out of Lainey's hand because I'm pretty sure you just impregnated her with your eye sperm."

"You're pretty funny, you know that?" I say on a laugh and take a sip of my beer.

I probably shouldn't laugh since the odds that I impregnated Lainey with my real sperm are much higher after last night. I've never gone bare with anyone, but fuck, I'm so glad it was her. Though I could have been wearing five condoms, and I know it still would have been amazing. Sex with Lainey is on another level.

Chandler lifts his beer. "I'm just glad Harper didn't witness it. I really don't want to listen to her rant all night about how you two are a bad idea."

My stomach clenches. I take a generous swig of beer to cover up how much that statement bothers me. I look back at him, and damn if he isn't watching me.

"You know I don't think that," he says softly, clearly seeing through me.

Chandler's a good guy. I could see him becoming a good friend. I'd really like to confide in him about last night, but I don't want to put him in the position of having a secret from his wife.

People start spilling into the living room, so I nod my thanks and head into the fray. I meet some of the other people, neighbors and friends of Kathleen's. I see some of my dad's friends are here, too. It seems their friend groups have merged successfully. It's probably an hour before I get anywhere near Lainey without a ton of people around us.

"Hey." I lean close and nudge her shoulder with mine.

She stiffens briefly and doesn't look my way. "Hey."

"I was told I eye-fucked you so hard that I probably got you pregnant."

"Oh, jeez." Lainey studies her sangria and finally looks at me. "Harper said that?"

"No, Chandler."

She shakes her head, laughing silently.

"I know we were safe, but next time we can be more careful if you want."

She jerks her gaze to me. "Next time?"

"I absolutely fucking hope there's a next time. You know as well as I do that next time would have been this morning if we weren't rudely interrupted."

She shrugs. "Maybe, but we were..."

"We were what?"

"I don't know. Still in our little tent bubble. Not in the real world."

"We can make more bubbles."

Her brows come together. "More bubbles?"

"Yeah, my bed, my couch, my shower, and my dining table would make great bubbles."

She laughs, and I lean in more, grazing the skin revealed above her shorts button with my fingertip. "Lainey..."

Her breath stutters as she sways into my touch.

"It was good. Really good."

"Yes," she breathes, her eyes softening even as they darken.

"There should definitely be a next time."

Her desire-filled gaze meets mine. "Yes," she whispers.

"Next time can be in a few short hours."

She smiles, a smile that says she thinks I'm crazy, but also says she's all in. Then she blinks as if she's coming out of a trance. "How do you do that to me?"

"Do what?"

"Make me forget everything."

"Lainey!" My dad barrels into the kitchen before I can answer her. "I heard you and Eli are dating."

She somehow manages to put space between us but glances at me before looking at my dad. "Not exactly. Our weekend date got cut short when he got sick."

"Yeah, Ben told me about that. Such a shame. He's like a second son, and I think you two would be great together. Don't you think so, Ben?"

I bring the beer to my lips. "Eli's great." I take a healthy sip.

If Dad realizes I didn't answer his question, he doesn't let on.

"Was there a love connection between you and Lainey's friend?" Dad continues, since he can't seem to let this shit conversation go.

"No, Dad. She's nice, but not for me."

"That's too bad. Wouldn't it be a nice story, friends all falling in love."

What about falling in love with your potential stepsister?

Last night might have been pure lust, but it also proved to me there's more to us than that. I don't just want her, I want to be *with* her—as much as possible.

Thankfully, one of my dad's friends walks up and the conversation turns away from our love lives. For the next few hours, we all mingle and eat, and I barely spend any time with Lainey. Eventually, all the guests leave, and it's only family left. Lainey's niece is watching a cartoon while the rest of us are sitting around the dining room table in the longest, most cutthroat game of Uno I've ever played.

My hands are so overloaded with cards I might need to grow another one to keep them all together. At this point, I'm ready for the game to end. End my misery. Lainey is next to me, and it's her turn. I brace myself for whatever card she's about to put down since she's responsible for ninety percent of the cards I'm holding.

She smirks as she lays down a Draw 4 card. The table erupts in laughter as I throw down my cards. "I'm out. I can't even hold anymore." Lainey's laughing so hard she's about to fall out of her seat. "Why? Why would you give me a Draw 4 when I'm holding half the deck? I didn't realize you were evil."

Harper wipes tears from her eyes. "Did we forget to tell you Lainey's a little competitive?"

"A *little*?"

That just spurs their laughter. "I'm never sitting next to her during Uno again. Actually, I don't plan to ever play Uno with you lot again."

They keep laughing.

"Liar," Lainey teases. "You love it, and you know it."

I glare at her, but don't say anything, because I do love it. I don't love losing, but the past hour has been the most fun I've had in a long time. Being an only kid, I didn't have these kind of family gatherings. Not that we didn't have our own fun, but since Mom died, things haven't been the same.

I glance at my dad, who has a wistful smile as he takes in the whole table. His gaze flits to mine, and his eyes look a little shiny. Before I can question him, he says, "I love this."

He says it loudly and earnestly enough that it grabs everyone's attention.

"I never would have thought a New Year's blind date would lead to this. That our two families would bond so wonderfully." He looks at me and there are definite tears swimming in his eyes. "With Ben being an only child, we didn't have boisterous holiday gatherings unless we had extended family around. After Poppy died, I'm afraid I didn't put a lot of effort into any holiday. But this..." He looks at all of us and takes Kathleen's hand in his, "this feels good. Right. We always wanted to give Ben a sister, and it's so nice to see him share a sibling relationship with your girls."

My stomach immediately drops. I cut my gaze toward Lainey, and she's somehow pale and flushed at the same time. Everyone at the table is silent, but my dad's words have touched them all. Kathleen and Harper are on the verge of tears, and even Lainey has a watery smile.

My dad turns in his chair so he's fully facing Kathleen and takes her other hand in his so he's now holding both of them. My stomach tightens, and my heart jumps into overdrive. Shit. Something huge is about to happen.

"How about we join our families officially?"

Oh fuck. Is he doing what I think he's doing?

"What?" Kathleen says, looking as shocked as everyone else.

My dad softly laughs. "That was my really poor attempt at asking you to marry me."

Lainey and Harper audibly gasp.

And I can't fucking breathe.

"Kathy, I never thought I'd want to marry again. I especially never thought I'd love again, but you changed everything. You came into my life, and it was like the missing puzzle piece clicking into place. We just fit. I know it's soon, so it's okay if you're not ready, but—"

"Yes!" Kathleen throws herself at my dad, enveloping him in a tight hug before they kiss. "I'd lost all hope of finding the one, then there you were. I found you, at last."

I subtly scan the table, trying not to lose my shit. Chandler appears surprised but happy. Harper's crying and has a genuine smile on her face as she watches our parents embrace. Lainey stares at our parents, her expression clearly dazed. It's probably the mirror image of what's on my face.

As our parents separate, the room erupts in congratulations as Harper and Chandler jump up along with our parents. Lainey and I are slower to join in. I glance at her again, but she's not looking at me, and I can't help but think it's on purpose. She's pasted on a smile, and it does a good enough job of reaching her eyes enough to look genuine, but I know it's not quite. Lainey moves to her mother and I meet my dad's gaze. He comes over to me with a sheepish expression on his face.

"I should have talked to you first. I wasn't really planning on doing that, not yet anyway. Are you okay?"

I swallow down the emotion clogging my throat. "I'm okay, Dad. If you're happy, I'm happy for you."

Tears flood my dad's eyes, and he wraps me in a tight hug. "I love you, son. This is the real thing. I know it."

I nod. "I know." I pull back. "I love you too, Dad."

We separate and I get caught up in hugs with Harper and Chandler before Lainey and I are faced with each other. She still doesn't look at me fully as she wraps her arms around me. Our hug is stilted and awkward, and I fucking hate it. I hate that she won't look at me. As we separate, I grip her arms so she can't escape me.

"Lainey..." Her gaze finally locks with mine. And now I wish it hadn't. Because what I see is a truth I don't want to face.

There will never be a next time.

National Meet a Mate Week

BEN

"I feel like I've lost a month of my life instead of two weeks," Eli says, as he takes a sip of the Old Fashioned I made him. "I don't think I've been that sick in my life. Ever."

"Yeah, I knew it was serious when you turned away Thai food."

I had dropped by with some food and Eli had taken one look at it and scrunched up his nose. Pretty sure he lived on canned chicken noodle soup for the past two weeks, though I learned Josie dropped off some homemade soup that he deemed worthy. It seems those two called a truce.

"If you want to buy some more for me, I'm game. My appetite is definitely back."

I snap my towel at him. "I just gave you a drink on the house. Don't push your luck."

Eli raises his glass. "Trust me, luck's not on my side."

"What are you talking about?"

"I wanted to make up for bailing Memorial Day weekend, so I asked Lainey out, and we met for lunch today."

My stomach knots. "Oh, yeah?" I hope my voice sounds

187

casual because that's the last thing I feel. I grab a glass to wash to keep me busy.

"Yeah, thought it would be a good idea to jump right in. I went straight up to her and kissed her."

"You *what*?" The glass launches from my hand and clatters into the sink, shattering. "Shit."

Eli raises his brows. "Thought I'd shoot my shot."

"And..." I prod, hoping his answer's what I want to hear.

"She kneed me in the balls."

"No way!" The word comes out in a burst of laughter.

"It's not funny. It hurt like hell."

I'm still laughing. I can't help it. "What happened after she kneed you?"

"She apologized. Said it was a knee-jerk reaction."

"*Knee-jerk* is right." I'm laughing so hard I brace myself on the bar.

"*Haha, puns are so funny.*" Eli says in a mocking voice as he raises his middle finger. "You're such a dickhead,"

"I'm sorry." I wipe the tears from my eyes as I try to control myself. "Then what?"

"We had lunch. Took the knee to the balls as a sign that I was officially friend-zoned." This time he takes a healthy sip.

I hope the relief I feel isn't written all over my face, especially since Eli seems to be watching me closely.

"I asked her what y'all did the rest of the camping trip."

"Oh, yeah? What did she say?" I gently pick up shards of glass out of the sink and dump them in the trash.

"She started acting weird. Didn't really meet my eyes. Kind of like you are now."

I look at him, his gaze heavy with accusation. "I'm cleaning up broken glass."

"Yeah, and it's broken because you freaked out I kissed her.

You could have just said you liked her and saved me the sore balls." He shifts in his seat, wincing slightly.

I open my mouth to deny his words, but I can't lie to my friend. "I'm not *supposed* to like her."

"Why not? Because your parents are engaged? Come on, isn't getting it on with your stepsister some sort of kink? Sounds kinda hot, actually."

Does he really not get the weirdness of this situation? "She doesn't want to fuck up their relationship, and I really don't either. If Lainey and I get together and it goes south, it could cause real problems."

"What if it doesn't go south?"

"I don't know. I guess that's the risk we're not willing to take, considering our track records."

Eli watches me with his glass hanging by his fingers. "When was the last time you really liked someone?"

"I've liked plenty of girls."

Eli cocks his head. "Come on. As much fun as you had as Frat Bro Ben, it was always a cover. You want the big love like your parents."

Shit. I don't have a response to that. It's true. "Yeah, well, after seeing all her mom's relationships with fuckboys go south, Lainey scares easily."

"So, Frat Bro Ben has to work for it now," he muses. "How the tables have turned."

I flip him off.

He laughs softly as he shakes his head. "Now that I think about it, I can't believe I missed the signs because it was crystal fucking clear you two like each other. I blame the flu for not catching on to all that Never Have I Ever bullshit. I have a strong feeling you two would both be drinking now with the sex question."

I keep quiet and concentrate on not dropping another glass as I clean it.

"Uh-huh. Nailed it."

"Lainey and I are just friends." If I say it enough times, it'll be true, damn it.

"Friends who fucked."

I shoot him a *watch-it* stare. The asshole smiles. I ignore him as I continue to clean.

"She sat in Poppy's spot, didn't she? That's why things got all weird when y'all were talking about it."

I don't confirm or deny a thing, but I don't need to.

He rests his forearms on the bar and leans close. "You've known this woman six months, and you've done things with her you haven't done with anyone else. You can call it whatever you want, but you two have been in an exclusive relationship."

I freeze. Damn. He has a point. Not that Lainey and I have been dating for six months, but we've been in constant contact. We've kissed. We've had sex. Maybe it's not a conventional one, but it's definitely some sort of relationship.

"Hey," Eli says, his voice sharp, forcing me to look up. His expression is sincere and serious. "I know your dad's happiness is important, but he wouldn't want you to give up on a chance for you to find yours."

LAINEY

Happy Birthday!!

Did you get your present?

BEN

Thank you!

You mean the T-shirt with Donald Duck on it that says Duck Around and Find Out?

LAINEY

How awesome is it that you share your birthday with Donald Duck Day!!

BEN

If you looked up the holidays for today, then you know what other day it is.

LAINEY

National Earl Day?

BEN

Try again.

LAINEY

National Meal Prep Day?

BEN

It's National Sex Day, and you know it.

Look, no offense, but I think you missed the mark on the holiday I'm really excited about sharing my birthday with.

LAINEY

Hmmm, must have missed that one.

BEN

Uh-huh. Sure.

LAINEY

You can celebrate by ducking yourself.

BEN

Oh, I will be. Just know…I'd rather be ducking you.

Lainey

. . .

JOSIE STARES AT ME OPEN-MOUTHED. "They're engaged? Are you serious?"

"As a fake heart attack."

She snorts, loving the reminder of my New Year's Eve saga. "Oh, my God. Girl, you fucked your stepbrother."

Several gazes swing our way in the small restaurant.

I lean forward and whisper hiss, "Why don't you say it a little louder?"

"Sorry."

No, she's not. "He's also not my stepbrother—yet."

"Wow. This is just...*wow*."

"It's not wow. I'm going to be stuck with my one-night stand for the rest of my life." My amazing, hot, funny one-night stand who I was starting to think maybe...

No.

No maybes. Not with Ben. Especially now.

"Okay, for one, there are people out there raising kids with their one-night stands, so at least you don't have that going on."

I do my best not to show that the possibility was higher since we didn't use double protection. I don't get consistent periods with my IUD, so I did take a pregnancy test a couple of days ago to make sure.

"And second, Ben isn't a one-night stand. You might have only had sex once, but he's not some stranger. You like him, as in really like him like you've never liked anyone before. I can tell. You would have never slept with him if you didn't."

"The lust is strong between us."

She shakes her head. "No, girl, that's called *chemistry*, and you know it. Why don't you give the guy a chance?"

"Because he's going to be my stepbrother!"

"Come on, that's not *that* taboo. It's not like you're blood-related or underage. You're consenting adults."

She's being so logical, and it would be so easy to allow it to sway me. I'm so fucking confused and conflicted. This thing with Ben doesn't exactly feel wrong, but there are so many things that tell me it's a bad idea. My DM's keep getting flooded with messages about him. Most of them saying he's a good time, not a long time. While I want to tell them all to go to hell, they don't know him like I do, those warnings keep popping up in the back of my mind. Then there's Mom.

"You should have seen my mom when Mike proposed," I tell her. "She said she finally found the one. They're so happy together, and he's perfect for her. For all of us. The other guys she's been either barely acknowledged us or didn't at all. Mike's all in, and Cassie's already calling him Grandpa. She even called Ben uncle."

"Aww..."

"See! I can't screw that up."

"*You* can't screw up *their* relationship, Lainey."

I don't mention that I've screwed up my mom's relationships before.

"Of course, I can. When have I ever got it right with a guy? I can't even get a holidate that works out."

"Yeah, but none of them are like Ben. Maybe that's the difference. Maybe that's what makes him...*right*."

No, I can't think of Ben as Mr. Right because what if I'm wrong? I was grossly mistaken about Isaac. I thought he was the perfect boyfriend. Turns out, he was the perfect boyfriend to several other girls, too. Isaac fooled me for two years, and I've only known Ben six months.

I can just see future holiday gatherings where Ben and I sit on opposite ends of the dining table, avoiding each other to the point of awkwardness. Or we'll have to take turns on holidays like a kid with divorced parents. Pursuing whatever this is any further spells disaster. I shouldn't have shared his tent. I should have never turned to him and begged him not to be my friend.

A text lights up my phone, saving me from responding to Josie. It's my boss asking where my Father's Day submission is. I was hoping I could skip the holiday since I've never celebrated it.

I sigh and put my phone back on the table a little harder than necessary.

"What?" Josie asks.

"I have to do a Father's Day post, and my boss wants to see my ideas. Maybe I should post a picture of me with my arm around the air."

Josie gives me a sympathetic look as she reaches over and takes my hand. I thought I stopped letting Father's Day bother me years ago, but this year it's hitting differently. Maybe because Mike and Ben are in my life. Not only do they have a great father-son relationship, but Mike has made a genuine effort to get to know me and Harper. In only six months, it feels like he's been part of our family for years. Like he belongs. Another reason I don't want to screw everything up.

"What about reaching out to Mike? Maybe you could do something with him?"

I don't hate the idea, but I don't want to interfere. "No. It's his day with Ben."

She tilts her head. "Do you really think Ben would mind?"

"I don't know."

"You know he wouldn't, Lainey." Her gaze narrows. "Okay, filter off."

Oh, crap. Josie doesn't withhold much, but when she turns off her filter, it means you're about to be hit with something you really don't want to hear.

She leans forward, her gaze steadily holding mine. "Stop

refusing to read the book because you're afraid of how it will end."

"What?"

"Read the fucking book, Lainey. Enjoy the journey. Don't think about the ending. Because a good book never ends. It stays with you forever."

As her words sink in, they lodge in the middle of my chest. My first instinct is to say I don't do that. But I do. It seems hardwired in me to flee at the first hint of trouble.

In the end, isn't it better that way, though? Of all things, I can't get *this* wrong. There's too much at stake.

Bald Eagle Appreciation Day

JUNE 20TH

BEN

Are you going out with Eagle today?

LAINEY

What? Where is that coming from?

BEN

It's Bald Eagle Appreciation Day. Seems like the perfect day to go on a date with a bald Eagle.

LAINEY

OMG! ROFL!!

Please don't tell my mother what day it is. I'll never hear the end of it.

BEN

You sure you don't want to give ol' Eagle a chance??

LAINEY

It's also National Vanilla Milkshake Day. I'd rather indulge in that.

BEN

Vanilla is so boring.

LAINEY

So is Eagle!

BEN

How do you know?

LAINEY

So, I might have gone to my mom's class then
on a coffee date afterward.

BEN

You didn't?

LAINEY

She totally tricked me! Said we were going to
brunch. I had to meditate about mimosas
instead of drinking them—which is totally not
the same.

Eagle talked WAY too passionately about Chai.
Oh, and he had talons. Like the longest toenails
I've ever seen. *gagging emoji*

Yoga is forever ruined for me.

And get this, his real name isn't Eagle.

It's Max Buffamonteezi. I saw the name on his
credit card.

BEN

I think I know why he goes by Eagle.

I'm laughing so hard my stomach hurts.

LAINEY

middle finger emoji

Father's Day

BEN

8:27 AM

ME

Hey, if you need anything today. I'm here.

LAINEY

Thx, I'm good. I stopped caring about Father's Day a long time ago.

LAINEY'S TEXT is still playing in my mind hours later. Her post a couple of days ago, in which she suggested activities for the holiday coming up, were all standard things that most people would think of. There was nothing personal in this one, and she usually adds a personal touch to show what she's looking forward to most. I think this day bothers her more than she wants to admit.

"You're up."

My dad's voice snaps me out of my thoughts, and I look down the fairway, completely missing my dad at the tee. "You're like a foot away from the hole."

"Yeah, it was a beauty of a shot. Too bad you were daydreaming and missed it."

"Sorry, zoned out." I grab my driver and move to tee up my ball. Golf is something my dad and I have always enjoyed together, though I didn't play during my college years. A Father's Day game has always been our tradition even if the course is extra crowded with many doing the same.

I swing, and the ball shanks left, nowhere near the green. My dad snickers as the ball descends towards the woods. "I swear, you seem to get worse the more you play."

"Thanks, Dad."

He slaps my shoulder as we grab our bags and head to our golf cart. "What's on your mind?"

"What do you mean?"

"Something's distracting you."

"My mind was just wandering."

"Is it the bar?"

"No, the bar's doing well. Far better than I ever expected." A small burst of pride swells in my chest. Even if I do wish some of the success wasn't because I made shirtless suggestive videos.

"A girl?"

I hesitate half a second too long.

He smiles knowingly. "Ah, it's a girl."

"Um, not like you think. I was thinking of Lainey."

My dad hits the brakes a little hard as we get to the wooded area where my ball should be, and we both lunge forward. "Why are you thinking of Lainey?"

"Because it's Father's Day. I reached out to her since she had done the same for me on Mother's Day. She said she was fine, but I have this feeling she isn't."

I get out and pull a club from my bag so we can finish the hole before the people behind us get mad.

"Would it make you feel better to know that I invited her and

Kathy to dinner with us?" my father says as we wait for the group ahead of us to finish up.

He has my full attention now. "What? When? Were you going to tell me?"

"It's only the fourth hole, son. I was going to get to it. Lainey sent me a Happy Father's Day text this morning, and Kathleen had told me it's usually a hard day for her, so I invited her. I hope you don't mind."

"No. Not at all. That's really nice of you, Dad."

"Well, I am about to be her stepfather." He laughs softly, his smile so full of joy it about steals my breath. "I still can't believe it. I'm about to have two stepdaughters and a granddaughter. Did I tell you Cassie asked to call me Grandpa?"

"She started calling me Uncle Ben." I smile, willing my sudden queasiness to go the hell away.

Impossibly, my dad's expression turns more wistful, and I say what's true and also bittersweet. "I'm glad you're happy. You deserve it."

But don't I deserve it, too? I want us both happy, I want to find a way to make this work for both of us.

His eyes turn shiny as he gives my shoulder a meaningful squeeze. It's time for us to tee off and focus on the game.

"I'm glad you're okay with everything," he says once we're back in the cart. "I know this all happened so quickly. I never thought I'd ever marry again. Not after your mom. But there was this...I don't know, just this peace in my heart when I met Kathy. I don't know how else to explain it."

My mind immediately goes to Lainey and the pull to her that I can't seem to stop. How so many of our moments are real and right.

He looks at me. "Have you ever been in love?" The question catches me off guard, and he must sense it. "Was there no one in college?"

I scrub the back of my neck. "I didn't exactly date in college." My dad immediately picks up on my meaning and doesn't seem surprised. "I loved Emily, I guess," I continue even though the words feel sour on my tongue.

A smirk forms. "You didn't."

"I think I said it at some point. We dated for a year."

"And I bet you said it because you thought you should, instead of meaning them."

I shrug, pretty sure he's right.

My dad has this faraway look in his eyes that's somewhat sad yet hopeful. Then he looks at me. "When you mean them, they're more than words. Because that person has marked your soul. And even if it's not forever, they still live with you. In one way or another, they changed you. And it will always be worth it."

"WHAT EVER HAPPENED WITH ELI?" my dad asks Lainey after we've polished off our drinks and appetizers at the restaurant later that evening.

A blush seeps into her cheeks and I have the distinct impression she's trying not to look at me. "Nothing, but he's a great guy."

It's the first time we've seen each other since our parents got engaged—since we had sex. It was slightly awkward at first, but we quickly slipped into the easiness we have with each other through texts. Honestly, simply being in the same room with her settles me like nothing else can.

"Really?" Dad's eyebrows shoot up. "I could have really seen you two as a couple."

"Yes, I saw the pictures of you two from your post. Y'all really look good together, and he's so cute," her mom says.

Lainey rolls her eyes. "Mom, you say I look good with every guy I've been on a holidate with."

"Well...you do. But if he's great, then what happened?"

Lainey's gaze pops to mine and back to her mom. "Nothing happened. It just didn't work out. He wasn't..."

"Soul changing," I say.

Lainey's gaze snaps to mine. Suddenly all the noise in the restaurant fades and there's only us. We're locked into each other, this invisible pull between us making it impossible to look away. Her mouth parts, and her breathing picks up. Fuck. I need to touch her. I need...

"No," she says, and it takes me a minute to realize she's agreeing with me.

I smile, the roar of the restaurant returns, and I remember we have an audience. I cut my gaze and pick up my drink. "You should tell him how you kneed Eli in the kibble and bits."

Thankfully, this does what I intend and takes the attention away from us.

"Lainey!" Kathleen exclaims.

"Now, this is a story I gotta hear." My dad leans back and laughs.

"It was an accident," Lainey insists.

"He tried to surprise kiss her," I tell them.

My dad shakes his head. "That boy. I swear, he never thinks with the right head."

That earns a laugh from me and Lainey.

"Lainey, he was trying to be romantic," Kathleen insists.

"Sexual assault isn't romantic, Mom. I didn't even know who it was until he was...folded over."

My dad, still laughing, reaches over and pats her hand. "Good for you, Lainey. I love Eli, but he deserved what he got."

Thankfully, our dinner arrives, and the conversation turns away from Lainey's love life. At some point, I glance at my dad and see he's looking at me with a thoughtful expression. My stomach knots. Was I too obvious? Does he realize Lainey's making a mark on my soul?

I'd love to just confess, but it's the last thing Lainey wants. That's what's been so hard about all this—fighting my feelings while respecting hers. Respecting my dad's relationship, too.

It seems like my feelings are doomed no matter what.

I push away my melancholy thoughts and refocus on our dinner. Once the bill is paid, my dad and Kathleen head to the bathroom so Lainey and I go outside to wait for them. She takes an extra step away from me as she stares at the parking lot. I shift and stuff my hands in my pockets. How did we go from being locked in and connected to this awkward as fuck moment?

"Thanks for sharing your dad with me today," Lainey says, her gaze darting in different directions as if she's afraid to look at me.

Fuck this. Needing to get us back on friendly ground, I close the distance between us and take her hand in mine, giving it a squeeze. "I hope it was a good day."

And that seems to do the trick because she immediately relaxes and meets my gaze. The smile she gives me in one hundred percent genuine. "It was." But the friendliness quickly transforms to more. The spark of heat we can't seem to escape ignites between us. We sway toward each other, and it takes all my willpower not to pull her into me and kiss her. Instead, I hug her and press my fingers between her shoulder blades. I feel the intake of her breath and hold on to her for a moment too long before I step back, letting my hand slowly fall away.

A swallow works her throat as her brown eyes zero in on my mouth. Damn. She's making it really hard to not kiss her right now.

"Ready?"

The sound of Kathleen's voice jerks us further apart. We

glance over to see our parents watching us with twin sets of guarded expressions. Fuck.

Lainey immediately moves toward her mom and exchanges a hug with my dad before they walk toward their car. We all met at the restaurant, and my dad's staying the night at the old house. I tear my gaze from watching Lainey walk away, but I'm caught.

One look at my dad, and I know he knows.

The walk back to our car is silent. I keep glancing his way, but his head's bent, seeming to be lost in thought. My stomach twists, and my forehead breaks out in a sweat. I'm back to feeling like a teenager and waiting for him to dole out my punishment.

"Ben..." he starts after we're in the car.

I want to tell him to stop. To not tell me what I'm feeling is wrong.

"It was a good day," he finally says and starts the car. I glance at him, and he gives me a reassuring smile.

"Yeah, it was." I turn back to look through the windshield. "That's it?"

"That's it."

National Kissing Day, National Limoncello Day - June 22nd

LAINEY

BEN

Your sister just told me to pick up fireworks and deliver them to some lake house tomorrow. TOLD me, not ASKED. I have no idea what's going on, but it's pretty clear I have no choice.

ME

OMG, I'm laughing so hard. It hurts.

BEN

Seriously, what is going on?

ME

Her annual 4th of July party. She gets really stressed about it, and Chandler is out of town for work, so I'm guessing you're next in line to help, big brother.

BEN

Why didn't she ask you? Sorry, I mean TELL you.

ME

Oh, there's no way Harper would trust me with the fireworks. They're a big deal. Plus, she knows you have a truck.

BEN

What are the odds I'd survive if I told her no?

ME

Slim to none.

BEN

Had a feeling.

ME

Totally kidding. Don't let her bully you into helping. She's a big girl.

BEN

No, I can help. But she could have asked nicely.

ME

She'll remember to be grateful eventually.

BEN

I'll pick you up tomorrow at 1pm.

ME

What? Why?

BEN

I have to pick up the fireworks at 2. It takes an hour to get to the place.

ME

I'm not going with you.

BEN

Yes, you are. It sounds like a shit ton of fireworks. I'll need help, and there's no way I'm doing all this without reinforcements.

ME

So, you're saying if you fuck up, you don't want all the blame to fall on you.

BEN

Exactly.

Come with me, Lainey.

Please. Pretty pretty, please. See how I can ask nicely?

ME

You told me nicely. That was not a question.

BEN

It was still nice. Come on, it'll be fun.

ME

Fine. Since you said pretty please

AS I CLOSE MYSELF INTO BEN'S TRUCK, I SECOND-GUESS MY decision to come with him. Okay, it's probably more like fifteenth-guessed. Even though it's been almost a month, I can't stop thinking about the fact we had sex.

It might have been hectic and rushed, but it was good. *Really fucking good.* I don't think I've had sex that satisfied me so much yet left me aching for more. Ever. I've practically worn out my vibrator reliving that night over and over.

After our parents' engagement, I swore to myself I would avoid being alone with him. But even being surrounded by family on Father's Day, we still managed to create enough awareness between us that I'm pretty sure my mom noticed. She didn't say anything, but there was this stilted silence between us the whole ride home—the kind of silence that reeks of disappointment and worry—the kind I was met with when she learned I'd been sabotaging her dates. I can't shake the feeling that Harper's fears from Easter could come true.

So, I've tried not to text him, but it's impossible to ignore his silly holiday texts—which are the highlight of my day. Proving I have no business agreeing to spend half a day alone with him—

especially with him looking hot as fuck in a fitted tee and athletic shorts.

He's plugging the address into his phone so it'll give us directions to the fireworks warehouse. Since they aren't legal in the city, we have a forty-five-minute drive out of town to purchase them.

Once he's done, he glances over. His gaze lands on my legs and slowly moves up my body. It's June in Texas, so the fewer clothes, the better, but considering how easily things combust between us, maybe I should have worn leggings instead of the running shorts that have hiked way up my thighs. "Hey." His voice is rough. Possessive.

"Hey." Damn. My voice sounds as turned on as his.

He clears his throat, tearing his eyes away from my legs and puts his truck into gear. Once we're cruising down the highway, he says, "Okay, tell me about this party. I'm assuming, after all this, I'm invited."

"Yes, I'd assume this is your official invite."

He shakes his head. "I didn't realize your sister had a lake house."

"It's not hers. It belongs to Chandler's parents. His family is pretty well off, and they've owned it for years. They used to host Fourth of July parties all the time, but they own a second home up north and leave Texas in the summer. So, Chandler and Harper took over hosting. She always stresses about it, and usually everyone pitches in to help at some point."

"Me included, I guess."

I glance over at him. "You're family."

He looks at me, and the air between us feels heady again. There's no denying the truth of my statement, and it's not only because our parents are engaged. He just belongs. And I don't know what to do with that feeling.

Especially when that feeling is so much more than familial.

I clear my throat. "Of course you're invited. You and your dad. Most of the party will be Harper and Chandler's friends. You'll see some familiar faces from Easter. Josie is usually my date, she'll be there, but this year, I'll—"

I don't exactly know why I stop talking or why it feels wrong to finish my statement. It's a holiday, so it shouldn't be a surprise to him.

"What?"

"Um, it's a holiday. I have a holidate."

The silence in the car suddenly feels thick and awkward. I watch as Ben flexes his hand around the steering wheel, his face completely impassive.

"I'm actually meeting him for dinner tonight to see..."

"See what?"

"That we'll be a good fit for the Fourth. Since they've all been flops, I thought a screener date would be good."

He nods, and a little grunt comes out of his mouth. "Think your sister will mind if I bring a date?"

A sick feeling fills me, and I have to force the words out of my mouth, "No, of course not."

"Great."

"Great."

Nothing is great. "Oh wait, don't you have to work?"

"Actually, I close on the Fourth of July."

"Really? Isn't it a huge drinking holiday for you?"

"Not for my bar and where it's located. Most people are at house parties or the lake. Uncle Red decided a while back that it wasn't enough business to make it worth staying open, so we close and let the employees enjoy the holiday. I wanted to keep the tradition."

"That's really awesome, Ben. I'm sure your employees love that."

"Yeah, they have to work most holidays, so it's nice to have a big one they can have off."

Thankfully, our conversation turns away from dating, and we get to the firework warehouse without further awkwardness. That is until Ben meets Chloe, the cute and bubbly woman helping us with our order.

I watch as he leans over the counter with a flirty grin and she does the same. I can't even process what they're saying, there's this sudden whooshing in my ears and my stomach churns.

"Chloe, are you telling me that an order this big made every year seriously doesn't warrant some sort of loyalty discount?" He takes her hand and presses it to his chest. "You're breaking my heart here."

I turn and walk away as a long-suppressed memory rushes to the forefront of my mind. I'm suddenly back in college, standing in the middle of campus, watching my boyfriend wrap another woman in a hug. Then there's the roar of my heart pounding when he presses his lips to her temple.

That's the moment he saw me. He stilled and smiled... smiled! As if I hadn't caught him with another girl. He spoke to her, and she walked off, before he headed toward me. I wanted to run. I wanted to scream. Instead, I stood there and waited. I didn't even move as he bent and kissed my lips.

"Babe, it was just a hug with a friend."

I blink, tears I didn't even know had formed slip down my cheeks. I shake my head. Not sure if it's because I don't believe him or because I do.

"I've known her since freshman year and haven't seen her in a while." He wipes away my tears. "Come on, Lain. Am I acting like someone who was just caught cheating, or like a worried boyfriend who wants to make sure his girlfriend is okay after seeing something that hurt her?"

I stare into his puppy dog brown eyes and see only concern.

Surely, if he was hiding something, I'd see it. I let the hug replay in my mind. His grin had been a little flirty, but he's kind of a flirty guy. He didn't touch her anywhere intimate. The kiss could be considered friendly. Maybe I am reading too much into it. Maybe it's my history of seeing my mom's asshole boyfriends making me distrustful.

"Promise?"

His lips twitch into a small smile before he leans in and kisses me, pulling me in flush against him. He slowly ends the kiss, his lips lightly brushing mine. "Who's my girl?"

"I am." I breathe into him.

I blink out of the memory. What a fool I was. I mistook his kiss for a promise instead of the diversion it was. Months later, after I truly caught him, I finally recognized all the moments he gaslit me.

And I fell for every single one.

I hate that watching Ben and Chloe interact brings all those feelings back. Or that I have no fucking idea how to process them. Should I even feel jealous or hurt when I keep pushing him away? When I'm going on holidates.

I press a hand to my belly and take a fortifying breath. Just woman up and go take care of Harper's order. I join the guys helping us load, keeping my distance from Ben and Chloe. When we're ready to leave, she hands over her card, making sure he knows her personal number is on it. I refuse to acknowledge the nauseous anger churning in my stomach—or the fact that I want to claw her eyes out.

"Here," Ben says as he hands over Chloe's card once we're back in the truck.

I stare, but don't take it. "Why are you giving me that?"

The venom in my voice has his gaze jumping to mine. "What's wrong?"

"Nothing." I adjust so I'm facing straight ahead and buckle my seatbelt.

"Aren't you going to take this?"

"Why? She gave it to you. She obviously wants you to call her."

His brows bunch. "I got it because she promised ten percent off next year's order if Harper places it before the Fourth."

I blink at him, remembering his comment about a discount before I walked away. I still don't take the card. "Ben, she gave you that card because she wants *you* to call *her*. You can't be surprised with how much you flirted with her."

He puffs out a frustrated breath, reaches for my purse, and stuffs the card inside then starts the truck. "It wasn't like that."

"She doesn't know that. You made her the center of your attention. Made her laugh. Made her feel good. Sure, you asked about a discount, but she's secretly hoping you'll call and ask her out. Her heart is going to jump every time she gets a text or call hoping it's you. Then when she realizes you used her, it's going to fucking hurt. It doesn't matter if she knew you less than an hour. And, yeah, she'll get over it, but every once in a while, you'll pop in her mind and remind her of that awful feeling. Your flirting isn't as harmless as you think."

I'm breathing hard and there's this ache in my chest as a thick silence fills the truck. He's staring at me, his expression confused and shocked and something else I can't quite decipher. I wait, but he doesn't respond. Instead, he puts the truck in gear and maneuvers us out of the parking lot.

His mouth is pulled tight, and I can't tell if he's pissed or being reflective. The longer we drive in silence, the more I want to say something. But I don't know what. I feel like the ball is in his court at this point. Eventually, he turns over his phone to me and tells me to pick a playlist. I do, desperate for anything to break up this stillness.

When we pull up to the lake house almost an hour later, his

impassiveness finally breaks. "Whoa, nice house," he says, leaning over the steering wheel for a better look.

It's not the biggest house on the lake by any means. It's an older craftsman style, but it's been updated inside and out, which has given it a more modern look. They also have a nice, manicured lawn.

"Yeah, it's pretty great, huh? Wait until you see the inside."

We unload the fireworks into the garage and head inside. The house was pretty much gutted, so the interior's an open concept. The kitchen is completely modern in a farmhouse chic meets lake-life way. I give him a quick tour of the place then we make our way back to the kitchen. Ben immediately moves to the area of the countertop that's covered in booze. My sister goes all out and has quite the variety. All the standard liquors plus a bunch of mixers and liqueurs.

"Now, this is a haul. I hope I don't get voluntold to bartend."

I laugh since it's something she'd totally do. "No, she actually hires a couple of bartenders."

He peruses the bottles and tips back a huge thing of tequila to look at the label and winces. "Don't drink this. It's shit."

"That's for the Jello shots."

His eyebrows raise. "Well, I'd advise against them unless you want your hangover with a massive headache."

"I usually stick to sangria. My sister makes a great one."

He glances over at the wine and nods, so I guess whatever wine my sister buys meets his approval. He grows quiet and the earlier awkwardness settles around us again. Well, hell. I don't regret what I said, but I hate this weirdness between us now.

Suddenly he turns to me, his gaze conflicted and tense. "I read her, okay?

I bunch my brows in question.

"Chloe," he continues. "I knew if I flirted, I could work a discount. She said Chandler's family have been ordering this insanely expensive order for the past fifteen years. It's just bad business not to do something for someone who has been that loyal." He pushes his hand through his hair in frustration. "It's a kind of like a sales tactic. I do it all the time at the bar. It gets us bigger tips. It makes the customers friendlier. It's part of the job. I'm not setting out to hurt people."

"Okay. I understand where you're coming from. It's only...I don't think you realize how charming you are and how genuine it comes off. You see it as innocent and fun, and it is for some. But for some, it's special. Who wouldn't want more of the gorgeous guy making them feel like a million bucks? Then when they realize it's a scam, they feel like chump change."

He grimaces. "Yeah, I'm getting that." He takes a step closer, reaching out and covering my hand with his. "But what I'm also realizing is it hurts you. And I'm sorry. I don't ever want to hurt you, Lainey."

My heart lurches even as this sense of comfort envelops me. Isaac never apologized. He only made me question my doubts. But there's no doubt at the sincerity staring back at me.

"Thanks. I do understand that you have every right to flirt and get women's numbers."

"Lainey—"

"And I might have had a bit of trauma response back there. I had a bad experience in college."

"Please don't discount your feelings."

I sigh. That's not what I'm doing. At least I don't mean to. But I have to acknowledge that I can't push him away then get jealous. "I'm not. I meant what I said. I guess..." I shrug, not sure I can fully confess that I hate the thought of him with another woman.

"Want to talk about it? The asshole that hurt you?"

I shake my head. Isaac has taken over enough of my day. I can tell Ben doesn't like my answer but nods. "I'm going to do better, Lainey. I've always had this natural charm. My mom started calling me her little charmer when I was barely out of diapers. But I'm going to be more conscious of my behavior. I can't say I want to be taken seriously if my actions scream Frat Bro Ben or Bare-chested Bartender."

I don't know how to respond. Because what I really want to do is throw my arms around him and kiss the hell out of him. He keeps surprising me, and yet I don't know how. He's been blowing my expectations of who I thought Ben Kelley was from the beginning.

He tugs on my hand, bringing our bodies closer. His vivid gaze holds mine, piercing me right through the heart. "And I *could* get other women's numbers. But I *don't want to*."

The rough intensity of his words steal my breath as a whole new set of emotions rush through me—all of them hot and needy.

And it must show on my face because his mouth curls into a sexy smirk. Fuck, how am I supposed to resist this man?

Thankfully, he doesn't call me out on it and leans away, giving me space.

His gaze returns to the counter full of alcohol. "Oh, look," he says, picking up a small bottle with yellow liquid in it. "Did you know it's National Limoncello Day?"

"And here I thought this was the one day we were together that wasn't a holiday."

He grins as he gently rocks the bottle back and forth. "What do you say? I think our firework fetching deserves a drink."

"I do love Limoncello."

"Let's see what I can make." He scans the bottles and picks up the cranberry juice. "I can do a Limoncello Cosmo."

He gathers the juice, Limoncello, vodka, and Grenadine. We find a shaker and he mixes everything, only adding a small drop of Grenadine. My gaze falls to his biceps as he mixes the drink. I love this part of his job. I could watch him all day.

He pours a little into a wine-sized plastic cup. "Taste this and let me know if you want it sweeter."

I take a sip. It's potent, a little sour, but good. "A tad sweeter."

He adds some of the Grenadine and mixes it again before dividing the drink between the two cups. He hands one to me then lifts his. "To National Limoncello Day."

"Cheers." I tap my cup to his and take a sip. "This is really good. It might be my new drink."

He shakes his head. "No. You're too complex for a vodka drink."

I raise my brows.

"Your cocktail would contain whiskey. Maybe a bourbon."

"Why's that?"

He takes me in, his body suddenly closer. "Because it's not only complex, but has a subtle intensity. It's spicy. Sweet. Earthy." His voice is smooth and velvety as he reaches out and twists a lock of my hair around his finger. "Like your autumn hair." His gaze lifts from my hair to my eyes, his blue stare powerful. "Trust me, Lainey, nothing about you is a vodka."

I can't move. Can't breathe.

"Ben..." I don't even know what to say. Or why I even said his name. This moment is full of all the descriptors he's used—intense, complex, spicy, sweet. And just as dangerous as the liquor itself.

He gives my hair a tiny tug before he lets go, his smile teasing. "Come on, let's go hang by the pool."

I'm thankful for the suggestion and the reprieve from all these blazing emotions. We take our drinks to the patio, where the house is really impressive. It has an infinity-edge pool and jacuzzi, a covered outdoor kitchen, bar-top seating, and, of course, a gorgeous view of Lake Travis.

"Let's go swimming," Ben says suddenly.

"What? No, we can't."

He glances at the glistening pool, which does look tempting and refreshing. The temperature is closing in on triple digits today, and we sweated tons hauling the fireworks. "Why not? I'm guessing this pool is going to be full of kids and parents during the party. Why not enjoy it now?"

"We don't have swimsuits."

"We don't need them."

My breath stalls. "We can't go skinny dipping."

"Again, why not?" He closes the distance between us. "I'd say it isn't like I haven't seen you naked before, but we didn't exactly get that far."

My cheeks flame as a surge of tingles rush through me at the memory of our bodies connecting—the way he filled me so perfectly. We were naked only where it mattered most.

His head dips, and his lips brush the shell of my ear. I shiver and bite back a moan at the barely there touch. "I've been inside you, Lainey. I think we can handle a little skinny dipping."

My breath catches, and it takes all my willpower not to lean into him and grasp his shirt so I don't melt into a puddle of lust. He pulls back, his face so close I can feel his breath against my lips. His bright blue eyes now stormy, matching the storm of emotions brewing inside me.

My gaze falls to his lips, and they quirk in a small half-grin before he lifts his drink to his lips. I watch as he takes a sip then swipe his tongue over his lips in a slow, sensual stroke. Jesus. The summer Texas heat has nothing on what Ben can do to me. I have to consciously resist the urge not to bring my hand to my pussy and give it the stroke it desperately needs.

A rumbly sound comes from him just before he turns away and heads toward the pool. He sets his cup down, grabs the back of his shirt, and tosses it on a lounger. He hooks his thumbs in the waistband of his shorts, and his head turns to the side, as if to see if I'm looking.

I sure as hell am.

Before I can prepare myself, he pushes his shorts and underwear down in one shove. Fuck me, he has a great ass. Round and tight. The memory of my fingers sinking into that ass, urging him to fuck me harder surges through me.

I hear a splash and blink out of the sexy memory in time to see him surging through the wavy surface. He brushes his hair back and wipes the water from his face, looking like a damn supermodel. The cocky expression on his face has my gaze dropping to the rippling shadows beneath the water. He closes in on the wall so I can't see anything, and I practically moan in disappointment. His grin widens.

"You coming in?"

No.

It's what I *should* say. Yet, I know I'm not. I come to the edge of the pool and set my cup near his, go to the deck box where the pool towels are stored. I drop a couple near the edge. "Turn around."

He tilts his head as if to say, *are you kidding me?*

"I'm not getting in unless you turn around."

He sighs, grabs his drink, and heads to the other side of the pool to look out at the view of the lake. I slip off my shorts and shirt, staying in my bra and panties. I can't abandon *all* my self-control—it's hanging on by a strand as it is. I sit and ease my way into the cool water, grabbing my drink then join him at the infinity wall.

He glances over and takes in my bra straps. "Cheater."

We glance back toward the view. "This is amazing. If I were Harper and Chandler, I would move here in the summer," he says.

"She'll stay for a few weeks, and her friends will come and

hang with her. But it's not super convenient to come and go, especially for Chandler's office."

"What about you? Do you ever come and stay with her?"

"I have before."

"Sometimes you two seem close, and sometimes not. Chandler mentioned she kind of took care of you growing up."

"Yeah, my mom worked a lot since she was raising us by herself, so it kind of messed up our sibling dynamic."

"I don't know, y'all can bicker like proper sisters."

I snort a laugh. "I suppose we do. She means well even if she drives me crazy. She just wants us all to be happy and safe."

"Safe?"

"Stable. She doesn't want me to fall in their footsteps. Struggling like Mom with men and jobs. Or like she did, constantly having to pick up the pieces."

"Do you feel like you're falling in their footsteps?

"I guess in a way. You know, what I talked about on Memorial Day weekend."

At the mention of Memorial Day, my mind immediately goes to what happened in his tent and not our deep conversation.

He closes the distance between us and turns me to face him.

"There were no poor decisions made that weekend," he says, his fierce gaze leaves no room for argument—not that I have one.

I float away from him a bit so I can take a full breath.

"You know today is another holiday."

I laugh, thankful for the change of subject. "I'm sure there are ten others, too."

"Maybe, but there's only one I want to celebrate."

Something in his voice ignites a low strum of tingles inside me. "And what's that?"

The mischievous grin forming on his lips tells me my body is on the right track. "National Kissing Day."

The tingles explode in a jolt of excitement and apprehension. "Seriously, Ben."

"Have I joked about any of these super important national holidays? You can look it up."

"Who do you plan on kissing?" It's a dangerous question, but I suddenly don't care.

"Hmm...there's this one woman whose lips I'd like to taste again." His gaze flits down to my lips, and my body heats.

"Again?"

"Yeah, I've kissed her before, and hers is different than any other I've had."

My chest suddenly feels tight. "Oh, how's that?"

"One kiss only makes me want her more. I can't stop thinking of doing it again, dreaming of it, too. When I see her, I pray it'll be the day I get to taste her again. Feel those soft lips beneath mine, feel the slide of her silky tongue against mine." He slips his arm around my waist, pulling me closer, but our bodies still aren't touching. He leans down, rubbing his lips over the shell of my ear. "Once I'm drunk on her lips, I want to taste the rest of her. I want to run my tongue along her neck and see if she moves it in a way that tells me she wants more." His mouth dips, and I arch so my neck's open and vulnerable. I feel him smile against my skin. "I want to hear the hitch in her breath because it feels so good. I want to kiss my way down her body until I get to her gorgeous tits." His hand trails up until his fingertips brush the side of my breast. "I want to reveal them and see the exact shade of pink of her nipples."

I can't breathe. He's making me crazy with want. "Ben..."

His hand wraps around my back again, his fingers slowly making their way up my spine, leaving a trail of tingles.

He stops in that one spot between my shoulder blades.

My reminder. I have the power to stop this. This one moment is my chance to stop things before they go too far.

Yet, every time he gives me this choice, I never stop him.

I move enough to let the water take me into him. My legs float up and around his waist. His cock, hard and hot, pushes into my center. Unable not to, my hips move, and I rub myself over his hard length. He growls and his hands sink into my hair just before he crashes his lips to mine. His tongue immediately sinks into my mouth and tangles with mine.

God, kissing him really is the best thing ever. His kisses are dream-worthy.

He yanks my hair and tilts my head back. The tiny sting of pain only sends hot tingles through me. His mouth trails down my neck, and I arch into him, allowing him more access. He moans in appreciation as he sucks my skin. For the first time in my life, I want him to leave a mark. I want this small claiming, even if it only lasts a couple of days.

His hands slide to my breasts and yank the cups of my bra, baring me to him. My nipples are hard and aching. He gently brushes a thumb over one hard tip. "Burnt rose."

"Is that a color?"

"It's yours." He dips his head and his tongue makes a slow, hot swipe over my nipple. My head falls back as I dig my fingers into his thick hair.

"Yes...more..."

His kiss turns more ardent. He sucks and nips and licks until I'm so hot I could boil the water surrounding us. He moves his attention to the other breast. I'm going crazy. It's not enough. I want more. I move my hips against him and wish I'd been brave enough to get into the pool naked. The thin lace of my panties is too much of a barrier. I want to feel the velvety skin of his cock against my pussy. I want to feel his thick head push inside me.

"Ben..."

"I know what you want, baby. What you need. But it's National Kissing Day. And today, I'm only kissing you." He moves us to the other side of the pool and sets me on the wall, pulling me to the very edge before spreading my legs. "There's one place I've been dying to kiss. So many nights I grip my cock thinking about having my face between your legs. My tongue sinking into your pussy, fucking you until your sweet cream fills my mouth. Show me, Lainey. Show me the lips I haven't tasted yet."

The man is going to make me come just with his dirty words instead of his mouth. This feels indecent, and I love it. I spread my legs a bit more, reach down, and shift my panties aside enough to completely expose myself to him.

"Fucking beautiful." His bright blue eyes are wild, his gaze locked on my most intimate place. "I can see how turned on you are. Your pussy is open and wet, begging for me. Isn't it, baby?"

"Yes," I breathe. I swear to God, if he doesn't touch me now, I might burst into flames.

His moan is deep. Guttural. The kind you make before you're about to taste the perfect bite of food. His head dips, and his tongue flicks out, slowly licking up my slit. It has to be the most erotic sight I've ever seen. He growls, as if one taste wasn't enough. He buries his face into my pussy, and my head falls back. I can't watch him anymore. If I do, I'll come immediately. As much as I crave the release, I want this to last, want to enjoy every second of him eating me out. My fingers sink into his hair and I rock my hips into his face. His tongue presses inside me, fucking me before he moves to my clit, ratcheting up my pleasure with every flick and suck. It isn't long before I feel my orgasm rushing forward. As if he senses I'm about to come, he lifts his head and gives my inner thighs a kiss.

"You taste so fucking good. I've never tasted anything sweeter than your cunt."

"God, Ben. Your mouth's obscene."

"You like it, don't you, baby?" He dips his head again and

teases his tongue between my folds. "This dirty mouth treats you so good, doesn't it?"

I moan.

"Tell me, Lainey. Tell me how much you like my filthy mouth. Tell me how much it turns you on. Tell me how much you want my mouth to make you come."

"Yes…I fucking love it. I could come just from your dirty talk. I'm aching…please, Ben. Make me come"

"You want to come on my face, baby? Want me to lick it all up?"

"Fuck, *yes*."

He sinks his tongue inside me again, fucking me relentlessly as I ride his face. His attention suddenly shifts to my clit, and I'm lost. I explode in a million fiery sensations as he grips my hips and slips his tongue back inside me, fucking me all over again. Fucking me until I'm slipping off the edge. He yanks into the water, my body plastered against his as he takes my mouth again. "Do you taste yourself? How sultry you are? How fucking delicious."

My hand slides over the firm contours of his stomach, down to his thick, hot, hard cock. "I want to kiss you, too."

A hard groan leaves his throat and he presses his forehead to mine. "This was for you. I wanted to taste you."

"And now it's my turn."

He groans again and his hand covers mine, easing my grip off his dick. "Don't you have a date to get to?"

Oh, shit. I'd completely forgotten. Not that I want to go on that date. No. I want to be right here with him. Kissing him. Sucking him. Fucking him.

"Ben…"

"Lainey, I'm not going to let you suck my cock then go on a date with another guy."

Oh God. He's right. Even if tonight is more of an interview than a date.

His beautiful blue gaze holds mine, promising me if I cancel, everything I want in this moment is mine. But at what cost?

No, I need to be responsible. For my job. For my mom. For my heart.

I pull away, the water suddenly cold. "We should probably clean up and get going. Harper will kill me if she sees dirty dishes all over the kitchen."

His jaw clenches. I get out and immediately wrap one of the towels around me, rushing back to the house as if I can escape the flash of hurt and disappointment I saw on his face.

I'm dressed and cleaning the kitchen when Ben joins me, fully clothed. We work together in silence and once done, we stand there, the want so thick in the room I swear I can almost see it.

He steps in front of me, his hands framing my face and lifting it to his. He gently kisses me. "National Kissing Day is *our* holiday."

I shouldn't find his possessiveness so sexy, but I do. "A national holiday only for us?"

His mouth quirks up on one side. "Yep. And you've already celebrated it today. No more celebrations are needed."

My body doesn't seem to have remembered it just orgasmed because it's now screaming for more. I really, really like Possessive Ben.

"Duly noted."

He shakes his head and grabs my hand, "Come on. You have a date to be bored at."

Fourth of July

LAINEY

"WHY CAN'T SHE BE AWFUL? OR YOU KNOW, HAVE SAGGY BOOBS," I say, as I eye Ben's date with the perfect pair of perky breasts.

Though date might not be the correct word. He introduced her as a friend and showed up with Eli in tow too. It's clear in the way he and Monica interact that they know each other well, but I haven't seen him touch her once. No flirty looks. Only friendly ones.

I can't help but think that this is his way of showing me he meant what he said last time we were here. While I'm here on a date I don't want to be on.

"The world isn't fair," Josie says. "And you really need to stop staring at Ben's date and pay attention to yours."

I scan the room for Gavin and spot him talking with Chandler. Gavin towers over him, as he's jacked in a pro-wrestler kind of way. He's so swole he looks like he's been stuffed into a thick coat and can't put his arms down.

"He's...um...interesting." Josie presses her lips together in an attempt not to say more.

Ha, that's being generous. I look at Josie. "Yeah, if you like working out and debating the benefits of whey versus egg white protein powder."

She laughs and nearly chokes on her drink. "I'm going to die, but that was totally worth it," she manages between coughs.

I feel like an idiot for leaving the pool with Ben for the most boring date ever. Not that Gavin noticed. He was more interested in telling me about the bodybuilding gym he's opening and the protein-forward diet I should follow for building muscle. I'm no fool. He wants to use our date solely to promote his gym. He's passionate about his work and lifestyle, and even though it's not my thing, I can respect that.

Though I wish I'd asked *what kind of swimsuit do you prefer* as one of my screener questions. I wasn't expecting the skintight, package-hugging shorts he's sporting. He pulls them off and has turned a few female heads, but there are kids here.

Gavin looks my way and smiles before motioning me over. Rocks settle in my stomach.

"See? Your date's missing you," Josie says with a barely contained laugh.

"Come with me." I give her an imploring look.

"Oh, I'm good. He already suggested beef isolate protein powders since I don't like whey."

I groan but put on my big girl panties and head his way, plastering on a smile. When I get to him, he wraps his arm around my waist. I stiffen, not expecting the move. The most we've touched is a handshake.

"Hey, there," he says, with a smile some might think is sexy—not me. "Missed you."

I do my best to keep the *what the fuck* out of my expression as I stealthily shift out of his embrace. "Really?"

"Yeah." His voice is rougher and there's something in the way he's looking at me that sends off an alarm in my brain. Abort! Abort!

I back up as he leans closer.

"Jello shots?" A handful of Jello shots are thrust between us.

I turn to see my brother-in-law with a big false smile on his lips, and I thank God my sister had the good sense to marry this man.

"Yes!" I pluck one from his hand, and he gives me a knowing nod.

Chandler holds out the other shot to Gavin. "No, thanks. I don't do artificial dyes."

On our intro date, I learned another thing about Gavin: to keep that body, he doesn't indulge in vices or anything that's not organic. I'll bet his cheat day and mine look very different.

"I'll take it." I grab the other shot, pop the tops, and swallow both in a matter of seconds. Gavin's looking at me a little shocked—and not terribly impressed. "I'll, um, go throw these away," I say, untangling from him. I turn and immediately lock eyes with Ben. He's across the pool, standing next to Eli and Monica. His jaw is clenched, and the grip on his beer looks lethal. Then Monica touches his arm, grabbing his attention, and he looks down at her and smiles. It's sweet and genuine, nothing that should twist my stomach in jealousy, but here I am.

I march up to the bar and ask for another sangria and Jello shot. The bartender hands me the shot first. As I pop the top, I hear, "Thought I warned you about those."

The brush of Ben's chest against my shoulder and the deep, velvety sound of his voice hit me harder than the Jello shot.

"I've decided to live dangerously," I say, before I use my tongue to loosen the Jello and suck the shot into my mouth. "You should try one. They're pretty good."

They're terrible.

"Lainey, you've just downed three of those with vile tequila in them. You're going to be sick."

At this point, I'd welcome puking over seeing him with his gorgeous date. Or friend. Or whatever she is.

"I'll be fine. They're not that strong."

It's a lie. The tequila's already numbing my brain cells, which is the only explanation for what I do next. I lean over the bar, swipe two more of the shot containers, tuck them into my halter top, and grab my sangria. I give Ben a big smile and turn back toward the party. I successfully avoid him for I don't know how long until somehow Gavin and I are playing ping-pong against him and Monica—who, of course, is really cool.

My hand-eye coordination isn't the best anymore, but I'm holding my own. I think. One of Chandler's friends comes up with a tray of Jello shots. Monica and I are the only ones who grab one, though I'm the only one who earns a look of disapproval from Ben and Gavin. With my gaze locked on Ben, I use my middle finger to loosen the Jello, stick my finger in my mouth, and swipe it clean. His jaw clenches. I suck in the shot. The second it shoots down my throat, I know it's a bad idea.

My stomach lurches. If I don't move, I'll throw up in front of the whole party. I manage a *be right back* and casually walk away, though nothing feels calm about what's going on inside my body. The second I set foot inside the house, I book it up the stairs and head straight for the primary bathroom where I know no one will enter. The closer I get, the more my stomach churns. I barely make it to the toilet. A rush of red surges from my mouth over and over.

"I understand Gavin's aversion to red dye now," I groan into the bowl.

Suddenly, my hair's swept from my face and a warm hand gently rubs my back. I know it's him. While I'm mortified for him to see me like this, I don't want anyone else with me right now. My stomach spasms, and I get sick a few more times before I think I'm finally done.

Ben hands me some toilet tissue to clean up my mouth. I do and fall back, leaning against his legs.

"Thanks," I say weakly.

"You okay?"

No. I'm a hot mess and embarrassed.

"Yeah," I manage, as he helps me up and leads me to the vanity stool. He rummages through the cabinets and pulls out a washcloth, wets it, then squats in front of me and gently wipes my clammy face. I can't look him in the eye. I feel so fucking stupid. "Are you going to tell me I told you so?"

"It doesn't seem like I have to."

I huff a laugh and look at him. He gives me a gentle smile, and I take the washcloth from his hand. "Thanks. I'm okay. You should get back to Monica."

He stares at me for a while before standing up. "Stay here, okay? Maybe go lay down."

I nod, and he leaves. I kind of hate that he listened to me, but I don't deserve his care. I look through Harper's drawers and thankfully find an unopened toothbrush and a tube of spearmint toothpaste. As I finish up, the bedroom door opens and shuts. I look over to see Ben is back, one hand holding a plate and the other a bottle of water.

"What are you doing?"

"The only thing I've seen enter your stomach all day is alcohol. Come on, you need to rehydrate and get some food in you."

I set the toothbrush aside and join him in the bedroom. He hands me the water, and I take a few small sips. Next, he's offering a cracker. I'm not sure I can eat anything right now, but I take a small bite. It goes down okay, so I slowly eat the rest of it. We don't talk as I nibble on a piece of cheese and a few more crackers. My eyes suddenly feel heavy after I get the whole bottle of water down. It feels like I'm in some sort of trance as I'm pulled onto the bed nestled next to Ben, then nothing.

Soft, gentle fingertips brush my wrist, caressing my skin. I open my eyes and realize I'm draped over someone. I look up to see it's Ben. "I slept on you?"

"Yeah. How are you feeling?"

"Better. How long was I out?"

"An hour."

I say what's true but not what I truly desire. "You should be with your date, not me."

"Is that what you really want?"

No. And he knows that. When I don't say anything, he sighs. "Monica knows where I am."

"She's okay with you going off with another woman?"

"I'm okay with the fact that she's married to one."

I jerk away to look up at him, but not enough to untangle our limbs. "What?"

He meets my gaze. "I've known Monica since freshman year when I tried to hit on her, and she responded by kissing the woman standing next to her. That woman's now her wife and had to work today. I invited Monica so she wouldn't spend the holiday alone."

"You brought a fake date?"

"I introduced her as a friend. Not a date."

"That doesn't mean anything."

"It does. I wanted you to know she wasn't a date. Has it looked like I've been on a date?" When I don't say anything, he continues. "If anyone brought a fake date, it was you."

"Gavin isn't a fake date."

He tilts his head. "I talked to him. This date is more about his gym than a love connection. However, that didn't stop him from trying to make a move."

I suppress a shudder at the almost kiss. "Just because he wants exposure doesn't mean it's not a real date."

One side of his mouth notches up. "You're cute when you lie." I huff out a frustrated breath and try to get away from him, but he pulls me back. "Just admit it. This is business, not pleasure. You move away anytime he tries to touch you. You downed two Jello shots to avoid kissing him, and you've done your best to avoid him."

"You're not cute when you're smug."

He barks out a laugh. "I so am, and you know it."

I don't get to respond because the door opens, and my mom walks in. And what she sees looks pretty bad—both of us looking sleepy and cozy with our half-naked bodies draped over each other. My mom's mouth falls open before that motherly look of disappointment comes over her face. "We've been looking for you. You left your date all alone. What are you even doing?" Her gaze jumps to Ben then back to me.

"Sorry, I had too many Jello shots."

"Yeah, I noticed." Her voice is tight and clipped, which is never a good sign.

"She just had a quick nap. She's feeling better now," Ben says, helping me off his body.

My mom's mouth flattens then she forces a smile. "Thanks for taking care of her, Ben. Why don't you go back to the party? I think your date has been looking for you, too."

Ben's mouth thins as he knows full well that isn't the case. He looks at me, his face full of concern. "You okay?"

"I'm fine. Go ahead."

He gives me a nod and squeezes my leg before heading out. My mom comes fully into the room and shuts the door. "What are you doing, Lainey?"

"I just got carried away with the Jello shots."

"That's not what I'm talking about. What are you doing with Ben?"

"Nothing. He was being nice."

My mom takes a step toward me, anger and worry on her face. "That's not what I mean, and you know it."

Shit.

"I was asleep until a few minutes ago. That's it," I say, hoping she doesn't notice I didn't fully address her statement.

But she notices. Instead of becoming angrier, her expression crumbles and tears fill her eyes. She covers her face with her hands. Oh shit.

"Mom." I rush to her.

"Lainey..." She drops her hands, and the devastation on her face is like a knife to the chest. "Mike is really close to his son. He'll put him above anyone else. Please don't mess with this like you did with..."

"With who?"

She looks away, tears streaming down her face.

"Mom?"

"Are you trying to...you know...like you did before?"

I shake my head. Fuck. She thinks I'm messing with Ben on purpose? To ruin her relationship with Mike? How could she think that now?

"Mike loves you. Truly. I can see that." Hell, anyone could. "I would never take that from you."

She takes a shuddering breath as a fresh set of tears start flowing. "If he walks away, my heart won't break, it'll shatter. Lainey, please...please, don't mess this up for me. I don't want to lose him. I *can't*." She's sobbing and working herself into a full-out panic attack. Seeing her like this is breaking my heart.

I pull her into a hug, guilt churning in my stomach.

"We're friends, Mom. We've gotten close because we're going to be family. I want you and Mike to be happy as much as you do. I promise."

I hug her tightly to seal my promise. To make sure I can't take it back—no matter how much it hurts.

Perfect Family Day

JULY 18TH

KATHLEEN

Hi family! We want you all to know we're getting married August 6th. Save the date!

MIKE

Willick Hall. 4:00 p.m.

HARPER

omg! Are you serious?

LAINEY

Wait? What? This August 6th?

BEN

Like less than 3 weeks from now?

KATHLEEN

Yes, this August 6th

LAINEY

But it's August. In Texas. No one gets married in August in Texas.

HARPER

Wow, this is so exciting!!

KATHLEEN

It's called an indoor wedding with air conditioning, Lainey. We decided we don't want a big wedding. Just immediate family and a few friends.

BEN

That's 19 days away.

MIKE

We're not getting any younger. Why wait?

HARPER

Mom! We have so much to do. Do you have a dress? What are Lainey and I wearing? We're your bridesmaids, right? Is there a reception? Food? What about Cassie? Is she a flower girl? What should she wear? There's a lot to do in a little amount of time.

KATHLEEN

Harper, take a breath. The venue takes care of everything. We're all good. I have a dress. I would like you and Lainey to wear something blue, whatever you want. Of course, Cassie is in the wedding. You can choose what she wears.

HARPER

But I thought we were going to go dress shopping together. Did you go wedding dress shopping without your daughters?

KATHLEEN

No, I have a white lace dress I bought years ago and have never worn. Why don't we pick out what Cassie will wear together?

HARPER

Okay. Yeah. That'll be fun.

MIKE

Ben? Lainey? Are y'all good?

BEN

Yeah, all good. Congratulations, guys! Really.
So happy for y'all

LAINEY

Yes, congrats!! This will be great.

BEN

Yep. Great.

HARPER

Can you believe this? She planned it without
us. WTH?

LAINEY

It's her wedding,

HARPER

She should have included us! This is huge.
She's finally getting married, and she just left us
out of it.

LAINEY

We're in the wedding, Harp. Don't make this
about you.

HARPER

I'm not making it about me.

LAINEY

Sure.

HARPER

At least I'm actually happy about it. You and
Ben sounded so fake. Could it have been more
obvious you two were freaked out by the date?

LAINEY

Of course, we're happy for them. She pulled the
rug out from beneath us. Who announces
something like that over text?

HARPER

It's probably good it's happening quickly before you and Ben do something you can't take back.

LAINEY

Okay, I'm done with this convo. Go take a Xanax, Drama Queen

HARPER

It's not drama if it's true. You can't mess this up by fucking your stepbrother.

LAINEY

middle finger emoji

CHANDLER

So, I hear we're going to be family sooner rather than later.

BEN

Yeah, really soon.

CHANDLER

You okay?

BEN

Yeah. Good. Why?

CHANDLER

Because I just listened to a Harper tirade about your mom's text bomb and how you and Lainey sounded less than enthused was a big part of it.

BEN

Ha! I think we were both shell-shocked.

CHANDLER

Them getting married doesn't mean it's a dealbreaker for you and Lainey.

BEN

I have a feeling it is.

CHANDLER

Shit, gotta run. Lainey must have pissed off Harper because she just threw her phone. Damn thing better not be broken.

BEN

So, this is really happening.

LAINEY

Looks like it.

BEN

You good?

LAINEY

I'm good. You?

BEN

Yep.

Good.

LAINEY

Good.

BEN

...

Chandler texted me. Sounds like our parents short-circuited Harper.

LAINEY

omg, yes. Her controlling nature can't take this.

BEN

Heard you pissed her off.

LAINEY

Told her to take a Xanax. She was making it all about her.

BEN

Hey, you know what holiday it is?

LAINEY

What?

BEN

Perfect Family Day

LAINEY

hahahahahahaha

Mike and Kathleen's Wedding Day,
National Sisters Day - August 6th

BEN

IT'S MY FATHER'S WEDDING DAY.

I don't know what I expected my emotions to be like today, but I didn't envision I'd mourn my mother all over again. It's like I'm realizing she's never coming back. Even though I logically know my father's love for her will never change, another woman has taken residence in his heart, essentially pushing aside the space my mother occupied. As happy I am for my dad and Kathleen, I can't shake the feeling, and I don't know how to get past it.

Then, there's Lainey. And the fact I might be mourning the loss of a future with her, too.

My dad stands in front of the mirror, adjusting his tie to the point it comes untied. The red tie was his only requirement for what he'd wear. I was a little surprised since the girls are all in blue.

"Nervous?" I go to him and make him face me so I can fix his tie.

"Yes and no," he says. "I never thought I'd want this again, but it feels right. I know it's been quick and possibly hard on you."

His gaze flicks to mine, and I hold it for a moment before going back to his tie.

"It's been good to see you happy, Dad. And I like Kathleen. You two are really good together." I hope he hears the truth in my words and doesn't sense my omission.

"That doesn't mean it isn't hard to see me move on, Ben."

I turn him so he can examine my work in the mirror, but he turns back to me. I look down at my shoes, emotion suddenly clogging my throat.

"So, maybe this seems a little weird, but I couldn't go through today without honoring your mom."

I look up at him. "What do you mean?"

He moves to the two boxes that contain the boutonnieres. "Your mom was my first real love, and she'll always be a love of my life. My marriage to Kathy isn't going to make that love go away. It will make it this treasured part of me, which allowed me to open my heart to love again." He opens a box. "When I thought of what flower I wanted to wear today, the only answer was a poppy." He pulls out a single red flower, and my heart lurches. Now, the tie choice makes sense. "It's silk. Finding fresh poppies was too hard, but that means we'll be able to keep it forever."

I gently take the flower, which has petals so delicate they almost seem real. The red bloom blurs as tears rush forward. "It's beautiful, Dad."

"Just like her."

I nod and swipe at my eyes, my dad doing the same.

"Here, let me put it on you." His hand trembles as he secures it to the lapel. Our tears continue as I return the favor. When I'm done, he takes my head in his hands and brings it down to his so our foreheads press together. "I love you, Ben"

"I love you too, Dad."

He gives my head a gentle squeeze before letting go. A

moment later, there's a knock at the door. Uncle Red comes in, and I leave so they can have a few minutes of privacy.

Stepping into the hall, I lean against the wall, close my eyes and take a few deep breaths. I hear the click of heels, then they stop. I open my eyes to see Lainey at the corner, worry creasing her brows. She's wearing a navy dress with a flowy, floor-length skirt. There's nothing overly sexy about it except the way the deep V accentuates her gorgeous breasts.

Fuck, she looks beautiful.

Our gazes meet, and she starts toward me. The tips of her shoes meet mine. Her fingers gently graze the poppy, and her hand cups my cheek. Her immediate understanding cracks something in my heart, and I take a shuddering breath.

She takes my hand and pulls me into the room across the hall. As soon as the darkness of the room envelops us, she pulls me into her arms, pressing her cheek to my chest as one of her hands immediately seeks out the spot between my shoulder blades.

Just like that, she's made everything better, and I know one thing for sure. All I need is her.

All I'll ever need—is her.

I slide my arms around her waist and sink into her, taking all her comfort—soaking up as much of her warmth and her scent as I can.

After a while, she leans back and looks at me. "You okay?"

"Much better. Thanks." I give her a squeeze, bringing her body further into mine.

Voices from the hallway penetrate our moment. "Where is she? The wedding starts in thirty minutes. She just disappeared." It's Harper's voice.

"She's probably in the bathroom or something," Chandler says.

"Where's Ben? Please tell me she isn't with him."

I immediately pull her into the room's closet so we're hidden in case anyone peeks in.

"He's with his dad," Chandler says, and I silently thank the man. Whether it's an assumption or a deflection, I appreciate it. I hear a noise that tells me someone opened the door then the voices fade as they move down the hallway.

Lainey sighs. "Harper has been a lot today. She's the wedding planner from hell that no one hired."

I laugh. "Hey, did you know it's National Sisters Day?"

"Well, if she keeps this not-the-bride-zilla behavior, I might not have a sister by the end of the day."

We both laugh softly, our gazes catching and locking. Our soft smiles fade as the air between us thickens and charges. I pull her into me even more. "Promise me something."

"What?"

"After the I do's, this won't change."

That little crease above her nose appears again. "I can't do that. After today...everything changes."

"It doesn't have to."

"Ben..." She pulls out of my arms. "My mother's happy."

"My father is too, but that doesn't mean we can't be."

"Yes, it does. I won't risk ruining their marriage. I don't think she'll ever forgive me if I do."

I sigh. "I don't think it's as big of a deal as you're making it out to be."

She's silent for a moment, and I don't like it. Like she's about to deliver a blow.

"When I was in high school, I sabotaged some of her relationships. I did it because I was tired of her picking them over me. When I told her that, it worked. She stopped dating and focused on me and Harper, though Harper was already in college."

"Okay," I say, not sure where she's going with this. "That sounds like a good thing."

"It was," she admits, but she suddenly seems tired. "But seeing us together on Fourth of July...she was scared I was trying to mess things up. She had a full-on panic attack. She loves your father so much. She finally found the one. Ben...I can't. We can't."

Tears choke her voice, and I hug her close.

Shit. The fact Kathleen actually said something changes things. While I still think things would eventually blow over, I understand why Lainey doesn't see it the same way.

I tip her chin up and hate the sight of her brimming tears. "I'll respect your decision, but please don't ask me to stop being your friend. I couldn't stand losing you completely."

A watery smile forms on her lips. "I don't want to lose you as a friend either. You're important to me, Ben. Please know that."

She rises on her tiptoes and places a gentle kiss on my mouth. I can't stop myself from kissing her back. It's soft and brief, with a bittersweetness that lingers on my lips. Yet, I can't think of it as a last kiss. I can't.

Twenty minutes later, I'm standing beside my dad at the altar watching Lainey come down the aisle, my heart racing but my head clear.

I can be her friend, but I'll never give up on the hope of being with her. This thing between us is so much more—it's inevitable.

Because I know, to the depths of my soul, that we belong together.

National Tell a Joke Day

BEN

It's National Tell a Joke Day

LAINEY

Oh, boy. Let me guess - you're going to tell me a really bad dad joke.

BEN

You seriously underestimate me. Ready?

LAINEY

Hit me.

BEN

Why do walruses love a Tupperware party?

LAINEY

Why?

BEN

They're always on the lookout for a tight seal.

LAINEY

Omg! That's so bad, it's good. You made me snort laugh.

BEN

What does a perverted frog say?

"Rubbit"

What do you do when your cat's dead?

Play with the neighbor's pussy instead.

LAINEY

omg!! That's so wrong! I'm laughing so hard. Do you only know dirty jokes?

BEN

They're the best ones.

What do you get when you jingle Santa's balls?

LAINEY

I don't want to know!

BEN

A white Christmas

LAINEY

Okay, you've officially ruined Christmas for me. My stomach is cramping I'm laughing so hard.

Okay, I got one. What did the hurricane say to the coconut tree?

BEN

What?

LAINEY

Hold on to your nuts, this ain't no ordinary blowjob.

BEN

hahaha! Good one!

What do you call a smiling Roman soldier with a piece of hair stuck between his front teeth?

LAINEY

This one is going to be bad. I can feel it.

BEN

A glad-he-ate-her

LAINEY

Yep. So bad. *eye roll emoji*

Why does Miss Piggy douche with honey?

Because Kermit likes his pork sweet and sour.

BEN

Whoa! Lololol! That is an image I don't need from my favorite Muppets!

LAINEY

Why didn't Barbie get pregnant?

Because Ken came in a different box.

BEN

What did Cinderella do when she got to the ball?

She gagged.

LAINEY

big eyes emoji

What is 6.9?

BEN

What?

LAINEY

A good thing ruined by a period.

BEN

Oh, shit! I just snorted water through my nose. Fuck, it burns. I can't stop laughing.

LAINEY

Mic drop.

National Bad Poetry Day

BEN

It's National Bad Poetry Day

LAINEY

Oh, no. I don't think I've recovered from joke
day. My abs were sore from laughing so hard.

BEN

This'll be good, I promise.

LAINEY

I thought it was supposed to be bad.

BEN

Roses are red

The sun gives off heat

If your legs are tired

Use my face as a seat

LAINEY

OMG! I should have known it'd be dirty.

BEN

um, of course

It's titled Ode to Being Suffocated

LAINEY

gif of woman with shocked expression

BEN

Mic drop

National Harper Day

AUGUST 30TH

CHANDLER

I can hear her screeching from across the house.

HARPER

Chandler, Cassie has a playdate at Phoebe's at 1. I'm going for a pedicure.

CHANDLER

Sigh. Okay.

HARPER

You can't drop her off. You'll need to stay.

CHANDLER

What? No. A bunch of moms don't want me hanging around. You've told me what y'all talk about. It'll be awkward as fuck.

HARPER

It'll be fine. It's only 2 hours.

CHANDLER

2 hours??

HARPER

Make sure Phoebe doesn't play with Cassie's baby doll. Cassie goes psycho on her.

CHANDLER

Are you kidding me? I'm not taking the damn doll then.

HARPER

You have to. They all play house together.

BEN

Have fun at your playdate, Chandler.

LAINEY

Happy Harper Day, Chandler!

CHANDLER

I hate you guys.

BEN

Don't forget to grab a cake on your way home.

HARPER

Oh, cake!! Red velvet, please.

CHANDLER

Harp, I can hear you laughing. Fuck you guys!

HARPER

That was too easy. *laughing emojis*

I'll handle the playdate, but I'm serious about the cake.

Labor Day Weekend

FRIDAY

Do you have a holidate for Labor Day weekend?

Technically, I have 3.

Technically?

Tailgating with Eric on Sat, coworker hang on Sun, and trivia at a brewery with Parker on Mon. What are you doing this weekend? The bar will be busy, I imagine.

Yeah, Sunday will be busier than normal, which will be good. It's National Chicken Month, so I'm pairing up with the food truck Cluckin' Good and opening early for brunch. They have amazing fried chicken honey biscuits. You should come by. Bring your friends.

I'll add that as an option.

BEN

Are you going to CTU game with Eric?

LAINEY

No. Tailgating and hitting a bar. I wish I was going to the game.

BEN

Then you should dump Eric and go with me.

LAINEY

What? You have tickets?

BEN

Yeah, wanna go?

LAINEY

Just us?

BEN

I only have 2 tickets, but don't worry, we'll be surrounded by a hundred thousand of our closest Toro friends

LAINEY

Funny. Ben, I can't cancel my date.

BEN

Why not? Your fans would love to see me as your holidate again.

LAINEY

Don't remind me. I'm bombarded by comments or DMs about you every day.

BEN

Really??

LAINEY

You're puffing out your chest right now, aren't you?

BEN

No...maybe.

Come on, I have some friends tailgating so I thought we'd hit that up before the game.

LAINEY

Frat friends? Is it at the house?

BEN

He was in the frat with me, but the tailgate isn't associated with it.

LAINEY:

Idk. I shouldn't cancel.

BEN

Did I mention my tickets are box seats?

LAINEY

What?? A private box? With a/c? How? Whose is it?

BEN

You want deets, come with me.

LAINEY

You don't play fair…and I'm apparently a slut for box seats since I'm about to text Eric to cancel.

BEN

You can be slutty for me anytime.

LAINEY

I'll tell him my boss said I need to go to the game. I can meet you just before so you have time with your friends.

BEN

Saturday is National Tailgate Day. No skipping.

LAINEY

Fine. See you tomorrow.

National Tailgate Day

LAINEY

I keep telling myself being alone with Ben all day is no big deal. We're friends, and friends go to football games together.

No. Big. Deal.

Except after weeks of exchanging texts, seeing him in person is a total jolt to my system. Every accidental touch and sexy smile zaps me like a live wire.

I'm so worked up I totally forget to be nervous about the tailgate until he puts the truck in park. Now that we're here, I think I could be sick. The last thing I want to do is be surrounded by former frat brothers. It's been years since Isaac humiliated me and broke my heart, and after my strong reaction to Ben's flirting with Chloe, it's clearly a wound that hasn't healed.

"Ready?" Ben asks, as he joins me at the back of his truck.

I nod, and to my surprise, he hesitates. He takes his hat off and runs a hand through his hair before replacing it. Is he nervous? I think he's about to say something, but instead he starts walking. The closer we get to campus, the more tense he gets. His mouth is drawn tight by the time we get to the rows of tailgating tents. Then, without warning, he stops and faces me.

"Um, so the people that know me...they know Frat Bro Ben."

Oh.

"I don't know how they'll act..."

My heart suddenly melts. Is he afraid he's going to revert back to his college persona, or that their stories might scare me away? I take a step closer and touch his hand with mine. "Hey, it'll be okay. I know Frat Bro Ben graduated."

He swallows as his blue gaze searches my face. "You do?"

As conflicted as my feelings for Ben are, I'm finally letting go of the fear that Frat Bro Ben will suddenly take him over again. Yeah, his flirting has bothered me and sent me into flashback hell, but there's no denying he was being genuine when we talked at Harper's lake house. And on the Fourth of July, he could have brought a real date or even flirted with Monica to make me jealous, and he didn't. Not to mention all the ways he's chipped away at his reputation these last eight months. I won't say it still doesn't scare me, because the Ben I know is seriously dangerous to my heart.

But I can't think about that part. I can only focus on the fact that he's my friend and he needs me to understand he's changed.

"I do."

My words release the tension in his body, and he squeezes my hand. "Thanks. Just don't be surprised if I become frat bro-ish. It might slip into place."

"If you become frat bro-ish, then I'll be sorority girl-ish."

He eyes me. "Were you in a sorority?"

"Nope, but I can totally channel what I've seen in clichéd college movies."

He chuckles. "Lord help us."

As we approach the tent, someone yells out Ben's name. "Now the party's started!"

Ben grins, though it looks reluctant as he shakes hands and bro hugs the guy. "Looks like the party's going just fine."

"Man, it's too bad we don't have a keg."

Ben's cheeks bloom with a deep blush as he turns to me. "Will, this is Lainey."

Will smiles widely and sticks out his hand for me to shake. "Hey, it's nice to meet you." He pauses. "You look familiar. Did you go to CTU?"

My stomach knots. I'm not sure why exactly, except being this close to fraternity members after so much time is bringing back memories. I suddenly want to ask Ben which frat he was part of. Surely, it's not the same one. "Yeah, graduated about four years ago."

"Me too. I probably saw you around campus then. So, how did you meet this guy?"

"Through our parents."

"Your parents set you up?"

"No, they got married," Ben says with a laugh.

"Oh, this is your stepsister. Thought she was your girl." Will's gaze bounces between us, pauses on Ben, who's slightly behind me, a panicked expression comes over his face. "Or, um..."

Ben claps Will on his shoulder. "Why don't you show us to the booze?"

Will looks visibly relieved. "Absolutely, it's over there. We've got liquor, beer, and plenty of barbecue, so y'all help yourselves.

We head for the makeshift bar, though Ben gets stopped several times. The lack of a keg is mentioned several times, and Ben seems to be doing his best to ignore it. After we get our drinks, we mingle. Ben keeps me close, his hand occasionally going to that spot between my shoulder blades. I don't think he's even aware of it, that it's some sort of comfort to him, which only makes me want him more. Everyone seems to be thrilled to find out he owns a bar now. I can tell the ones who seem genuinely happy and those who probably will stop by to try to get free drinks.

Will makes some introductions, so I'm officially known as the stepsister to most of the group. As nervous as I was, this hasn't been that bad. Ben has loosened up, too. There's a bit of frat bro vibes, but it's more reminiscent than obnoxious.

I return to the bar to make another drink, and Ben joins me. "How are you doing?"

"Good. Everyone's been nice."

He nods. "Yeah, it's not bad."

I raise my brows at him. "So, the keg thing?"

He dips his head. "Yeah, keg stands were something I used to do."

"I know. Once it was brought up, I remembered hearing about them. I was a senior, though, and had stopped going to frat parties. I know a bet was involved."

He looks at me, his expression embarrassed as he rubs the back of his neck. "Yeah, it was stupid. And not all the bets were cool. I mean, they always agreed to it, and I didn't bully anyone, I promise. I...."

I put my hand on his arm. "Stop." I pull him so we're facing each other. "Everyone does stupid and immature things in college. I know Frat Bro Ben had a reputation, but it wasn't a cruel one. And I know *you*. You would never let some alter-ego compromise your true principles."

He visibly swallows, takes my elbow and pulls me closer, and dips his head until the brims of our hats touch. "Thanks. I didn't realize how much I needed to hear you say that."

I want to pull him in my arms and never let him go. I hate that I made him doubt himself because of my fears. Though I'm glad I spoke up, maybe it's time for me to tell him about Isaac. He deserves to understand why it bothered me so much.

Some noise erupts behind me. It sounds like someone the whole group knows has shown up.

Ben looks past my shoulder, and a distasteful sneer forms on his face. "I hope this asshole doesn't see us."

"Why?"

"He's this dick who was in my frat. He was a senior when I was a freshman, so I wasn't around him a lot, thank God. I almost didn't pledge because he was such a tool, but everyone else made it worth it. They even considered kicking him out before I got there, but he didn't do anything wrong other than be a douchebag." He shakes his head, clearly not agreeing.

"What did he do?"

"He catfished all these girls. Dated them all at the same time. Fed them a bunch of lies about himself."

My stomach tightens and I feel like I'm floating outside of myself. No. No way. This can't be happening.

"One night, he got bold and thought it would be fun to invite them all to the same party. He asked them to pretend they didn't know each other as some sort of sexual role-playing game, but it was really so he could sleep with them all in the same place and not get caught. He slept with two of them before one of the girls figured it out and called him out in front of the whole party."

I press a hand to my tightening chest. It's weird to hear a summary of the worst night of your life. A story that barely touches the hurt and humiliation I felt. Or how that night, Isaac destroyed my trust. In men. In myself.

"That's not even the worst part."

No. It wasn't.

But before Ben can continue, he says, "Oh, shit."

"Ben!"

As sweltering as it is, my whole body turns to ice at the sound of Isaac's voice.

"Hey, Isaac," Ben says with a forced smile.

"The man who gave me a run for my money," Isaac announces, as he closes in on us and shakes hands with Ben.

"Nah, man. You were in a class all your own." Anyone who knows Ben well would catch the insult in his tone, but I doubt Isaac will. He's way too egotistical.

Now that he's close, I inch back, hoping I can slip away without him noticing. I don't think Ben has any interest in introducing me, which I appreciate.

But I don't move fast enough. Isaac turns his attention to me. "Hey, I'm Isaac," he says, extending his hand.

Though I don't want to, I turn to face him. His eyes go wide for a second, then his hand drops, and he opens his arms wide. "Lainey!"

Are you fucking kidding me?

He leans forward as if he wants to hug me, but I step back and extend my arm, stopping him. He lets out a laugh. "Oh, come on, don't hate the player, hate the game."

"I have no problem hating both."

He leans forward again, but Ben is suddenly between us, his hand on Isaac's chest, pushing him away from me. It's not an aggressive push, but it gets the point across. "Hey, she made it clear she doesn't want you any closer."

Isaac scoffs but steps back. "Lainey, we had two good years. Why dwell on one night?"

I let out a harsh laugh. I have about a dozen comebacks to point out all the ways he wronged me and the other three girls, but there's no reason to voice them. He's a narcissistic psychopath, and doesn't care who he hurts along the way.

"Watch out, Isaac. One day you're going to piss off the wrong woman and find yourself without your favorite appendage. Not that it would be a *big* loss or anything."

Some light laughter spills out around us. Isaac's cocky smile falls and his gaze narrows. It seems I had a comeback after all, and it struck a nerve. He attempts to move, but Ben extends his arm, making sure he stays put. Suddenly, Will is there, clamping his hand on Isaac's shoulder. "Hey man, time for you and your friends to head out."

I glance behind Will and spot a couple of guys glancing our way with hangdog expressions. One of them says, "Let's hit up another tailgate before the game."

Isaac glances at them, back at Ben, and then me. "Whatever." He opens his mouth to say something else, but Ben clearly presses his hand harder into his chest.

"Better leave before you say something I'll make you regret." Ben's tone is full of barely controlled anger.

Isaac's jaw clenches, but he steps back and walks away with his boys. Ben watches him, staying physically between us.

Will comes forward. "I'm so sorry, Lainey." It hits me why he thought he knew me. He was at that party. "He wasn't invited. I could never stand the guy. Unfortunately, word gets around, and I can't control who shows up."

"It's fine. Thanks for asking him to leave."

He nods and gives Ben's shoulder a squeeze before leaving us alone. I look at Ben, whose face has paled. He runs a hand through his hair and steps closer. "Fuck, Lainey, you let me talk about that story like—"

"Like it wasn't mine? Like I wasn't one of the Virgin Four?"

I gave Isaac my virginity, along with three other girls in less than two years—possibly even more. The girl I'd seen him hug on campus had been dating him for over a year. The other two girls from that night had been with him about six months. The way he was able to string us along while we all attended the same college was genius on his part—genius but psychotic.

Ben's face contorts in a mixture of pain and anger, and he takes my hand. "I should have fucking decked him."

"While that would have been fun to see, I'm glad you didn't."

I just want Isaac out of my life and out of my head. He's lived there rent-free for far too long.

"Let's get out of here."

His grip tightens and we move, not bothering to say goodbye to anyone. He leads me away from the stadium and toward the nearby art building. He tests the door and when it opens, he ushers me inside. The hit of A/C is glorious. A few people have congregated in the hall, enjoying a break from the heat, too.

Ben leads me up a staircase, and we wind through several empty corridors until he finds a bench where we're completely alone.

We sit.

He hasn't let go of my hand once.

We lean against the wall behind us and sit in silence for a long time.

"He didn't...did he force—"

"No. I was just a naïve eighteen-year-old who fell hook, line, and sinker for his lies." I puff out a laugh. "The ironic thing is I thought I was an expert on fuckboys. I'd seen so many come in and out of my mom's life that I could spot them a mile away. But, Isaac put them all to shame. He always had an excuse. He'd make me feel like the crazy one for questioning things. Then, he'd shower me with so much affection all my doubts disappeared. How could he cheat if he was doing all these romantic things and spending so much time with me? Most of what he told me about himself wasn't even true. He made up a completely different persona."

Ben stiffens, his hand clenching mine before he lets go and sits forward, resting his elbows on his knees and cradling his head in his hands. "Fuck. What you must think of me."

I take my time, searching for the right words. "I don't know if my fear of being manipulated like that again will ever fully go away." I swallow. "But...I *know* you. I know you weren't cruel like that."

He shakes his head still in his hands. "I'm sure some of the girls I slept with wouldn't see it that way. Even if they knew the score, I'm sure it hurt to be cast aside."

"See? *That* is what sets you apart. Isaac could have apologized today. I'd still hate him, but knowing he'd grown up and recognized he was a dick might have given me a bit of closure. There's no changing a narcissist, and you are the furthest thing from that."

He leans back, looking at me. "I'm sorry, Lainey. Sorry he hurt you. Sorry I quit college and wasn't there to kick his ass or stop him or—"

"Ben." I put my hand on his arm. "No one in that whole party—the entire frat—stopped him. It wasn't a secret he was dating multiple girls. I'm sure he had help keeping up the charade. No one warned any of us. The only reason I figured it out was because I wanted to be good at his little game. I wanted him crazy and desperate with need because he couldn't find me. So, I stayed hidden and watched. I couldn't even believe what I was seeing. Convinced myself he didn't take those girls in that closet and fuck them. It took me eavesdropping on the second girl before I believed it. No one cared what Isaac was doing."

"I'd like to think I would have."

"Me, too."

A long sigh escapes him. "I wasn't like him, Lainey. I flirted and charmed, but I didn't lie. I didn't want a girl to sleep with me because of a lie. I wanted them there because they wanted to be."

"I know."

He holds my gaze. "Promise me you do. *Promise me.*"

The raw need I see in his eyes, the earnest pleading in his

voice, it almost breaks my heart. And I can't deny him. "I promise."

He takes my hand again, but this time, he brings it to his lips and kisses it. I want to lean in and kiss him to reassure him, but the weight of my promise holds me still. Because this isn't a promise to believe him—it's a promise to trust him. Since Isaac, I haven't wanted to trust any man, I don't think I've even really tried. As much as I've resisted trusting Ben, he's more than earned it. And giving it freely feels wonderful.

Which makes the fact that we can never be more than friends all the more painful.

So, I don't kiss him. Instead, I change the subject. "You've left me in suspense long enough. It's an hour before kickoff. Whose box are we going to be in?"

He smiles and his gaze softens, and I think he's glad to move on, too. "Logan Mackenzie. He's a former player."

My mouth falls open, and I straighten. "Um, yeah, I know who Logan is. I might have already graduated, but the list scandal was all over the news." Logan Mackenzie and his girlfriend made headlines when a college bucket list containing several sexy items was leaked over the internet.

"Yeah... maybe don't mention that."

"Of course, I wouldn't. It was ridiculous such a huge deal was made of it. How do you know him?"

"I'd met him and his roommates at parties and had some classes with them. I know Ally, too."

He's referring to Logan's girlfriend, but there's something about the way he says the last bit that makes me think there's more to the story. "How do you know her?"

"We sort of went out. Not really. It was just one date. Not even a true date, actually."

"Well, that's clear as mud. Are you trying to say you slept with her?"

He laughs. "No, definitely not." He stands and pulls me up with him. "Come on, let's head to the stadium, and I'll tell you." Once we're back outside, he continues, "I had a crush on her. She would come into Cafe Jolt all the time when I worked there. She was my date to a frat party my senior year, but..."

"But?"

"But I was Frat Bro Ben." He shrugs.

We walk in silence for a bit before he starts talking again. "Ally was cool, but I let Frat Bro Ben take over and ended up putting her on the spot and embarrassing her. In the end, the whole thing helped me realize I needed to grow up."

"But you're friends enough for them to invite you to their box?"

"Yeah, we're good. It's not like I was heartbroken or anything. That night was a turning point for her and Logan, too. After that's when they started *listing*."

"So, Frat Bro Ben brought them together," I tease.

His grin's sheepish. "I guess so. It was still embarrassing and a kick to the ego."

We enter the stadium and when we get to the box, the room has a decent amount of people milling about. No one I immediately recognize. Ben leads me further into the room and I spot Ally Worthington. Her face had been all over the news about a year and a half ago. I always thought she handled the backlash well. She even got a center set up on campus to help students manage social media and their mental health, as well as a safe place to deal with bullying—on campus and online.

"Ally," Ben says, as we approach.

Ally gives him a big smile and hug. "I'm so glad you could make it. It's really good to see you."

"Yeah, thanks for the invite. This is awesome."

"I know. I'm still getting used to the fancy boxes. I never visited my mom's box because, you know, it would have been so uncool as a student." She laughs and rolls her eyes at herself. Ally's mom is also the president of CTU.

"Hey, this is Lainey." Ben pulls me closer. "Lainey, meet Ally."

Ally's expression is just as friendly as she greets me and folds me into a hug. "So nice to meet you."

"It's really nice to meet you, too." I almost gush over her like a celebrity, but I keep myself in check. We all chat while we get a drink then Ben sees someone he knows and excuses himself.

"How do you two know each other?" Ally asks.

I laugh and she gives me a curious look. "Sorry, it's the question of the day. We met when our parents got high and went to the hospital because they thought his dad was having a heart attack. Now, they're married."

Ally's mouth drops. "Seriously?"

"Yep."

She starts laughing. "Wow, what a story. And now you're stepsiblings."

I scrunch my nose before I think not to. "We are."

Ally looks at me a little thoughtfully. "Don't like that label?"

"I guess you could say it's hard to think of ourselves as that." I glance over at Ben, who's at the bar talking with someone, but as if he senses me looking, he glances over. His mouth hitches up in a smile, but there's a fierceness and possessiveness in his gaze that sends my heart galloping.

It's been there ever since Isaac tried to touch me. And I have a feeling it isn't going away.

"I bet it is."

I blink out of our stare. Ally wears a knowing smile on her face as she glances between me and Ben.

Thankfully, I'm saved from further conversation because Logan walks in. Logan's now in the NFL and about to start his second season with the New Orleans Revelers. I get a quick introduction, but he's quickly swept up into working the room. I meet more people, some friends, and some university big wigs. Mostly, Ben and I stick together. Logan stays through the first quarter of the game before he heads to the sidelines. By the fourth quarter, the Toros are ahead by eighteen points, and everyone is more involved in conversations than the game. Ben's talking to some other former players by the bar, so I sit with Ally.

"I like this Ben." She glances over at him and looks back at me.

"The real Ben," I say emphatically. It feels so good to finally have zero doubts about that.

"Yeah, I thought so. This is more the guy I've seen since our date—" She looks at me a little stricken as if she revealed something she shouldn't have.

"He told me about your date." I laugh, keeping my tone light, and she sags in relief. "Can I ask you a question? Why did y'all keep talking to him if the date was such a disaster?"

"It wasn't so much that. The whole frat vibe wasn't my thing. To be honest, no one would have been my thing but Logan. It became clear when Ben kissed me."

"Oh, y'all kissed?"

Ally's eyes go wide. "I thought...well, it was sort of an ambush. It was awful." Now she looks mortified all over again. "I'm sure he's a good kisser. It was just a weird moment, and I was so into Logan—"

"Ally," I say to stop her panic rambling. "It's fine. I know he's —" I stop from admitting how I'm intimately aware of how good of a kisser Ben is.

Ally's expression immediately turns from panicked to amused. "You know, he's...?"

"That he's not for you. Obviously."

"Hmm-mmm."

"You didn't answer my question. How did you become friends?"

She shrugs. "We just did. I'd see him at Cafe Jolt, and he was as cool with me after the date disaster as he was before. I think he realized Logan and I were the real deal before we did. We all stayed in touch. It's easy to be friends with him."

It is. It's also easy to be more than friends with him. What's not easy is *only* being friends with him.

National Fried Rice Day, National Queso Day - September 20th

LAINEY

ME

It's National Fried Rice Day and National Queso Day. Both my faves!! Why do they have to be on the same day?

BEN

Have both

ME

It's an odd combination

BEN

One for lunch and one for dinner.

ME

Hmmm, that's not a bad idea

BEN

It's a great idea! Let's go to The Hub. Best queso in town. And I know a great Chinese restaurant by the bar. We can do takeout for dinner.

I READ HIS TEXT AND SET MY PHONE DOWN. HE WANTS TO EAT lunch and dinner together? That's not exactly what I had in mind when I texted him. I shouldn't have even started this text. I've told myself to put distance between us since Labor Day weekend, but we can't seem to stop texting each other. He invited the whole family to the bar on National Stepfamily Day and we debated on the best chocolate for Choose your Chocolate Day—his favorite are fudge brownies. We even texted in pirate-see for Talk like a Pirate Day. He's been friendly—too friendly.

No blatant flirting. No touches, not even a graze of hands. It's exactly what I asked for when our parents got married. So why can't I seem to escape this aching sense of disappointment? I love being his friend. But I also miss his kisses. I miss the feel of his hand pressing between my shoulder blades—making me feel safe and reckless at the same time.

BEN

Come on, it's just food.

ME

A whole day of food.

BEN

Um, yeah. That's a perfect day.

ME

True.

I'M GOING TO HELL.

ME

Okay, I'll meet you at The Hub in an hour. Sound good? I'll have to get some work done between lunch and dinner, though.

I can't help the smile that forms. God, it sounds so nice. So nice I should say no. But I won't. Because I miss him. And I want to spend time with him. And I don't really know what to do with all that except go with it.

An hour later, we're at The Hub with a large bowl of queso between us.

"What do you have to do for work today? Any upcoming holidates?" Ben asks as he dips his chip.

"No, thank God. I'm so glad there's a holiday break."

He bites back a smile but still looks way too happy about the fact I don't want to go on a date. I ignore him and stuff a chip into my mouth.

"You could write a post about National Queso Day," he suggests.

"Since there aren't many holidays between now and Halloween, I'll probably have to include these silly holidays and find dates."

"I can't believe you'd spend these crazy holidays with anyone else but me." He presses his hand over his heart.

I throw a chip at him, and he laughs.

"You know my dates are your favorite." He gives me a flirty grin while I pretend that isn't true. "So, still not liking this job like you'd thought?"

I swirl a chip through the cheese. "Not really. Checking out all the new, hip places in town is fun, but it's also draining. I don't want to be 'on' that much. Writing the posts is okay, but I don't want to be a writer. So, here I am, bored again. Why can't I find something that really excites me?"

"Look at it this way, you now know what you don't want to do."

He has a point. I always focus on how I keep getting it wrong that I don't think about what I do learn from each failed attempt. "That's true."

We split a burger so our lunch isn't solely chips and queso. Afterward, we head to Red Poppy, and Ben gets me set up in his office. I'm working from the couch while he's at his desk. He's in and out as he works on inventory. At some point, we're both on the couch working. We share some smiles and heated looks, but mostly it's just nice. Natural.

My legs are propped on his lap as I work from my laptop. He was reading until a moment ago when he tossed the papers away with a sigh and is now rubbing my sock-clad feet—which feels amazing.

"What is it?" I ask without looking up.

He's silent for a moment before saying, "I've been thinking about doing something for my mom's birthday here at the bar, but I'm having a hard time getting something going. Last year, it wasn't until I was halfway through the day that it occurred to me I named the bar after her but didn't do anything to acknowledge her birthday."

"I think that's a great idea. When's her birthday?"

"October first, which also kicks off Breast Cancer Awareness month. I should do something to raise money, but there's a part of me that doesn't want to dwell on what killed her. Kind of terrible of me since it could really help others, huh?"

"No, I get it. You want to think of her before she got sick."

His gaze roams over my face, settling on my lips for a few beats longer before returning to my eyes. "Yeah, that's it. That's exactly it."

I set aside my laptop and take his hand in mine. He lifts our joined hands and presses a kiss to my knuckles, his grip tightening. The raw need in his eyes hits me so thoroughly I want to cry. The need to crawl fully into his lap and hug him to me as tightly as I can nearly overwhelms me.

He clears his throat and looks away. "Anyway, it's not that far off, so I should get on the ball and figure out what all I need to do. Get the word out. I don't understand how I want to do something so badly yet can't seem to make myself do it."

"Let me do it," I blurt out.

He looks at me, confused. "What do you mean?"

"I'll organize it. If you give me access to your socials, I'll do all the marketing, and I can even mention it on my blog. Let me do it all. You focus on creating a signature cocktail for the night. I know you already have the Poppy, but let's do a specialty birthday drink. The proceeds from the cocktails can be donated. What do you think?"

My brain's already churning up ideas I'm dying to write down.

His brows bunch. "I can't let you do all that."

"Yes, you can. You just said you're having a hard time with it, so let me do it. I already have some really great ideas." I'm practically bouncing in my seat.

"What are they?"

"No, sir." I shake my head. "Let me do this for you. I promise you'll love it."

His eyes roam my face again. "This excites you."

Damn. It does. I really do enjoy the hands-on part of marketing—even if this is a slightly different situation. "Yes, it really does."

"Okay, you can do it."

I can't help myself; I launch at him and hug him. "Thank you, thank you."

When I pull back, our faces are close, and the intensity from earlier is back. Neither of us are breathing as we stare at each other, fighting for what we both want. He releases a breath and uses his hand to brush my hair away from my eye. "I'm not sure you've noticed, but there's not much I'll say no to when it comes to you."

This man. This man's going to melt my heart and my brain cells.

Fuck.

How am I supposed to resist him when he says things like that? He presses the special spot between my shoulder blades, and I know he's about to do something I should say no to, but won't. Because I want it as much as he does.

"Kiss me, Lainey."

"I can't." I don't know how I found the willpower to say those words.

"A kiss to seal our deal."

"You don't play fair."

"Never said I would."

His gaze bores into mine, his fingers pressing further into the skin between my shoulder blades, a reminder it's still my choice.

I lean in. "Just one."

He doesn't disguise the raw heat in his eyes. "Better make it good."

I brush my mouth against his. I do this over and over before I finally let my tongue trace his lips—then I seal it with a real kiss. It's slow and sultry, us each sipping and tasting from each other. It's the kind of kiss you never forget. The kind you relive at night. The kind you think of years later with perfect clarity.

When I pull away, I look into his gorgeous blue eyes and know I'll never forget the pure desire and want reflecting back at me. The promise I'm too afraid to fully acknowledge.

Shit. I really shouldn't have kissed him.

We untangle and get back to work. Two hours later, I have a three-page list of ideas for Poppy's birthday. Jan shows up for work, and I pull her aside to discuss everything I want to do and how I want to keep it a surprise for Ben. She's all on board. I haven't been this excited about work in a long time. I like that I'm creating something real and will be a part of the results.

Ben orders our fried rice, and we tuck ourselves back onto his office couch with our bowls. It really has been the perfect day. I don't remember the last time I enjoyed a workday more. I wish I could spend all of them here with Ben.

"Thanks for today," I say.

He glances at me then, a soft smile on his lips. "It was a nice day."

I want to tell him it was the best day. That no one has made me feel this comfortable and good before. I want to tell him he scares me in a way I've never been scared. I want to tell him he's soul-changing.

"Hey." He nudges me, and I blink out of my thoughts and meet his gaze. In those blue eyes, I see understanding. He knows I'm feeling more than I'm saying. He is, too. "We can do it again. Any time you need a day like today, just say the word, okay?"

I nod, even if I know I won't. I can't. I don't know if I can walk away from another day like this without losing my heart.

Poppy's Birthday - October 1st

I NEVER REALLY THOUGHT OF MYSELF AS A CONTROL FREAK, BUT handing over mostly all the decisions about my mom's birthday celebration at the bar has tested that. While I've collaborated on a few items, Lainey hasn't divulged any of the details. Meanwhile, my whole staff knows everything. She asked me to not look at Red Poppy's socials the last couple of days. It's been hard, but the last thing I want is to ruin her surprise. I'm supposed to pick up my dad and arrive at the bar an hour before opening.

She asked my dad to ignore socials as well, so when I pick him up, he's nervous, too. Kathleen isn't with us, but she'll be there. I love her support and understanding of his love for my mom.

"You don't know anything Lainey has done?" my dad asks on the way to Red Poppy.

"Not really. I had to come up with a specialty cocktail and do a little write-up about Mom and why we're celebrating, then she'd fill in the details. Did she ask you anything?"

My dad shakes his head. "No."

"I think she talked to Uncle Red."

My dad's staring out the window, his mood more subdued than I like. "You never really said why she was handling all this."

"She saw I was struggling with organizing it. Besides, she went to school for marketing. I think she was excited to do it."

"Are y'all still spending a lot of time together?"

I glance at my dad. There's a bit of a knowing look on his face, but it's his inquisitive tone that has me worried.

I keep my gaze focused on the windshield. "Some. Not a lot. Is that a problem?"

"No, son." I can't tell if he's answering exactly what I'm asking. "You two are family now."

My hands tighten on the steering wheel, but I don't dare look at him. I'll reveal too much, like that my definition of family, when it comes to Lainey, is very different than his.

I find a place to park that's not in the back employee lot since Lainey asked me to meet her at the front entrance. When she sees us, her face lights up with excitement, but the fact that she's wringing her hands together tells me she's nervous.

"Hey," she says almost breathlessly. She hugs my dad then me, and I immediately press my hand between her shoulder blades. She instantly relaxes, and when she pulls back, I don't let her go fully.

"It'll be good, Lainey."

A little blush creeps into her cheeks. "Shouldn't I be the one reassuring you?"

"If you're this excited and nervous, I know it'll be great."

The way her expression softens in appreciation...man, she's so fucking beautiful it hurts. As much as I don't want to let her go, I release my hold on her. She blows out a nervous breath. "Ready?"

We both nod, and I'm suddenly nervous, even though I have full confidence she knocked this out of the park. She opens the door for us. Dad and I share a look before I gesture for him to go first. I hear his gasp right before I step in and release my own. She's transformed my bar into what looks like a Broadway musical set. Hanging from the ceiling are upside-down black umbrellas with iridescent streamers and twinkle lights hanging from them to look like rain. It's *Singin' in the Rain*.

"It's Poppy's Favorite Things," Lainey says as the song *My Favorite Things* from the *Sound of Music* fills the room.

I can't believe it. Several Broadway playbills hang on the walls, and I recognize all of them as ones Mom saw and liked. Different musicals play on the few televisions I have mounted around the bar.

"The DJ's only playing music from the '60's and'80's, plus musical soundtracks. I hired a caterer who's working out of a food truck outside, and they're only serving appetizers."

She's included all the things I told her about on Mother's Day and more. She goes on and I walk through my bar in a daze, taking in all the incredible things she's done. While much of the bar's interior is already red, she added many gold accents. There are even more poppies than usual, too.

"Fuck, Lainey." Emotion clogs my throat. I glance at my dad and the tears streaming down his cheeks. When I look back at Lainey, her expression clouds with uncertainty. I swallow down my threatening tears. "This is perfect."

Her whole body relaxes. "Really?"

"You've done more than I ever could have imagined."

She presses a hand to her heart as her eyes turn glassy. It takes all I have not to touch her. To pull her to me and never let go.

"I wanted it to be more than a remembrance of her," she says, her tone soft and contrite. "I wanted it to be a celebration she would have thrown for herself."

My heart beats so hard it feels like it hits my ribs. And I know, without a doubt, I've ended my fall.

I love her.

I love her beyond words. I love her beyond measure. I love her so fucking much I don't know how I'll live another day without her by my side. In my bed. In the center of my life.

I want to pull her to me and kiss the hell out of her. Tell her how I feel. Make her mine. Instead, I let her lead me to the bar where she shows me the cocktail menu.

"I renamed your specialty cocktail list to musical titles. The one you created is the Singin' in the Rain."

I smile. I'd done a Tequila Sunrise mimosa in honor of the Good Morning scene. "I thought of it when I picked that drink."

"I know. I was hoping you'd do something that fit that movie. You exceeded my expectations."

"You've exceeded ours." My dad pulls Lainey into a hug then takes her head in his hands and kisses her forehead. "Thank you for this beautiful tribute. I see exactly why Ben put his trust in you. If you'll excuse me, I'm going to take a stroll and look at your wonderful work."

My dad moves toward the playbills.

Lainey's cheeks flush. "I should go get our families in your office. I wanted you and your dad to take it all in by yourselves first." She hurries toward the hallway before I can grab her and kiss every last drop of uncertainty out of her. A minute later, Uncle Red, Harper, Chandler, and Kathleen spill into the main area of the bar and we all greet each other with hugs.

Uncle Red claps me on the back. "So proud of you and what you've done with this place. And Lainey, she sure is something." He smiles as he takes in the room. "I like her. I like your new family."

"Yours, too."

He smiles. "They're all very welcoming."

Jan announces a pre-opening toast and motions us toward a

row of Singin' in the Rain cocktails on the bar. Everyone in the room, including staff, takes one.

"I want to thank you all, especially Lainey, for this magnificent birthday celebration. My mother would have loved it." I raise my glass. "To Poppy."

Everyone raises their glass and says, "To Poppy."

From there, we spring into action to make sure everything's ready for opening. Our families settle into a VIP section Lainey's roped off. I finally pull out my phone and thumb through the brilliant social media posts she created, which have gotten a lot of attention. It bodes well for a really busy evening.

And it is.

For a night full of music of a generation far older than most of the patrons, everyone seems to be loving every last detail of Lainey's event. Dancing has even broken out in the courtyard. Lainey's talking with Eli, who even got teary-eyed when he saw what she'd done with the bar. My mom had been like a second one to him. The song changes and *Waiting for a Girl Like You* by Foreigner fills the air. Before I question it, I make my way to Lainey.

Her eyes round as she must see the determination in my gaze. "May I have this dance?"

She blinks. "Do you think we sh—"

"Yes. We definitely should." I take her hand and lead her to the dance floor where people have already coupled up. I pull her close, letting my arm slip around her waist. Her eyes roam my face, and I don't know if it's all the twinkle lights she's hung, but there's a soft glow to them that makes me believe her feelings for me mirror my own. I want to tell her that this is our song now. That's she's been the girl I've been waiting for.

That she's it for me.

Instead, I say, "Tonight's magical, Lainey. Thank you."

"I'm so happy you love it." Her smile's finally genuine like she believes me. "I loved every minute of planning it. I really wish I could have met her."

"She would have loved you." But not as much as I do.

Her smile turns even more dazzling. "I'm going to take that as the highest compliment you could have paid me."

I pull her into me until our bodies are flush against each other. We sway to the music, but I can't look away from her. "Do you have any idea how hard it is for me not to kiss you right now?"

Her gaze falls to my lips. "Maybe." Her voice is soft and breathless.

"We could, you know?"

"Ben...please." I can't tell if she means please yes or please no. Honestly, if I were to ask her, I don't think she'd know.

"Lainey," Kathleen says, suddenly next to us, and we jump apart. "I want you to meet someone who needs to leave soon." Kathleen's gaze shifts to me, and I don't like what I see—a mix of panic and determination. "You don't mind, right, Ben?"

Yes, I really fucking mind, but I can't say that.

"Of course. I'll be over at the bar." I let Lainey go, and though it's childish, I want to haul her to me like some petulant child and yell *she's mine* at the top of my lungs.

Kathleen takes her by the arm and pulls her away from me. I stare after her, and a huge sense of loss swamps me. I glance at my dad who is standing off to the side, his expression concerned as his gaze flicks from me to his wife and the woman I love.

Why do I have this sinking feeling that there's broken hearts ahead of us all?

National Hug a Kevin Day

OCTOBER 10TH

CHANDLER

It's National Hug a Kevin Day. It's finally my day, baby!

BEN

Um, that's not your name.

CHANDLER

Kevin Chandler Stevens

Harper, prepare to hug the fuck out of me when I get home.

And by hug, I mean...

gif of man gyrating his hips

HARPER

Omg, Chandler. Stop!

LAINEY

Harper, are you going to "hug" him hard?

BEN

Are you going to "hug" him all night long?

HARPER

Y'all are the worst!

CHANDLER

We need to hug, Harper. We need to hug badly.
It's been too long since we've hugged.

HARPER

Yeah, well, our kid is a big ol' hug blocker. We
need a hug vacation.

LAINEY

Take one!

HARPER

When? It's not that easy, Lainey.

LAINEY

I swear I can hear the censure in your text. I'm
just trying to help you hug your husband.

HARPER

I know. Sorry.

CHANDLER

Man, y'all have put a giant wet blanket on my
holiday.

BEN

What about a Vegas vacation? I'll be there the
29th-1st for a Restaurant & Bar Expo. Y'all can
join me. I'll be busy during the day, but my
nights are free. I can even get tickets for the
food and drink exhibition.

HARPER

Oh, that sounds awesome, but it's Halloween. I
can't miss trick-or-treating. There are only so
many dressing-up years.

CHANDLER

Yeah, thanks for the offer, Ben, but Cassie has
already picked out her costume.

BEN

Totally understand.

LAINEY

There are direct flights on the 29th & 31st and it'll get you home on Halloween at 1pm. That would give you plenty of time to be ready for trick-or-treating. Y'all should go. I'll watch Cassie.

HARPER

We can't. Or could we? Chandler?

CHANDLER

If we're back early, I don't see why we can't.

HARPER

Really??

CHANDLER

Let's do it!

HARPER

happy dance gif

HARPER:

You're not babysitting, Lainey. You're coming with us. I'll get Mom and Mike to babysit.

BEN

Dad would love that.

LAINEY

I have a Halloween holidate. I can't.

HARPER

Dates happen at night. You'll take the same flight as us.

CHANDLER

Yeah, Lain, that excuse isn't going to work. Vegas, baby!!

LAINEY

Fine, I'll go. But I don't want a room near yours.
I do not want to hear y'all hugging all night.

HARPER

Deal!

CHANDLER

Harp, we should hug it out tonight to celebrate.

HARPER

You put Cassie to bed and I'll hug you real
good.

LAINEY

For the love of God, pls stop.

HARPER

Sounds like someone needs to get hugged.

LAINEY

Hug You!

National Martina Day - October 29th

"PLEASE TELL ME YOU'RE KIDDING?" HARPER'S WIDE-EYED WITH that big sister look of shock and disappointment—a look she's perfected.

"Okay, I'm kidding."

Harper huffs as she twists and turns in her airplane seat. "I'm serious, Lainey." She lets out a frustrated growl. "Where the hell is the seatbelt? I hate the middle seat."

"It's your hug holiday. You have to sit next to your husband," I reply, making sure she hears the note of teasing. Maybe a night of solid hugging will get her to simmer down.

Chandler moves and helps her look, pulling the belt from where it was caught between the seats. "I'll trade with you," he offers, and I don't know if I want to laugh or sigh in awe. Chandler has a good half a foot in height on Harper. Sitting in the middle will practically shove his knees into his chest, but he'd totally do it for her.

"Babe, please," she replies, though the sweet offer deflates her frustration. She leans in and gives him a peck on his lips. Unfortunately, one moment of marital sweetness didn't end her tirade, and she whirls to face me. "You can't stay in the same room as Ben."

"Why not?"

Harper does the one eyebrow arch. "You know why."

I roll my eyes. "Harp, we're friends."

"No, you're stepsiblings."

"We can't be both? Stepsiblings can't share a room?"

Harper sighs again. "I saw y'all at Poppy's birthday celebration. Hell, the whole bar sensed the electricity between you. Did you notice the song that was playing when he grabbed you to dance? Mom was practically having a panic attack."

Like I need the reminder. Mom gave me a *please don't fuck this up for me* look before she introduced me to some random guy she'd met.

The problem is that my feelings for Ben have grown roots and started wrapping around every part of my being. Do I think rooming with him is a good idea? Not really. But it seemed pointless for me to get one all by myself, considering how little time we'd be in the same place together.

"It just makes sense, Harper. He's going to be at the Expo most of the time so why would I get my own when I'll practically have his room by myself? It saves me money, too."

"Because you're going to get into one of those situations where the only room left has one bed. Then all your naughty bits will start touching, and next thing you know, you're *hugging*."

I could really make her head explode and tell her our naughty bits have already touched, and they like each other *a lot*.

"We're staying at one of the largest hotels on the strip, not a roadside motel during a snowstorm, so calm your rom-com mind. There's two beds, Ben's confirmed it." I won't admit my disappointment at that fact.

"It's a bad idea."

"Oh my God!" I dig in my purse and pull out my ear buds, making a big show of shoving them in my ears and turning toward the window.

She's still talking, but now it's muffled. Out of the corner of my eye, I see Chandler take her hand and kiss it, and her attention finally turns away from me. Sadly, it's not the last time she brings it up during the almost three-hour flight. By the time we're in a cab to our hotel, I'm imagining stuffing her into a barrel and tossing her into Lake Mead.

I turn my back to her and text Ben.

ME

We're en route to the hotel. Say a prayer for Harper. I'm ready to take out a mob hit on her.

BEN

Whoa. Long flight?

ME

You have no idea. Thank God it's National Martini Day. I'm ordering several as soon as we arrive.

BEN

It's not National Martini Day. It's National Martina Day.

ME

Oh. Well, see, that shows you how crazy she's made me. Just call me Martina today.

BEN

Martina with a martini?

ME

Exactly!

BEN

lol. I'm at the hotel now. I'll meet y'all in the
lobby. That way I can give you a key and show
you our room.

OUR ROOM. I shouldn't like the sound of that as much as I do.

ME

Sounds good. ETA: 8 mins

WE WALK INTO THE LOBBY, and Ben's sitting at a small table off to the side. He immediately joins us with a martini in hand. It takes all my energy not to kiss the hell out of him. He hands the drink over with a smile.

"Hey, Martina," he murmurs close to my ear before placing a kiss on my cheek.

"Whoa, where's mine?" Harper asks.

"Here you go." Ben leans in and kisses her cheek.

"I meant the martini."

"Oh. Well, Martina here sounded desperate. Don't worry, I got you one too." He turns and picks up the other martini from the table and hands it to her.

"Martina?"

"Inside joke," he says.

Harper gives me a look that says, *see, this is a bad idea.* I don't engage but lift my martini in toast, then down half.

"Welcome to Vegas," Chandler says, as he accepts a beer from Ben.

Harper huffs a sigh and downs most of her martini in one go. Chandler shakes his head and maneuvers her to the reception desk as Ben and I head to the elevators. I polish off my drink on our way to the twentieth floor.

Ben steps close and takes the glass from my hand. His expression is a combination of warning and amusement.

"Are you going to tell me what to do now?"

"Nope," he smirks. "It's Vegas, baby. If you want to be Martina Martini, go for it."

I laugh. "What happens in Vegas..."

"Exactly."

We arrive at our room and it's nicely spacious with Ben's stuff all tucked away neatly.

"What happened between you and Harper?"

"This." I gesture around the room. "She's harping on what a bad idea it is."

"Harping." He snorts a laugh. "You mean us sharing a room?"

I shoot him a sly look. "She thinks our naughty bits are going to touch. Her words."

A seductive smile forms. "Our naughty bits do like each other. We could arrange a playdate for them if you want."

I point at him. "Behave. I refuse to prove her right."

"Harper loves to be right. Don't you want to make her happy?"

"Trust me, she'll take no satisfaction in this. Hopefully, Chandler's hugging the hell out of her, and she'll be in a better mood for dinner."

Ben throws his head back and laughs. God, he's gorgeous when he lets go like that. If I'm being honest, I could go for a quick hug right now. As if he's read my mind, Ben closes the distance between us.

"Does Martina need a hug?" He reaches out and runs a finger down my arm, letting it trail to the small of my back, pressing just enough that my body falls into his. I close my eyes as his head starts to dip toward mine and his lips brush my cheek. "What do you need, Martina? A long, gentle hug or do you want it quick and hard?"

My breath shutters out of me on a low moan. Any remaining space between us is gone. My whole body is pressed against his, and his hand traces up my back to our spot.

"I'll hug you anyway you want. Anywhere. Anytime." His rough voice brushes my ear before his tongue teases the sensitive spot on the underside of my jaw. I arch my neck, giving him more access as my hands fist his shirt. Right as he sucks on my skin, a loud knock at the door has us jumping apart. We stare at each other, breathing heavily. What the hell just happened?

"Why the fuck did I give her our room number?" He runs a hand through his hair. It hits me then that it's probably Harper and Chandler. So much for Chandler hugging her senseless.

There's another knock which spurs us into motion. Ben adjusts himself in an attempt to hide his arousal and takes a seat at the small table in front of the window. I move for the door, smoothing a hand over my hair and pressing it to my stomach to calm it. I want to hate Harper's impeccable timing, but it's probably for the best.

I open the door with a smile and Harper immediately narrows her gaze. "Interrupting something?"

"Ben was just giving me the best hug ever."

Chandler slaps his hand over his mouth to stop himself from laughing while Harper rushes past me and into the room. She takes the room in, looking for signs that we really "hugged," but the beds are pristine.

I look at Chandler and whisper, "Thought you two would be in your room hugging it out by now."

"Me too." There's an edge of annoyance in his voice.

"I wanted to tell you our room number and see what the plan is," Harper says.

I bite my tongue so I don't say she could have texted that. The last thing I need is to raise her suspicions more.

"Actually, I was just about to tell you I have an event tonight, and I won't be able to join you. But I was able to score tickets to a Cirque Soliel show if y'all want to go," Ben says.

Harper squeals. "No way!"

He goes to grab an envelope from the desk and hands it over. "All yours."

Harper launches herself at him and wraps him up in a hug—a real one. "Thank you so much. I wish you could join us."

"Me, too. I actually have to get back now. There's a workshop starting in half an hour and it takes forever to walk through the casino. Tomorrow night, I'm completely free and we can do the food and drink exhibition together."

"Great." Chandler grabs Harper's hand and drags her to her door. "It's hug time."

Harper's giggles can be heard even after the door shuts behind them. Hopefully, she'll get off my back for the rest of the night.

I face Ben to find his crossbody bag draped across his chest. I paste a smile on my face so my disappointment doesn't show, but I can tell he doesn't buy it. He pauses at my side on his way out, leaning down close to my ear. "Don't be too disappointed, Martina. After I leave, you can always hug yourself."

And I totally do. I was tempted to text him proof, but as soon as the thought entered my mind, I chastised myself. Martina's a bad influence on me.

I do leave the bed unmade, though.

I make my way to the casino, hit the slots, and sip on more martinis. After Chandler and Harper hug their brains out, they join me, and we grab dinner before the show. It's a great night, but I feel like a complete third wheel. When we get back to the hotel, Chandler and Harper immediately head up to their room, and I decide Martina has had enough martinis and should probably tuck in as well. After I shower and slip into bed, it's after midnight, and Ben still isn't back.

I try to go to sleep, but the desire to see him overrides any tiredness. When the key card clicks, my stomach lurches in anticipation. I don't move though, pretending to sleep. He quietly moves around the room, and I swear he pauses by my bed before going into the bathroom. The shower starts up, and his belt clanks against the tile floor. I squeeze my eyes shut, remembering the sight of his ass before he jumped into the pool. The shadows of his hard cock underneath the water. It really is a shame I haven't seen it fully yet. Or felt it bare in my hands.

The thought of wrapping my hand around his cock sends a surge of wetness between my legs. I really want to be in that shower with him, on my knees, as he feeds me his cock. I want his hand tangled in my hair, holding me still as he fucks my mouth. I want to suck him so hard he loses all control. I want to feel his cum shooting down my throat.

I bite back a groan and rub my legs together—and that's when I hear it. A deep moan coming from the bathroom. My eyes fly open and I still, listening as carefully as I can. I hear it again. A moan followed by a muttered *fuck*. Then...

Lainey

Oh, damn. He's jerking off—and thinking of me. I'm aching so hard now I can't ignore it. I push my hand into my panties, shuddering as I easily slip in between my folds. Fuck, I'm so sensitive. So wet. Messy sounds fill the room as I rub myself. Ben's groans have gotten louder and cruder, and I rub myself faster, harder. My release builds so quickly I'm going to come soon. But, I want to hear him first. I want to come with him.

"Fuck...yes...Lainey..."

The unmistakable sound of him coming has my own moan leaving my throat as I work myself even harder. My orgasm hits me so hard that I arch off the bed, but I refuse to stop. I don't let up, riding the perfect combination of pleasure and pain until I fall back on the mattress, panting. Holy shit. That was way more intense than my earlier solo ride.

I finally get my breathing under control by the time I hear the shower cut off, but my body still vibrates from the release. I haven't even removed my hand from my panties, which I realize when he opens the door to the bathroom. I keep pretending to be asleep, but not sure I'm doing a great job of it.

I hear him move around the room and get into his bed. I don't think he's lying down though. No, I have a feeling he's looking at me.

"I know you're awake."

I open my eyes and turn my head toward him. My eyes are still adjusted to the dark so I can see him sitting on the edge of his bed. He's wearing pajama pants but no shirt. His expression is tense, which is surprising, considering he should be feeling pretty relaxed. My whole body feels like jelly.

"Did you hear me?"

The longer I stay silent, the more the room charges with tension. "Yes."

"Did you only listen?"

"No."

He leans forward and rests his elbows on his knees. Even in the dark, I can see the intensity in his expression. "Give me your hand."

Oh, fuck. Another raging ache fills me and it's so hard not to rub myself all over again. Instead, I pull out the hand I touched myself with from under the covers and extend it toward him. He brings it up to his mouth, and his breath tickles my fingertips. He's smelling me and teasing each finger over his lips. He lets out a low sound as his silky tongue licks my skin. He slips several fingers into his mouth, sucking hard. We both moan shamelessly. His tongue swirls around my fingers, sucking and biting until he's licked every bit of my cum off each one.

He presses a kiss to my palm before letting go of my hand. "Heavenly."

Without another word, he gets fully into bed and turns his back to me as I lie there, more turned on than ever.

I toss and turn, wondering if I should get myself off again. Or go take a cold shower. Or jump in his bed.

"Lainey, go to sleep or I'm joining you and hugging you into the bed so hard you'll never find your way out of it."

I freeze and force myself not to move again.

October 30th - Mischief Day

"Come on, Harp. Let's go back to the room." Chandler pulls Harper to him, his hand dipping down to her ass.

"But I want another drink." Her words are slurred and whiney.

I cut out of the conference early so I could spend time with everyone on their last night. We had plans to hit up a club after the food and drink exhibition, but we stayed longer than I imagined, drinking and eating. We're all already halfway, or in Harper's case, fully drunk.

Chandler gives his wife a hot look that makes me a little jealous. "No. You want to hug your husband before we leave in the morning."

Harper's eyes light up and she wraps her arms around his neck. "I do like hugging," she says before sealing her mouth to his.

Ugh, I want to head to the room with Lainey and spend all night hugging the fuck out of her. I haven't been able to stop thinking about how she got off to the sound of me getting off. I'm dying to bury my face between her legs and taste her all over again.

Lainey makes a gagging sound at her sister and brother-in-law, forcing them to break apart. Harper turns her attention to me. "Come on, time for bed for you, too. You don't need to drink any more than I do."

"I'm not going back yet." Lainey crosses her arms stubbornly.

"Well, you don't need to stay out," Harper says with a pointed look between us.

I throw an arm around Lainey's shoulders. "Yeah, we should go back to the room."

Harper blinks a few times as her inebriated brain comprehends what I said. "Wait. No."

Lainey throws fuel on the fire and wraps her arms around my waist. "We should call it night. I could really use a good night hug."

Harper looks like her head is about to explode.

"Come on, Harp, they're messing with you. Let's go." Chandler gives us a frustrated glare. Harper tries to protest, but he kisses the hell out of her, successfully distracting her and leading her to the elevators.

"That was too much fun," Lainey says, as she steps away from me. "Now what?"

"More drinks are probably a bad idea," I say.

"Probably."

But if we return to the room, I have a feeling we'll make worse decisions. Not that I would mind. Staying out drinking feels like the safer choice.

I grin at her mischievously. "Then we should definitely do it."

She returns a matching grin. "Definitely."

We decide to hit up a club after all, and the next couple of hours becomes a blur of drinks and dancing. When we fall onto a sofa to take a break from the crowds, Lainey pulls out her phone and groans in frustration.

"Oh my God! Harper is checking in. What the hell is her deal already? Why didn't Chandler hug her unconscious? I should make it look like we're naked and send her a pic."

I lean in and brush my lips over the shell of her ear. "Or we could just get naked." I give her earlobe a quick nip, and she gives me a side eye. I can also tell she liked it. "It is Mischief Day."

She rolls her eyes. "You and your holidays. What's Mischief Day?"

"It's like a prank day."

Her eyes light up. "That's it! I know what we need to do. We need to pretend to get married!"

I laugh. "That'll give her a heart attack."

"Oh my God, it's perfect." She gleefully starts swiping her phone screen again.

"What are you doing?"

"Googling what you have to do to get married in Vegas. Do you need a license, or do you just show up?"

"I have no idea, but we don't need a license if it's a joke."

"Oh no, we need a license. That'll make it so good. I want to freak the fuck out of her."

The rest of the night is a blur of cab rides, more drinks, laughter, Elvis, and a really good kiss. There's only one word on my mind before everything goes completely blank.

Wife.

Halloween

I DON'T EVEN HAVE TO OPEN MY EYES TO KNOW I'M A THOUSAND percent hungover. My head's pounding. My mouth feels like cotton. My stomach's rolling. And the only thing my aching brain has the strength to ask is, what the hell happened last night?

The more the question rolls around in my brain, the more my stomach churns, which doesn't bode well. I open my eyes and I'm in a dark room I don't recognize. Hints of sunlight peek around the blackout curtains, so it's daytime. Where am...oh, shit.

Vegas. Hotel room.

Ben.

As soon as he enters my thoughts, I realize I'm not in the same bed as the night before—and there's a distinct weight across my waist. Oh my God. Did we have sex? I lift the sheet and find my breasts are bare, but I have on panties. That's a good sign, right?

I drop the bed covers and that's when I see it. A gold band sparkles around my finger. I grab my hand and realize gold's an overstatement. The ring's probably one step up from plastic.

Suddenly, a memory of snagging it from a gumball machine comes into focus. A barrage of images hit but only two stick out: a marriage license and Elvis.

I jackknife in bed, grabbing the sheet to keep me covered. "Ben! Ben!"

He startles awake, shooting straight up like I did, a mixture of confusion and pain on his expression as he presses a hand to his forehead. "What?"

I hold up my hand. "What the fuck did we do last night?"

He stares for what seems like hours, blinking as if he's trying to get his brain to work. "Um...I think we got married."

My heartbeat roars in my ears.

"It was a joke for your sister. Mischief Day. Remember?"

His recollection slows my thundering heart as it all comes back to me. I wanted a picture with a marriage license at a Vegas chapel to send to Harper. That was all we were going to do. Just take a picture with Pastor Elvis.

"We're not really married, right?"

Ben runs a hand over his face as he shakes his head.

"And we didn't have sex?"

He looks at me then, noticing for the first time I'm topless under the sheet. He's shirtless too and I hope he's wearing boxers. He lifts the sheet. "I have underwear on, and we were so plastered, I would have had whiskey dick."

"You sure we didn't try? Drunk people do stupid stuff."

He looks around the room. "No, I kinda remember you taking off your top. We got in bed. I think we kissed goodnight. That's it."

Goodnight, husband.

The sudden memory spikes my heartbeat. Okay, focus on the positives. Not really married. Didn't have blackout sex. I glance at the clock. It's 6:00 a.m., which is way too early for me to be up, considering how late we probably went to bed. But there's no way I'm falling back to sleep. Not when I leave for the airport in less than three hours.

"I'm going to shower. Will you, um, turn around?"

He falls back onto his pillow and slings an arm over his face with a groan. I get up, grab my things, and take a shower. Twenty minutes later, I emerge feeling a smidge better, but no amount of hot water will cure this hangover. Ben's up and the curtains are pulled back, the room filled with natural light. He's standing at the table in a T-shirt and sweats, looking down with a furrowed expression.

"I'm done."

His head snaps up and he's blinking like he's not fully functioning. "I went to the vending machine and got some Gatorade." He points at the nightstand.

"Oh, bless you." I go grab it as he gets his stuff to shower. I start packing because I don't know what else to do with myself. I'm afraid to look at my phone, but I eventually find it and plug it in. Of course, it's dead. Did I send pics to Harper? Surely not, or she'd be knocking down the door. Though to be fair, it is only six-thirty in the morning.

I sit on the bed and drink my Gatorade, willing my brain to remember. There was an Elvis. I was adamant about getting a picture. I remember laughing a lot. And...we kissed.

My wife.

My heart starts going crazy again, and I don't know what it means. Am I excited he called me his wife? Does it terrify me? Maybe a bit of both? Hell, did he even say it at all? My brain's so full of fuzz I can't be sure of anything.

Well, except for the ring on my finger. I look down, unsure why I didn't take it off while I showered. Ben steps back into the room and notices me looking at the ring. I glance at his hand, and he has a band around his ring finger too—that he also didn't take off. I jerk my gaze away and take a big drink of Gatorade.

He drops off his stuff at his suitcase and sits on the bed across from me. The past twenty-four hours seem to replay as we stare at each other, and next thing I know, we're laughing. I mean, how ridiculous are we?

As we calm down, he says, "Look, we need to—"

Suddenly, there's a pounding at the door. We both freeze.

"Lainey! Open the damn door now!" Harper's voice comes through.

"My phone was dead, and I was too afraid to look at it," I tell Ben.

Harper pounds again.

He winces. "I would be, too."

We sit there for another beat before I force myself to answer the door. Time to face the consequences of my actions. I open it with a big smile on my face. "Hey, sis."

My chipper and dressed state definitely throws her off. She's wearing a hotel robe with a serious case of bedhead. Chandler's behind her wearing clearly thrown-on clothes, looking miserable.

"What the fuck did you do last night?" She shoves her phone at me, the screen displaying a crisp picture of me and Ben smiling with Elvis between us. I'm holding up a marriage license. She bulldozes her way into the room, and Chandler gives me a frustrated look. The fact he's not amused tells me I might have crossed the line.

"Couldn't y'all have just hugged and called it a day?" he says as he passes me to follow his wife. Yeah, the joke is officially over.

"Calm down, Harper. We didn't really get married. It was a joke."

"Lainey, there's a marriage license in this picture." She points to her phone.

"Yeah, that's what makes it funny."

Her expression is incredulous as she screeches, "That's what makes it legal!"

"But we didn't really get married. We only took the picture with it."

Harper blinks a few times. "You got a license but only took a picture with Pastor Elvis? He didn't actually marry you?"

"Right."

"Um, Lainey..."

I look over at Ben, who appears a little ashen, his expression possessing an edge of panic. My stomach immediately knots. "What?"

"That is what I was about to tell you. The license...is signed."

"Yeah, we had to sign it to get it."

"No, it's signed *by the chapel*." He picks it up from the table and I realize that's what he was looking at earlier. He holds out the white paper and I snatch it from his hands. Sure enough, it's signed.

"But...but we just took a picture."

He runs a hand down his face. "I think we did more than that."

I shake my head as I try to unlock my memories through the haze of alcohol. "We kissed, but it was for the picture. There were no vows."

"I'm not so certain about that."

"No, I would have remembered if we'd gotten married. We laughed with the Elvis. We took a picture with him. He told us to kiss. He..." I look at him, and my words fall away.

"Lainey...I'm pretty sure we got married."

"Okay, stop. This isn't funny." My throat's getting smaller and smaller as I stare at Ben. This is a joke. I couldn't have gotten married in Vegas. How stupid is that? "There's a video. Didn't we take one?"

I go to my phone and power it on. No one speaks a word as I

wait. I ignore the barrage of messages popping up from Harper and go to my pictures. Among the many drunk candid shots of us and Elvis, there's one video. I click it and hold out my phone for us all to see.

Ben and I are giggling, clearly not sober. I have a bouquet of fake flowers in my hand and a cheap veil on my head.

"We need a picture wedding," I tell Elvis. "Quick and easy."

"You want to marry this man?" Elvis asks.

"I definitely do," I say, and burst into giggles.

Elvis turns to Ben. "You want to marry this woman?"

"Yes, *thank you very much*," Ben replies in a horrible Elvis impression and we're laughing all over again.

"Under the state of Nevada, I pronounce you man and wife. Kiss your bride."

We both look at him, then each other, and burst into another round of laughter.

"We need a picture!" I say way too loudly.

Someone says something off-camera. I wrap my arms around Ben's neck and kiss him. At first, it's awkward as I knock him off balance, but he quickly gains control, and holy hell, the kiss turns hot as fuck. Ben's hand slips up to my acnestis, and my hands dive into his hair, tugging him closer. Elvis says something unintelligible, we break apart laughing, and the video abruptly ends.

I look at Ben. "That could not have counted."

"Of course, it counted," my sister shrieks. "You both said yes! It's signed. You're married!"

Oh. My. God. I married my stepbrother.

Cliche Day - November 3rd

LAINEY

I GRAB THE CARTON OF ICE CREAM OUT OF THE FREEZER, YANK OFF the lid, and open the cabinet to get a bowl. Changing my mind, I close the door and grab a big spoon from the utensil drawer. My eyes land on the faux gold band on my ring finger. I moved the ring to my right hand when I had to go on the Halloween date I set up before I went to Vegas. And again for the Day of the Dead festival. Yep, I went on two dates less than twenty-four hours after getting married. I'm already a shitty wife.

I'm not even sure why I'm still wearing the ring.

Maybe as a reminder that I'm a red-hot mess. If I hadn't insisted on a marriage license to make the joke look authentic, I wouldn't be in this situation. Drunk logic is so stupid. I jam the spoon into the ice cream and scoop up enough to give me a brain freeze but stuff it in my mouth anyway.

Back in the living room, I settle on the couch and start the next episode of the reality show, *Below Deck*. Other people's drama is way more entertaining than my own. Ben didn't want me to leave Vegas, but I needed space. Surprisingly, Harper was great on the flight home. She didn't yell or lecture but held my hand and told me everything would be okay. I don't know if she believed it, but at least she didn't kick me when I was down.

Ben has texted and called several times since then, and I've ignored them all. That's pretty much been my M-O about everything since getting back. I've channeled my inner ostrich and buried my head deep in the sand. If I don't think about it, then it really didn't happen.

When there's a knock at my door, I know it's him. I'm honestly surprised it's taken him this long to show up since he got back from Vegas two days ago. I set my ice cream aside and get up to look through the peephole. Ben's standing there with his hands on his hips, his agitated expression fierce enough to break through the door. I open it, and he gives me a quick onceover, interest flaring before he quickly masks it.

"Sorry to come by unannounced, but my wife's going on dates and ignoring my calls."

"Funny," I say dryly.

"True." He gives me a pointed look.

"Don't remind me."

Something flashes across his face, and I wonder if I hurt his feelings. I step back so he can come in. He takes off his coat and tosses it over the back of my dining room chair, paces my living room like a caged tiger before he finally stops and looks at me.

"We have to talk."

"Probably. More than anything, we need to get an annulment. Have you happened to research it yet?"

"No."

"Yeah, I've been in this sort of shocked daze. I guess I owe you an apology. If I hadn't insisted on the license, we wouldn't be in this situation."

He runs a hand through his hair. "Yeah, about that..."

I suddenly notice he looks nervous and guilty, like he did when he told me the license was signed the other morning.

"So, um...things have been coming back to me. And..." He meets my gaze. "I watched Elvis sign it."

It takes a few seconds for what he said to sink in. If he watched, then he knew he was sealing our fate as a married couple. "You watched him sign it...and you didn't stop him?" My voice is way too calm, considering my body's vibrating with anger.

He rubs the back of his neck. "No."

"What the fuck, Ben! Why not?"

"I don't know." He throws his arms up in surrender. "It was like it was all happening in slow motion, and I was stuck. I couldn't move or talk. Then, it was done."

"What were you thinking? That we would just be married?"

"I don't think I was really thinking at the time. But... yeah...maybe."

I blink at him. "What does that mean?"

He shrugs, and looks at me sheepishly. "We could stay married."

I fist my hair and turn away from him. Am I living in a sitcom? This can't be my life. Has he lost his mind?

Finally, I face him. "Know what today's holiday is?" I don't wait for him to answer. "It's Cliché Day. That's us." I point between us. "We're a fucking cliché. We got drunk and married in Vegas by Elvis."

"To be fair, it would probably be more of a cliché if we got divorced."

"Ben! We can't stay married! *Our parents are married.*"

"I'm aware."

I blink. How does he not see this as an issue? My mom begged me to stay away from him and I went and fucking married him. I'm the worst daughter in the world.

"Stop pretending this isn't a big deal. We could ruin our parents' marriage for a stupid pretend holiday." I motion between us. "That's all we even are. A bunch of holiday texts and wrong holidates."

"No." His head snaps up as he stalks toward me. I backpedal until he cages me against the wall. His eyes are steely, his jaw tight with tension. "*Don't.* It's been almost a year, Lainey. A year of becoming friends and sharing moments together that we haven't experienced with anyone else. I've been *inside* you, Lainey. Don't fucking dismiss those holidays. Each and every one of them led us to this moment."

Just like that, everything changes between us.

Heats.

Pulls in tight.

He's so close, I can't breathe. He leans in and brushes his lips over my cheek before moving closer to my ear. "I know you like no one else." He tips my chin up, his grip intentional, as he leans back enough so our eyes meet. "Say it, Lainey."

When I stay silent, his hand trails down to my neck as his lips feather kisses over my face. Everywhere except my lips. His thumb rubs up and down the column of my throat before he applies a little pressure. Just enough for my body to turn volcanic. My hips thrust against him as I arch back, giving him even more access to my throat.

"Say it, Lainey." He presses his cock into me, his lips hovering over mine.

"No one knows me like you."

As soon as the words leave my mouth, he kisses me, his hand tightening around my throat. It's a punishing kiss. No finesse. No seduction. But it's passionate. Needy. And that's what makes it perfect. He rips his mouth from mine, drops his hand, and kisses down my throat. Though maybe kiss isn't the right word. It's more bites and nips and hard sucks. I have no doubt the evidence will be on my skin for days.

"Did you kiss your dates?"

My heart lurches at the pain I hear beneath the anger. "No. Never. I never kiss them. You know that."

A possessive grin forms on his lips. "I do. Because you're mine."

He grabs the hem of my shirt and pulls it over my head, then rids me of my bra. He kisses down my chest, pulling a nipple in his mouth, sucking hard. I arch into him on a whimper, sinking my fingers into his hair. My body's on fire. I want his touch everywhere. And as if he heard me, he gives my yoga pants and panties a harsh tug and jerks them off me. His hands grab my thighs, spreading me just before he buries his face in my pussy.

"Ben...fuck..."

My knees buckle, and he puts pressure on my legs to keep me stable as he feasts on my clit.

He moans and pushes his tongue inside me, fucking me in the most delicious way. He's relentless, and it feels so damn good I know I'm not going to last long.

"Yes...right there. I'm going to come."

His fingers dig into my thighs even harder as he attacks my clit again. And I come. Hard. I've never been eaten out so roughly, but I love every second of it. I ride his face, milking every ounce of pleasure he's giving me. When he finally pulls away, he has to grab me so I don't slip down the wall.

He shoots me a self-satisfied smile as he wipes his mouth with the back of his hand. "Delicious." Then he pulls his shirt over his head.

"What are you doing?"

"I'm going to fuck my wife."

And all my insides turn to molten lava.

"Ben...we can't."

"We can." He unzips his jeans and my gaze dips to his gorgeous body.

Finally, I get to see him fully naked. When he stands straight after kicking his jeans off, I take in his beautiful cock. It really is a thing of beauty, thick and long, but not *that might break me* long. I've never wanted to taste a cock as much as I want to taste Ben's.

"Jesus, you can't keep looking at it like that, or I'm going to come. And I really want to sink into that sweet pussy of yours."

He grabs me by the neck again and kisses me, hard and fast, before ripping his mouth away, and suddenly, I'm being turned and dragged to the couch, where he bends me over the back of it. He moans as his hand gently roams over my ass. "Fucking beautiful."

I feel him slide his cock over my pussy, still wet and aching. "If you don't want me to fuck you, you know how to stop me." He leans forward and kisses me between my shoulder blades, his cock pressing hotly against my ass. "Stop me, Lainey."

He knows I won't. I don't want to. I want this as badly as he does. I always want him. I don't think I'll ever not want him.

I push my ass against him. "Fuck me, Ben."

"Fuck me, *husband*," he corrects.

That word from his lips should be like a bucket of cold water on this moment, but my pussy throbs. A sharp slap sounds, and my ass stings, the pleasure pain forcing a moan up my throat.

"Fuck me, husband."

A guttural sound leaves him right as he pushes inside me. I cry out at how full I feel in this position. His cock feels like silky steel inside me. He grips my hips tightly and fucks me as relentlessly as he ate me out. It's hard and messy and so damn good that I never want it to end.

"Fuck...Lainey...my good little wife. You like how your husband fucks you?"

Holy shit. I had no idea that I'd have a married kink, but his words are making me insane. I clench around his cock. "Yes. You feel so good. Don't stop."

He groans and fucks me even harder. "Oh, I'm not. I'm going to wreck this pussy."

One of his hands slides from my hip. A moment later, a wet finger slips between my ass cheeks. "Has anyone ever touched you here, wife?" I feel pressure as his finger slowly presses inside.

"No," I moan the word, unable to form more. The pressure and pleasure building inside me is almost too much. But I love it. How brutally perfect he's fucking me. How deliciously full I feel.

"One day, I'm going to wreck you here, too. And you're going to take it like the good wife you are."

At that, I fly over the edge. I come hard and loud. His fingers dig into my hip as he pistons in and out of me furiously and comes along with me.

"*Fuck*." He slumps over me, and we stay like that for a good while, all labored breaths and slick skin and spent bodies. He finally pulls away and takes my hand, leading me to the bathroom. He starts the shower and pulls me under the stream when the water's warm. We wash each other, not saying a word the whole time. When we're all dry, we get into bed and tangle our limbs together, facing each other.

"What are we doing?" I ask him softly.

"Cuddling."

"Ben, I'm serious."

We shouldn't have done that. Yet, I don't regret it. I can't even make myself feel guilty about how I've broken my promise to my mom. It felt too good. Too right.

"I don't know. I...I'm not ready for it end. Are you going to tell me you never want to do what we just did again?"

I sigh, unable to deny the truth. "You know I do."

He sits up so he's leaning on his elbow. "Then let's keep doing it. Let's have a honeymoon."

"A honeymoon? What are you talking about?"

"We take our two weeks of fucking our brains out like every married couple. Except we stay here instead of doing it at a tropical resort."

Panic fires up in my heart, but I can't tell if it's bad or good. "Let me get this straight. You're suggesting a two-week fuckfest, then what? We get the annulment?"

"Yeah. Sure."

That sounds very dangerous. It also sounds really fun. Two weeks of pure, hot sex with Ben sounds like paradise.

"The sexual tension's never going to die between us if we don't get it out of our systems. We'll just find ourselves back here at some point in the future." He traces a fingertip down my cheek. "At least if we do this, we'll know. We'll be able to get over it."

I bite my bottom lip, seriously contemplating his proposition. This feels a lot like drunk logic. Neither one of us is drunk, though, so I don't know what it says about me wanting to agree.

His gaze flicks to my right hand, which is lying on the pillow between us. He trails his fingers over my ring and slides it off.

"Give me your other hand."

We stare at each other for a few moments before I move so I can give him my left hand. He slips the band on my ring finger. "Lainey, will you be my wife for the next two weeks?"

I stare at the cheap ring. My finger will probably turn green before the honeymoon's over, yet I don't hate the idea of my skin being marked. His proposal is probably the worst idea ever, but I can't seem to say no.

"I will."

Honeymoon Day 3 - November 6th

"HOLY FUCK!"

Lainey straightens from tying her shoes and turns to face me. "What?"

"No, no, no. Do more of that." I take her by the shoulders and bend her back over, taking in the sight of her ass.

"What's wrong with you?" She laughs, looking over her shoulder at me, her hands braced on her thighs.

"Baby, what kind of leggings are these? Jesus. You can't do this me. I can't take it."

Her grin breaks wide. She tries to right herself, but I push her back down and run my hands over the rounded globes, giving her cheeks a hard squeeze.

"Would you stop?" She stands, still laughing. "They're my workout leggings."

Like hell. "There's no way you're going to the gym wearing those. Every guy there will stare at your ass."

She gives me a sassy look.

"I'm serious, Lainey. Fuck." I try to check out her fine ass again.

She playfully pushes at me. "Okay, they might be butt enhancing leggings. They give my flat girlie a little oomph."

"Your *girl* doesn't need enhancing. She's perfect the way she is."

A crooked grin forms as she raises her brows at me. "The tent in your pants says otherwise. I think the leggings are doing their job."

"Baby, I always have a tent in my pants when it comes to you." I stalk toward her until I have her backed up against the front door. "And your mighty fine ass in those tight pants reminded me I haven't been inside your pussy in eight hours." I hook my fingers in the waistband and pull down.

"Eli and Chandler are supposed to be here any minute." Her hands press against my chest. "I gotta leave before they see me."

I'm seriously regretting keeping the tee time we made at my mom's birthday celebration.

"Eli's never on time, and Chandler's picking him up. Plus, we have fifteen minutes. I'll be done in five." I yank her leggings and shoes completely off and start working my belt.

"Five whole minutes? You sure know how to woo a girl."

I shove my pants past my knees, not bothering to take them off, and push her fully against the door. I spread her legs, and my finger easily slips inside her. "Baby, you're already wooed." I fuck her a few times with my finger, and her eyes flutter close. "Now I'm going to rock your world."

I wrap her leg around my waist and line my cock at her entrance. She cants her hips and wraps her other leg around me. I thrust up, my eyes shutting at the tight squeeze I'll never tire of.

"Fuck, yes." Her head falls back against the door.

"That's right. Take my cock like a good little wife."

"Give it to me harder."

"Shit. *Fuck.*" This woman will be the beautiful fucking death of me.

"As you wish, baby." I give her exactly what she asks for and fuck her so hard the door's banging on the hinges. I bury my face into her neck, murmuring dirty sweet nothings as she moans and urges me on. Then she clenches around me, and I'm lost.

"Come now. Come all over my cock."

And my hot as fuck wife obeys. She screams through her release and that's all it takes for me to lose it. I swear we're going to knock the door down as I pump into her, filling her with my cum. When it comes to her, I turn absolutely primal. Fucking feral. The idea of my cum filling her—marking her as mine—I need it as much as I need air. We fall into each other, the room overly silent except for the rushes of our labored breaths.

When we finally separate, she says, "Well, you got my heart rate up."

"I did. Go crawl back into bed and relax. No need to go to the gym. I'll work you out again when I get home." And revel in every fucking second.

She gives me an exasperated yet playful look. "I've been flat on my back for three days. I've got to get out and move."

"Baby, you've moved plenty, and I recall several times when you weren't on your back at all."

"Stop it." She picks up her leggings and shuts herself in the bathroom. I pick up my pants and follow her.

"Hey, let me in. I need to clean up, too. We're married. It's okay if you pee in front of me."

"No, it's not. We're in the honeymoon stage."

I chuckle. "Fine."

A minute later, the door opens and those fantastic leggings are back on, hugging the thighs I've love to be between. Her hair's a tangled mess, and her face is flushed. "The freshly fucked look suits you. Keep it on so the men staring at your ass at the gym know you're taken."

She frowns like she thinks I'm being ridiculous, but there's a twinkle in her eyes while she's doing her best not to smile. She's been like this a lot since we started honeymooning—carefree and relaxed. Happy. I love it.

Hell, I love her.

I wish I could tell her and not freak her the fuck out. For now, I'm going to enjoy this time together. I lean down and give her lips a quick kiss before gently smacking her ass on my way into the bathroom. She pretends to be outraged, but the curl of laughter gives her away.

I clean up and straighten my clothes, though my pants are more wrinkled than before. I pull my golf clubs from the hall closet. With my lease up on my apartment in December, my father offered me his house. I wasn't sure I wanted to live in the same place I grew up in, the one my mom was sick in, but it's hard to pass up a great house that's paid for. Plus, I really didn't like the idea of selling it. Since Dad moved in with Kathleen, we decided to make it our honeymoon house. And I really love having Lainey here with me. I've talked to her about what I'd like to do to update it, and she even went with me to the paint store to pick out swatches, which are taped up on the walls. I'd be lying to myself if I said I didn't want to make this place *ours*.

When I return to the living room, Lainey has her shoes on and her overnight bag over her shoulder.

"You could leave some clothes here so you're not going back every day," I offer, wishing she'd move in with me. I want her here, every night curled up in my arms, and every morning when I wake.

Her smile dims as she seems to think this over. "I suppose I could do that. I'd be living out of a suitcase if this was a real honeymoon."

I wish the fact she doesn't think this is real didn't sting. I just have to remind myself that this was our agreement—one I came up with. "Right."

"Okay, I need to go before Chandler gets here and sees my car." She opens the front door. "Oh, shit."

Lainey's curse has me looking up to see Eli leaning on the half wall of the front porch, starting a slow clap with a knowing smirk on his lips. Chandler's standing next to him, but his head's dipped, avoiding our gazes.

"Fuck," I mutter.

"I'd say," Eli says with a huge grin.

"How long have you been standing there?"

"I caught the whole show." He hooks his thumb toward Chandler. "This one plugged his ears and ran."

"Oh, my God." Lainey covers her face with her hands.

"Lainey, if we could avoid looking at each other for a few days, that would be great," Chandler says, his head still down.

"Works for me." She turns to me. "Bye."

Her gaze goes to my mouth like she wants to kiss me goodbye but decides against it. So, I grab her by the waist and press a quick kiss to her lips. "See you later."

The blush on her cheeks deepens and she rushes off. Once she's shut inside her car, Chandler looks at me. "What the fuck, man? You're supposed to be getting an annulment, *not having a freaking honeymoon.*"

"Whoa, wait!" Eli pushes off the wall. "You're fucking married?"

"Jesus." I run a hand down my face. I totally forgot to warn Chandler not to mention my marriage to Eli. I knew I should have canceled this tee time. Now I've got four-plus hours of listening to them giving me shit ahead of me. I go grab my clubs and step out on the porch.

"You got married in Vegas and never told me?" Eli demands. "That was over a week ago."

"Been a little busy."

Eli gives me a murderous look. "You couldn't come up for air from fucking your *wife* to give your best friend the news? Hell, I would have settled for a text."

Chandler groans. "Is it too early for beer?"

"It's beer o'clock as soon as we step on the golf course." And I'm having several.

"Thank God."

"Um, hello?" Eli waves a hand in my face. "Are you just going to ignore me?"

I sigh. "I'll tell you everything in the car if you'll stop fucking yapping at me."

Eli thankfully shuts up. Once we're in the car, I tell him everything about Vegas and fill them both in on what's happened since we got back—minus the sexy details.

"Wait. She wants an annulment, but you convinced her to have a honeymoon first?" Eli asks.

"It's not like I twisted her arm. She's a willing participant."

Chandler glances at me from the driver's seat. "You know this is an epically bad idea, don't you?"

"I don't know. Feels pretty good right now." I smirk at him, and he winces and shakes his head. Yeah, I'm in trouble. It's only been three days, and I already don't want this to end. I knew I was putting my heart on the line when I suggested it, I just have to hope that in the end, it'll remain intact.

We make it all the way to the ninth hole when I putt an Eagle before Lainey's brought up again.

"Damn, man. Married life clearly agrees with you. Your golf game's never been better," Eli says. "Or maybe it's all the regular p—"

"Stop." I glare at him.

"You realize I heard your dirty talk."

"Eli." I glare, my tone full of warning.

"Fine." He shoves his putter into his bag, and we all get into the cart.

"What exactly is your end game?" Chandler asks. He's on his third beer, so I'm now the cart driver. "Do you think Lainey will magically decide she wants to stay married after this so-called honeymoon?"

"I don't have an end game."

Chandler gives me a doubtful look. "Don't give me that. I know you don't want the annulment."

He's one-hundred percent correct, but I don't say anything. I love Lainey and I'm married to her. Why would I want to end it? Yeah, I get that it's too soon. That doesn't mean it won't work. She's my best friend. She's the best lover I've had by far. She's everything I've always wanted in a partner. I'm happy. She's happy. It's meant to be, damn it.

"See! I'm right." He points at me. "It's written all over your face."

I give him a look but remain quiet.

"The honeymoon will end, and the reality of the situation will come bearing down on her again. She's not going to change her mind, Ben," he says gently.

Okay, maybe that's the fear I refuse to recognize. Maybe I'm living in a fantasy. But maybe, just fucking maybe, the fantasy can become a new reality. One where we belong together.

National Happy Hour Day, Honeymoon Day 9 - November 12th

LAINEY

THE RED POPPY IS CRAZY BUSY. IT'S NATIONAL HAPPY HOUR DAY, and the people are out for it. It doesn't hurt that Ben has some awesome drink specials. Watching him mix cocktail after cocktail, how smoothly he moves behind the bar...

So. Fucking. Hot.

With Josie and Harper here with me, I'm doing my best not to drool. Thankfully, they're in the middle of some story, so I can take a moment to watch him.

He grabs the shaker and looks up, a scorching, dark look coming over his face as he starts shaking. I zero in on his folded-up sleeves and sexy forearms and immediately have to press my thighs together. He maneuvers the shaker in a jerk-off motion right as he finishes. My eyes go back to his face and his confident grin. He knows exactly what he's doing to me. He pours the drink and delivers it to the customer. A few minutes later I get a text.

BEN:

You like the way I shake, wife?

ME

You shake good. Real good.

I look up and see him smile at his phone.

BEN

Are you wet?

ME

Soaked.

BEN

Fuck. You weren't supposed to go that far. Now I'm going to have to mix drinks with a hard-on.

ME

Think you'll get a break? I can take care of that for you.

BEN

Jesus.

"WHAT ARE YOU SMILING AT?" Harper says, and I jerk my gaze up. She looks from me to Ben as he slips his phone into his pocket. "Are you two texting each other?"

"No."

She casts me a doubtful look. "Have you filed for an annulment yet?"

Thankfully, Chandler has kept our honeymoon under wraps. I think he's more worried about Harper having an aneurysm if she knew than he cares about protecting me. Harper is back in controlling mode. She sent me the link to get an annulment with instructions. Turns out we could have done it that last day if I'd stayed in Vegas.

I pick up my drink. "I'm working on it."

Just need to get through our fuckfest of a honeymoon first.

We've been going at it like the world's about to end. Even with our different schedules, we've managed to do it at least twice a day. We finally had to take off yesterday to give our naughty bits a rest. But that didn't stop me from sleeping in his bed last night. He slipped into bed at some god-awful hour in the morning, kissed my neck and promised to lick me awake. I woke up first, fully intending to let him sleep, but he pulled me onto his face and told me to suffocate him. I gladly did.

"I still can't believe you got married without me," Josie pouts. "I've waited my whole life to wear a bad bridesmaid dress and throw a raunchy bachelorette party."

"You can throw her an annulment party instead," Harper suggests with a pointed look at me.

I barely resist the urge to toss my drink at her. I'm getting really tired of her shit. Yes, the whole Vegas wedding was crazy and stupid. But it doesn't feel wrong anymore. Actually, every day I spend with Ben is starting to feel more and more right.

"Seriously, Lainey, it doesn't take this long to fill out a form. What's stopping you?"

My husband's amazing cock.

Oh, and the fact that I'm falling in love with him.

But I don't want my sister's head to explode. Or really admit to myself that this honeymoon has gotten completely out of hand.

"Harper, please stop. Ben and I are working on it."

She huffs a sigh. "You can't let Mom find out. This will kill her."

A tingle of guilt fills me. I do hate lying about all this. And the stronger my feelings for Ben get, the more I worry about how my mom would handle it. Would it really be the end of the world if we stay together?

Thankfully, Jan comes up with a second round of drinks and

distracts Harper and Josie away from my marriage. I glance back at the bar to see Ben talking with a woman. She's leaning over the bar, all up in his space, and my stomach clenches. I've gotten better with my knee-jerk reactions since Labor Day, but I can't seem to get rid of these queasy feelings when I see him flirt. The flirting I witness now is nowhere near what it used to be. It's light and sweet instead of leading and promising. He also got rid of the red napkins and pen, which this woman seems to have an issue with since there's a black napkin dangling from her fingers.

Seeing the black napkins for the first time had me ducking into the bathroom before he could see me burst into tears. We haven't talked about the gesture, but it was further proof that he's serious changing his flirty ways. That he's serious about me.

Lord, I'm in so much trouble with his man.

Whatever the woman says to Ben, it has him shaking his head. He flashes his hand and wiggles his ring finger at her. Fuck, that was so sexy. My pussy clenches as a swell of possessiveness rises in me.

She says something that makes his brows rise in surprise. But whatever it was, he didn't like it. He leans forward, says something with an intent expression before retreating with a smirk on his face that screams he's done with this conversation. But she apparently isn't because she pulls something out of her purse then quickly pops halfway over the bar and stuffs something into his shirt pocket.

Oh. Hell. No.

He backs away, his expression clearly annoyed, but she flounces off before he can respond. His gaze zeroes in on me, a slight panic widening his eyes.

I glance at the woman, now with her friends laughing. Our gazes catch and she stills, glancing between me and Ben before sending me a smile that's either flirty or cocky.

I look back at Ben, his whole body is rigid and emitting distress. I raise my brows at him and ease off the barstool. "Running to the bathroom," I toss to the table, not waiting for a response.

Before I can even get to his office door, he grabs me by the elbow and spins me around. His blue gaze penetrating as he takes in my face just before he opens his office and shuts us inside.

He cages me in between him and the door. "Talk to me."

"Is that what you really want?"

Confusion flashes across his face before determination takes over again.

"Wife." His voice is rough with warning and my pussy practically purrs. She's such a slut for the endearment.

I reach into his pocket and pull out a glossy business card, glancing at it "It seems Amy found a way around the black napkins."

"I didn't ask for that."

I hold his gaze. "I know."

His body relaxes enough to tell me he was worried. I twirl the card in between my fingers. "For a therapist, she doesn't seem to have any moral issues with hitting on a married man."

He smirks. "After she saw my ring, she told me my wife could watch."

I stiffen. And resist the urge to march to her table and go all UFC on her.

He plucks the card from my fingers, tears it into pieces and lets them fall to the floor. "I told her I only fuck my wife."

His hands grab my wrists, pinning them above my head. "Because my cock is yours. Only yours." He presses his hips into mine, letting me feel exactly what's mine.

My breath stutters.

"Feel that, wife? Every inch. It's all yours." He leans down, feathering kisses along my jaw and down my neck.

"Yes," I breathe as I allow him more access. "Such a good husband."

The sound he releases is deep and guttural. Animalistic. Fuck. I'm so turned on I'm feverish and lightheaded.

"You need to let me go."

He pulls back, his eyes questioning.

I give him a saucy look. "I can't show you good I own your cock unless I'm on my knees."

His fiery gaze goes dark. He releases my hands and I sink to my knees. He hisses a curse as his hands sink into my hair. I work his jeans and underwear until his cock springs free. I'm practically panting to have his cock in my mouth. I lean forward and lick him from base to tip.

His grip tightens. "Fuck, Lainey."

I swirl my tongue around his head, licking up his precum.

"That's it, baby. Own me."

I wrap my lips around him and suck hard before releasing him and very gently scraping my teeth against his velvety skin. He shudders, his fingers clenching my hair tighter.

I look up at him. "You want me to own this cock?"

"Yes."

"Then you're going to let me fuck it. Brace your hands on the door."

He groans as he follows my directions. I take his cock in my hands and slowly jerk him off. His hips thrust forward, and I stop. "Nope. You don't move."

He lets out a shuttered breath. "Yes, wife."

Fuck. I love it when he dominates me, but I had no idea how much it would turn me on to be the one who dominates him. My pussy's soaked and throbbing with need.

I press a chaste kiss to the head of his dick. "This cock is only mine," I say, then take it fully in mouth, sucking him deep into my throat.

He lets out a guttural moan and his body tenses, as if he's struggling to stop himself from moving. "That's it, wife. It's yours. Take it all."

I lick, suck, and use my hand on him until his body's vibrating with need. And that's when I release him.

"Lainey," he begs. I look up and his expression's part pain, part need.

"Now I'm going to let you fuck my mouth. But you aren't going to come until I do."

His gorgeous blue eyes are practically gone, his pupils are so blown. Everything in his demeanor shows how tattered his control is. And it makes my pussy throb harder.

"Yes, wife."

I almost come right then. Having him at my mercy like this is so damn sexy. He's mine. *Only mine.*

I shimmy my skirt up over my hips until my pussy's exposed, and he groans. "Fuck, you haven't been wearing underwear this whole time."

"Nope. And I'm so wet my thighs are slick."

He groans. "Open your mouth. *Now.*"

I smirk.

"Please, wife."

I lean forward and lick up the length of his cock. "My good husband," I open my mouth, and he grips his cock, feeding it in as his other hand tangles into my hair.

"My naughty wife. This cock was made for your perfect mouth."

I moan around him and his control snaps. He fucks me roughly, pushing his cock all the way to the back of my throat over and over. His grip on my hair becomes almost painful. But I love it. My pussy aches so much I might come from the coarse, raw sounds he's making. I love how crazy I make him.

I put my hand between my legs, and I'm so wet my fingers slip right off. I try again, and my clit's so sensitive it borders on pain, but it's a sweet one.

"Yes, rub that pussy. Damn, I can hear how wet you are. You like owning this cock, don't you, wife? Owning me."

I moan and he almost pulls out of me before sinking back deep in my mouth. I want to edge myself, forcing him to do the same, forcing him to wait before he takes his pleasure. But I can't. I need release. I need to feel his cum shoot down my throat.

"It's all yours, Lainey. Every inch. Every drop of cum. It's all fucking yours. Let me give it to you, baby. I want you to fucking suck me dry."

His words immediately push me over the edge. I cry out around him, waves of pleasure crashing through me over and over. He groans, and I feel him swell inside me just before his cum fills my mouth. His thrusts become harder and faster as he rides out his climax and I suck every drop of him down. When he pulls out, he's shuddering and bracing heavily against the door, his breath labored. After a moment, he pulls me up and presses me into the door, taking my mouth in a savage kiss.

He rips his mouth away from me so roughly, it's as if he has to make himself do it or he never would. "I like tasting me on you." He takes my chin and gently tilts it down so I'm looking between us.

"Look," he demands. His cock is still jutting out, glistening from my mouth with a ring of red at the base from my lipstick. "Look at how you marked me, wife. So fucking pretty."

My God. Every time he opens his mouth, he wrecks me.

He lets go of me, tucks his cock back into his boxer briefs, and pulls his jeans up. "It's going to stay like that the rest of the night."

Fuck.

Once he's dressed, he kisses me roughly again, but when he pulls away this time, he presses his forehead to mine. "I'm yours."

He tugs the hair at the base of my head as an exclamation mark on his statement before he moves around me and leaves. I brace myself against the door and bring a shaking hand to my lips, the delicate skin tingling and swollen from being used so thoroughly. I have no idea how I'm supposed to recover from this. I don't know if I will. Or want to.

I eventually use his bathroom to wash up. My lips are puffy and lipstick's smeared. My mascara's smudged, and without a brush, there's not much I can do to my hair. I look thoroughly fucked. I smirk at my image and leave his office.

As soon as I get back into the main room, I lock eyes with Amy. I use my thumb to wipe the side of my mouth and let it trace my bottom lip before giving her a sly grin. Her cheeks bloom red, and she quickly looks away.

I suppress a laugh as I turn toward my table and find Harper looking at me with a mixture of anger and hurt. She jerks out of her seat and storms out through the patio doors.

Shit.

Time to face the music. I follow her out and find her pacing in an empty corner before she whips to face. "What the hell are you doing, Lainey?" Tears glisten in her eyes and her voice is full of anguish. My God, you'd think I just kicked a puppy, not fucked my own husband. "Well, now I know exactly what you and Ben are working out before you sign the papers."

"We decided to have a sort of honeymoon first."

Her expression turns incredulous. "Are you fucking kidding me?"

"It's only for two weeks. You know, to get it out of our systems."

She pushes her hands through her hair and turns away from me before turning back. "You're delusional if you think this is no big deal."

I don't appreciate the dig, but there's no denying she's right. Ben is nowhere near out of my system—and I don't think he ever will be.

I take a breath. "Okay, yeah, I like him. Would it really be so horrible if we date?"

Her eyes practically bug out. "Date? You're *married*."

"We can figure that out."

She shakes her head. "I knew you were going to make Mom lose another good guy. I knew you would fuck this up for her and crush her heart all over again."

"What the hell are you talking about?" I know for a fact I never made my mom lose a good guy.

"Danny!"

Danny? I search my brain for who she's talking about, and it hits me she's talking about the guy I overheard on the phone with another woman. It was the last guy I got rid of before I confessed what I'd been doing to Mom.

"He was cheating on her."

"No. You were wrong. You overheard him talking to his daughter."

My stomach twists. "Mom never told me he had a kid."

"She was young. They were taking it slow with her."

"Okay. That doesn't mean I crushed Mom's heart. They hadn't been dating that long. A few weeks?"

Harper huffs a laugh. "They'd been talking for months before they decided to start dating. They were in love."

I shake my head. No, that can be right. I would have known.

"They worked together. That's how they met. She broke it off with him when everything blew up. He begged her to give him a chance to prove to you that he was serious about her. Eventually, she quit because it was too hard to see him every day and not be with him."

"Why didn't she tell me all this? How do you know all this?"

"I visited when you were away, and she started drinking wine then crying and it all came out. He'd texted her earlier that day telling her still missed her and it had been a year since they broke up. The next morning, she begged me not to tell you."

I think I'm going to be sick. A whole year and he still...

"By the time you went to college, he'd moved on and was engaged. It killed her all over again."

Tears blur my vision.

"Do you see now why I kept warning you away from Ben? If this goes wrong, you're going to break her heart all over again. I can't watch her sink back into that kind of despair. It was hard enough to pull her out then, she's married now. If she loses her husband because of you—"

"Stop!" I press my hand to my chest, but it does nothing to ease the pain piercing through my heart.

"Lainey..."

"It's not serious. It's just sex. I've got it under control, okay?"

It might be the biggest lie I've ever told, but maybe the more I repeat it, the more I'll make it true.

National Unfriend Day, Honeymoon Day 14 - November 17th

BEN

I LAY IN BED WITH LAINEY CURLED NEXT TO ME. THE ONLY LIGHT IN the room is the glow of my digital clock. It might not actually tick, but it's all I can hear. Each passing minute—each second—feels like a vice tightening around my heart. At the stroke of midnight, will she leave me? Do I get to keep her until morning? Do I dare confess my feelings?

In a twisted version of irony fucking me over, it's National Unfriend Day.

The day is actually about self-care and eliminating anyone on social media who doesn't bring you joy. But nothing about the holiday feels freeing for me—not when I have this fear wrapped around my throat that I'm about to lose the most important person in my life.

Things shifted between us on National Happy Hour Day. When we were in my office together, it felt like we were finally on the same page. That we'd claimed each other and had no plans to let go. Then something happened and it's felt like she's been holding back ever since, even if she's still staying in my bed every night.

Lainey stirs, her leg draping further over mine. Her hand

starts moving slowly up and down my chest. We'd fallen into exhaustion after our last bout though I've only pretended to sleep.

We've been frenzied and desperate for each other from the moment we woke up, as if we were racing the clock, though neither of us acknowledged it.

Lainey shifts again, curling into me. I move so our limbs tangle and our mouths find each other like a magnetic pull. This kiss is different than the others we've shared these last several days, unhurried and full of the emotions she's been denying. She rolls over me until her body straddles mine, and my hands dive into her hair as I deepen the kiss. She opens her legs further and reaches down, lining my cock with her pussy. I push my hips into her as she sinks down on me. Her wet heat clenching around me is the best fucking thing in the world.

We don't move but stay like that, simply needing to be connected. Our kiss softens as we savor each taste, each gentle meet of our lips. I trail my lips down her jaw to the column of her throat before returning to her mouth. The kiss ends slowly, our faces still close as her hand comes up, cupping my cheek.

With our gazes locked, she starts moving. She fucks me slowly, letting my cock almost slide out of her before sinking back down. Tiny whimpers escape her as she sits up and rides me. She's fucking glorious with her head thrown back and her gorgeous tits thrust forward as she grinds down on me. Unable to help myself, I grip her hips and drive up into her. She lets out a loud, broken moan, then falls back down, bracing herself over my chest, and we curl into each other, our hips thrusting together.

Our breaths mingle as our foreheads meet. This isn't like any other time we've fucked. It's more. Sensual. Emotional. Vulnerable.

True.

I take her mouth again and pour all my certainty—my *love*—into the kiss. As if she understands, she kisses me back with a ferocity that begs for more. A spike of pleasure shoots up my spine, pure need urging us both, fueling us to move faster. Harder.

"Lainey..." I moan against her lips, unable to hold back much longer.

"Yes...yes...now..." She comes around my cock, her body shattering over me. It's so fucking good I explode inside her.

"Fuck...Lainey..." I shudder, letting her pussy drain every ounce of cum inside me. "Take it. Take all of me."

She cries out even louder as she continues to ride me before slowly coming to a stop, then slumps into me.

I wrap my arm around her, gently squeezing her into me as our breathing calms. That felt life-altering so I should be floating on cloud nine. Instead, the bliss is shadowed by a fear working its way around my heart that things aren't going to work out the way I want. When she places a gentle kiss on my chest, I squeeze my eyes shut.

Don't leave.

But my fear's realized when she eases off my body, leaving me cold and anxious. The bed lightens as she gets off. I open my eyes and push up on my elbows as she picks up the T-shirt she's been wearing all day—my shirt.

"Want breakfast?"

She looks over her shoulder at me, then glances at the clock. "At eleven-thirty at night?"

I grin at her. "We've burned more calories than we've eaten today."

She smiles at that, but it's soft—almost reluctant. Six hours ago, she would have laughed.

She grabs her underwear from the floor and sits back on bed as she shimmies them on. "I should go."

"No. You should stay."

She doesn't move but doesn't look back at me. My heart hammers in my chest as I wait for her to respond.

"Ben...this is our last day, and you know it. Honeymoon's over."

I take a fortifying breath and decide to shoot my shot. "That doesn't mean we have to be over. What if we talk to our parents about us?"

She stiffens. "No."

"Lainey—"

"Ben, this was only two weeks. To get it out of our systems." She looks back at me with an expression I'm all too familiar with. Not long ago, I was the one giving women this look. I was the one who never saw things as anything more than temporary, and now I'm the one begging for a commitment. Karma really is a bitch. "There's no us."

Those words spear me right in the heart, but I push past the pain and move until I'm right behind her, holding her gaze. "We've been us-ing for much longer than two weeks and you know it. Am I out of your system?"

Her mouth flattens, and she looks away.

"Exactly. You're sure as hell not out of mine." I try to pull her into me, but she shrugs out of my hold and stands.

"It's time to move on and end this farce of a marriage, Ben."

"Farce? Has any of this felt like a joke? I think we've been pretty good at marriage so far."

She laughs, though it's clear she's not amused. "That's because all we've done is fuck. There's a lot more to marriage than good sex."

"*Phenomenal* sex. And I know that. I think—"

She shakes her head. "That's the problem. We didn't think. Our marriage was a prank gone wrong. None of this was serious."

Fuck. Everything out of her mouth is like a sledgehammer to the chest. "Are you fucking kidding me? How can you say that, especially after what just happened in this bed? This was serious before we ever got married, and you damn well know it."

A moment of strained silence falls between us before she finally whispers. "It's not that simple."

She walks away, finding her pants and slipping them on. Then she starts filling her bag up. Each item she stuffs inside breaks another piece of my heart.

I get out of bed, shuck on my sweatpants, and go to her and turn her so she's facing me, but she keeps her head down.

"It *is* that simple. You want me. You have feelings for me but are too fucking scared to admit it." I tip her chin up, forcing her to look at me. "Stop running and tell me the truth."

Her eyes turn glassy, but there's a stubborn tilt to her chin. "I'm not running."

"The fuck you aren't. Tell me you don't want this."

She closes her eyes. Tears seep through and trail down her cheeks. "Ben...please."

My hands shake, frustration and anger bubbling inside me. "You have to stop hiding behind our parents' relationship. This—"

Her eyes snap open. "Ben, *stop*. My mom's finally happy, and she doesn't want us together. I can't fuck this up. Not anymore than I've already done. I was wrong about one of her guys in high school. He loved her and I took that away from her. *I can't be wrong again.*"

Wrong again? What does that mean?

She pushes away from me and goes back to packing, and I can practically feel my heart fracture. Maybe I need to stop dancing around the truth and tell her how I feel. She needs to know she can walk away tonight, but it won't change that I love her. That I know in my soul we belong together.

I reach for her hand, but she retreats from my grasp.

"Lainey, I—"

"Ben, stop pushing."

"Hear me—"

"Acnestis!"

The word strikes like the thrust of a sword. Almost silently but with sharp precision. An agonizing numbness fills me. Of all the times she's used the safe word, she's never wielded it as a weapon. Maybe I forced her hand, pushing her until it was an act of desperation. But, fuck, her aim was true.

And there's nothing I can do but watch her walk away.

National Have a Bad Day Day

NOVEMBER 19TH

Harper has put you in charge of dessert for Thanksgiving. She assumes picking up a pumpkin pie from the store will be easy enough.

BEN

I'm not coming.

You're coming.

BEN

No. I'm not.

You have to. It's the first Thanksgiving since Mike and Kathleen got married. Harper's going out of her mind trying to make everything perfect.

BEN

I would think Harper would love that I'm not there. I'm not exactly her favorite person right now.

CHANDLER

She might think y'all are making a big mistake, but this is Thanksgiving. All family required. She just wants y'all to pretend you aren't hugging. And married.

BEN

We're not.

CHANDLER

Not married?

BEN

Not hugging.

CHANDLER

Since when?

BEN

Two days ago.

CHANDLER

Oh. What happened?

BEN

Honeymoon's over.

CHANDLER

Wow, you're a fountain of information.

BEN

What's there to say? We were fucking, now we're not. The annulment papers hit my inbox today, so the marriage will be over soon. Are we done now?

CHANDLER

Sure. Don't forget the pumpkin pie.

BEN

You can tell Harper she can go shove her pumpkin pie.

CHANDLER

Hey, I get you're upset, but don't make me leave work to kick your ass.

BEN

Sorry. It's National Have a Bad Day Day, and I'm having one.

CHANDLER

You get a pass this time. Try that shit again, and we'll have a problem. Happy Have a Bad Day Day. See you Thursday. With pumpkin pie.

BEN

I like apple.

CHANDLER

IDGAF as long as you bring a pumpkin one; otherwise, Thursday will be Bad Day Day— Harper style.

BEN

shudders

Thanksgiving

WALKING AWAY FROM BEN WAS THE HARDEST THING I'VE EVER done. But I can't be selfish anymore. Knowing I truly ruined my mom's happiness once has been like a knife constantly twisting in my heart. I promised her I would stay away from Ben, that I wouldn't mess this up for her, then broke that promise without a second thought. I can't let another one of my mistakes turn into devastating consequences.

It doesn't matter that Ben doesn't feel like a mistake. I can't take that risk. Not when I'm always wrong.

So, I filled out the annulment papers and sent them to Ben then promptly ran to the bathroom and threw up. He hasn't responded and I don't know if it's like a soothing balm to my aching heart or makes me want to scream until I have no voice. I need him to sign it. To end this pain.

I'm just glad my body knew it needed to be in protective mode today and has gone completely numb. I'll see him for the first time since that night, and only with the pain anesthetized can I face him and pretend I'm not shattered in front of our parents.

It'll also make me forget that I'm here with the date from hell.

Yeah, bringing a holidate to Thanksgiving is a dick move, but my boss forced my hand. She handpicked the date since she wanted me to run the Turkey Trot this morning, and invited him to *my* Thanksgiving dinner—a fact I learned *after* the race. What was I supposed to do? It's my freaking job.

A job I'm hating more and more with every holidate I have, and Pete might be my worst one yet. I'd rather poke my own eye out than spend another minute with him. I've never run a race in my life, and my boss decided to pair me with a running enthusiast. Pete spent the whole trot running ahead then coming back to "tease" me about how slow I am—while criticizing everything from my running gait to the adorable Thanksgiving themed outfit I was wearing. Fucking asshole.

I lift the mimosa to my lips and drain half. I put too much OJ in this thing.

Harper gives me a death glare.

We haven't exactly talked since that night at Red Poppy so bringing a surprise guest to Thanksgiving dinner has thrown her into a complete tizzy. I've tried to help, but all she's done is give me the silent treatment and flit around me, not letting me do anything.

I would go into the living room and watch football, but that's where Pete is. So, here I am in the kitchen, numbing the pain as quickly as I can.

"Are you going to get drunk or actually help?" Harper snaps.

I point at her drink that's half gone. "You're having one too. And I've been here for fifteen minutes, but you've barely acknowledged me. What do you want me to do?"

Harper sighs and looks around the kitchen as if she's trying to figure out what I'm capable of doing and not screwing up.

"You can butter the rolls. And mash the potatoes when they're ready."

Freaking Cassie could handle that. My sister really needs to unclench, but I don't say anything and get to work. I ignore the fact she's eyeing me to make sure I butter bread properly. She eventually turns her attention to the casserole she's preparing. The welcome silence lasts all of ten seconds.

"I can't believe you brought a date to Thanksgiving. Our stepbrother, *whom you're married to*, will be here any minute. After all I told you the other night, you really thought getting a date would be the best course of action. Are you insane?"

"Geez, Harper, I thought you'd be happy I was with someone other than Ben." I drain the rest of my mimosa.

"Lainey," she says in warning.

"Harper." I serve her tone right back.

She aggressively starts chopping an onion. "You could have told me you were bringing someone instead of just showing up with him."

"I told you I didn't know until two hours ago, and I couldn't exactly turn him away. It's for work."

"You couldn't have texted me?"

Instead of answering, I grab the bottle of champagne from the ice bucket and pour another glass.

She shakes her head. "What the hell were you thinking? Oh, I'll bring a date to Thanksgiving where the husband I fucked for two weeks will be sitting across the table from me. It'll be fine."

"I'm actually doing my damnedest not to think. Or feel." I take a healthy sip of my mimosa. Though can you really call it that without the orange juice?

Harper looks at me and her expression softens. Suddenly, I feel like crying. For days, I've felt gutted. I could really use my sister right now.

But she doesn't come to me.

She sets down the knife. "That's the thing, Lainey," she says softly. "You never think. You just make one impulsive decision after another. Maybe if you stopped and thought things through, you wouldn't keep getting it wrong. Seriously, who makes sure to get a real marriage license for a prank marriage? If you put that much effort into any other aspect of your life, you might actually be succeeding instead of floundering from one ridiculous job to another and dating all the wrong men."

Whatever sentimental sisterly feelings I have evaporates. She took every single one of my insecurities along with my already raw emotions and threw them in a shredder to make sure I felt every shred of pain.

Well, unfortunately for her, she also stirred my anger. And that emotion is definitely one I can handle.

"So sorry, we can't all be *perfect* like you."

"I'm not perfect. It's just—"

"Oh, trust me, I *know*."

Her brows snap together. "What the hell does that mean?"

"It means you're the last person who should be casting stones, and you know it."

Harper's eyes narrow in anger, but I also see a flash of hurt. I refuse to feel bad. Not after what she said to me. I'm fucking sick of her and her righteousness, especially when she's no saint.

"At least I learn from my mistakes. Instead of making them over and over again."

"God, you're such a bitch. I have no idea why Chandler hasn't left you yet."

My arrow strikes deep. Harper stills. Anger and hurt radiate off her. She's not the only one who can tap into someone's greatest fears.

"Get the fuck out of my kitchen." Her voice sounds calm, but her composure's hanging by a thread.

I grab the bottle of bubbly and my glass. "Gladly."

I join Pete and Chandler in the living room. Chandler takes one look at me and the bottle in my hand and immediately heads to the kitchen.

Pete glances at his smart watch. "When are we going to eat?"

"I don't know." I flop back into the cushions. "Who's playing?"

He looks at me like I've asked the dumbest question in the world. "Dallas. They play every Thanksgiving."

His condescending tone makes me want to pour my champagne over his head, but I'm not wasting good bubbly on him.

"Right." I give him a tight smile.

Suddenly, his arm goes around the back of the sofa and he pulls me into him. What the hell? He's barely been civil to me all day, and now he's trying to cop a move?

"You see, Dallas and Detroit play every Thanksgiving, but not each other." He continues to mansplain football to me as if I've never seen a game. I'm starting to think my boss hates me. This guy is a complete douche.

Thankfully, Mom and Mike show up so I'm able to escape his embrace. I introduce Pete to them, and they both seem confused I brought a date, but my mom quickly looks thrilled. I can't quite get a grip on Mike, but he engages Pete in conversation about the football game, so I take advantage of the distraction to grab the champagne bottle and slip from the room. With my mom in the kitchen with Harper, I seek out Cassie in her playroom.

Coloring with Cassie turns out to be the perfect distraction. Even though I polished off the bottle of bubbly, I've done a damn good job of staying inside the lines. When Cassie decides the pictures could use glitter, I don't stop her. This earns me a frustrated look from Chandler when he checks on us. I'll feel bad about it tomorrow. Today, I'm going to enjoy the satisfaction of hearing Harper shriek as soon as she sees her glitter-bombed daughter.

I head to the kitchen since Harper is now preoccupied and find a bottle of wine. I pop the cork and look around for my glass. When I don't see it anywhere, I decide I don't need one. I return to the living room, where Mike and Pete are still watching the game. I'm pretty sure my mom is helping Harper and Chandler with the glitter situation.

"Who's winning?" I tip up the bottle.

"Is that a different bottle?" Pete asks.

"Yeah," I answer as if he was stupid for asking.

The doorbell rings and stops him from replying. Mike gets up to answer it, and I don't know why it surprises me to see Ben walk in. But the sight of him steals my breath and my traitorous heart lurches so hard, it's as if it's reaching for him. He looks good—except his eyes look as tired and drawn as mine.

His dad gives him a hug and says something I can't hear. Ben looks at me, and I raise my bottle in toast and take another drink. Then his gaze flicks to the couch.

Pete stands. "Hey, I'm Pete."

Ben ignores his extended hand and frowns at me. "You brought a holidate to Thanksgiving?"

"It's a holiday, Ben."

His mouth flattens before he shifts the pies in his hands and shakes Pete's hand. "Hey, man."

"Now that everyone's here, think we'll eat soon?" Pete asks generally to the room though his gaze falls on me.

"Probably," I reply, and take another healthy swig.

"Good. I want to eat before you pass out at the table."

Ben's shoulders stiffen, and his gaze turns hard. "What the fu—"

"Ben! So glad you could make it." Harper sweeps into the

room. She gives him a hug, and he hands over the pies, which she gushes over.

"Oh, good. Miss Perfect is okay that they're store-bought."

Harper glares at me. Ben takes me in again, his brows furrowed. "What happened between you two?"

Harper waves a hand, dismissing the question. "Dinner's almost ready. Just have to mash the potatoes."

I face her. "That was my job."

"Well, you've been preoccupied with booze and glitter. And your *date*." She gives me a tight smile.

"*You* kicked me out of the kitchen. I can handle mashing potatoes."

Not letting her protest, I go to the kitchen and find the pot of potatoes already cooked and ready to be mashed. Harper comes in, and I'm fully expecting her to try to stop me, but she doesn't. I mash while she goes in and out of the room to set the table.

When all's done, I head to the dining room and bring the wine bottle with me. I remove the wine glass beside my plate and replace it with the bottle. "I don't need this," I hold out the glass to Ben, who's now standing next to me. He gives me a grim look as he takes it.

I settle in my chair as Pete takes the one on the other side of me. I suppress a shudder. He doesn't bother looking at me, as he's too busy taking in all the food on the table. This guy must really love Thanksgiving.

Harper comes in. "Oh, good. Y'all found your seats," she says as if sitting me between Ben and Pete is her evil plan coming to fruition.

"Nice and cozy," I reply, refusing to show her my irritation that I'm sitting between my husband and my date.

Harper scowls and heads back to kitchen. I look over at my mom; her expression is a combination of disappointment and embarrassment. I grab my napkin, slowly unroll it, and set it in my lap, unable to look up. I know I'm behaving badly. I can't seem to stop. Or care.

"Lainey, what's going on with you and Harper?" My mom leans forward, her voice soft but full of the emotion reflected on her face.

"Nothing."

Her mouth flattens. "Whatever it is, it's enough. It's Thanksgiving."

Harper returns with the rolls while Chandler brings in Cassie in a completely different outfit and straps her into her booster seat. An awkward silence falls over the table once everyone is seated.

Mike clears his throat. "How about a prayer?"

Everyone murmurs their agreement. We all bow our heads, though Harper's gaze clashes with mine and we glower at each other. As Mike goes on about the importance of family and how thankful he is, I steeple my hands as if praying, then slowly bend all my fingers except the middle ones which I turn toward Harper.

"Amen," Mike says. and we all repeat it.

I pick up my wine bottle and toast it to Harper. She picks up her wine glass in a way that has her middle finger aimed toward me.

Everyone starts passing around dishes and filling their plates. The conversation turns to how good everything tastes.

"This cornbread dressing is amazing, Harper," Mike says.

"Yeah, it's *perfect*," I say, and give Harper an overly sweet smile.

"Thanks." She returns my smile. "Sorry the potatoes are lumpy. Mashing potatoes isn't that hard, but of course, Lainey manages to get it wrong."

The whole table freezes, and the tension's thicker than the gravy. That's it. She wants a war? I'll give it to her.

"At least I'm honest about my imperfections." I look at my mom. "Remember when I visited Harper at college during her freshman year?"

"Lainey!" Harper hisses, the grip around her knife so tight I can see the white in her knuckles.

"Come on, honey. You can watch *Tangled* while you eat." Chandler quickly sweeps up Cassie and disappears.

"Showed up to her dorm to find out she wasn't living there. No, Miss Perfect was shacked up with *two* guys, and they weren't just roommates, if you know what I mean."

My mom gasps as Harper shoots up, her face red. "You fucking bitch!"

I stand and face off with her. "That's right, Harper had her own little reverse harem going on."

An animalistic sound leaves Harper's throat before she shouts, "Lainey and Ben got married in Vegas!"

As soon as the words are out of her mouth, she realizes what she's done. I almost laugh. For all her talk about me screwing up, she's the one that spills the beans to Mom.

But I can't take any satisfaction in it when my mom makes another anguished sound. I glance at her and she's white as a sheet. Mike looks equally shell-shocked.

"Wait! You're married?" Pete stands, looking at me with disdain.

"Oh, shit," Chandler mutters, as he returns without Cassie.

"Please tell me that isn't true," my mom says to me, her eyes glassy.

Before I can answer my mom, Pete stands "You're married to your stepbrother and on a date with me. What is wrong with you? Should have known you were crazy when you showed up to the race in a turkey tutu."

Another gasp fills the room.

In a blink, Ben is in between us. "Talk to my wife like that again, and you're going to be eating Thanksgiving dinner through a tube."

Pete raises his hands up in surrender, stepping away from the table. "You're all crazy." Then he sneers at me like I'm trash. "I only agreed to this date for the food anyway."

All of a sudden, Pete's face is covered in cranberry sauce and dressing. I turn to see Harper and Chandler staring at Pete with murderous expressions, their hands dripping with berries and clumps of cornbread.

Holy shit.

"Take it to go, asshole," my sister yells, and I almost laugh out loud.

Mike closes in on Pete and points his half-eaten turkey leg at him like a sword "You need to leave. *Now.*"

Pete wipes food away from his eyes and dumps it on the floor. "Gladly. Fuck you all."

As soon as he turns his back, we all grab food and hurl it his way, hitting him in the back. Even my mom threw a roll at him. He pauses then blazes for the door, slamming it behind him.

My mom finally breaks the silence. "Please tell me this is all joke. You two really didn't get married."

I sigh. "It was a mistake. It was supposed to be a prank on Harper, that's it. We're getting it annulled."

"Not before they decided to have a honeymoon and fuck for two weeks," Harper adds.

"Jesus." Ben wipes his clean hand over his face.

Whatever truce we had over our hatred of Pete is over. "At least I fucked my husband and not two guys at the same time."

Next thing I know, cornbread dressing strikes my face. "Brother fucker!"

"Step!" Both Ben and I yell. I grab two handfuls of mashed potatoes and hurl them her way. "Suck on my lumpy potatoes, Miss Not So Perfect."

It's now an all-out war. We're throwing food at each other and slinging insults even faster. An arm wraps around my waist, and I'm yanked away from the table.

"Control your wife," Ben orders, as Chandler grabs Harper to stop her from crawling over the table to get to me.

"Control yours!" Chandler fires back. "She started it!"

"Oh, like Harper's innocent. She must have started in on Lainey as soon as she walked in, or she wouldn't be downing wine from the bottle."

"Hey!" I fire at Ben, as a blob of cranberry sauce hits him in the face. I catch Chandler with his hand in the crystal bowl.

"That's it," Ben growls. Keeping his hold on me, he grabs a handful of mashed potatoes and hurls them across the table, hitting Chandler in the chin. Harper nails me in the chest with dressing, suddenly, it's complete chaos. Food is flying everywhere. We're all screaming at each other. Mom and Mike are yelling at us to stop, but we're too far gone.

Chandler flings more cranberry sauce at Ben. "If you'd gotten this annulled right away, none of this would be happening."

Ben dodges the sauce, throwing me off kilter as I grab more potatoes to throw at Harper.

"I couldn't!"

"Why not?" Harper yells.

"Because I'm in love with her!"

Suddenly, it's as if a bomb dropped in the middle of the room. The silence is deafening, save for my pounding heart. Yet, it doesn't drown out Ben's words. The incessant beats somehow amplify them.

Until their echo is all I hear.

Harper's raised hand full of dressing falls and she slumps in Chandler's arms. I glance at our parents, standing back from the table, looking as stunned as I feel. My body goes limp, and Ben tugs me against his chest. I turn, needing to see his face, needing to confirm he really said those words. The mix of fear and honesty in his expression tells me I heard him correctly.

"You can't love me," I whisper, fearing he'll take it back.

His expression softens. "I can." He cups my jaw, using his thumb to swipe away errant food. "I do. You can call our marriage a lot of things, but it's not a mistake. I can't think of my future without you in it."

"Look at what this marriage has done." I gesture to the food carnage scattered across the room.

"So, our first Thanksgiving was a little bumpy."

I huff out a laugh, unable not to. "Don't you mean lumpy?"

He smiles. "See? We're already laughing about it."

I shake my head. "But it's not funny. This was horrible and mean and..." Tears fill my eyes. I can't even look at my sister right now. "It won't work. Then we'll ruin their marriage, and I can't have that on me. I *can't*. Not when I've already ruined my mom's happiness once."

"Lainey..." my mom says.

I look at her. "Harper told me about Danny. How I messed up. And I'm so sorry, Mom. I never meant to keep you from someone you loved."

My mom's silent tears turn to sobs, and she buries her face in her hands.

"See," I say, turning back to Ben. "Look at what I've done."

"No. That's not about us. We haven't done anything wrong. We're just two people who have fallen for each other."

"But I'm always wrong. I've been wrong about every job I've had. I was wrong about Isaac and every other guy I've dated. Danny."

"But you're not wrong about me."

"You don't know that."

His jaw clenches. "I do know that, Lainey. And you fucking

do too if you would just stop listening to your insecurities and the people who keep throwing them in your face." He glances at my sister and my mom before bringing looking back to me with an impassioned gaze "Listen to your heart."

"I can't. That's led me to hurting people I care about and getting hurt myself. If I would stop and think—"

"Lainey, you're focusing on the wrong mistakes." He takes my hands in his. "Your heart hasn't steered you wrong. It steered you away from things that didn't fit, and right to where you belong. It steered you to me."

Tears blur my vision.

"Nothing between us has been a mistake, Lainey. And you know it. All you have to do is admit it."

The sounds of my mom crying. The erratic beat of my heart. The fear that whatever I do, it's going to be wrong. It's all lodged itself in my throat, choking me. Suffocating me. Why can't I trust the words I want to say?

As my anguished silence stretches, Ben's expression goes from hopeful to devastated to cold detachment. My heart cracks as he releases my hands and steps away, and I know I just made my greatest mistake yet.

Tears pour down my cheeks as the chokehold on my throat releases and all the feelings I've been denying myself rush forth. I grab his shirt to stop him. "Ben—"

"Acnestis."

I inhale sharply. He's never used our safe word.

"No." The resolve in his voice has my stomach sinking. "You've told me over and over all these months and I didn't listen. But your silence...it's loud and clear. Acnestis." The word comes out soft, but firm.

He let me go every time I said it, so I do the same.

I unclench my fingers from his shirt and step back. I'm vaguely aware of him walking away and the sound of the front door opening then the finality of it closing. The next thing I know I'm sprinting through the house and closing myself in the bathroom and emptying the contents of my stomach. For the second time in a week, I curl up in a puddle of tears on a cold bathroom floor.

"WAKE UP, LAINEY."

I feel a nudge on my shoulder as I blink my eyes open. I'm still on the bathroom floor and only the little bit of pride I have left has me pushing up to sitting. Because honestly, I'd rather not move. I wish I could melt through the floor and disappear. I look up to see my mom squatting down trying to help me up.

"I can do it," I say softly and get myself to standing. I wince when I see my reflection in the mirror. I'm still covered in food from our fight. Now it's all caked on and crusty.

"Come on, I'm driving you home."

I don't question her, and follow. I'm surprised the house is mostly dark, it's even dark outside.

"What time is it?"

"Eight."

Damn. I slept on the bathroom floor for about five hours. What a disaster I am. And I owe my mom a big apology. An explanation. Instead, I get in the car, fasten my seatbelt, and stay silent. It's apparently my M-O today.

Thankfully, my mom doesn't seem to want to talk any more than I do. When we arrive at my apartment, she walks me inside, guiding me to my bathroom. "Take a shower and change."

Her tone has been soft and gentle this whole time which makes it really hard to judge where she's at with the whole *Thanksgiving food fight and married to my stepbrother* thing. I stand under a stream of hot water and stare into space, trying not to think of all the ways I screwed up today. I turn off the water when it turns cold. My skin is red and raw from how long was in the shower and it takes all my energy to get dressed and not crawl into bed to let oblivion take me.

Instead, I return to the living room where my mom is sitting on the couch with two mugs of tea on the coffee table.

"It's Chamomile. Hopefully, it's not too cold now."

I pick up the cup and take a sip of the lukewarm tea. "It's fine. Thanks."

We stay like that for a while before I finally work up the courage to speak. "I'm sorry."

"You're going to have to be specific. Drinking wine by the bottle? Ruining Thanksgiving with a food fight? Revealing your sister's secrets? Lying about your feelings for Ben?"

"All of it. And what I did to you in high school." I swallow. "Most of all, I'm sorry if I ruined things between you and Mike."

My mom lets out a long sigh. "Lainey...actually, I owe you an apology. I was so ashamed I wasn't the mother you and your sister needed, I couldn't even apologize or tell you that I'm glad you took the actions you did. Yes, Danny and I had feelings for each other, and I did struggle with missing out on that, but you were always more important. I had to step up and prove to you that you and your sister are my world. My number one priority. Because you are. I'll never forgive myself for making you doubt that."

"Mom, I forgive you. Please don't—"

"Baby, I love you for that. But this is on me. I've gone through a lot of therapy, and I've forgiven myself for a lot, but this is one thing that I've accepted but can't quite forgive. And I'm okay with that. What I'm not okay with is that I got caught up in old insecurities when I saw you and Ben getting close."

I swallow as tears threaten again. "I really did try to stop what was happening. I never wanted to hurt you. Or you to think that I was purposely trying to."

My mom puts her mug on the table then does the same with mine before taking my hands. "I never thought that. I let my fears take over. When Mike came along, and it was all going so perfectly, I kept waiting for something to come along and mess it up. I latched onto you and Ben. It was wrong. I was wrong."

Tears fill her eyes. "Seeing you two together today...I couldn't believe I was so selfish that I was keeping my daughter from the man she loves. Yeah, I was scared at how Mike would react, but quickly realized it didn't matter. Ben was right. What's between you two has nothing to do with us. Mike and I will be just fine. We did have some big conversations this afternoon and agreed we could use some couples therapy to help us communicate with each other. Mostly, we're hurting for our children."

"I fucked up, Mom. I love him and was too afraid to admit it. And now I've lost him."

"Oh honey," she pulls me into her and hugs me tightly before pulling back and taking my face in her hands. "If I've learned anything in this life, it's never too late to right a wrong."

Black Friday

LAINEY

I stare at my television screen. The CTU game's on, but I couldn't recall a single play. I can't even focus on the score to see who's winning. All I can do is relive everything that happened yesterday and today's repercussions.

One, I lost my job. Pete complained about the food fight, and I woke up to an email terminating me, effective immediately. While being unemployed will eventually cause me to panic, I can't seem to give a fuck right now. I was planning to quit in the new year anyway.

Two, how I treated Harper makes me feel like throwing up. Her few months of walking on the wild side in college was our secret, and I never judged her for it. Harper let her freak flag fly for the first and only time in her life, and I loved it. As hot as being with two guys might sound in my romance novels, it's not something I'd ever dare to try. Hell, I can't even handle one guy.

Which brings me to number three—Ben. And the email that just came in from him that I can't make myself open. I already know what it is. I already know it's going to hurt—even if I deserve it.

I need to click on it like I'm ripping off a Band-Aid. Get the pain over with.

I swallow and close my eyes, my chest feeling so tight it physically hurts. I tap on the email, hold my breath, and dare myself to read his message.

There they are. The signed annulment papers. But the pain is nothing like pulling off a Band-Aid. No, it's deeper. Soul-wrenching deep. And all I can do is pull my knees up and wrap myself into a fetal position.

I was happy. I was in love—*am* in love.

And I fucked it all up.

I hurt him to the point of using our safe word. I was stupid to think it was only for me. That I was the only one at risk of being hurt. How fucking selfish of me. And now, I've lost it all.

A knock at my door tears me from my spiraling thoughts, and I freeze. Could it be...

Another knock sounds. "I know you're in there."

It's Harper. Knowing her, she'll probably camp out on my doormat if I don't answer. As hard as it's going to be to face her, I have to. I have to make things right.

I open the door, and there she stands with a pumpkin pie in her hands. I immediately burst into tears. She starts crying too and pulls me into a tight hug.

"I'm sorry," she says between sobs.

"Me, too. That was awful of me." My chest heaves. "I'm so sorry. I had no right."

Fuck, I may throw up.

"Me, too."

We pull away, and I move to let her in. She immediately goes into Mom Mode and starts making coffee. Thankfully, she says nothing about the state of my apartment. We eventually settle on my couch with pie and coffee and watch the game. This is our usual Black Friday ritual—pie, football, and online Christmas shopping.

While I appreciate the break to get our emotions under control, I don't want to avoid yesterday any longer. "Are you and Chandler okay? I'm sorry if I—"

She waves her hand at me. "Chandler knows about my freshman year craziness." Relief fills me as tears rush forth. God, I would have never forgiven myself if I messed with her marriage. "He wasn't exactly happy with my behavior yesterday either. Or for the last eleven months. I've been especially controlling and awful lately." She looks at me. "I was the one that was wrong about you and Ben."

My heart pinches at his name.

Harper shakes her head. "I was more concerned about myself, because I couldn't handle it if Mom spiraled again. I'm a mom now and it's been so fucking hard, and I'm constantly worried I'm doing it all wrong and...I just can't be that girl I was in high school again." She blows out a breath and looks at me with watery eyes. "Ben was right about how I was treating you. It was unfair and awful, and I'm really fucking sorry."

I pull her into my arms and hold her close. I hate that I didn't realize how much she was struggling with motherhood.

"I think we all need family therapy."

Harper laughs and eases out of my hold, wiping her eyes. "Yeah, probably."

"Please don't feel like you can't talk to me when you're having a hard time, Harper."

She nods. "Thanks, I know I should. I promise I'll be a better sister to you."

"Me too."

She gets rid of the rest of her tears and looks at me with renewed determination. "Okay, we need to figure out how to fix the World's Worst Thanksgiving and get you and Ben back together."

I press my hand to my chest as the pain blooms all over again.

"I think I finally pushed him too far. He signed the annulment papers."

Sympathy fills Harper's expression. "Do you want to stay married?"

I sigh. "I know I want to be with him. But our relationship is basically based on failed dates and a drunken wedding. How can a marriage last on that? Maybe it's best that he signed."

Harper's silent for a moment. "I met Chandler when I was living with Drake and Ethan."

I blink. Those are her Reverse Harem boys, as I like to call them. "Okay," I reply, unsure where she's going with this.

"He needed a place to crash for a while, so he stayed with us."

The almost shy yet leading tone of her voice has me sitting straight. "Wait. Do you mean...was he part of your...?"

"No." Then cocks her head. "Kind of."

I swear my eyes feel like they might pop out of my head like some cartoon character. "Chandler? *Really*?"

She shrugs. "He wasn't a stranger to group play, but that's not the point."

"It isn't?" I push my hand through my hair trying to comprehend that my cinnamon roll brother-in-law has a group kink. "Oh my God, you have to tell me more. No, wait. I don't know if I want to know because it's *Chandler*. Do y'all still...?"

"God, no! Lainey, focus. The point is we met under very crazy circumstances, and our relationship wasn't easy at first. I had a lot of growing up to do and getting over my own shit, which I clearly still struggle with, but we worked at it together. We still do. As much as I question my threesome phase, I don't regret it. It brought me to him. Hell, look at Mom and Mike and how their first date went. Don't you see? Maybe it isn't about how it happens. It's about how right it feels."

And Ben feels right. He has all along and all I had to do was tell him.

"Listen to Ben. All those wrongs were just leading you to what's right. You're fucking amazing, Lainey. You don't settle for anything less than the best for yourself."

Emotion clogs my throat. This is the Harper I've needed all year.

My tears start all over again. "Except I pushed the best away."

"It's not too late."

"That's what Mom said, but I really hurt him. I kept him at arm's length all year, yet he kept wooing me, finding every single crazy holiday in the world just to text me. And all I had to do was fucking tell him I loved him back."

Harper smiles and sits up straighter. "It's simple then. Woo him back."

My breath stalls then my heart seems to whoosh back to life. That's it. It's perfect!

I don't think it's going to be simple, but it's not only exactly what I need to do, but it's what he deserves. I'm going to stuff a year's worth of love and courtship into one month and pray he forgives me.

National Bartender Appreciation Day - December 1st

EVERY DAY SINCE THANKSGIVING HAS FELT LIKE NATIONAL HAVE A Bad Day Day's been on repeat. I've been slogging through the days, pretending the fact Lainey still doesn't trust what we have is right, real, isn't like a dagger stuck in my heart. Pretending that signing those annulment papers wasn't like twisting and sinking that dagger even further into the wound. Pretending that signing them wasn't a mistake, even if I knew I had to do it.

It's been less than a week since Thanksgiving, which fell late this year, but it's felt like years. Did she send in the signed papers? Are we officially done?

Another stab of pain echoes in my chest. I'm afraid this is going to become a chronic condition without Lainey in my life. Not that she will truly be out of it since she's my stepsister. I talked with my dad after the mess of Thanksgiving, and he apologized for not addressing the situation with me when he saw it happening. Apparently, both he and Kathleen were worried how us getting together would affect their relationship. In the end, I think everything that happened helped them realize they needed to communicate better. And they both threw their support behind me and Lainey. I just don't know if there's anything to support anymore.

I look at my phone in my hand and set it down. As much as I want to text her, I'm not ready. My feelings are still too raw, and I don't know if I can control them yet. Plus, there's nothing to even say. I made my feelings clear, and she made hers. Thinking there's something to hold on to is a hope I should probably let go of.

I push out of my office chair and my phone lights up with a text. I glance down to see it's from Lainey.

My heart stutters to a stop. I'm not sure how long it takes me to sink back into my chair and pick up my phone. It feels like it weighs a thousand pounds in my hand. I hold my breath as I open the message.

LAINEY

> It's the first Friday of the month. Know what that means?

I don't. But guessing it's some obscure holiday. I don't know if reverting back to our holiday texts is good thing, or if I should feel insulted she's ignoring what happened over Thanksgiving. Before I can reply, she does.

LAINEY

> It's National Bartender Appreciation Day!

That does surprise me. I find myself typing before I think too much about it.

ME

> Huh. Had no idea.

LAINEY

> What? I thought checking what crazy holiday it is was the first thing you did in the morning.

ME

It was. Yesterday was National Personal Space Day, and I thought maybe I needed a break from the holidays, so I turned off the notifications.

There's a long pause.

LAINEY

Would you be willing to take a break from the holidays this whole month?

I have no idea where she's going with this. Is she talking about us? Just the holidays?

LAINEY

Like don't look up the holidays.

ME

Why?

LAINEY

I know I have no right to ask this of you, but could you trust me?

I bark out a laugh, the bitter sound filling the small room.

ME

Jesus, Lainey. Of all the things to ask me after the shit show on Thanksgiving, you ask me that?

LAINEY

You're right. I don't deserve your trust, but I'm hoping by doing this one thing, you can allow me the chance to earn it back.

While I can appreciate that she wants to earn my trust, it pisses me off that she still hasn't acknowledged she hurt me. That after all that happened between us this year, she still thinks it a was a mistake.

LAINEY

You don't have to decide now. Or even say anything. Just enjoy your day. There's a package coming for you and your staff. Have a great night!

I toss my phone on the desk. Usually, I'm never ready to end our text conversations, but I'm glad she signed off—which tells me I'm not quite ready to forgive and forget.

An hour later, I get the package, and the first thing I see is a banner that says National Bartender Appreciation Day. Several T-shirts have sayings printed on them that she's labeled for the staff. Jan's has *Appreciate this Badass Bartender.* Mine says *More than a Bartender. Appreciate this Bar Owner.*

Fuck. She could have gone the Bare-chested Bartender route; instead, she knew exactly what I needed. I don't know why exactly she wants me to ignore the national holidays, but my curiosity is getting the best of me.

ME

Got the package. Everyone loves their shirts. Thanks.

LAINEY

Hope you know that you deserve it all. You can have it all.

Except you.

LAINEY

Oh, and one thing I need you to know…I don't want personal space from you, Ben.

The big thump of my heart is the first beat I've felt in days.

Let's Hug Day

DECEMBER 3RD

I received a pair of humping reindeer with a note that says, Happy Let's Hug Day. Please tell me this is from you and not a sick joke from Chandler.

LAINEY

I couldn't let you miss out on Let's Hug Day.

BEN

I don't know what to say.

LAINEY

Really? I was expecting a lot of euphemisms.

LONG PAUSE.

LAINEY

Well, I hope it's a good day. Just maybe don't tell me how you celebrate.

BEN

How are you celebrating? Holidate?

LAINEY

No. I don't work for What's Good, ATX anymore.

BEN

What?

LAINEY

Yeah, they fired me before I could quit. Pete the Dick didn't think the food fight was funny. Neither did my boss.

BEN

Damn. Sorry.

LAINEY

I'm not.

Longer Pause.

BEN

gif of virtual hug sent

LAINEY

Thanks. Your hugs are the best. Best I've ever had.

National Letter Writing Day

DECEMBER 7TH

Dear Ben,

It's National Letter Writing Day, so I thought I'd forgo a text for an actual letter. Writing a letter is surprisingly harder than texting. The act of putting pen to paper immediately becomes more intimate. More raw. It's so easy to bypass emotions with texting, or pretend an emoji really signifies what we're feeling. So, in this letter, I'm going to lay all my emotions on the line. I miss our usual texting banter. Your silence is so palpable, I can feel it pressing down on me until I can't catch my breath. I can imagine it's not unsimilar to what my silence felt like on Thanksgiving.

But, it's okay. I asked for the chance to earn your trust, and I don't deserve witty and flirty comebacks. Yet.

That's why I'm courting you.

Yes, that's what I've been doing all week, and I don't plan to stop anytime soon. I let my insecurities and fears cast doubts for far too long, even when my heart had none. I pushed you away, yet you never gave up on me—on us. You wooed me all year. Now, it's my turn.

Buckle up, baby. I'm about to court the fuck out of you.

Yours,
Lainey

National Brownie Day

DECEMBER 8TH

BEN

I just got a big package of brownies. Part of your courtship, I assume?

LAINEY

Happy National Brownie Day!

BEN

There's like 50 brownies.

LAINEY

Brownies are your favorite.

Which flavor do you like most?

Long pause.

LAINEY

The answer is the dark chocolate sea salt caramel, btw.

BEN

Nope. It's the triple chocolate. It made me moan.

LAINEY

Too bad I missed that. Though I'm more partial to your grunts and growls.

...

...

LAINEY

I can imagine all the naughty responses you're biting back.

It's okay. I'll wait until you're ready.

BEN

growls

National Ding-a-Ling Day

DECEMBER 12TH

BEN

Yesterday I was delivered a noddle ring—which has to be the weirdest way ever to eat pasta. And today, I wake up to a box on my front porch full of bells with penis-shaped ringers. I wasn't sure things could get any more bizarre than Noodle Ring Day.

LAINEY

Oh, just you wait.

BEN

Seriously…the penis bells…why??

LAINEY

Because it's National Ding-a-Ling Day! Duh!

BEN

Gotta admit, that wouldn't have been my guess.

LAINEY

I couldn't think of something ditzy like the true meaning of a ding-a-ling, so I went the bell/penis route. It is Christmastime, after all.

BEN

Sure. Because nothing screams Christmas like bells with cock ringers.

LAINEY

Every time a ding-a-ling rings, an angel creams.

BEN

Fuck! I just choked on my coffee, and now my nose burns like hell.

Where did you even get these?

LAINEY

The internet is a weird and wonderful place.

National Ugly Sweater Day

DECEMBER 15TH

BEN

A company named Langford Event Services has hacked into Red Poppy's social accounts and organized an Ugly Christmas Sweater Night at my bar without my permission.

LAINEY

Is it really hacking when I already had the passwords?

Don't worry, I ran it by Jan first.

BEN

I know. She showed me the sweaters you gifted my whole staff. I'm not wearing that sweater.

LAINEY

You're so wearing it.

BEN

It's an upside-down snowman with a dangling carrot and ornaments hanging from its hat.

LAINEY:

I remember. I spent a lot of time picking it out for you.

BEN

What if people try to touch my "ornaments" or suck on my "carrot stick?"

LAINEY

Um, I know you like that.

BEN

Yeah, but only from a certain someone.

LAINEY

Lucky girl.

PAUSE.

LAINEY

Stay behind the bar. That'll be your carrot-blocker.

BEN

You're funny.

LAINEY

I know ;)

BEN

I was being sarcastic. Have you seen the amount of comments these posts have gotten? I'm going to be slammed tonight.

LAINEY

You're welcome!

BEN

I don't know if I want to wring your neck for going behind my back or kiss you for what will clearly be a successful evening.

LAINEY

I vote you kiss me with your hands around my neck.

Pause.

LAINEY

I'll wait while you adjust yourself.

Long pause.

BEN

How about you spill the tea about Langford Event Services?

LAINEY

Long story short, I decided it was time to do something that truly excites me, and organizing Poppy's party helped me realize what that was. You helped me realize that. Lots of stuff is still in motion to make it official, but I've had some help getting the ball rolling. Tonight, I'm working Chandler's holiday work party.

Red Poppy's Ugly Christmas Sweater Night is on the house, btw. ;)

BEN

So...sounds like pelting Pete the Dick with turkey and dressing was a good thing.

LAINEY

For sure!

BEN

Good. Because I have 100% no regrets.

Also, I'm really proud of you, Lainey. I think this is going to be perfect for you.

LAINEY

Thx. I think so, too.

Pause.

LAINEY

So, when I stopped by Red Poppy, the black napkins caught my attention all over again.

BEN

Why? Did you think I would switch them back to red because we're not married anymore?

LAINEY

No.

Though you have every right to.

Pause.

LAINEY

That's not why I'm bringing it up. I stopped and stared at those napkins because I thought about the first time I saw them. And how I never told you how much it meant to me that you switched them.

I went to the bathroom and cried that day. You took such care of my feelings and…and I didn't do the same for you. I'm so very sorry for that.

Long Pause.

BEN

If you had never taken care of my feelings, I wouldn't have fallen in love with you.

LAINEY

Now you've made me cry again. You're really good at the grand gestures.

BEN

grand gestures?

LAINEY

Big romantic moment. Significant.

BEN

Is that what this courting thing is? Are you grand gesturing me, Lainey?

LAINEY

Oooh, that sounds naughty.

BEN

Lainey.

LAINEY

Speaking of naughty, wanna see my ugly
sweater for Chandler's party?

*pic of Lainey wearing a sweater with a
gingerbread man going down on a gingerbread
woman with saying, 'Tis the season to be
naughty*

BEN

Fuck...Lainey...

...

LAINEY

You'll always be my gingerbread man, Ben.

National Chocolate Covered Anything Day

DECEMBER 16TH

Is this what I think it is?

What do you think it is?

Chocolate-covered nipples.

It's what you think it is.

Happy National Chocolate Covered Anything Day!

One guess on whose nipples they are. *devil emoji*

Lainey, you're killing me.

Go ahead and give them a lick.

Fuck.

LAINEY

After that, bite them nice and hard. They love that.

BEN

Jesus. This is torture.

LAINEY

It's not torture. It's courting.

BEN

You court so dirty. And I like it.

Blue Christmas Service Day, National Coquito Day, Winter Solsitice

DECEMBER 21ST

LAINEY

I wondered how I would handle our courtship today, knowing it's the anniversary of your mom's death and it would be a tough day for you. But sometimes the answer really is in these wonderfully strange holidays.

Today is Blue Christmas Service Day. It's for those who are struggling with grief and joy during the Christmas season. I emailed you a list of churches holding services today. I'm unsure if this is something that will bring you comfort or not, but maybe it could help shoulder the grief. And if you need a real shoulder, I'm here.

A FEW HOURS LATER...

BEN

I went to one of the services, and it was exactly what I didn't know I needed. Thank you, Lainey.

LAINEY

You're welcome.

Another couple hours later...

BEN

Lainey…I don't know what to say. You've blown
me away today.

LAINEY

You don't have to say anything.

BEN

Yes, I do. You took the hardest day of my life
and made it beautiful. Walking into Red Poppy
took my breath away. The twinkle lights. The
Christmas trees. The lighted snowflakes and
icicles. The angel hanging over my mom's
spot… made me cry like a fucking baby.

It's absolutely enchanting, Lainey. It's like
walking into a Winter Wonderland.

LAINEY

Wait until the snowmaker machine shows up.
Happy Winter Solstice!

BEN

What? Really?

LAINEY

Don't worry, I have people coming to clean up
after you close.

Oh and also, Happy National Coquito Day!

BEN

That's why Jan suggested I create a Coquito
martini?

LAINEY

We agreed the drink would pair perfectly with
the Winter Solstice theme.

BEN

It's hard to complain about you and Jan planning events without my knowledge when they're this amazing. I have a feeling once tonight's pictures hit the internet, Langford Event Services will be in high demand.

Pause.

LAINEY

I didn't do this for the exposure.

BEN

I know.

But I'm going to make damn sure everyone knows who made this happen.

Because you deserve it.

LAINEY

Thank you, but all I want is for you to have a good night, Ben.

BEN

I will.

Pause.

BEN

Thank you for courting me, Lainey.

LAINEY

It's been my pleasure. Truly.

Christmas Eve

I'VE HEARD FROM LAINEY EVERY DAY THIS MONTH, YET IT'S 5:00 p.m. on Christmas Eve and nothing. I hope that means I'll get to see her.

My dad and Kathleen invited me over for Christmas Eve dinner, not mentioning if anyone else is coming, and I've been too chicken shit to ask. Too afraid of how disappointed I'll be if Lainey doesn't show up. I'm so desperate to see her, it might crush me.

She said she was going to court the fuck out of me, and she did. She sent carolers to my bar on Caroling Day and had the whole place singing. I got some seriously questionable cookie cutters for Cookie Cutter Week. I didn't realize how much I needed her to pursue me. To prove her feelings are as real and strong as mine.

It's been seriously hard not to interact with her over text like we have all year, but I needed to see her courting through. Then the twenty-first happened, and it took all my willpower not to find her, wrap her in my arms, and never let her go. I couldn't believe she even remembered the anniversary of my mom's passing. She gave me the joy of Christmas back, allowed me to grieve and enjoy the holiday that was my favorite until six years ago. She made me fall in love with her all over again.

If I don't see her tonight, I'm going to say to hell with this courting dance and hunt her down.

When I arrive, Kathleen's all smiles and warm welcomes, though maybe a little nervous, too? While we've cleared the air since Thanksgiving, we haven't seen each other since. Is this residual awkwardness, or does she know her daughter's courting me?

I push aside my questions and step into their house, which is all decked out in Christmas decorations and a tree covered in white twinkle lights. As I take it all in, I notice some things from my childhood scattered about. Things I haven't seen since my mother died. My dad didn't bother with a Christmas tree the first year after she passed, but when I brought a three-foot tree to his house the next year, he took the hint and put a few things out. But it wasn't the same.

I go to the table where a nativity scene is laid out. My mother painted this set. I pick up the Mary figurine and smile at the glued hairline break in her praying hands where I'd dropped it as a kid.

"I hope you don't mind that I set out some of your mother's things," Kathleen says, as she comes up next to me, her small smile hesitant. Maybe this is why she's nervous.

"No, not at all. I haven't seen them in years." I gently place Mary back beside the manger.

"Your father thought it'd be a nice surprise."

"It is. Thanks."

"I was thinking that when everything is boxed back up, I'd give it all to you to use next year. But if you don't want to, I can use them here."

"I'd actually love to have them. I miss not decorating for Christmas. I wasn't helpful to my mom when she decorated, but

I loved what she did." And I miss it. I miss her. "What you've done here...it feels like Christmas again. Thank you for that."

She smiles and hugs me tightly.

After that, Kathleen impresses me with a Christmas-themed cocktail, and we all settle in front of the tree and chat. She says there's a casserole in the oven, so dinner isn't quite ready. They haven't mentioned Lainey or Harper, and I'm about to burst out of my skin with curiosity. I'm trying to play it calm and cool, but my leg won't stop bouncing and I don't think I'll be able to hold back from asking for much longer.

Then I hear the sweep of the front door opening just before a high-pitched screech.

"Merry Christmas!" A shrill voice rings out from the front hallway that can only come from Cassie. She barrels into the living room, yelling for her grandparents.

My stomach jumps into my throat as I stand, waiting to see who else emerges from the hallway. Harper and Chandler follow behind their daughter, their arms full of gifts. Our parents greet them with smiles. After Chandler puts his stack of presents under the tree, we shake hands and give each other a half hug. Harper comes up and hugs me, and it's nice to have her as a friend instead of a foe. She pulls back, and her mischievous smile has my skin tingling. I look beyond her to the hallway and hold my breath. It's probably only two seconds, but it feels like years before Lainey steps past the wall and into view. I don't know how it's possible for my heart to race and stop at the same time, but it does.

"Merry Christmas, Ben," Harper whispers before she steps away.

I can't tear my gaze from Lainey as I watch her make her way toward her mother. The room's brimming with chatter, but I can't hear a thing. I can only watch and wait for her to get to me. And finally, it happens. Her beautiful brown eyes are on me. The way her chest stills then rises again makes me wonder if her heart's going as crazy as mine.

She gives me a soft smile and steps closer, then falls back, seemingly unsure if she should hug me. "Merry Christmas, Ben."

"You're here," I say instead of returning the sentiment, really hating she's not in my arms right now.

Her smile's wide and bright. "I'm here. There's nowhere else I'd rather be." With that she leans forward again, yet still hesitates. So, I take a step toward her, hoping she'll take the hint. I'm desperate for a hug.

Fuck that, I'm desperate for *her*.

She steps into me, her hand snaking up my back until she presses on our secret spot. We both instantly relax into each other. In this moment, everything's as it should be. Just us. Where we belong.

She gives my back a last caress before pulling back. All the chatter in the room hits me again, and chaos ensues. Cassie's shaking presents and talking about Santa. Kathleen recruits the girls to help get dinner on the table. Chandler's in charge of opening wine while my dad keeps Cassie occupied, which he does happily.

I can't seem to move. She's here. We're all here. Together.

I press a hand to my chest and try not to cry like a baby. I didn't realize how much I missed family until now. Tonight, a new tradition begins, and I hope it means Lainey will always be by my side.

Lainey sits across from me at dinner, and we can't stop sneaking glances. Her smiles are shy and uncertain. I didn't exactly put myself out there in her courting texts, though, to be fair, she hasn't truly declared her feelings either. And I really need her to.

Once we're back in the living room with dessert and drinks, Cassie immediately goes to the tree, inspecting the presents.

"Can I open my present now?" she asks, jumping up and down like a kangaroo on crack.

"You don't open them tomorrow?" I ask.

"We have a tradition that she gets to open one gift on Christmas Eve," Harper says before giving Cassie a pointed look. *"Our pick."*

Cassie deflates slightly at the reminder then nods and continues to jump. Harper picks out a particular present and hands it to her. "Here you go."

Cassie tears into it, revealing Christmas-themed pajamas that immediately get tossed aside for a Vet Doctor Barbie doll with a dog and a cat. Cassie jumps up and begs Chandler to open the doll. As soon as Barbie is free, Cassie takes off to another room. Once she's out of earshot, Chandler whispers that tomorrow they're going to give her the dog she's been begging for and shows us all pictures of an adorable spaniel mix puppy. Harper proceeds to hand out presents to everyone else in the room and we all discover we have pajamas matching Cassie's.

"Be prepared for a cheesy family photo in about an hour," she declares.

"I'm just glad they don't have an upside-down snowman on it," I say, prompting everyone to laugh. The pictures of me in my ugly Christmas sweater were a social media hit, and the comments were ruthless—as were the texts from everyone in this room.

"So, there's one more Christmas Eve present to give out." Lainey goes to the tree, grabs a big box, then turns to me. "This is for you."

"Me?"

She smiles and nods. I glance around the room, and our families all look like they're trying not to smile. I take the present, which is a decorated box with a top that lifts off. The first thing I see is a bag of gummies with a sticky note on it that reads, *Caution: Can cause fake heart attacks.* Then there's my hospital bracelet as well as a lavender Pick Your Poppy bracelet from Valentine's Day, and a mask from Mardi Gras.

I look at her. "It's from your holidates."

She shakes her head. "From *our* holidates. Keep going."

As I dig, I spot mementos from all our holidates and texts—a small bottle of Limoncello, a Jello shot, a book of dirty jokes, and more. At the bottom of the box is what looks like a photo book. I open it, and it's pictures of us with snippets of our texts throughout the year, including her courting texts. I stop at the picture of me reaching up and touching the angel above my mom's stool from the Winter Solstice. I run a hand over the picture before turning to the next page. There, with no other notes or pictures, is our marriage license.

"You should have included the annulment papers next to this," I say with a laugh.

"I can't."

My brows snap together. "What do you mean?"

"I never submitted them."

I swear the air thins. "That means we're still married."

She smiles, though it's a little unsure. "We are."

I don't know what this means, and I'm too afraid to hope. Lainey sinks to her knees in front of me. My heart kicks into overdrive.

"Ben, this year has been the best of my life. The truth is, I started falling for you the moment you took my hand on New Year's Eve. And with every holiday that passed, I fell more and more. You might have been the wrong holidate, but you were the only one that ever felt right. You were the only one I ever wanted. I'm so sorry for hurting you. For not trusting myself enough to say what I knew in my heart. Ben, you're all I want, all I need. So, no. I didn't annul the marriage to the man I love."

My heart is thumping so hard and fast I wouldn't be surprised if the whole room could hear it. I can't believe it. I'm afraid to. "You want to stay married?"

"I do." She takes my hands in hers, her brown eyes tinged with an edge of fear. "Do you?"

I lean down and take her face in my hands. "I do, but only if you're sure. It's okay if you're not ready. We can date properly. We—"

She places a finger over my mouth. Her gaze softens and the earlier fear clears. "I'm not going to lie. It's scary, but it's a good scary—the kind that excites me. I don't want to go backward. I only want to move forward with you." She leans in until our mouths are a breath away. "Husband."

Raw need rockets through me, and I can't resist her a moment longer. Our mouths clash in a kiss that's full of love and carnal desire. It's been too fucking long, and neither one of us hold back. She raises up on her knees, and I yank her closer. If she crawled inside me, she still wouldn't be close enough.

A loud clearing of a throat stops us. Damn, I totally forgot we were in front of our whole family. We reluctantly pull apart, our gazes locked with a mixture of amusement, love, and lust.

"You totally grand gestured me," I tease her.

She tilts her head with a playful smile. "Of course. How could I court you properly without one?"

"I love you, wife." I lean in and give her a quick kiss. "Can we hug now?"

Harper and Chandler groan as Lainey gives me a saucy smile. "We should definitely hug, husband. I think we deserve a nice, long, *hard* hug."

New Year's Eve

LAINEY

"IT ALREADY HAS HALF A MILLION VIEWS."

My mouth drops open, my stomach knotting as I look at Jan. "You're kidding me?"

Jan shakes her head with a huge smile on her face. "The video was hot, if I do say so myself." Jan's responsible for filming and editing the video. "Way hotter than any Ben did by himself."

A flush rushes through me, unable to believe so many people have seen the sexy video. Ben hadn't made a Bare-chested Bartender video since before Thanksgiving. And after we officially got together on Christmas, he told me he didn't want to do them anymore. He wants to shift away from the playboy image. However, Red Poppy's Instagram page was flooded with comments and DMs wanting the next video.

So, we sat down and tried to figure out a way to keep the videos without Ben feeling like he needs to be a sex object to make his bar succeed. What we came up with so far is Red Poppy only posts one video a month, unless he wants to do more. And while the video will still have sexy vibes, he's going to keep his shirt on, and he'll slowly transition the posts so they aren't all blatant thirst traps. Some of the other bartenders are

390

going to start participating, too, making the video any way they'd like.

But before we start implementing these changes, Ben had an idea for how to end the year. He wanted to make one last sexy video—with me.

"I want everyone to know I'm taken, that I'm yours. What better way to do that than with the introduction of your cocktail?" he'd said yesterday after he'd told me he was adding The Lainey, a bourbon-based drink, to Red Poppy's permanent menu. This was right after he presented me with a pretty pink cocktail topped with egg white foam in a coup glass, declaring it was mine. The cocktail includes Limoncello and cranberry bitters, among other juices, but I loved how it wasn't only my cocktail, but included parts of our story, too.

Then he told me his idea for the video, and I couldn't help but love it. Never did I imagine it would get so much attention in just four hours.

Ben returns from the back room with a box of booze in his arms. He's made sure to have all hands-on-deck tonight so they don't drown like they did last year. However, we don't anticipate a pot gummy-induced fake heart attack.

"Ben, it's hit half a million views," Jan squeals. "Wait. We're almost to 750k."

His eyes round as he sets the box down. "No way!" He looks at me and I can tell he's trying to gauge my reaction. "Are you okay?"

"I think so. It's fast."

"Faster than what I've ever gotten, but this video was way sexier." He gives me a hot look, reminding me exactly what happened in his office earlier to celebrate the making of it. My already fired-up body heats even more.

"Behave," I mouth to him.

He laughs and closes the distance between us to pull me into his arms "Never," he says before he takes my mouth in a searing kiss. And we kiss. And kiss.

"Oh God, please stop. You're reminding me that I'll be slinging drinks and not kissing anyone at midnight."

We reluctantly part at Jan's words, but we still have goofy smiles on our faces. Ben hugs me to him as he pulls his phone from his pocket. "I gotta see this."

He pulls up our video, seeing the insane amount of comments and likes. We browse through the comments, and they don't disappoint. From naughty to funny, they're all awesome. Ben plays the video again, and though I've lost count of how many times I've watched it, I still can't believe how incredibly sexy it is.

The way he feeds me an orange slice. The way his thumb caresses the bump at the end of a lemon, strategically placed in front of my breasts—and my head falls back as if he'd actually touched my nipple. There are shots of him touching me in various places—his hand on my stomach, around my throat, over my lips—our new wedding bands featured prominently.

This morning, we surprised each other with new rings. Ben's is solid platinum and mine's a gorgeous solitaire diamond with an infinity twist band filled with smaller diamonds. I couldn't have picked out a more perfect ring. Not only does it suit me, it suits us.

The video ends with both of our hands pushing the coup glass toward the camera, the drink becoming the focus as Ben and I blur in the background. Yet it clearly shows Ben's hand sinking into my hair before he kisses the hell out of me, while my hand fists his shirt and raises it enough to show a hint of skin as words fill the forefront of the screen: The Lainey...Red Poppy's New Permanent Menu Addition.

"Fuck, my wife is sexy," Ben says as he presses his lips to my temple.

I laugh. "My husband's no slouch."

Ben sets his phone on the bar top and pulls me back into him so our chests are pressed together, his expression suddenly serious. "It's been a year since you walked through those doors. I would have never guessed that this New Year's Eve, I'd be married to the love of my life."

My heart flutters and I go up on my tiptoes to place a soft kiss on his lips. "I know."

"Best year of my life. I can't wait to start another best year with you, wife."

"Me either, my husband."

His mouth quirks up. "I knew charming shirtless bartenders were your thing."

A Note From the Author

Thank you for reading THE WRONG HOLIDATE! I hope you enjoyed Ben and Lainey's story! If you have time, please consider leaving a review. It would be much appreciated. xoxo

CONNECT WITH CATE!

https://linktr.ee/cateashton
www.cateashton.com

Books By Cate Ashton

PERSONALLY YOURS SERIES

YOURS IN LUST

YOURS TO PROTECT

CTU SERIES

OFF LIST

Behind the Story

When I started this story, it had no connection to any of my previous books. It was a complete standalone I'd started, hit a wall with, and stopped. During Off List edits, it was mentioned to me that it would be fun to see Ben, the fuck boy frat bro character, fall in love. That wasn't even on my radar, but when I came back to my holidate story that was still stagnant, it hit me this should be Ben's story. So, I renamed the MMC to Ben and started reworking the story.

The character Chandler was always in this book, as he was my favorite character from Friends. However, the name is so iconic, I'd planned to change it eventually (though it was getting harder to come up with a new name for that character as he'd really become Chandler in my mind). Then, in the middle of edits, Matthew Perry passed away. And I knew there was no way I could change his name now.

Friends is my favorite TV show. It's pretty much been on my TV every day since it premiered. It's my comfort show. It's my background noise. My family makes fun of me, I watch it so much. To say the show and the actors in it have a special place in my heart is a massive understatement. And when Matthew Perry died, I was devastated. He's the only celebrity death I've cried over. Since I now had two characters with names from Friends (Chandler & Ben), I decided I'd have a little fun and make sure every character had a Friends connection as a tribute to Matthew and the special place the show has in my heart (and millions of others).

It was a little hard as some characters I couldn't rename (or didn't want to) so I had to get creative. Not only does every character have a name from Friends, but there are also some other Easter eggs within the story. Did you spot them all?

Here they are:

Ben Kelley - Ross's son, Ben (most famously played by Cole Sprouse)

Lainey Langford – Langford is Matthew Perry's middle name.

Harper Langford Stevens - Paul Stevens, Ross' college-aged girlfriend's dad (Bruce Willis)

Chandler Stevens – Matthew Perry

Mike Kelley – Mike Hannigan (Paul Rudd)

Eli Burke - Richard's last name (Tom Selleck)

Josephine (Josie) Lecroix – Feminine version of Joey (referenced in The One with Ross' Teeth), Lecroix, last name of Joey's roommate, Janine (Elle Macpherson)

Kathleen Langford Kelley – A nod to Kathleen Turner as Chandler's dad and Kathy, Joey & Chandler's girlfriend (Paget Brewster)

Cassie Stevens - Monica and Ross's cousin (Denise Richards)

Jan (Red Poppy bartender) – Janice, Oh. My. God. (Maggie Wheeler)

Bar Employees - Nora (Chandler's Mom, played by Morgan Fairchild), Tyler (for actor James Michael Tyler who played Gunther), Bonnie (Ross' girlfriend played by Christine Taylor)

Mona (NYE, Miss Red Dress) - Ross' girlfriend (Bonnie Somerville)

Duncan (Lainey's Mardi Gras date) – Phoebe's "gay" figure skater husband (Steve Zahn)

Dr. Elliott (ER doctor) – Elliott Gould (Jack Gellar, Ross and Monica's dad)

Dr. Wheeler (April Fool's Day doctor) - Charlie Wheeler, Ross' girlfriend (Aisha Tyler)

Vince (Kathleen's former BF) - When Phoebe dates two guys at same time (The One with Ross' Thing)

Jason (Kathleen former BF) - When Phoebe dates two guys at same time (The One with Ross' Thing)

Danny (Kathleen's former BF) – Neighbor Rachel dates with inappropriate sister (George Newborn)

Isaac (Lainey's frat ex) - copy shop guy (Maury Ginsberg)

Ryan (Lainey's St. Pat's date) - Phoebe's submarine guy (Charlie Sheen)

Mrs. Abbott (Harper's neighbor) - Last name of Phoebe's bio mom (Teri Garr)

Tim (Lainey's ex mentioned in Cinco de Mayo) - Monica's bad sous chef that Phoebe dates (Kevin Rahm)

Phoebe (Cassie's playdate friend) - Lisa Kudrow

Uncle Red "Gary Redford" (Ben's Uncle) – Phoebe's cop boyfriend, Gary (Michael Rapaport)

Chloe (Firework warehouse employee) – Copy place girl and Ross' 'on a break' hook up. (Angela Featherstone)

Rachel (Mardi Gras scene) – Jennifer Aniston

Monica (Ben's 4th of July date) – Courteney Cox

David (Lainey's first holidate, NYE) – David Schwimmer (Ross) or David, Phoebe's scientist boyfriend (Hank Azaria)

Max Buffamonteezi (Eagle) - The other scientist in The One with the Monkey (Wayne Pere) and "British" Amanda's last name (Jennifer Coolidge) in The One with Ross's Tan

Gavin (Lainey's 4th of July date) – Rachel's maternity leave replacement (Dermot Mulroney)

Eric (Lainey's Labor Day date) - Ursula's fiancé (Sean Penn)

Parker (Lainey's Labor Day date) - Phoebe's overly positive date (Alec Baldwin)

Will (Ben's frat friend) - Rachel's high school enemy (Brad Pitt)

Pete (Lainey's Thanksgiving date) – Monica's billionaire Ultimate Fighter boyfriend (Jon Favreau)

Drake and Ethan (Harper's RH boys) - Drake Ramoray (Joey's Days of our Lives character) and Ethan, Monica's underage date (Stan Kirsch)

Poppy (Ben's Mom) – roommate Joey slept with (Nikita Ager) The One with the Sharks – this was an original name I didn't want to change but happy to see it was a Friend's character name, even if it's not spoken.

Jill (Cinco de Mayo waitress) – Rachel's sister (Reese Whitherspoon)

Amy (pushy woman at bar) – Rachel's sister (Christina Applegate)

Willick Hall (where Mike and Kathleen get married) - Carol Willick, Ross' ex-wife (Jane Sibbett)

Other Easter Eggs:

Going Commando in Easter scene– Joey in The One Where No One is Ready.

Vegas Wedding – When Ross and Rachel get drunk and married, The One in Vegas.

Not liking Oysters (Lainey's failed Valentine date) – Phoebe's date Parker wants her to try oysters at Jack and Judy's anniversary party, The One in Massapequa.

Cate has been in love with love stories for as long as she can remember. It never occurred to her to be a writer until she realized she was constantly making up love stories in her head and she enjoyed that far more than anything else. So, she put fingers to keyboard and hasn't stopped.

Cate likes her romance with a dash of humor, a punch of emotion, and heaps of heat. When she's not writing, she enjoys spending time with family and friends, finding new places to visit, and curling up with a book (naturally).

Cate resides in Texas and living out her own HEA with her husband, two children, and pandemic pup.

Acknowledgments

This story was a lot of fun to write, but no book of mine is without my village of help. Thanks so much for indulging my questions and constant indecisiveness.

Dolly – Thank you so much for seeing Ben's potential in being the star of his own book. He might just be my favorite hero yet.

Abigail – You've been such a help from editor to overall supporter and advisor. And you're the best cruise roommate ever! Can't wait to see you soar in this next part of your publishing career.

Tracie – Thanks so much for your incredible last-minute edits and story insight (and tough love) that absolutely made this story better.

Rebecca – Thanks so much for being my beta reader and helping me shape this story. Your support has meant the world to me.

Catherine, Cheryl, Tracie – Thanks so much for being my sounding board for the dreaded blurb writing. I always appreciate your insight.

Shellee – As always, I appreciate your first look into my books that help me rein it all in.

Mitxeran - Thank you so much for the beautiful cover!

There aren't enough words to express my love and gratitude to my family and friends. You're my supporters. My cheerleaders. My shoulder to lean on. My sounding board. You are simply what keeps me going. I love you all.

www.ingramcontent.com/pod-product-compliance
Lightning Source LLC
Chambersburg PA
CBHW031829310726
48972CB00005B/1218